Ropen Island

Lois Buchter

This novel is dedicated to my favorite

two people in the world,

Richard "Mark" Buchter and Carol Spencer Smith

who have always cheered me on from the sidelines.

I've been a lucky girl…

Prologue

Dark skies turn the Miami horizon purple-black, as the building storm clouds race in across the bay. Increasing winds carry the damp smell of rain, confirming the intensity of the impending maelstrom. Just outside of the multi-storied reception area, Dr. David Lane leans against the glass. His deep blue eyes glance at the onslaught. He stands transfixed, holding a large mixed drink in his hand. He silently welcomes the harsh weather.

In the next room, a mourning crowd of professionals gather. Folding seats occupy the center, and an open bar is at the far end of the room. Servers wordlessly top off drinks around the atrium. Black suits and designer collections set the bar high for the physicians in attendance. Hushed conversations dominate as a life suddenly ended is remembered. An elaborate easel highlights an image of an attractive woman in her fifties and the words:

In Remembrance of Dr. Jeanne Lane
Pioneer Physician
Pediatric Transplant Program
University of Miami Medical School

A large floral arrangement and signature book sit to one side as people take turns signing in. Mournful glances come in his direction.

Dr. Lane takes one last gulp from his glass as he turns from the view over the bay and enters the reception. He pushes down the burning sensation in his stomach, commanding it to calm. "Just get through this," he hisses through his teeth. He tries not to make eye contact with anyone.

His son, Eric, twenty-four, quickly joins him. He wears a navy blazer, looking like he could be on the cover of GQ. He puts his hand on his father's shoulder. "Dad, you doing okay?"

Dave takes a deep drink. "Has Mack arrived?" He scans the room. "What time is it, anyway? This thing ever going to start?" "Don't worry. I just got a text from him. His flight is in. He should be here before everything begins." Eric squeezes Dave's shoulder. "We're here for you, always."

A somber mood fills the room as people talk in whispered tones. An elderly woman, with garish makeup, approaches. Her mouth down-turned in a grimace. The room effortlessly parts, then closes in her wake. Her wrists are a cacophony of jangling bracelets. A perfect accompaniment to her teased helmet-like hair. She approaches Dave and Eric.

"God, Atilla the Hun has arrived," Dave whispers to Eric.

Eric steps in front of his father as a surge of protectiveness hijacks him. He focuses on a smear of orange lipstick at the corner of her mouth. "Aunt Nancy, so nice of you to fly in. Haven't seen you since our reunion at the ranch two years ago. You're looking fit as ever."

Nancy looks Eric up and down. "You're getting too good-looking for your britches, young man. All the Lane men are just too smart for the rest of us. Give us a hug." They embrace, but she keeps her eyes on Dave. "Where the Hell is Rob? Did you run him off again?" Nancy straightens Eric's jacket. "Now, you, have you finished your degree in…?"

"Geology. My field is geology, remember?" Eric tries to stay out of kissing range.

"Yes." Nancy turns to see the large portrait of Jeanne. "She was one of the nicest people I've ever met, but we all thought she was going to wind up with Rob."

Dave winces and turns his back to Nancy. His thoughts go back to their childhood. Not once in my life could that woman keep her big mouth shut. He tightens his lips shut. Boiling hot, anger churns in his gut.

Eric hands her a large cocktail. "I think you need a drink."

"There was never a contest between us," Dave hisses as he turns to get another drink from the server behind him. Nancy lowers her voice to Eric. "Bull. There has always been a contest between those two boys, for as long as I can remember. I think Rob once tried to push Dave out through the crib railings."

Eric stifles a nervous giggle. "I believe it."

Nancy's eyes water as she reaches for his hand. "I'm sorry for your loss, Eric. She did such important work for those kids, and she was an incredible mother to you two." She dabs her eyes. "Have they charged that driver?"

Dave stands to one side listening but doesn't take part in the conversation. He shakes the hands of those arriving, saying quiet platitudes.

"We've been talking to the police for the last two days. They're supposed to charge him today." Eric scans the room. "Have you seen Unka Rob? Haven't been able to reach him."

"No telling where he is after that ridiculous incident at the conference. I think he may be having a nervous breakdown or something. He threw his credentials down the toilet. I can't believe he left a successful practice to go chase after monsters or some sort of nonsense."

"He's been telling me stories of things that go bump in the night since I was a kid. He's got a passion for - the unknown. Mom used to tell us to 'follow your dreams'."

As she drones on, Dave fantasizes about holding Nancy down when they were children and stuffing dirt in her mouth.

"Last I heard, he closed down his lab and was out somewhere in Peru looking for God knows what." Nancy adjusts her dress and smiles as a good-looking surgeon nods to her as he passes. She leans in closer to Eric. "Have they talked?" Eric shakes his head.

A well-dressed executive stops in front of Dave and puts his hand on Dave's shoulder. "How are you doing?" Dr. Anderson pulls him out of the stream of people coming in the doorway and away from Nancy.

Dave shrugs and nods a greeting to someone. "This is all a dream. It never happened."

Dr. Anderson winces. "It's a blow to all of us, Dave. The staff would like to talk to you. Sometime next week? They want to start a foundation in Jeanne's honor. Funding to keep her work going." Dr. Anderson takes a long drink. The ice in his glass clinks. "I'll have Cynthia reach out to you on the scheduling. You need to take a block of time off. Let me know what you need, and I'll arrange it."

Dave nods and walks away. He returns to Eric. Nancy is still droning on about their upbringing. His thoughts return to a childhood mantra, "If she says one more inappropriate comment, I may strangle her in front of witnesses". He watches her with scorn as she talks with distant relatives nearby.

Eric turns to Dave so he doesn't see Nancy but can instead focus on the large portrait of Jeanne, and her smile. His heart hiccups, then shatters once more. This isn't happening. How could I lose her? She is going to come walking through that door any second.

Hot anger swells inside his chest. He rubs it to push the feeling back. Dave finishes his drink.

Eric shakes the hand of another couple. "Thank you for coming." He notices Dave's hand shaking as his father switches to a tall glass of water.

For the fiftieth time, Dave checks his watch. *Where the hell is Mack?* Nancy moves in beside them. "Family sticks together, no matter what. If you need me to do anything, let me know."

He responds with a deadly look in her direction.

"Can this thing move any slower?" Dave says in a deadpan voice.

Eric elbows him as a disheveled Mack comes in the door. His wrinkled suit hangs loosely on his tall frame, as he shakes the moisture off from the storm. Mack scoots his suitcase next to the bar, grabs a drink, and Dave immediately pulls him into a bear hug. Eric takes Mack's drink as the two embrace. Tears flow easily. Eric embraces them from behind.

Nancy pushes them gently to the side, away from the others. "Why don't you three take a moment in the corner?" She hands them a fist of napkins. They move beside a large potted palm.

"I can't believe it. I just talked to her on Saturday. She was so excited about a successful transplant with one of her patients. She was alive, so alive, and happy." Mack unwraps a folded handkerchief from his pocket and uses it. Eric and Mack bookend against Dave. He holds onto them tightly for over a minute. Mack gives him a comforting tap on the back as Dave releases a deep exhale.

"God, I didn't expect it to hurt like this." Mack tries to dry his eyes and scans the room. "Where's Unka Rob?"

"I should just chuck it all. Go to a remote beach. Learn a new trade." Dave looks at the crowd as a minister walks to the front of the room. The crowd moves to the seating area. "Research might do you some good, Dad. Get away for a while. Recharge. But let's not talk about that now." Eric coaxes Dave to move to the front of the room.

Nancy scans the faces in the crowd. "I don't see Rob. Mack, have you heard from him?" Mack shakes his head.

Dave fumes and looks around one last time. No Rob. So much for family sticking together. He looks up to the front of the room to a large projected screen filled with Jeanne's images. A woman who had floated into his life as a sort of ethereal being. This isn't how it was supposed to go.

A hush falls over the crowd as the minister steps to the podium. The truth of his words hit Dave like a lightning bolt. "We are here to honor the life of a special woman, healer, activist, educator, and mother, Dr. Jeanne Lane."

For **Dave**, the intensity of his pain turns the room into a blank wall of static white.

CHAPTER 1

TWO YEARS LATER.
PAPUA NEW GUINEA, 2005

The six-seater Cessna sputters and dips as it hugs the coastline and banks a turn toward a clearing near the beach line. After passing a steep mountain peak, the endless panorama below turns to deep shades of green sliced with chocolate rivers. The plane's cabin is filled with five research scientists, who all hold on to support straps that hang from the ceiling on the bumpy descent.

Dave sits behind the pilot's seat and after two hours of noxious fumes from the engine, he's glad to see their destination unfold. He watches the faces of his crew as they struggle against their seatbelts. The only woman in the group, Isabelle, tracks their progress with a folded map of Papua New Guinea, the lettering PNG stands out. Her pen streaks across the page as they drop several feet at once. She looks up to Dave, annoyed.

He calls out to the team, "Almost there!" He watches the anxious eyes of his colleague, Dr. Z, holding on to an air sickness bag with white-knuckled hands, looking twenty years older under the stress.

Two grad students accompany them, both with the beginnings of thick stubble on their jawlines. Billy, a more than enthusiastic photographer, has his Canon lens pressed up against the glass window, partially blocking Drew's view. They emit contained excitement of five-year-olds as they compete for viewing of the salt-water crocodiles basking in the sun along the river. Nearby, a wide range of mountains stretch across the mainland like an exposed spine.

Billy is animated. He smiles at the densely forested and topographically forbidding carpet of green before them. His eyes dance with delight as he shoots. "Did you see those crocs down there?" He sighs a breath of relief at knowing he really is here. It isn't a dream.

Drew, a typical graduate student letting his first beard grow, uses his elbow to clean the window on his side of the plane. "Yup, salt-water crocodile, Crocodylus Porasus. They are widespread in this area. We'll find New Guinea crocs in the freshwater ahead. They are smaller, but still have a nasty bite."

Billy pauses for a moment, notes their size even at altitude, and says under his breath, "Look at those snappers." He grins, thinking about their adventure and what the next few weeks will reveal. How many submissions can he send to *National Geographic*? He will have to call his buddy who interned for the magazine when they get back.

Dave checks the fork in the river against the map in his hand. He leans into the pilot. "What do you think, land in about fifteen?" The bush pilot nods at Dave and flips several switches on the dashboard. Dave tries not to look at the rust-lined compartment they've been crammed into, and the loose screw dancing around his feet. Surely, the casement body must be missing more screws? His technical mind flashes to lift, drag, and landing before reviewing the bios of the crew behind him one more time.

It had taken Dave over a year to get the grant and pull together the team. He had needed to get out of the rat-race of board meetings and administrators. Nothing had been working since Jeanne's passing. His temper was short. Conversations were shorter. Forget trying to sleep a full night, no matter how tired he got. He had tried cutting the alcohol, but that didn't go well. After moving and downsizing, he knew it wasn't the environment. HE had to change. After he limited the drinking to one drink per week and spent almost a year closed up in the lab, working on the schematics of blood testing following a lead Jeanne had mentioned at their last dinner together, he quieted the pain. He kept sane by replaying that moment in his mind a million times every night in the lab. As the test results continued to improve, Biometrix made the call and offered the grant specifically for him, and he finally had his first full night's sleep.

Drew calls out over the loud hum of the propellers, "I watched *Romancing the Stone* too many times when I was a kid." He clicks photos out the window, with his own camera. He had promised Dave he would look out for Uncle Z and be the extra eyes on statistics needed for their data. They couldn't afford any screw-ups on this trip. It was a one-time deal. "Can't wait to get out there!"

The plane lurches forward and drops fifty feet. Z pulls the bag to his face but doesn't use it. Isabelle pats Z on the leg and catches Dave's eye as he talks to the interns. He smiles at the crew. "I'm going to remind you of that in a week or two." He gives Z a "thumbs up" and turns to take in the surroundings. Stands of Melaleuca, a paper bark eucalyptus, stretch across the land to the base of the mountain before them. To the right, a large garden of sugar cane, bamboo, yams, and vegetables is enclosed by a bamboo fence at the edge of a village. On one side of the clearing, mud huts on poles create a small community. At the beach, about a dozen long, thin, dug-out canoes line the water's edge.

The pilot calls out over the loud roar of the prop, "Brazza Delta. We need a second fly-over after they've cleared that stretch of beach from the crocs. Everyone sit tight. We're gonna land."

Below them, villagers run toward the crocs, waving, and yelling as a group. The remaining three crocs finally move into the water with a swishing of their tails.

The plane turns, dips, and makes a bouncing landing on the strand of a long beach. It taxis to a bit of a rise and powers down.

Dave unbuckles as they wait for the pilot to unlatch the door from the outside. He bends over, looking out the side window, and murmurs a prayer of thanks on arriving. *Finally, away from it all*, he thinks. He looks at the team briefly. Their optimism over the trek before them would soon show in tight lines on their faces and muscles pushed too far. How would they hold up? That was the real question.

He closes his eyes and calls out an affirmation to Jeanne in his mind to *get the samples and keep the crew safe*. The dangers here are real and right in front of them.

Dr. Zahir, known affectionately as "Z", stands and stretches. He folds the barf bag back into the seat pocket and rubs his hands along his trim white beard. "Guess this is the point of no return." Deep wrinkles in his pants make him look even shorter than his 5'4" frame. His thoughts turn briefly to his wife waiting at home for him in Boston. She would be reading the paper at the kitchen table right now.

Isabelle smiles at him. "This is a lifelong dream of mine," she says, in a strong English accent that rolls off her tongue like butterscotch. Short brown hair frames her face, accenting her brilliant blue eyes. "Heading into the deep on a real scientific exploration." She sighs. Years of sitting behind a desk in London and dreaming of this day made her realize she needed to find a new job. Something that would get her out more and make a difference. She would prove Stephanie's words wrong. She could make things happen when she wanted to.

Dave addresses the group. "We're behind schedule already. So, let's not dally. And get your gear where it needs to be. We are burning daylight." Dave looks out the window. "Looks like our guide, Malcolm, is here and ready to go. Everybody set?" They all gather their items and give their backpacks a final zip. Isabelle rubs in a line of suntan lotion quickly all over her face.

The door opens, and a blast of heated humidity hits them all. As if on cue, they put their sunglasses and hats on in unison and move away from the propellers, cradling backpacks and holding onto miscellaneous gear packs. A small group of village children ran past to help with their luggage.

Isabelle comments, "Bloody brilliant," as she scans the area.

Dave shouts above the slowing engine sound. "Don't let the children touch the equipment." He waves his hands, motioning for the young villagers to step back. The team makes a protective circle around the gear as they watch a rugged man in his early forties step forward from the tree line. He calls out "NOGUT!" in a booming voice, which stops the children in their tracks. They sit and watch the newcomers as the man approaches.

Z stops one child from touching a bag. "I've got it." He looks at the seated group and puffs up his chest. "No one touches the communication gear but me." Adjusting his shirt away from his body, he steps forward, holding his arms out like a barrier. Z wipes away a line of sweat. He knew this was his last chance to forage, to feel the rush of adrenalin, and to have a true adventure. He didn't want to bring Drew, but he needed a break from their routine as well, so here they were, and he had promised his wife he wouldn't kill him.

A child takes the man's hand as he walks to the scientists at the landing. "Wet liklik," he says, to the child who runs off to be with the others. "Welcome to Brazza River. I am Malcolm Hadu, your guide." He spreads his hands wide as he talks, smiling, with white teeth blazing against his dark skin. Padded shoes with soles made from old tires cover his feet. Isabelle returns the smile as one child hands her a flower. "Lovely. Simply lovely. What a welcome." Isabelle sighs and adjusts her sunglasses. "Dreams do come true."

Dave steps forward and holds out his hand for Malcolm to shake. "Glad to see you, that's for sure! I'm Dr. David Lane, leader of the exploration."

Malcolm takes his hand. "Good to meet you, mate. Everyone will have to help unload the plane as your delay put us behind schedule. If you will separate your things into food, clothing, and gear, we can load the canoes." He points to three separate areas on the beach next to three large dugout canoes. "Let's see what you brought?"

Within seconds, the team is sweat-drenched. Dave's silver hair is plastered to his scalp. He wipes the moisture from his bald head and readjusts his baseball hat. His long arms hang a large backpack, dropping the last item onto one of the piles, and then he rummages through his pack. Facing away from the group, he holds up a laminated sheet with basic contact information on one side and a large map on the other.

Billy reaches for it, but Dave holds firm. "I've got it," he grumbles as he stands and faces the group. His joints pop loudly as he turns. "Everyone has the same sheet in their info pack." His eyes narrow. "Let's get one thing straight now. Don't anyone touch my stuff."

They all watch Malcolm briefly look through the piles and efficiently stack everything into three canoes. His speed is amazing.

Billy's constant camera clicking echoes across the valley floor and bounces back from the rock wall on the other side. The truth of their situation is all around them as they stand in silence looking at no-man's-land.

Isabelle hands Dave a freshwater canteen, which he drains before returning it to her. "Thanks," he says, as he stretches his arms above his head. "I'm getting too old for this hands-on stuff. Maybe I ought to go back to the university and the soft life after this." He grins at Isabelle. "Sure, you're up for this?"

Isabelle continues to take photos with her phone. "I love it here." She motions to Malcolm and says, under her breath while looking at Dave, "Malcolm is well known, we're lucky to get him." Malcolm turns and smiles at the team. "I had to pull heavy favors with my central World Wildlife Federation office to even get permission to go into the west at this time of year. See what a ten-year employment bonus gets you? He's everybody's go-to guy in this area."

Dave stretches his shoulders and then offers her a hand with her gear. "I've heard that Malcolm is an incredible guide. Believe me, we're going to need him. I'm rusty with field work." He watches the proficient efforts of Malcolm as he tucks the gear into each canoe. Finally, out of sight of phones, computers, and endless meetings, Dave takes a deep breath and lets it out slowly.

"Not me. I'm based out of the London office and monitor palm production stats. Really exciting stuff. I live to get out here. This is my third year of foraging out of the office and into the wild. Doesn't get wilder than this." She lifts the gear with an experienced hand. "Have you been away from academia long?" she asks.

"I had to do something different with my life. Plus, there's only so much BS you can put up with around campus politics and fundraising. I gave the department twenty years. This new gig with pharmaceutical research makes my soul sing. The data looks promising. I set my own hours, pick the research projects I want to drive on, and bill them accordingly."

Dave and Isabelle drop the last of their gear beside the canoe. "I look forward to getting to know everyone better on this trip." Isabelle sneaks a quick drink from her canteen.

Dave smiles as he watches the crew. *We might just pull this off,* he thinks to himself. There was a sense of satisfaction niggling at the edge of his brain. He'd like to end his career in research on a high note and get the accolades for the department research and scientific papers that would follow. After that, he didn't know what he really wanted to do.

Malcolm stands back, satisfied that the canoes are packed. Drew and Billy hand him the last of the gear.

"I'm sure we'll all have brilliant connections on this excursion," says Isabelle, as she continues to pull information out of Dave. "Do you have any kids?" They talk as they watch Malcolm re-pack things and several of the children take off running after large blue butterflies.

"Yes, two boys. Mack is finishing his master's degree at Texas A&M, in environmental engineering. He's a die-hard Aggie. Eric has a little more adventure running through his veins. He finished his master's in geology, has a great job he loves, and has a steady girl." He pauses briefly. "They don't need me anymore. How 'bout you? What's life like in London?"

"London has a vibrancy to it. The city seems to hum with life. Sometimes maybe too much life. And I absolutely love history." She shelters her eyes as she scans the area. Z, the oldest in the group, walks over and momentarily staggers. His feet turn in the deep sand they are standing in.

"Good heavens." Isabelle steps to his side. "Sure, you're okay, Dr. Z?" She takes a step closer to him. Billy and Drew join them.

Sweat drips off Z's short wiry beard. "No worries, tired, that's all. Please call me Z. Looks like my canoe is ready. I tell you what, knowing we are about to get into that water with those crocs is making my heart beat a little faster." He gives Dave a nervous look. "Dave has been trying to get me on site for years. I'm hoping to have real adventures on this trip. You did promise?"

Dave shakes his head and smiles. "Well, I did promise a long time ago." His thoughts go back to a younger, energetic Z, back in college. He had gotten more serious with age, but the twinkle in his eyes was still there.

After checking his watch, Dave calls out. "We're even after this. Drew and Z take up the rear. Isabelle, you're in the lead canoe with Malcolm, so you'll have to be on snake watch. Billy and I are in the second with the communication gear." He tries not to get distracted by a loud splash in the water from the crocs.

"Didn't mean to interrupt you guys." Z gingerly gets into his canoe. He pads his knees with a rolled-up T-shirt. "Sure, you don't want me with the gear?" Z points to the pile as Dave finishes placing a tarp over the electronics.

"I've got it, Z. You just worry about keeping up with us. Our arm muscles will be killing us by the end of the day." Dave stretches out his arm, giving it a good extension. *I am not too old for this.* "But it's only five-to-six weeks, right? Hope everyone did their conditioning. We will know if you didn't."

The rest of the team steps into their primitive dugouts. Three large crocs move into a fan pattern on the far bank. Z watches them closely as he wipes the sweat from his brow. He pats the side of the canoe. "Did you carve these out for us?" Z looks at Malcolm.

"Naw, we borrow out here. No problem." Malcolm holds onto Isabelle's hand as she settles in. "But don't tap the boat. That can attract the crocs." Isabelle's eyes go wide as she looks over to Z and pulls her hands in, keeping them close to herself. Dave tries to distract Z. "Isabelle is telling me how much she loves history and living in such an old city." Dave settles into the rear seat with Billy in front as they push off the bank.

A constant stream of clicking noises comes from Billy's camera as he takes hundreds of photos. Everyone cranes their neck to the primal vista before them as they enter the first gorge on the river while continuing to monitor the crocs following them.

Dave touches Billy on the back with his oar. "I expect you to dip your paddle into the water, not take constant photos. I'll give you some leeway, but put some muscle into it."

The team talks back and forth between canoes. Z's shirt is soaked as he tries to engage Isabelle. "Well, if you love history, you're in the right place. I just finished reading an article about a civilization on the eastern side of the island. They're dating pots from that era at sixty thousand years." Z's voice quivers slightly as he responds.

Isabelle giggles. "Not what I think of when I say history. My history is more geology-based. Guess it's all in your perspective and interest." A large croc bellows from across the river and five animals hit the water at once. It cuts Isabelle's conversation short. Frozen, they watch in amazement at the primitive scene before them. "At least we don't have to worry about hippos."

"It makes me think we're back in time, watching nature at its best." Z looks around in awe. "Just listen to the jungle calling out to us." He cups his hand behind his ear. They listen to the mix of alarm calls coming from the canopy.

"It will take years to truly understand what the jungle is telling you, but I'm happy to translate." Malcolm slices his paddle into the water with precision.

Isabelle grins. "Last summer, I was part of the aid contingent in the Eastern Highlands Province with the New Tribes Mission group on the south end of the island. Worked with several Americans finishing up some Peace Corps programs. But it was all village life-oriented and water system development training. Heading out into the deep is something I've dreamt of doing. Back at headquarters, we call it 'the deep'." She frowns, looking at an extra-large croc. "Funny, but in my dreams, there weren't any crocs."

"There never are, are there?" says Dave. They stroke their paddles in unison as they pass the predators. "I just hope we don't get in the middle of any tribal conflicts."

Isabelle takes a handkerchief out of her bag, wets it, and drapes it around her neck. Z watches her and, with caution, quickly dips his bandana in as well. He looks at her with concern. "Sure, you're okay? The natives can be quite possessive with single women. I don't understand it really, but I've heard of some unsettling encounters," he said, as he looks at a large croc moving in their direction. Z rests his oar for a moment. "Isabelle, I'd like to be your "stand-in husband"'. Grab my hand. My wife doesn't have to know."

Dave touches the back of Billy with a sweep of his blade. "If you don't stop taking pictures and start paddling, I may have to re-think our arrangement." Billy paddles with earnest.

Malcolm turns to Dave. "You know, that's not a bad idea. Isabelle, as the only woman in our group, all eyes will be on you. Bunking with Z and acting like a wife will elevate your safety." Dave smiles. "Isabelle, you can have your pick from our group." He spreads his arms wide. A flock of white birds flies from the tree canopy behind him.

"Z will be fine, and I won't tell my girlfriend about it either," she says, as she pulls ahead with her strokes.

After another hour, Dave smiles at his team as he recalls the monumental effort it had taken to get everyone signed up, not to mention winning the grant. Months of paperwork, meetings, and research documentation brought them all to this tiny point on the globe. The initial testing in the lab had shown such promise. Getting viable blood samples from three types of bats could lead to a cure for diabetes. Ending his career in research on such a high note would be something he could be proud of. He could author papers for the next five years and think about retiring to that honeymoon coastal cottage he had purchased for Jeanne twenty years ago. She would have liked that. He wouldn't be the guy sitting on the porch, though. He'd have to keep his mind active, or he would go nuts.

A field of crimson bushes lay on either side of the team as they cruise along the river. From the top of a stand of eucalyptus, a flock of sea eagles quietly watch the canoes pass. They are massive and frightening as their heads turn in unison, looking like something made in a Disney animation lab.

"Just pretend it's the Jungle Cruise ride at Disney World," Drew shouts over to Billy. He points out the sea eagles to Billy, who immediately focuses on them. A curtain of trees hangs over the river, so they keep to the middle. Now and then, they get a glimpse of a bank of white puffy clouds on the horizon.

"Karkar Island is off to the northeast from here," Malcolm shouts. He points with his paddle, then dips it seamlessly into the water. "Everybody, try to pick up the pace. Day one of a six-week excursion and we're behind schedule." With renewed energy, all three units move forward.

Dave shouts to all. "After that 4.9 earthquake on the 19th, we've been having quite a few minor tremors in the area. The data show that we're in for another eruption. By the way, that information is not in your packet."

As if on cue, there is a rumbling sound in the distance, and the surrounding water vibrates, splashing a little water up the side of one canoe. "That's another slight tremor. Nothing to be concerned about," exclaims Malcolm. "I just got back from visiting family over at Gubin Hospital. No worries. Everything is fine there. They had one floor collapse with the big earthquake of 2020. Nothing to collapse out here."

Billy was watching a large croc that had been following them. It submerged with seismic activity. He looks around nervously and yells to Drew. "Did you see that big yellow one back there?" Drew smiles and gives him a little wave. He turned, watching the back of his Uncle Z, sometimes feeling his eyes on him, just waiting for him to screw up again, after almost catching the lab on fire last semester. *He couldn't be blamed for everything, could he?*

They paddle for hours before Malcolm calls out to the group. "We'll have to pull in for the night and set up camp. It'll be dark soon. Hydrate yourselves now because we'll be getting busy in about half an hour." Malcolm drops a fishing line off the back of their canoe, never missing a beat of his paddle. Dave and Billy are alongside them.

"Won't that attract the crocs?" Isabelle watches the taunt line. "Yes, it will if I leave it in too long." Malcolm tugs the bamboo pole with a flick of his wrist, and a nice sized peacock bass lands near Isabelle's feet. In a flash, he stabs the fish, and it stops flopping. "It's the movement and vibration that will attract the crocs, not the smell. Inside the dugout, don't even tap your foot."

Malcolm puts the line back into the water. "Good to know." Isabelle looks at her shoes and the bleeding bass. "My last assignment didn't offer to go this deep." Purple, blue, and gold scales flash as the last rays of sunlight hit the bass. "That's a beautiful fish. But now, I'm almost afraid to breathe."

Malcolm catches her eye as he responds. "We don't have any big predators other than the crocs, but there are vipers, and poisonous tree frogs that can do you in. Don't underestimate even the smallest creature when we get on land."

After hours, the sun lowers on the horizon, and Dave calls over to Malcolm. "Don't want to be out here too late. Can we find a landing?" Malcolm moves them toward shore. As they pull up, Malcolm announces, "Let's camp." They stop in a small clearing with a slight incline up from the water's edge. The deep blue-black water swirls and pools in the inlet. The evening sun sets with a brilliant orange streak across the sky, illuminating dark storm clouds in the distance.

Dave calls out as they tie down the first tarp. "Camp meeting tonight." Drew efficiently sweeps the area clear with a cut off branch, then digs a fire pit using a broken branch. The loose sand gives way easily. Billy does his part by collecting firewood when he isn't distracted by the foliage around them. The others put up their tents for the night. The mood lightens when Billy whistles the theme song from the *Andy Griffith Show* as he strings a tarp over the fire area.

On the side, Dave, Z, and Isabelle secure the tents and make sure the communication gear is safely secured. Isabelle strings her hammock between a few trees and drapes the mosquito netting around.

Silently watching the team and the gentle rustling coming from their left, Malcolm eyes a creature moving along the foliage. He squats over the fire pit and digs a small hole at the base, placing a handful of large sweet potatoes wrapped in banana leaves inside. He builds the fire over it, then puts the fish to cook over the flames. "It should rain in about twenty minutes, so get your gear inside as soon as possible." He calls out, "Will probably rain all night."

The team looks up to see clear skies overhead through a filtered canopy. A few eyebrows are raised, but they secure their gear, anyway. Later that evening, as everyone huddles under the cooking fire canopy, Dave addresses the group. The rain falls in torrents around them. Isabelle swats a flea on her leg and flicks it off into the brush.

"We are at the point of no return, Dave muses, as he turns to the group. If anyone wants to make a call, now is the time to do it. As I mentioned before, in your packet, satellite coverage is limited the farther we go." Z coughs and motions for Dave to continue. "Watch your bites and use your antibiotic cream on every open cut. Infection can start easily out here, especially on your feet. When we hike, your hot, wet boots will be a good breeding ground for infections. Blisters will happen to all of us. If you can keep a pair of socks dry, do so. I don't want to amputate any toes." Dave winces for effect.

He stirs his tea and takes a deep drink. "There will be times of complete exhaustion on our trek, and we will take the most direct routes: straight up or straight down. That means little zig-zagging back and forth up those steep mountains. Sometimes our trail will only be wide enough for one foot with gut wrenching drop-offs to the side. You'll face deep gorges and raging rivers below. If you hit a wall of exhaustion, let me know, or let Malcolm know."

Z groans out loud as he fidgets with a headlamp. "Drew, that's why I brought you here." He hands Drew the headlamp. Billy fiddles with his slingshot.

Dave continues, "We hadn't planned on this stop. We'd hoped to make it to the village, but it's another two hours upstream. If we can, we'll stay in the smaller villages, but prepare yourselves. It will be mud and hills, hills and mud, for the next three-to-four weeks. Every morning we'll meet at the breakfast fire for the day's itinerary. If we can get forty blood samples from our key targets, then our mission will be a success. Are there questions or observations to share?" Dave looks directly at Billy, who isn't paying attention.

Billy takes aim with his slingshot at something moving at the perimeter of the camp and lets it fly. A squeal cut short in the darkness and almost immediately, three flashlights lit up the area. A one-foot rat lay dead nearby. They go over to inspect the animal.

"Specht's Mosaic-tailed Rat, I believe," Z leans over the body. He grabs it by the speckled tail and holds it close to his flashlight. "Great, it's a threatened species." Drew frowns at Billy. "Sorry, it was a reflex," Billy says dejectedly.

Dave shakes his head and rubs his forehead. *Why did I bring him? Give me patience, Lord. Jeanne, I can hear you saying, 'Be' nice.' Billy promises to hold back on his impulses, and on the first night, he lets it fly.* Dave sighs in frustration.

Billy keeps his head down, not making eye contact with the rest of the crew as Z throws the body of the rat into the river and returns with a length of netting in his hands. "Extra netting," he says, as he throws it on the ground.

"Let's not lose sight of what we're here for." Dave looks at each member. "This isn't a cheap hike in the woods. Everyone has a role to play, a significant role. Isabelle will document deforestation. Z is our communication expert and biologist. Drew, you will assist Z with specimens and documentation. Billy, I want photographs of everything unusual or key to our research. Especially any new bat species that we may find." Billy gives a "thumbs up."

"As I told each of you, our goal is to get the blood samples and stats from those key bat species. Everyone will take turns in the nets. Refer to your documents if needed. Gloves are mandatory when handling the bats. I don't want to send anyone for rabies shots. We will have a review of the process with the first few animals. But you all will be proficient with the process in a short time. Questions?" Dave scans their faces.

Malcolm points to the cooking fire and the pot of water boiling. "Hydration is the number one thing that will keep you going. If you don't empty both canteens by lunch, I will know. Don't go ANYWHERE alone. Everybody got their compass?" Each member stands and shows off their belt compass.

Isabelle joins in. "I am looking for any areas of deforestation. Please, keep your eyes on the watch for them." Dave brushes off his pants and points to Drew. "Drew, you, and Billy, climb up the hill and stretch out the netting for the evening. We may get lucky and catch our first bats."

Drew and Billy take the netting, push their broad-billed hats down on their heads, and walk into the foliage. The rain stops, but the trees drip heavily onto them. Dave sits and reviews his documentation.

Isabelle moves toward her tent, but then stops and turns back to Z and Dave. "Z, would you have a little extra netting that I may use tonight?" She takes a step forward. "I thought I might fashion a sort of perimeter around my tent in case any of those crocs decide to explore our camp. I don't want to disturb the specimen netting." She ponders the hammock she set up versus the tent with the zipper.

"Yes, I have a second net, if you're careful with it." He rummages through his pack. Z's attention turns to a sound in the tree next to his tent. He turns his headlamp to the tree where a pair of eyes reflect at him. A black-spotted cuscus freezes in the light's glare half-way up the tree, almost hidden in the foliage.

The jungle quiets in the night, but movement sounds become more apparent. Malcolm scans the camp and walks the perimeter. Isabelle stops him and points to her hammock. "Would it be safer to sleep in the hammock or the tent? How close will those gators come up from the water?" He smiles at her. His white teeth reflect in the campfire. "Since it's raining, you might want to use the tent. I'll be sleeping in my hammock."

Dave holds his light firmly over the animal. "No telling what we are going to find." Isabelle steps forward, saying, "Isn't he cute? Look at those incredible, enormous eyes."

"I think he's a cuscus," says Z.

Malcolm calls out from the fire. "Yes, and he's good to eat. Do you want me to take care of it for you?" He holds a sharpened stick in his hand. "We could have him for breakfast." In a huff, Isabelle whispers, "I refuse to eat monkey."

"No, let's let it go this time. You fixed a fine dinner this evening. Is there anything you need, Malcolm?" Dave moves toward the campfire. Malcolm shakes his head. "Got it covered, mate. Remember, this is my home. I've got extra kindling for the fire. That should keep the crocs away." Dave puts his hand on Malcolm's shoulder. "Anything at all. Let me know. I'm going to bed." He walks over and unzips his tent. "Keep an eye out for Billy, will ya? His enthusiasm can get away from him. He's the only one I'm worried about."

Dave calls out from his tent. "Early wake up tomorrow. See you at sunup. If we catch something, let me know." Isabelle stands looking at her netting and places several sharp sticks in a circle about her tree base and hammock. She looks at Z. "Do you think the crocs will come up this far?" "We're all in trouble if that happens." He walks to his hammock and grabs a big stick. Tucking it in against his body, he settles into his hammock and closes his eyes.

In the middle of the night, a ruckus awakens the complete camp. Drew stands outside his tent and throws rocks into the bush. Malcolm watches from his hammock next to the simmering fire, but the others are quickly wide awake and are there too, standing close by. Malcolm gets up and puts another log on the fire. Isabelle stands close to Malcolm, wide-eyed.

"What is it, for God's sake?" Dave wipes the sleep from his eyes. Billy's hair is at all angles. The coals from the campfire illuminate the area with low light. Z looks sheepish and nods in Drew's direction. "Rats," says Drew.

"Yeah, well, they might not bother you, but you didn't wake up to a rat sitting on top of you," Drew mumbles, out of breath. "And this wasn't like those cute little rats that we feed to the snakes in the lab." He wipes the spittle from his face with the back of his hand. "I can't believe you got me out here." He looks at Z with malice. Z rummages through their tent, then steps back outside to join them.

Isabelle audibly shivers. "Rats?"

"Was your tent zipped?" asks Dave calmly.

"It was hot when we got back from securing the nets, and I might have left the door open to get a breeze going." Drew wipes at his chest and cleans his hands on his pants.

"Next time, keep the tent zipped. No telling what might venture inside!" Dave turns and enters his tent. Billy is close behind him. "Now, do you see why following directions is important?" Dave flops down on his thin sleeping bag as Billy carefully zips the screen closed on their tent. As they lie down, Drew's silhouette is backlit by the campfire. Billy turns and watches Drew pace and stop, pace, and stop. "He's just standing there," comments Billy. Dave turns his back. "Not my problem. Get some sleep. You're going to need it." After a breath or two, Dave snores.

The sky lightens with the first hints of sunrise, and there are soft sounds of birds awakening. Dave stirs. He hears the snap of the campfire roaring and crawls out of the tent to join Malcolm near the embers. He watches Malcolm set more logs on. "Morning," he says, looking around the quiet campsite. The river shimmers chocolate in the morning light.

"Mate." Malcolm squats near the fire and throws a pot of water on to cook. The water in the pot swirls a dingy brown. A variety of vegetables lay on the ground beside him. He peels them expertly with a large knife. "If you have another pot, I'd love a cup of hot water. I'm a tea drinker." Dave pulls a tea bag from his shirt pocket. "Anything happen last night?"

"Not that I know of." Malcolm chops a sweet potato into small chunks. "There is some evidence that one croc came up close, but the fire protected us." Dave sees the dirt-marked trail from the water's edge up about twenty feet to the fire. He looks over to Isabelle's tent. An array of broken sticks circles her area as if it would stop an army of pigmies.

Malcolm takes a saucepan, adds some water, and puts it on to boil. "I'll make extra boiled water for everyone to fill up canteens each morning. But you'll have to remind them. I'm not anyone's mother." The purification tablets he adds to the pot. It hisses and bubbles, turning the mixture a light tan. Drew stumbles from his tent carrying his backpack, which he plops down nearby. He sorts through his gear, lining up all the contents in the dirt.

Dave walks over. "Checking everything out?" He watches Drew hold up the strap and thinks that this lesson will be good for everyone to keep their tents zipped. "Yeah, those darn rats chewed through a bit of the strap on my backpack. I think it will still hold, but I'm trying to repair it with my first-aid needle. It's not quite strong enough to go through the nylon." He shows the damage to Dave. He throws down his needle and digs into the remnants of his bag. "Where's my duct tape?"

"I've got a bit. Let me get it." Dave unzips the tent and shakes Billy's foot to wake him. Billy groans. "What time is it?" Dave rolls up his bag, saying under his breath, "Time to get up and make the donuts." He smiles as Billy's eyes get wide and then close again.

Dave rifles through his backpack pockets until he finds a small roll of duct tape. "Found it," he calls out. He shakes Billy's foot again. "Hey Billy, go check in with Z up the hill. Let's see if we caught anything." Dave leaves the tent door open and walks back to Drew, throwing him the roll. "Use it sparingly," he says. Drew catches it and nods.

Isabelle steps briefly into the woods, sweeping the area with a stick as she moves. She re-enters camp quickly while zipping up her pants. She rolls up the netting, checking the ground for tracks. A look of alarm flashes across her face when she sees the footprints and tail drag of a large croc across the camp thirty feet from her area. Dave joins her and helps take down the security and netting. He knocks over some spike sticks. "Nice defense system. How'd you sleep?" he asks. "Not as restful as I hoped. After we do some of that hiking, I know I'll sleep really well."

They walk a few steps to Dave's tent and take it down together.

"I'm going to need to get photos of that foliage before we leave." Isabelle points to a large bush at the perimeter. Billy's singing in the distance diverts her attention from the foliage. Then, from the bush, they hear Z hollering. "Do you have to wake up the world?"

With his strap repaired, Drew steps over to check on the tarp covering the electronics. He gives Dave a "thumbs up" before joining Malcolm near the fire.

Everyone watches Billy and Z return to camp. They enter as knights returning from war, holding up the entanglement netting and two large squirming bats. Their gloved hands twist as they try to keep the bats from getting tangled in the nets. Dave calls out to them, "Great, I'll get my gear." He picks up his medic bag and rushes to their side. *This is exactly why we are here.* Dave beams as he looks over the bats. The largest bat has a wingspan of two feet.

"Let's see what we've got here," Dave says, approaching Z. "Check out the yellow eyes and ears. I still can't get used to them." The bat twists awkwardly and tries to take a bite of Z. "Careful, you don't want to go through more shots." The bat twists again and almost bites Dave before he throws a towel over its eyes. Z gets a better grip with his gloved hand. "Tube-nosed fruit bat with a face only a mother could love." He holds the animal so everyone gets a good look at it. The caramel-colored creature has a protrusion on its nose and a face that looks like it flew directly into a wall.

Billy struggles with his unhappy bat. It is much larger than the first one. Drew walks over with his gloves and takes the creature from him. "Big-eared mastiff bat?" He calls out to Dave.

"Yup," says Z. "We're going to have everyone watch for the first sample. It will only take a few minutes and these boys can be on their way home."

Dave grins at everyone. "I just need a few minutes to get a blood sample and take a few stats." Dave uses a fallen branch to hold the bat steady. He adjusts the towel holding the bat and gently takes a blood sample and measurement. "Be sure to get the blood sample from near the joint at the shoulder." Everyone watches closely as he takes a small blood sample with the edge of a knife. He clips a metal tag to the bat's foot. "That's all there is to it." Dave lifts the bat, and it takes off. "Be sure to note all the measurements. Hopefully, we'll get our target on this trip."

Malcolm calls out to everyone. "Hey, bring your canteens over, and breakfast is ready." No one moves toward the campfire as they watch the second specimen being tagged. Malcolm shakes his head and fills his own banana leaf plate. He mutters as he takes the first bite and thinks about the way they first contacted him about the trek. He had been back in the city center to fill out paperwork for a friend's surgery and aftercare, when he ran into the director of the Forestry Research Group. Past tours into the deep with teams from the lab had been some of his more enjoyable excursions. As a personal favor, Malcolm had agreed to contact Dr. Lane, hoping to be hired full-time by the research group.

He watches those around him, the intensity of their interest. They seem like a good bunch, but how will they be after a few weeks out, without their comforts? Most Americans are soft, unable to withstand the rain, bugs, and crocs for any length of time. Behind him, a bird of paradise call floats in the morning's symphony. It's too early to tell if this would be a good trek or one of the many disappointing ones. He takes another bite of breakfast and waits for the crew to join him.

The disassembling of the camp takes a little longer than Malcolm would like, but it's only their second day. He shows the younger men how to strap the covering over the equipment and they do a pretty good job of duplicating the knots.

After canoeing for about an hour, Billy and Dave paddle up beside Isabelle and Malcolm in the lead canoe. "Could you smile for me, Isabelle?" Billy asks, adjusting his lens. Different-colored blue and yellow wild butterflies have landed on her wide-brimmed hat. Flame of the forest trees are in full bloom behind her, splashing streaks of red throughout the jungle. Large white orchid petals dot the shoreline. "Lovely, isn't it?" shouts Isabelle toward Dave.

"Some aren't." Dave pulls a large, fat leech off the side of his leg and tosses it into the water. "But you are stunning, Isabelle." He points to her hat. "Take it off for a second?" With a questioning look on her face, Isabell lifts the hat. Her face lights up as she studies the butterflies and dragonflies in front of her. "I didn't even know they were there." Extending her finger, one crawls on. Billy takes another shot. Isabelle exclaims, "Now this would be the hat to wear to Ascot!" She gently places the hat back on her head and poses for Billy.

"This one is for my department head for my next proposal. He can't turn down funding with an image like this!" She turns, giving Billy a great profile. Dave adds, "It just needs a spray of palm fronds for back up. How did you get interested in Aceraceae?" Isabelle turns toward him. "Wow, I'm impressed. Most people don't know about the study of perennials and acaules."

Dave scratches his itchy scalp. "I read up on each member of the crew. You came highly recommended by the World Wildlife Foundation." He watches her eyes light up. "Palm trees have become my passion. Especially when they are being decimated in such large numbers." She points to a patch of palms spread across the hillside to their left. Malcolm breaks out into a native song, "Ol Singsing Bilong Lotu na Bilong Ol Pikinini." His voice floats across the water. "It helps to sing to give the villagers a call, so they know we are coming." He winks at Isabelle. "Better than a phone call around here."

Billy's camera clicks at a collection of colored water snakes who dance across the mirrored surface in front of them. "At this rate, the village should be about a half an hour up on the right. Malcolm nods to Dave. He continues to sing as they paddle.

A break in the foliage shows a misty cloud shrouding the mountain tops in the distance. Paddling in the humidity feels like swimming in pudding. Dave watches the number of times each member stops and takes a drink. "I'd like to spend the night and see if we can get a few men to carry our gear." Dave reviews the mounds of gear displayed in each canoe. "What do you think? Can we pick up three or four porters? Will there be a problem with some of the unrest between the tribes?" He turns toward Malcolm.

"Things have settled down, but the conflicts are more on the west coast. I haven't been up this river in two years. Change happens quickly out here. Let's see how it goes when we get there, mate." Malcolm pulls ahead with his paddle strokes. In less than an hour, shadowed figures emerge from the deep underbrush beside them.

"Wa," shouts Malcolm, as a naked man wearing a horims (penis sheath made from a gourd) raises his hand and steps out from the jungle. He holds a long spear in his hand. In response, Malcolm calls back, "Wa." The man has a string around his waist that helps keep the gourd sheath close to his body. The gourd is over a foot long. Naked young boys run along the trail in front of him as they race into the clearing ahead.

A handful of women leave their huts and walk toward the crew as they pull up to the bank that serves as a make-shift dock. Nearby, a large bird roasts on a pit near the center of the village. To the right of the clearing, a new building is in the early stages of construction. Its long stilts are holding it in place. There are crude carvings displayed on the huts. Small, fenced garden areas are next to each hut.

"Wa!" Malcolm waves as he jumps out of the canoe and pulls it to the bank." He looks at Isabelle and softly says, "Stay in the boat until Dave and Z are beside you." "But I've got to pee really bad." She squirms uncomfortably. "Hold it a little longer," Malcolm says, as he walks up the bank.

A small group of tribal men stand behind the chief. The women are bare-chested and wear either a grass skirt or a skirt made of twisted bark strings. When they smile, most have missing teeth. Some men wear old, dirty, ragged cargo shorts, or some grass skirts, but most wear only the horims. Most of the kids wear old, beaten T-shirts or nothing at all.

Malcolm walks over to an elderly gentleman who stands to one side. After a few minutes of conversation, the man smiles and escorts the crew to the main area of the village. After gesturing and talking in the crude language, arrangements are confirmed for the porters and for securing their canoes until the return portion of the trip.

The enclave village includes about a half dozen grass-thatched huts, two of which larger than the rest. Malcolm tells the crew that one lodging is for the men and the other is for the women, children, and pigs. A round cooking hut is a bustle of activity as smoke bellows from the opening in its ceiling. From their perspective, it appears to be on fire. Nearby, pigs roam the public area like pets.

Z and Billy secure the canoes at the water's edge, then stand guard while Isabelle relieves herself. "They look like head hunters," Billy whispers, as Isabelle rejoins them. Z shakes his head. "No, these aren't, but I'm sure we'll meet some."

Dave joins Drew and Isabelle. They watch the villagers become more comfortable with them. Drew stands with his hands on his hips. "I could buy a wife for four pigs here. Think of how many wives I could afford?" He does his best Yul Brenner impression of standing with his chest out and legs spread wide. Dave tries not to laugh. Drew grins at Billy, "Dude."

Malcolm motions for Dave to come over near the chief. He strides over and nods his head in greeting, as Malcolm had shown him how to do. "I set everything. They've given us one of their huts for the night." Malcolm accepts a gourd of fermented berries from the chief. He takes a sip, then passes the drink to Dave. He struggles not to cough but finishes the drink and smiles at the chief. His thoughts trail back to the video feeds he had watched on YouTube over some of the tribal interactions. He wills himself to keep his motions slow and controlled.

The chief motions for the porters to come forward. Three wear grass skirts and one is naked except for a bright orange plastic horim. They are strong young men who appear to be in their twenties and early thirties.

Dave sees Billy giggling and raises his eyebrow in a warning. Billy stops abruptly. *That kid is going to kill me*, he thinks to himself. Better to get them busy than to have them just standing there. Dave points to the solid hut in front of them. "We are using this for the night. Go ahead, store the gear." He picks up his pack and places it inside the doorway. The rest of the team follows his lead.

Dave catches Malcolm's eye. "Should we unpack the electronics or keep them nestled in the canoe?" Malcolm raises his voice so that everyone hears. "If you don't want to lose your valuables, keep them close. Absolutely, unpack the electronics."

A woman enters the hut with a make-shift broom and sweeps out the interior as they unload. She giggles as she quickly leaves.

Z and Drew are first to the canoes with the team behind them. "Let us do this. It's better if only Drew and I touch the gear. We know what to watch for." Z hands Drew the satellite-phone backpack as Dave and Isabelle re-secure the canoes. Isabelle motions to look at Billy, who is surrounded by topless teenage girls and kids. His red hair is interesting to them. They try to touch it. Billy kneels down giving them more access to his hair.

Z smiles. "That could solve my problems. Drew could stay here, and I wouldn't have to worry about him and my grant anymore." He pauses. "I probably shouldn't be getting those ideas. My wife would kill me for letting her nephew do that." "What?" Dave says. "Nothing," says Z. "Just doing some daydreaming out loud."

One of the new porters speaks broken words of English, and he relishes saying them repeatedly, "We go 'morrow, go 'morrow." Dave nods a greeting to him and his buddies.

A group of children cluster around Malcolm as he enters the camp with an armful of netting. The children pelter him with questions about their journey and how far they are going. Dave pulls out his laminated sheet with the images of the bats on it, which the children study intently. As the sun sets, they are called into the hut to join the village for dinner and are served first by the women in the tribe. Billy looks perplexed at the food offered and whispers to Drew, "I wonder if it's human or mammal?"

Dave's thoughts drift away as he remembers sitting around the campfire with his wife and two boys in the outback of Australia and how the boys had once argued over a laminated map. He smiles and shakes himself back to reality. He looks around at the happy community and smiles.

The chief rests his feet on top of one pig and pats it while they eat. Isabelle inquires about the women of the tribe who have missing fingers. One has no fingers left on her hand, but a thumb. Malcolm explains, "It is a custom for widows to lose a finger. This lessens the pain of heartbreak when focusing on the loss of a finger instead of her man."

Stories are shared with the crew through Malcolm's translations. They are fascinated and watch as Malcolm explains that the researchers aren't here to kill the bats. Just study them. The children spend a long time looking at the images of the bats and eventually take turns drawing their own images of bats in the sandy foot of the hut. Many of the sketches are detailed. Billy takes photographs of their work. As the skies darken, a teenager talks to Malcolm.

"Apparently, they want to know if you are here to catch the Black Death?" says Malcolm. "It's a legend around here. A large flying bat who feasts on dead bodies and crocs." Billy giggles and shakes his head. "It's the Creature from the Black Lagoon." He accepts a banana leaf of fried noodles from one of the cuter village girls, who blushes when he smiles at her. Another girl touches his red curly hair, snickers, and runs away. It isn't long before one of the curious children points to Billy's slingshot. He shows the kids how to use it. The children are delighted with Billy and his toy.

On another edge of the hut, Drew lets a child listen to music through his ear buds.

"What does the Black Death look like?" Dave asks the excited teen. He tries to sketch a black lagoon creature for the kids in the sand.

The villager beckons Dave to follow him outside, which he does. Z follows, but the rest stay inside as a storm lights up the skyline. In the glow of the evening fires, the tribesman draws with a stick in the damp sand, a crude drawing of a large, winged creature with a huge crest on its head. The animal didn't seem to have legs, just feet attached to wings.

In a burst of lightning and a sudden wind, Z looks at Dave and exclaims with shock, "Looks kind of like a Pterodactyl, or some other relative of the Pterodon." Z studies the drawing closer with his flashlight. "Where did you see this?" asks Dave. His stomach drops with a lurch. He grimaces, bracing himself as his body stiffens, knowing that they stepped off the cliff of reality into something unknown. A sea of faces from the science community dismissing, and laughing at, their research flies across his mind.

CHAPTER 2

Malcolm stands in the hut's doorway. "Where did you see this?" he asks again. "How big?" The villager quickly points toward the mountain and marks the outline of the wingspan on the sand. When he finishes, the wingspan is close to twenty feet across, and includes three toes, ribbed wings, a head crest, and a long sharp beak.

Lightning flashes again, and the heavens open up, obscuring the drawing in seconds. They all quickly run inside. "When did you see this Black Death?" Malcolm asks. The man gestures while he talks for about five minutes before Malcolm can translate. He soon has everyone's attention as he relays the conversation. "His brother died two years ago. They buried him back up the hill in one of their sacred areas. Two days afterward, they found the grave disturbed and pieces of his body in the general area. When they went to re-bury him, an aerial attack swooped down from a tree and lifted one boy. Hito went to his rescue and was burned with acid on his arm. He points to a young man nearby and the father shows them his still healing scar.

"Ask him if the story is true?" Z asks. Malcolm repeats the questions, then asks if anyone else in the village has seen the creature. The boy nods. One hand raises in the small group, an elderly man with an exceptionally long gourd. He spoke for a few minutes. Malcolm translates.

"He says that years ago, while out hunting at night, he saw three of them together. He heard a loud swooshing sound and went to investigate near a clearing. There, he saw three of them flying away. They are like fire."

Malcolm asks them questions before he clarifies the response. "He says they glowed, like a fire." Z steps forward. "Bioluminescence, they had a bioluminescence?" he asks incredulously.

Dave shakes his head in disbelief. He looks back to the sketch in the sand as it disappears. Drew, who had turned off his iPod, comments from across the room, "There are no known mammals with bioluminescence." Dave groans as he sits. His knees pop as well. "Great, I'm back in my brother's world." *Keep it together*, he silently urges himself.

"What do you mean?" Isabelle scoots closer.

Dave sneers, "My brother left a well-paying job in biology to become a cryptozoologist. He's been talking up stories of Pterodactyls for years. Had my boys convinced by the time they were seven that they still flew. In fact, my son, Eric, is out exploring with him now somewhere in South America, chasing after some lead or another. He made the family name a laughingstock when he ditched a promising career in biomedical research to go chase after the unknown."

"You know," says Z, "they have no reason to make this stuff up, and they certainly don't know that they've drawn us an animal who supposedly has been extinct for thousands of years." Z walks over and inspects the young man's burn scar.

Later that evening, the chief invites the men to sleep in the "men's hut," but they decline. Everyone settles down in the visitor's hut, which they soon find is infested with fleas. As normal breathing sounds fill the hut, Billy comments softly under his breath. "Lions and Tigers and Bears, oh my."

"Shut up, Billy," Dave says, as he swats a circus of fleas on his chest.

Silence fills the air for a minute. Across the room, Drew answers, "…and Pterodactyls too."

In the early morning hours before daybreak, Z rifles through his bag, checking the charge as well as a beeping on the satellite phone. Carrying the bag with him, he returns to his bed area and softly shakes Dave awake. "We've got a message from your son, asking you to call."

Instantly awake, Dave asks, "Which one, Mack or Eric?"

Fiddling with the knobs, Z replies, "Eric." and turns the unit on as Dave lies back down. Z looks over to Isabelle, who softly stirs. "No, we can call. Give me a minute. I've got it recharging now." He sighs. "Can't sleep. Keep thinking about the creature they described, and these damn bugs."

"I know," Dave grumbles. "I want to talk to that guy again before we leave." He swats a flea and smashes it between his thumbnails. "I think I'll get up and see how Malcolm is doing. He's probably starting the campfire about now, anyway. Maybe I can get in a quick clean-up and scrub off some of these bites?"

"We all could use it, I'm sure." Dave rises. "Hold on, I'll join you. Best not to go to the water's edge without someone with you." They exit the hut to find Malcolm setting a pot of water on the community fire pit. Both say, "Morning," as they squat down by the fire and check their bodies for remnants of the night's feasting. "Top of the day," says Malcolm. "I'll have some tea ready for you shortly."

Dave laughs. "Really, top of the day?" Z grumbles. "Sorry, didn't sleep worth squat." Malcolm throws another log on the fire, and it sparks.

"Thanks, Malcolm, appreciate your thoughtfulness." Dave joins Z as they step down toward the boats. "I'd like to talk to that villager again before we leave, and I need to make a call on the satellite phone as well." Dave glances at the phone, charging, and the villagers moving about. He looks back at Malcolm.

Malcolm calls out, "No problem, I think. We can make it to the missionary village in Kantu by nightfall if we don't have too much rain today." They all look at the sky, which still drips from the deluge of rain from last night, but patches of blue-sky filter through, above them.

Their porters enter the camp. One carries a dead neon-blue and black-stripped monitor lizard. Another has part of the netting and a very agitated large red flying fox. The third porter holds onto the rest of the netting and two bats. Dave quickly grabs his bag and wakes up the rest of the crew.

"Holy crap!" calls out Z when he sees the lizard and walks over to the porters. "I've seen nothing like that before. The coloring is absolutely amazing. And look at the s-s-size of it," he stutters, and the porter lifts it up for the others to see as they tumble out of the hut. "Must be close to four feet! "Billy, get your camera and take a bunch of shots of it asap," Z calls out.

Billy stumbles out of the tent and tries to get his shoes on. "Shoot, that is one beautiful lizard!" He ducks back inside and grabs his camera. Malcolm laughs after talking to the porters briefly. "Hey, Dr. Z, they think you want to eat it." Z waves his hands "No, but tell 'em we want to study it." Z places the lizard on the ground before them.

Dave yells, "Drew, get out here and see this."

Isabelle and Drew both exit the hut at the same time. They glance at the lizard but walk over to Dave and the two bats the other porters have. "Now, that's a bat!" Isabelle exclaims as Drew puts on gloves and takes them from the porter.

"He's one of the largest, if not THE largest. It won't help our database, but I can't help but tag him and get a sample anyway." Dave works on the creature while Drew holds the bat's head between his gloved hands. Z joins them, gathering the stats. "You know, there is an exceptionally rich diversity of reptiles in New Guinea with over 170 known species. We may just have come across number 171." Z sighs in appreciation as he keeps glancing at the lizard. Dave finishes evaluating the bat. It takes off with a big swish.

"The bio-diversity of this area is like walking back in time." Isabelle stretches and looks longingly at the mountain range before them. "I am totally enraptured with the Papua, the deep." Isabelle inhales deeply. "It even smells exciting. Kind of a damp earthiness, vanilla and citrusy. I can't quite put my finger on the whole thing."

Dave secures his data. "I know what you mean. I kind of like the way you call it 'the deep.' It's fitting." He zips up his bag and turns to the crew. "Okay, since we're all here, everyone eat a substantial breakfast and check your water supplies and your bites. We all got them last night. Our porters will take the heavier packs, and I want each of you to carry one piece of our scientific gear. Z, you'll oversee the communications, and Drew, take extra care with the sonar equipment." Everyone nods in agreement.

Isabelle reaches for the banana leaf stir-fry breakfast concoction from

Malcolm and holds out her antiseptic pen. "Make sure you tag all those itches you got last night," she says, to the group, as they gather their things together. She even dabs areas on Malcolm, who looks surprised at her interest.

Some villagers shuffle out of their huts to join them by the fire. Strong smoke bellows from the nearby cooking hut. Billy watches a man skin the lizard and photographs the whole thing. The tribesman expertly cuts the skin down to strips. Billy takes a section of the discarded hide, which he folds and bands on to his straw cowboy hat.

Malcolm gathers their gear for departure, keeping one eye on the activity in the camp and choosing porters for the items. Over by the canoes, Z sets up the satellite system. He calls Dave to his side and hands him the satellite phone receiver. "Dr. Dave Lane here. Over," he says, into the mouthpiece. Static fills the line. Drew adjusts a knob, clearing the line.

"Dad, it's Eric. Got news! Renee and I are engaged. Wanted you to know it. Over." "Wonderful news, Eric. Where are you? Over?" Dave asks with lips pressed against the receiver. "El Tajin–Veracruz. (static) Here with Unka Rob. We found undiscovered Pterosaurs carvings on the Mayan (static). It's exciting. Over."

"Seems your mythological creature might have relatives here as well. Just got off the Brazza River, and we're heading to the Kantu camp tonight, in New Guinea. Over." Dave has a firm grip on the microphone. Static fills the line for a moment before a different voice interrupts. "-- new sightings? Can you confirm? Over?"

"Yeah Rob, believe it or not, recent sightings, but they're not too recent. Maybe months ago. Looks like I'll--" Dave says, as the phone goes dead in his hands. Drew tries several dials on his receiver box, but the line remains lifeless. "Sorry, looks like we didn't charge it enough. We can try later." Z puts the gear away. "I'll keep the communication gear with me. You know, it's not a new system, but it should work okay. We had it cleaned and re-calibrated before we left Boston. I re-checked the emergency pack last night. It's in good order." Z motions for Drew to join them as he adjusts the gear.

Billy drops his backpack and shows off his hat, doing mock poses. "I'm itching to get going. Can we go?" Billy rocks on his feet. Drew takes a photo of Billy with his hat as he clowns for the camera. "Yeah, might as well get underway. I wanted to talk to that villager again, but we can catch him on our return," Dave throws his backpack on. "Everyone, let's head out to the deep!"

Billy bellows, "Wagons Ho!" He takes a step and pauses. Drew and Dave stand next to him as they wait for Isabelle and Malcolm. "How are you doing? Everything good?" Drew nods and adjusts his pack. "What's the deal with you and Z? He seems to have a short fuse for you." Dave looks at the water and the space ahead of them. Drew looks at Z. "I know. He's not happy to have me along, but he's my uncle. I kind-of set his lab on fire last spring and he hasn't forgiven me for it." Drew adjusts his pack while holding onto the main communication box.

"You did what?" Dave exclaims and turns to Drew. His eyes catch the porters in the rear, each loaded as if it weighs little. Dave turns to look at Z. God, I would lose control if that happened in my lab. He should have told me about it. I'm going to have to talk to Z later. Billy grins ear to ear. "Dude, how'd you do that?" Billy smiles. "Hope it was worth it?"

Drew takes a deep breath. "It's a long story that involves excellent wine, a cute girl, and some outta control sex. Never light a candle close to research papers, especially when those papers aren't yours." He leans toward Billy, and adds, - "Totally worth it." He smiles wickedly as they move out.

The wide track through the brush soon narrows to a footpath snaking muddily through a gap in the tree line. The canopy above their heads closes in, blocking the sun and any breeze. All of them are sweat drenched within the first thirty minutes. They start their ascent up the first mountain range. Along the way, the vegetation changes to lower canopy trees. The progress is slow as they traverse swollen creeks and a large, ominous river. Isabelle negotiates the crossing with the help of one of her porters, who walks backward in front of her, holding her hands. The porters' ability to walk quickly, quietly, and without fear on narrow, slippery, muddy trails is amazing. "I'm so glad we could get the porters," Dave says, patting Malcolm on the back as they stop for a break. "That porter, Gupty, he handles that pack like its nothing." He smiles at the burly man and nods an acknowledgement to him.

Continuing on, after the first break, Dave smiles as they all step to a rhythm that works. This is how it's supposed to be, he thinks to himself. They are all keeping up and the complaining has been minimal.

During the afternoon's rest, Malcolm calls out, "We're making good time today, but I think we're in for some rain later. Better to keep going." There is little resistance from the team as they reload and follow him.

Isabelle checks her reference materials against the flora samples she holds in her lap. "This stuff could keep a researcher going for years." She holds up the leaf and puts it into a zip-lock bag. As she bends over, Dave calls out, "Hold it right there. Don't move." Isabelle freezes. Dave walks over to her, drops to his knees, and gently grabs a large leech attached to the top of her back leg, just above the short line. A little blood mars her leg. He holds it out to her, drops it on the ground, and steps on it.

"Sorry, it looked pretty nasty," Dave says, as he checks the bottom of his boot and his own legs.

"Thanks, Dave," says Isabelle, as she rubs a generous amount of antiseptic over the area. She winces as the chemical burns for a second on her skin, before continuing, "I can't believe I didn't feel it."

Dave calls out to the group, "Everyone, do a double-check for leeches while we are here." They dispatch another one from Billy's leg. He takes a photo before Drew squashes it.

Later in the afternoon, they come across three birds of paradise bathing in a river. Their long bright yellow tails catch everyone's attention, and Billy has a field day taking their photos. They watch the brush for signs of a female, but no one can find it. Dave practically has to drag Billy along when they start up again.

Dave cuts into a wild ginger plant on the edge of the trail. He tucks the large root into his belt after showing it to Malcolm, who agrees, "Ginger, it's one of my favorites." Then, every chance he gets, he uses the knife to cut into chunks of clay stuck to the bottom of his hiking boots. They are constantly encased in thick mud. One-pound sections of reddish-brown globs break off with each effort.

At one stop, Malcolm points out a tree kangaroo high in a neighboring tree. Everyone watches the animal, as they catch their breath. The sounds of the deep jungle surround them. The caramel-colored creature looks at them with interest.

Later in the afternoon, Isabelle rubs her thighs and leans against a large broccoli type of plant. "Glad I did that extra cardio at the gym these last few weeks," she exclaims, but soon is swatting biting ants that swarm from the plant and onto her hip. Drew sprays her down with RID insect repellant. "Sorry, it's rather nasty smelling, but this stuff works."

Malcolm comments, "It will help get rid of the mossies too, but you'll need to put on more sunblock." He turns to those still sitting down. "Everyone better apply another dose of sunblock. The sun here is different, and you'll need to put a fairly good amount on every couple of hours."

Billy huffs. "I'm so drenched, that I feel like a human sprinkler system." Everyone laughs. "I think I've drunk two gallons of water and I have yet to pee. It's all seeping out of every pore available on my body. "And, mossies?"

"You know, mate, mossies—skeeters, whatever you call mosquitos."

"It's better to be protected. Thanks, Malcolm, for the reminder." Dave sprays himself down and gives Z's arms a dose as he holds his out. Z walks with Dave for a while down the trail before he asks, "How are you doing? Or, should I say, how are we doing?"

"Better than I thought." Dave nods as he talks. "I haven't been too dictatorial have I?" Z smiles and takes a second before he answers, "I'll let you know after a few weeks."

Malcolm scans the path ahead. "In the village, we will have to get permission to trek through to the Enga Highlands. Please don't wander from the path once we get closer to the village." Everyone looks at Billy. "What? I stay on the path." It fills Billy with indignation. He huffs as he walks past them, clenching his jaw.

Dave bites his lip, resisting the urge to say something to soothe Billy, but he can't think of anything to say anyway. He knows dreadful things happen when you're angry, and not paying as much attention as you should be, so he keeps watch over Billy, mimicking their calls. High in the canopy, parrots screech in response to Billy, and the primeval palms sway overhead. Remnants from the earlier shower and a breeze bring a cascade of droplets down onto them. They press on to the village.

Again, Malcolm sings as he leads them forward. Soon the path widens to an area of logs laid across a muddy area. The barefoot porters cross with ease, but Z slips and falls into an area of waist-deep mud. He is a mess of bruises and scratches and is covered in thick mud by the time they pull him out. The clay screams a strange suction sound as it releases him. "Swoock!"

Z congratulates himself on keeping the communication gear safe above his head. "If I didn't have to hold on to it, I probably could have caught myself," he mumbles. "I'm gonna need a high pressurized nozzle to get this stuff off."

"If you clean it afterward, I can loan you my loofa sponge." Isabelle walks past him and resists touching him all-together.

They approach a clearing illuminated in a shaft of silvery light as a gang of children wearing beads around their necks run up to greet them. Malcolm calls out "Wa!" and several children hug him under the watchful eyes of a tribal man standing farther down the path. As they step closer, a scattering of straw huts perched on stilts stands at the bank of a nearby lake. Pigs run freely through the village. Many of the pigs wear brightly colored beads around their necks as well. A thin, tall, elderly white woman greets them.

Malcolm smiles and walks over to her quickly. "Kennedy, Miss Kennedy," he says, with deep affection. Her long gray hair hangs loosely down her back. Threadbare khaki pants and a thin T-shirt complete her attire. "It's been a long time, " she says, as she hugs him. They touch their foreheads together in tribal greeting.

They converse in the native language for a minute before she turns and welcomes those around. "Welcome to Kantu Village. I'm Kennedy Bastrop, and I've lived here with the Kantu for over twenty years. They are my family." She cradles a young boy of about five next to her and rubs his head lovingly. "What can we do for you?" She smiles as she takes stock of Z and his dip into the mud.

Dave moves forward. "Dr. David Lane, and this is my research crew. We're on our way farther north into the highlands to document wildlife. Would it be all right to set up camp over there for the night?" He points to a cleared area just up from the lakeshore and nods.

She says a word to a man standing nearby. He looks relatively young to be considered a chief, but there are no old people in this village, as far as they can see, other than Kennedy. "This is Boas. He's the leader of Kantu, and he has given you permission. You can set up camp." Kennedy puts her arm around Malcolm and says to the team, "Please join me for dinner when you are finished." She and Malcolm walk away and toward a hut. The simple native structure is on poles, about eight feet off the ground. Malcolm follows her inside.

After a dinner of river fish, rice, and sweet potatoes, Kennedy stirs the fire. Boas joins them, as well as three women that Kennedy identifies as his wives. He sits on the thatched floor. His dark eyes reflect the gleam from the small fire burning in the middle of the room. He wears a strand of pig teeth around his neck and sits cross-legged, showcasing his decorated penis gourd. Some men wear worn shorts. A collection of books sits on a shelf behind him.

"God called me to help the people of Kantu to hear the word of God. I've been here translating their language and translating the scripture into books they can read. The Kantu know little about the outside world, but they know Christ and His light. He makes a real difference in their lives," she says as she offers them another round of drinks. "In the PNG, people are responsible for each other in their community. There is no sense of the individual." She notices they are not drinking. "Please, you must drink a lot to replenish your system."

"We have begun the foundation work on the new literary center. We'll have room for equipment, a library, a workroom, and storage. I've got a team coming in from the Christian Church Outreach next month to finish it." She smiles at Malcolm. "Imagine what we can do here, Malcolm. You could join me?"

"Thank you, Miss Kennedy." Her offer genuinely touches Malcolm. Dave notices a connection between them. There is an awkward pause in the conversation.

"I've set up the ELOD scan tonight near the netting, and the phone is fully charged if you want to try your son again," says Z as he joins the group. "It fascinated the kids. Billy's out standing guard by the unit." Drew pipes in.

"A phone," Kennedy sighs. "Could I…. Would you mind if I put a call through? I haven't talked to my family in a long time." Dave nods. "No problem at all, Miss Kennedy. We'd be delighted for you. Follow me." Dave and the group adjourn to the campsite.

Billy meets them wearing his infrared goggles. Close by, Isabelle scrubs herself at the shoreline with a thin bar of soap. She washes everything, including the clothes she wears. Soon, the children join her on the beach.

Drew uses a leafy branch to move a pile of pig dung to the other side of their camp—and the squadron of flies that accompany it. Two Tiki torches illuminate the area on either side of the equipment where a cluster of children huddle as they look at the green screen of the sonar scan. Billy shows them the radar scanner ELOD by throwing rocks into the air. The kids cluster around him asking for more. "Move back children," cries Kennedy, in their native language. The children obediently oblige, returning beautiful, innocent smiles.

After Kennedy finishes her phone call, Z hobbles toward the group. "I'm afraid that one of these gashes isn't looking too good." Isabelle immediately brings him closer to the torches to examine a tear on his thigh.

Dave watches Z. *Will he hold us back? Maybe he should stay here?* His mind races through a thousand scenarios. Each one has them waiting on Z to catch up. He shakes his head to clear the images and watches Isabelle's careful administration.

"Let me see. No, that doesn't look good at all. I'm afraid you're going to need stitches. Want me to take care of it?" she asks as she steps into her tent and grabs the First Aid Kit. "I'm not an expert medic, but I'm sure I can doctor this up pretty cleanly." Dave steps over to look at the wound closer. "Definitely needs some stitches and an antibiotic."

Z tries to look at it himself, but the angle is awkward for him. "Yes, please. Amazing that the mud held it all together. It didn't even bother me until I washed up." Z sits down and holds his leg out straight.

Across the courtyard, Billy explains the concept of the Echo Location Observation Device (ELOD) with a flip of a switch to Kennedy and she tells the children what it can do. Billy puts on his night vision goggles and makes a monster's face. Kennedy and the children laugh with delight. She is amazed at the detail on the screen and calls for the children to line up, so they can take turns looking through the lenses.

Drew brings out his set of goggles and soon he is imitating a bat flying in the sky, so the kids can see him. Dave relaxes next to Z and watches Isabelle stitch him up.

"Pretty clean stitches, Isabelle," he says with the last pull of the black thread. Miss Kennedy joins them. With a sigh, Dave asks, "is it always so peaceful here, Miss Kennedy?"

"It's glorious, isn't it?" she replies, as Isabelle hugs one kid, who sits next to her and another child offers her a beech nut, which she accepts. "I worry about too much outside influence, though. They have everything they need here and are happy. They know God and his love."

To the side, Isabelle whispers to Z, "Does she realize that she is an outside influence?" Z nods, as he watches Kennedy. "Best not to get involved with tribal politics," he whispers back to Isabelle.

She pauses. "I've heard that in the farther west there have been incidents of clashes within the tribes. And people have been disappearing in settlements to the south." She rubs the head of the child, who now is curled up in her lap.

"We heard some interesting stories about a large flying creature that sounded close to a Pterodactyl back at the Gimi settlement." Dave pats a pig stretched out next to him. It grunts a cheerful response and stays stretched out. In the distance, the screech of a loud bird interrupts the quiet of the surrounding night. Everyone stops briefly to listen to the jungle night sounds.

Unaffected, two of the older children bring the group two large toads and a bit of sugar cane. The sugar cane is cut into bite-sized pieces and distributed among the team. "The frogs are for your breakfast," Kennedy says, under her breath. "Pterodactyls, interesting concept. I've not heard of them but let me ask around and see if anything surfaces."

Billy whoops with excitement as he watches two bats fly into their netting on the ELOD. "Cool, check it out. That's the first time I've seen it in real time! Want me to bring them in?" he asks Dave and Z, as he flips a switch and turns the unit to a low light lens, recording the activity on the netting. The screen glows red, illuminating the two bats struggling.

"Yes, have Drew help you, and bring 'em in. We may have found a sweet spot this close to the water." Dave rises to get his kit. When he returns, he sees Isabelle throwing rocks up into the air over the water. A large bat swoops down from the star coated sky, grabs it, holds on to it for a second, and then drops it into the river below. Soon the kids join her, and rocks are flying over the water as they watch it on the display. Isabelle smiles. "My brother used to do that all the time when we were kids."

"You've started a new past-time," says Kennedy. "You've brought us good fortune and we're having a rare, rain-free night."

At breakfast the next morning, Malcolm stirs the campfire coals, adding more kindling to the fire. Dave joins him outside the tent. "Think we might stay here one more day. Will the porters be all right with that?" Dave pours water to boil. "We caught seven bats last night. That's a good count. Thanks, by the way, for asking about the porters."

"Did you catch the bats you are looking for?" Malcolm asks, as he secures his hammock.

"Two were. The rest will be interesting in the database. And I think letting Z's leg rest for a day will be good, before we head uphill." Dave picks more clay from the bottom of his boots. "Is the muck always so thick?"

"Yes, always. Sometimes it's worse." Malcolm places yams, vegetables, and rice on to cook. "I will let the porters know we are staying here today."

Later that morning, a small exploration team heads into the jungle to document foliage with Isabelle. Soon, many of the villagers join them, but on a hunt. With an expert's eye in the group, they return with a huge black wallaby for dinner. The children are an immense help to Isabelle. She shows them what she is looking for and they scour the area like ants. "What we need is about ten more kids, and I'd have enough work to keep me busy for the next few years. I can't believe what we are finding," she comments to Dave.

"It's a magical place, that's for sure." Billy returns to the campfire, holding the hand of one kid on the way back. Across the camp, Z remains lounging in one hammock. Beside him on the floor is a collection of assorted leaves, dead frogs, and a make-shift cage with butterflies in it. "Welcome to Kantu zoo", he calls out to the group. "The little ones have been bringing me presents all day." A woman smiles at Z. She holds a two-year-old in a sling around her waist. "Kennedy tells me that this one," Z says, smiling and pointing at the woman, "has eyed me for her next husband. My wife in Boston may get fed up with my explorations. I might have to stay for a while."

Dave stifles a laugh. "Good to see you on the mend."

Smoke pours from the cooking hut as women stoke the fire. Near the river, Z watches a man skin a wallaby. "That's an endangered wallaby." Z stumbles out of the hammock to watch the dissection with Dave. The children laugh and play around them. Dave ruffles the hair of one child as it runs past and laughs out loud. He looks up when he hears a zippered tent sound and watches Billy step out naked. He casually walks over to the team wearing a gourd covering his penis. "This isn't as comfortable as it looks," he says as he shifts things around.

Z muffles a laugh and then lets it loose. Isabelle laughs the loudest, as she says, "That's bloody brilliant!" "You've gone native!" Dave bursts out laughing and leans over to hold himself upright. Billy's white buttock stands out like a beacon. "Who talked you into that? "Dave adds, as he continues to giggle.

"Asan, over there, thought I needed to look more manly," says Billy. "Drew," Dave calls out. "Bring your camera over here, quick." Isabelle continues with bouts of giggles every time she looks at him. "I can't... just can't."

Billy poses like a runway model and strikes moves for the camera. They all have a good laugh over it before Billy gets frustrated with them. "Laugh it up. They've got more gourds for you too," says Billy, as he walks away. His white cheeks stand out like a target in the woods. He decides to change back into western attire after several hours of snickering.

After dinner of roasted wallaby, Dave lays out the plans for the next morning. "Let's get up early and be ready to go by sunup. We've got a lot of vertical climbing to do, and with the lack of rain last night, we should be able to make it into Enga if we push hard. The Enga people are known as tree people. They live more remotely and have less outside contact, and it won't be as congenial as here," Dave says, with a grin in Kennedy's direction.

The porters sit cross-legged on a straw floor beside the fire and sing and chant as the evening ends. The crew beds down to the sounds of the porters' song.

Later Malcolm shakes Dave awake. "You've many bats in the netting," he whispers.

Dave is instantly awake. He rolls over to Drew, sleeping next to him. "Wake up. Time to catch some bats." He puts his boots on outside the mosquito net. A scurry of rats escapes to the safety of the bushes. He zips the tent closed. Drew mumbles, "Good thing we bedded down together last night. I don't think I could have stopped laughing had Billy laid down next to me." They both grin and soon are laughing.

Drew checks the digital equipment, displaying six bats in the netting. "Think I'll just take my gear over there and, we'll evaluate each one and then release them." Dave adjusts his goggles and turns them on. After a few close calls on sliding in the deep mud, they make it up the hill overlooking the raging river below. They tag and take specimens in a pleasant rhythm.

Billy stumbles into the netting area. He yawns as he watches Dave and Drew. "How's it going?" he says, as he helps Drew release the bat. "We're getting some results. This is number five!" Drew kneels on one knee and looks up across the horizon. "You know, I keep forgetting to look up. I'm so concerned about what's around my feet or in the surrounding foliage, that I'm missing those stars. Just look at that carpet of majesty out there. It's beautiful."

He continues, "Dr. Wilson, you know, the guy who runs the observatory, told our class that there are more galaxies out there than grains of sands on all the beaches in the world." "Seriously? Let me take a moment or two for that to sink in." Dave releases the bat and watches the Milky Way above him. "And that's just one. We've got a lot to learn on this grain of sand, for sure."

Billy stands next to him. "Makes you feel kind of small." They both nod and watch Billy swat a mosquito on his thigh. "Science can be a humbling experience," Dave says, as he adjusts his goggles, keeping his eyes on one area on the horizon. He stops. "WTF, do you see something glowing out there?" He points to the north near the mountain range they would hit the next day.

"Where?" Drew squints as he looks at the horizon. "In between that range of mountains near the foliage line, about 9 o'clock." They both focus on the area. "Yeah, I make out three glowing objects," Drew says. "Wait a minute, make that four." They watch for about a minute before the objects disappear behind the mountain range. and out of sight. "Let's finish up here and get back to camp," says Dave. "Think it's the Black

Death?" Drew asks as he keeps scanning the horizon. He tries looking with and without the goggles. He adjusts the lenses one more time. "I can't make out anything other than a bouncing- glowing orb."

"Man, I should have brought my camera with me." Billy waits for a turn from Dave's binoculars. "I don't know," Dave says, as the last bat takes off. "No one with any electronics out here except us, that's for sure. Next time, bring the Canon with you, the one with the good zoom lens."

He scans the horizon long after Drew and Billy have gone back to camp. Quietly, he makes his way back to his tent. After lying there for a while, he puts his penlight in his mouth and studies the map. *What in the hell is out there?*

CHAPTER 3

Later that morning, under overcast skies, they reach an altitude that leaves the thick jungle behind. A granite mountain range spotted with moss and saplings sprouting from every nook and cranny blocks their way. "Every time we reach the summit, I keep thinking we've made it, but there appears another peak higher in the distance." Z leans on his walking stick. A breeze blows through, and the air cools them, bringing out goose bumps against their damp skin. Z looks over the horizon. "It's beautiful, but never-ending."

Malcolm stops the group for a moment. "Time to put on your ponchos." They all breathe heavily. Dave places his hand on Z's shoulder and asks, "Z, how's the leg?" Z shakes his leg and gives it a stretch. He adjusts his covering, home-fashioned and made from tree bark, for the communication gear, and gives it a little pat. "This works pretty well, and while I can feel the injury, it's not bad." He adjusts his poncho over it. "I'm fine. Really."

Billy snaps photographs of the purple-hued mountains in the distance. "Hey, there are some caves up there," he calls out to Dave farther ahead. Dave walks back to him and lifts his mono-binoculars to the cliff. "Yeah, I've heard about those caves. I read up on the history, and there were reports of Japanese hiding out in the cave system in WWII. Can you imagine locals hunting the Japanese on these trails?" Dave scans the area carefully, focusing on the nearby hill. "The Japanese took strongholds in parts of the island. You may even see some old equipment scattered throughout the jungle. I noticed Kennedy had an old bomb shell as a flowerpot back at camp."

Z interrupts, "Yeah, that's a horror movie in the making. Can you picture, during the war, being hunted out here by head hunters?" He takes a deep breath as he looks around. "Wasn't there some story about a bunch of Japanese who ran out of food and were chased through the swamps by gators?"

Billy stops scanning and looks at Dave. "Really? That would be a hard decision. You are starving. Do you go forward into the swamps to be eaten by gators or stay where you are to be eaten by headhunters?" "Really, we don't need to put those thoughts into our heads. That didn't happen, did it?" Isabelle looks over at Dave.

Malcolm tightens his poncho. He looks grim as he says, "Yeah, it happened. Almost a thousand Japanese went into the swamp, and only twenty came out." Isabelle stands immobilized, looking at the vast expanse of swamp below them. She shivers, making it difficult to get her poncho on. Drew helps her get everything settled. She whispers to him, "I'll watch out for you around the gators if you do the same for me?" He nods an affirmation and turns to the trail.

Her thoughts turn to the ideal version of trekking with the team that she envisioned. *What was I thinking? There is real danger here. What if Malcolm leaves us? Could we forage on our own? Could we find our way back to any sort of encampment? What if my footing slips, and I just kept going off the side of the cliff? Would I be food for the gators?* Her heart beat hard in her chest. She could feel it. A thousand men eaten by gators?

Her partner had begged her not to go, but her stubborn streak hit and, after talking about going into the deep for years, the opportunity had finally presented itself. It was part of the reason for their breakup. She had to prove this to herself. That she was just as good, no better, than the research analysts back at the office.

Hours later, hard rain peppers them, then it turns into a downpour. Malcolm urges them onward in silence. The porters in their bare feet have a better feel of the land and slip less on the trail.

"Going up is hard, but the going down part is extremely hard. My head hurts," Isabelle complains. "I'm concentrating so hard, that I'm busting a headache." She massages her temples, while under a rock ledge overhang. Malcolm makes her a walking stick by whacking off the tip of a sturdy limb. She accepts it graciously. Malcolm whispers to Billy to keep his camera away at the village until he checks with the elders. Dave watches the conversation and gives Billy a raised eyebrow to confirm the message.

Everywhere on the steep downward trail, there are slippery logs, large tree roots, and rocks. They cross a rushing stream, then climb straight up and out of a gorge as the rain lessens. Malcolm and the porters urge them onward with short sixty-second rest periods. Finally, after five hours, they emerge from the jungle and reach a point on the trail that overlooks a small village of huts perched high in the trees.

Malcolm calls out, "We're here. Stay calm. No sudden movements as we approach the camp. You will notice, the Enga men don't wear the gourds. Try not to stare. They are a beautiful people once you get to know them." Malcolm stops on the trail and cautions them, before walking through a palm-peat bog with a narrow trail only a foot-width wide. At the end of the bog, Malcolm stops again. Dave is right behind him.

A menacing warrior with a large nose ring stands down the trail, waiting for them. As they approach, he points his bow at them. The group freezes. The jungle noise stops. Dave doesn't breathe until Malcolm walks forward, speaking a different dialect. After several heart-stopping minutes, Malcolm motions for them to follow him into the village. They are all on high alert.

Billy says, under his breath, "Holy sh--! Sure, would like to photograph him." Dave squints at him. "Really, a headhunter appears on our path, and your first thought is to get a photograph of him? Not that our lives may be in danger?"

As they catch up to Malcolm, other menacing warriors step onto the path. The warriors stop before the team sees a muscular man who stands in defiance. Everyone stops. There is no reading his harsh expression or even his age. Two strips of dog teeth, fashioned into a necklace, runs across his chest. Billy's hand goes to his camera, but Dave holds his hand back. "Idiot," Dave cautions. "Don't."

The horns of a large goliath beetle and boar tusks decorate the man's nose. On top of his head, he wears a flat hat made of intricate weavings of bamboo fibers coiled into his hair. Another thin belt of small dog teeth encircles his waist. His chest has been oiled to a sheen.

"Yeah, beautiful," mumbles Billy to Drew, who walks up beside him.

Isabelle holds onto Z's hand as they walk into the village center. The group stops together and waits as Malcolm has a sit-down meeting with the chief on one side of the main area. Anxious minutes pass before he returns. Z tries to give Isabelle a reassuring smile, but she isn't buying it.

"Well, they distrust any unknown visitors, but I'm known to them. I have been working with them over the last seven years. We've received permission to be on their lands and continue in the morning," says Malcolm. "We can set up camp here, but it might flood if the rains come in strong." From their position, they watch a hut high in the canopy as it sways in the breeze and are soon engulfed with a powerful aroma of pig manure. Their campsite adjoins the fenced pig encampment.

"Pigs are excellent watchdogs," Malcolm says, as he builds a spot for the campfire. He points to the area nearby. "Start setting camp." Dave is the first to move as the others cluster together. He monitors the surroundings as he works. The rest of the team slowly moves into action as the pigs squeal, watching every movement of the tribe.

Off to one clearing, men of the village bring in long strips of a sago palm to a work area. They use hand axes made from fist-sized chunks of hard, dark stones sharpened at one end and lashed with a vine to a slim wooden handle. Once the men pummel the sago to a pulp, the women knead it with water to produce a dough they mold into bite-sized pieces and grill over an open flame. Isabelle watches them intently after finishing staking her tent.

A cooking hut nearby is a beehive of activity as smoke curls from the rafters. Billy asks Malcolm, "Think it would be okay to take some pictures?" Dave motions for him to wait as Malcolm walks over to the elders. He returns shortly. Dave didn't realize he'd been holding his breath for part of the time. "You may take photographs of those who seem agreeable. They think your white skin and red hair are quite unusual. If they ask to rub it, let them. Isabelle, stick close to Z in this camp, just to be sure. Even at the latrine."

Isabelle looks around with even more alarm. "They look like headhunters," she whispers to Malcolm. "They probably were." His response makes them all look twice at the encampment.

Soon Billy has the children giggling, and the mood eases considerably.

Dave watches him intently, waiting for the next screw up that could get them all killed. He walks over to Billy. "You realize what a risky situation we are in, don't you? Don't relax too much." He points to a lethal trio of sharpened blades stuck in the ground nearby. Billy nods his head. "I'm being careful. Look, they are already more friendly."

As they set up camp, Malcolm warns them that the trail ahead is flooded and much of the area is knee-deep in mud. "Tomorrow you might need snorkels." "He's not kidding, is he?" Drew says, while helping Z secure the tarp over the campfire and a separate one for the electronics. Isabelle pulls a log over to be close to the fire. She sits there hugging her knees. Finished with the tarps, Drew sits next to her while Z stands behind her.

"This is pretty creepy," Drew says, repeatedly as he tries not to look anyone in the face.

The porters stay to themselves and don't mingle with men in the tribe.

Later that evening, the chief invites them into one hut and the sharing of sago grubs. At eighty feet off the ground, there is an escape from the heat and biting insects. It takes some coaxing with Isabelle, to get her off the log, but the mood has relaxed since their arrival. She follows the team up the ladder to the platform balcony. The view takes their breath away. "No wonder they live up here," says Isabelle, as she takes in a spectacular sunset streaked with orange, pink, and blue. She tries to communicate how beautiful it is to the owners of the hut.

"Mu calla," says Malcolm, on her behalf. One of the chief's wives nods her head in agreement. Dave sits next to Malcolm. He keeps his eyes down in respect, as Malcolm warned him to do.

Inside the hut, woven palms cover the floor. The women sit on one side, and the men on the other. On one wall, an assortment of stone axes are displayed. A bedding area and make-shift kitchen or food prep area cover a quarter of the room. The prep area has utensils made from bamboo shards, shells to hold water, and heated stones to re-heat foods. A hearth area made from strips of clay-coated rattan is suspended over a hole in the floor so someone could quickly hack it loose, to fall to the ground, if the fire burns out of control.

Billy munches loudly on a sago worm. "Tastes kind of nutty." He smiles at the group. "They are superstitious, believing sorcery and forest spirits can cause death," Malcolm talks in a faint voice. "It wasn't long ago; they still ate people. But only people they didn't like, or enemies from other tribes." Malcolm acts as if it is not unusual. Many of the crew lose their appetite over the corn mush they offer with pill bug sprinkled on top. "They used to eat brains of animals mixed with sago worms, out of skulls."

Trying to be polite, Isabelle takes a bit of the corn mush, but can't bring it to her mouth." Billy elbows her and points at a human skull used as a bed pillow. "Holy shit, Batman," he says. Dave gives him a "look" which makes him stop pointing. Drew is wide-eyed at seeing the skull. There is a level of anxiety for all of them, until the meal is finished, and they can excuse themselves and go back to their tents.

Isabelle looks at her shaking hand when her feet touch the ground. "Look at this, I'm a mess." Her memory flashes back to the urging of her partner not to go on the trip. She pushes it back out of her mind.

Z snaps her back to reality by saying, "I'm turning in early. Lovely wife, Isabelle, care to join me?" He holds out his hand to her. She blushes and takes his hand. Z looks back over his shoulder. "Drew, you can bunk in Isabelle's tent."

"Thank you, Z. I may even have to spoon a little with you," she says as she stops for a moment, using her flashlight to scan a collection of wood to one side of the camp. She walks over and examines it more closely. "Agar wood." She runs her hand down one of the tree trunks. "It's very costly, and one thing the WWF is watching. I must have Billy take a photo in the morning, in better light." *Are they harvesting the Agar for local consumption or for someone else?* She would have to ask Malcolm his thoughts.

"Did you see the carvings done on that pole?" Z nods toward the ornate artistry. "Yes. Incredible. Did a thesis on it. Back in the '60s, German collectors had a nasty run-in with some tribes over their carvings. My advice is to look, but don't touch," she says, as they walk up to the others.

Dave grumbles as he adjusts things in and outside his tent. Everyone can hear his frustrations. Drew settles in his tent and calls out, "At least the pigs will be our lookout. They are pretty smart creatures." A strong odor of pig filth wafts through the camp.

Billy tries to lie down next to Dave, but after the third shuffling, he takes his bedroll out and re-zips the tent's net opening, closed. The anxiety of sleeping in a head-hunter camp is hitting Dave full blast, and they all feel it.

Dave listens to his footsteps recede as Billy approaches Drew. Dave adjusts himself again, spreading out his arms, enjoying the solitude of the space while trying to cover his nose with a bandana. It doesn't work, and he tosses it aside. He knows that the smell is going to imbed itself into every pore like a parasite.

"Okay, if I bunk over here, Drew?" Billy's words float across the small camp. "Can I borrow your hammock?"

"Sure," says Drew.

Billy throws his bedding in. "He's a grumpy bear tonight, and I'm tired." He takes the hammock out and strings it up quickly.

"Billy, I have to get up at first light to check the nets."

"No problem, I won't sleep at all, anyway. There is nothing like sleeping in a head-hunter encampment to stir your adrenaline. My heart is still pounding like a sledgehammer." Billy sighs as he lays down.

The next morning, Billy, Drew, and Dave document their bat catch and quickly return to camp. Malcolm and the porters, ever vigilant, cluster around the campfire, boiling water, and refilling canteens.

Dave watches Isabelle and Z near a cluster of palm trees. She motions for Dave and Malcolm to join them. They walk over. "Look at that. Have you ever seen anything like it?" She points to a collection of talons that are nailed to the post of the tree. They are a varied assortment of sizes, colors, and species. One talon foot is blue, and three times the size of an eagle's.

"Wow, now that's a talon." Malcolm inspects it. "Not cassowary either, I'm not sure what this is?" Malcolm converses with one of the taller children standing nearby. He asks them what bird it came from. "They say it's from the Black Death, one who tried to capture a child."

Soon, the rest of the team joins them. "What's going on?" Drew is the last to arrive. He takes measurements and photographs of the talons on display. He identifies several species from the other claws. Z and Drew argue over the items. "Black Death?" asks Z.

"Ask them what it looks like." Malcolm steps away to talk to the children and the one man who is nearby.

Billy gets his second camera to take more photos. He adds a pencil for perspective of the 16-inch item. The skin has a blue-gray leathery tint to it. Billy touches it repeatedly. Dave catches his hand. "Look, but don't touch." It took his mind seconds to register what he was looking at. Nothing made sense. He was adamant about his prep for the trip and knew every large species on this island and the areas adjoining. "This doesn't fit." He repeats it several times before Malcolm walks over to see what the fuss is about.

Malcolm echoes the message from the tribe. He pauses. "Sounds like your mysterious creature. They say it belongs to a large, winged spirit that hunts at night. He has a long sharp beak with many teeth and a big horn on top of his head. They told me he is big and can lift a man. The beast took a child several feet off the ground. His father rescued him by cutting off the foot, and that's how they escaped."

Z takes a measurement from the tip of the talon to the back of the foot. He scribbles the information on a flip pad and does some calculations. He looks up, raising his eyebrows. "That would give it a wingspan of almost…thirty feet!"

Dave feels his world shift. A moment of dizziness hits him. He shakes his head, trying to clear his mind. It can't be! Dave gets closer to the talon. He feels a fiery anger rising within, but, with effort, he controls it. "Great, just great," Dave mutters. "This is my brother's world, not mine. I am a man of science, damn it!" He turns and walks away, commenting over his shoulder, "Let's get going, everyone! We don't have time to waste. I will not turn this expedition into a laughingstock!"

Z grabs Malcolm's arm before he turns to leave. "Ask them when this happened?" he asks urgently.

Dave yells, "Leaving in fifteen!" In less than a minute, Dave has two of the tents down and ready for packing.

Malcolm kneels down in front of the child with the stick. He notices her mother watching from the balcony above. He quickly joins the team in closing camp. Isabelle has Billy discreetly take photos of the woodpile. She poses in front of it with a big smile before they rush back to the campfire to pack up the last remaining items. The porters are ready before the rest of them. Dave watches them, noticing they are watching the skies in the expanse before them.

Malcolm whispers to Z as he walks by, "He said the claw was two weeks old."

CHAPTER 4

Z's feet hold to a steady rhythm as his mind wanders. *If the talon foot is two weeks old, where does such a monster creature live?* Biology is his specialty. He needs cells, blood, anything that can be looked at under the microscope. *What will the cells look like?* Now, he wished he had scraped cells off that talon with his knife. *What subspecies can we link the creature to? A new species of Pterodactylus?* Few fossils remains have been found in the fossil records because of their fragile hollow construction. If he remembers right, remains uncovered in Germany, several years ago, were dated to the Late Jurassic Period. He can't wait to get back to the lab and his computer. His fingers itch in anticipation.

His research is rusty on Pterodon, other than it fed on a variety of invertebrates and vertebrates. He remembers the wings were formed by skin and muscle membrane stretching from a long fourth finger to its hind limbs. There were no bones in the wings, just collagen fibers. He scanned his memories of a childhood fascination that led to his career in biology. *Will we actually see the creature?* He smiles at the thought and looks over to Dave leading the crew, who hasn't said a word since they left camp.

Later that morning, as they traverse through areas of dry, and wet trails, the porters cut down logs to help negotiate through the deep sago bog glades. Herds of water rats swim through the swamp nearby, their orange incisors catching the light. Billy takes exceptional photos of them while balancing precariously on a log. Dave nods his approval, even though Isabelle calls out her concerns several times until he gets the shot.

On the remnants of an old animal trail, they cross a rickety make-shift bridge that sways down to the water. The aged natural bridges are totally underwater. Drew makes a spear out of a bamboo pole, and this makes him the official 'croc watcher' according to Dave, even though Malcolm says there aren't any crocs in the area this area.

At one point, Drew almost completely loses his footing on a muddy crossing, but one porter grabs the strap on his waterproof backpack in the nick of time, keeping him from going into the bog. Both men fall back into Dave, and with lightning quick reflexes, Dave grabs the communication box, so it doesn't land in the dink. He scowls over the incident. They take a longer rest than usual to recover and hydrate afterwards. It is another hour before Dave gets his anger under control and apologizes to the crew.

Repeatedly, the trail takes them across mud banks infested with leeches. They regularly stop after each passing for leech checks. Dave makes everyone circle in front of him after each crossing. On a strange side note, the porters have few leeches compared to the field team. Malcolm chirps up, "Maybe they just don't like our blood, aye, mates?"

After trekking until the sky turns to dusk, Malcolm announces they have reached Yafufla. It is nothing but a small line of stilt huts overlooking a small inlet lake fed by a picturesque waterfall. This village is much smaller than Enga Village that they left earlier. The tension is low as they approach, and Malcolm converses with the men who come out to greet them. One native wears shorts, the others are naked save for necklaces of prized pigs' teeth, and leaves wrapped about the tip of their penises. A tall 100-foot pole in the center of the village is decorated with vines and flowers.

Dave stands protectively in front of Isabelle, but she grabs Z's hand as they walk into camp and whispers to him, "Thanks for being my stand-in husband."

In the swamp lands surrounding them, massive Banyan trees and sago palms dot the area. The Banyans have huge dramatic above-ground dark-red root flares at the base of the trees. The canopy of the trees above drips with long gray strands of Spanish moss. It makes for a striking artist's pallet composition against the picturesque backdrop of the lake.

As Billy and Drew approach, several young native women smile at them. They wear the same sago palm skirts as the women did in the last village, but have strange circular scars the size of large coins running the length of their arms, around their stomachs, and across their breasts. Dave whispers to Malcolm, "What's all over their skin?" "The marks make them look more beautiful." Malcolm sighs. "Think of it as a tattoo."

They come to a clearing, close to the encampment. "We'll camp here," Malcolm says. Dave is the first to drop his bag, but they are all happy to drop the gear. He catches his breath by turning to the beautiful sunset over the mountains and the clean village around them. Malcolm joins him at the vista point. "I spent time at this camp last year. We shouldn't have any problems."

"What's the pole for?" Isabelle motions to the unique carvings on the tower. "These are the birdmen. 'Voladores de Papantla' Dancers of the Sky. They swing off that pole for their celebrations," Malcolm says, with admiration in his voice. "It's really something to see. I will ask if they have plans to fly soon."

"Wish we could see that," Billy says, as he stands next to Dave.

"I can't wait to clean up a bit." Drew drops his pack and looks at the water longingly.

Not too far out of the village, a small group of men topple a palm. The sound of their shouting echoes. An enormous snake falls out of the tree. In a flash, one man kills it with a sharpened bamboo pole. They hold it up for the women of the village to see. As if he were having a victory dance, a tribe member slams his heel against the tree flares producing a thumping sound that adds more echoes across the jungle. "That lets the people of the tree house know they are coming home." Malcolm smiles.

"Kind of like, Tarzan," Billy says, as he sets up his tent.

"Better hurry with getting the camp up. Those thunderheads to the north may hit us heavy tonight." Malcolm points to a cloud cluster on the horizon.

"It's so beautiful here. I just want to sit and take it all in." Isabelle sits on a log and takes a deep breath. She exhales loudly. "At least this village doesn't feel so hostile." The scream of cicadas pierces the surrounding air, followed by the answering call of birds in the distance.

In minutes, all four tents are up. The porters cut lengths of bamboo and string one tarpaulin over the bundle of supplies. A tarp loosely covers the now raging fire pit and dinner cooking area. Another blanket covers the loosely hanging hammocks for the porters. Children giggle and watch at the corner of their campsite as the crew members get things ready.

Later, the porters, with their serene smiles, take turns at the water's edge cleaning their feet and legs. A collection of makeshift spears lean into the sand along the bank nearby. Z and Drew can't keep their eyes off them and soon Z walks over to inspect. There is a collection of sharpened bamboo poles of varying sizes on display. Dave joins them, looking longingly at their craftsmanship.

"Pig arrowheads." Z points to an assortment of broad-bladed tips. "For birds and monkeys."

Malcolm notices their interest and joins them. "Fish arrowheads."

Malcolm touches the tip of a thin pronged spear. "Nicely done."

Drew looks at the largest tipped spears. "I'm guessing, but is this cassowary bone?" It has six barbs carved on each side and a dark bloodstain coating the tip.

Z steps through the water to the other side of the grouping to get a better look. "For much larger prey."

Malcolm turns the spear in his hand. "That blade would do terrible internal damage." The arrowhead is the size of his hand as he holds it up next to the spear.

Dave whistles. "Impressive." He lifts the blade into his hand several times.

Malcolm steps back to throw a dead wallaby onto the fire over a make-shift grill. The hair singes in a flash, snapping and sizzling.

Dave turns quickly. *How in the world did he already catch that?* "Guess it's wallaby for dinner tonight." He crinkles his nose. "I'm still trying to get used to it. Hope I can get it down without gagging. I keep imagining a large pasta plate and a fine wine. Gotta stop doing that." Drew and Z nod their agreement.

As the sun lowers, Billy dances with one child in the clearing. The children's laughter over his robot impersonation can be heard throughout the camp, and Billy quickly snaps photos of the children in the fading light.

Z walks back through the ankle-deep shallow water and cleans up a bit. "We need to work on the night shift and categorize some of the bat data, now that we have stats to work with." He splashes the water vigorously as he washes.

Drew joins him. "Yeah, I noticed peaks already on the sugar levels. They might be off. It's worth a look." He washes up.

After finishing, Z steps out of the water and inspects his healing injury.

Dave walks toward them and asks, "What levels are off?"

"It's probably nothing," Drew says, as he steps into the water to his knees and washes his feet. In a flash, the water explodes around him. A flash of green scaly skin and white barbs, jet through the foam as a crocodile GRABS his arm. The teeth snap with a loud CLAMP. A violent tug of war begins. The croc pulls Drew two steps farther into the water. Its green and black skin flickers in the now turbulent water. Drew screams, "HELP!" The creature pulls him deeper as it twists and pulls at the same time.

Z, only meters away, moves like a Ninja. He turns, grabs a spear from the beach and, with a giant leap, lands beside the croc, impaling the spear through the back of its cone-shaped head.

Dave splashes down next to him, bayonetting the beast seconds later. *NO! No one is dying on my watch*, Dave says to himself as he scans the water for more creatures. His heart pounds in his chest.

The croc stops moving. Dave and Z, with the help of Malcolm, and Billy, pry the jaws off Drew's severely mangled arm and lay Drew on the beach to inspect the damage. His complexion has gone pale. Isabelle runs over with the First Aid Kit. She immediately starts a tourniquet.

Drew sucks in a breath as she tightens it. "Thanks guys," he says, in a shaky breath.

"You were lucky, Drew, very lucky." Z turns to inspect the croc the natives have now pulled up on the beach beside him. "That wasn't a large croc."

"Big enough, man." Drew breathes out deeply as he looks at the seven-foot creature laying out full length beside him. "Funny, it doesn't even hurt, just a lot of pressure and pulling." His elbow bone sticks out, and a shredded section of muscle is missing. Drew tries to regulate his breathing and not look at the wound. Instead, he watches the natives turn the animal belly-up. They cut it open, and one of them skins it with an expertise that is extremely efficient. The skin on the croc's back has a series of raised scars running down it.

Drew looks at Billy. "Dude, can you take a photo for me? Gotta have something to remember this moment." He turns to watch Isabelle lifting a bloody rag off his arm. "Can you move me back to camp? I think my legs still work. They may be a little wobbly, though. Don't like the idea of bleeding all over the beach. There might be another croc."

Drew bites his lip. *That isn't what I meant, but where can they take him? I hate the idea of activating the emergency rescue account. The policy coverage costs more than I make in a year. What will the hospitals in the area even look like?* He pictures his mother's face when she finds out about his injury. It surprises him when the first moan falls from his lips.

A rumbling fills the skies over him as the first drops fall. In seconds, a torrent of rain encompasses them. As quickly as possible, they all help Drew back to the tent camp and gently lay him down on a thin blanket. Everybody clusters around the opening of the tent, trying to stay out of the rain. They watch Isabelle clean the wound. Billy goes back down to the beach.

"Look at those snappers," Billy says, as he walks past the croc. Thick yellow and brown teeth leave a permanent grin on the croc. He shelters the lens from the rain as he takes the photo.

Z brings the satellite phone in next to Drew and flips the switch, activating the emergency tracking device. "I'm hopeful we can get someone at the Missionary Evacuation Service Center on the coast." Z checks the equipment. "I'm going to see who I can get on the phone."

Drew shakes his head. "Maybe it's not that bad? Are you sure?" Z looks up toward Dave.

Dave nods. God, his arm looks terrible. Shaking the thought from his head, Dave points for Billy to re-tie a tarp as he repeatedly checks the power setting on the phone. He paces outside the tent, leaving Z to engage the system. Thankful for something to do, Dave accepts a banana leaf of steamed noodles and vegetables from Malcolm.

"It must have come in with the latest rain storm." Malcolm looks him in the eye. "I've gone swimming here before. So have the natives." He watches Dave eat and continues, "Did you see how fast Z jumped to the rescue? He was like Superman or something." Dave nods, lost in thought.

Z fidgets with an array of knobs. "Should only take a minute or two. Let's give it a second." Drew's breathing steadies. Isabelle kneels next to him and offers him more water. Worry fills Z's face. He moves his hands nervously. "My sister is gonna kill me forever. There won't be a holiday event without this being mentioned. You can count on that."

Drew lifts his head and looks at Z. "I talked to her before we left, Uncle Z. She will be fine." He closes his eyes for a minute. Z walks over and takes his other hand. "I've got you," he says, softly. Drew smiles, keeping his eyes closed. "You moved like a ninja. Guess all those Kung Fu movies didn't go to waste?" Z pats his shoulder gently. "You rest. We've got help coming."

After dinner, Isabelle joins Dave at the campfire. She whispers, "He's lost a good amount of blood, and I've stopped most of the major bleeding sites, but the tearing inside his arm looks horrible. He's going to need a doctor. I've given him a pain reliever, but we have little to give him. He's in for a long night, I'm afraid."

A Howler monkey scream echoes through the camp. An answer calls from the other side of the lake. Dave paces. "Let me try the evacuation center again. Last word they gave me, they were trying to get a helicopter unit out and said they would call back if they completed the repairs to their unit." Dave turns the phone back on.

As the rain turns to a drizzle, Malcolm walks over. "The chief accepts your gift of the crocodile, and they are asking about the condition of young Drew. How's he doing?" Malcolm sits down and watches Dave as he continues to adjust the dials.

"We've got to helicopter him out of here. He could lose that arm. Please let them know what we are planning. I don't want them to think we're working any magic. They have seen helicopters before, haven't they?" Dave jumps as a garbled voice tunes in. "Dr. Dave Lane here. Over."

"Dad, Dad… it's Eric. Renee and I are coming to join you. We should be there around ten if the weather clears. We can take out your injured guy. I've chartered a heli out of Kiunga. We've triangulated your location. You, okay? Over."

"Eric, how in the world? I thought you were in South America?" he yells into the phone. Eric is here? What the Hell?

"Tell you about it tomorrow. Over." Eric says as the line dies.

CHAPTER 5

Maybe it could work out? Dave has a million questions running through his head. *Eric is here? What about Drew's arm and the surgery that will accompany it? Are the forms he filled out with the government for the evac properly done? What nightmare is Drew in for? If Jeanne were here, she would know what to do. God, if Jeanne were here, I wouldn't even be here.* The adrenaline is running high through his system. He can't turn it off.

Dave steps over a sleeping Z near the campfire and hands a cup of coffee to Isabelle as she unfolds herself from Drew's side. She looks tired beyond reason. Dave stretches beside her. She adjusts the mosquito netting covering Drew. "Let him sleep." They walk to the other side of the campfire and whisper.

A thin stream of color lightens the skies to the east. "I wonder if we'll get caught in a deluge again today." He checks the wetness of the soil under his feet. Dave whispers, "How's he doing? I'm almost afraid to ask."

"Well, he started a fever about an hour ago, but I got him to drink extra liquids, and he kept his dinner down. That's about all I can do." She picks up a stick and stirs the coals, popping her neck and kneading the muscles in the back of her neckline. "Heard your son is coming to join us."

Dave takes over the massaging. "I'm rusty at this. Haven't touched a woman in... a long time." Isabelle smirks. "Too much information." She smiles as he pops her neck. "You've still got the touch." His large hands work the stress out of her muscles. Dave talks as he works. "I can't believe it. My son must have left the site in Venezuela as soon as I talked to him. He's a good kid and a decent addition to our team. He's worked beside me for years. I don't know Renee too well yet. Anxious to finally meet her, though. There's nothing like getting to know your future father-in-law deep in the jungle. I hope I'm not too frightening." He sighs. "Let me know if I get out of line, please." He pats her neck, signaling the end of her message, and checks the echo locator unit. It's showing an empty screen.

"Billy caught thirteen bats last night. Thirteen! And eight of them were Otomops Papuensis." He winks at her. "I'm going to call them 'Otto's.' They're our best chance of finding the cure."

Malcolm carries a load of kindling to the fire. It is a mixture of wet and dry wood. He plops it down without making too much noise. "Everything is drenched." He pulls out a little strip of rubber tire from the bag around his waist and lights it as he restarts the kindling. "I only use the bits when we can't get any dry kindling. It's going to smoke something awful."

"That's a great idea," Dave says. "I'm going to remember that in the future. You must have learned from someone very skilled. I couldn't have picked a better guide. There's an old television show where a guy always saves the day by using only his wits and everyday-things that anyone would always have around, anyway. You're like MacGyver—the jungle version. So glad you're with us. If you're up for lessons, I'm game."

"It's something they showed me as a kid. Those tire chips will save your life." Malcolm turns to fill the water containers. "Sometimes, I just know what I'm looking at. The jungle will provide. If you truly see."

Dave walks down to the water's edge with him. They both watch the sunrise and scan the water for more crocs. It's so peaceful here. Hard to believe the danger lurking under the surface or in the history of this place. What they saw last night was primeval and raw. "How are we doing? I mean, so far on this trip? Think we can endure for the entire time?" Dave turns, shadows visible under his eyes. His lack of sleep is showing.

"God turns out the lights and then he turns them back on." Malcolm smiles. "I am always amazed at how quickly things change out here." A cacophony of bird songs moves like a giant sound wave toward them. "You've got a good team. They care about each other. There is no bickering. That's a good sign, mate. And they listen when you need them too." Dave catches his eye. "I noticed you didn't answer my question."

Malcolm returns a sly smile, turns, and starts working on the fire.

Scratching his collection of mosquito bites, Dave turns and walks away. "Well played, Malcolm."

Later, as Malcolm puts together breakfast, three of the porters gather around talking in their native tongue. Malcolm joins them. He motions for Dave to join him. "What's the plan for the day, boss?"

"Well, first we need to get Drew on his way to the hospital. Do you think we can make it into Tenery Village if we leave about noon? According to my contacts and the map, there is some sort of old abandoned camp area near there." He swallows the last bit of his hot tea and puts the still smoking tea bag into his pocket.

Z dozes by the communication gear with one hand resting on top of it. His mouth is open, and a bit of drool is hanging from his lip. Billy takes a quick shot of him before giving Dave an okay sign.

"Let me ask about the trail ahead." Malcolm steps over to a cluster of village men standing near a collection of buttress tree roots. Massive vines travel the length of the tree, giving the children an easy climbing hold. Laughter from the porters rings out across the village green. Their warm smiles are easily given.

Earlier than expected, they hear the helicopter approaching. The noise puts the entire village on edge, and people scatter. An unusual call sounds ("WHOO-IEEE, Whoop, Whoop") from the chief's hut, people scurry to watch from the doorways of their huts. The engine hovers over the lake briefly before setting down in a section of the cleared beach. Dave moves forward to greet them. He is all smiles and anticipation as he approaches the area. It will be good to see my boy and meet Renee. Eric and Renee quickly jump out, followed by several bags of gear landing with a SPLAT. On the other side of the helicopter, a medic in a flight suit pulls out a transport cage and efficiently moves toward the camp. Dave points to Isabelle standing by the tent and the medic moves in her direction. The blades on the helicopter continue to slowly spin.

He takes a step forward and is engulfed in a big hug from Eric. After they embrace, they shake hands, and then hug again. Dave turns, and in a flash, scoops up Renee and spins her around. She laughs, pats his massive chest, and kisses him on both cheeks before he puts her back down.

"You must be Dad!" Renee laughs again. "So happy to meet you!" Her heart is bursting with happiness. After two years of almost non-stop traveling with the research team and now, with Rob and Eric, they seem to bring you up into conversation every day. What Dave would think of this or that, or old family stories from when they were young, and Eric's adventures as a teen when he started being interested in cryptic events. *She feels like family already.*

Malcolm and a porter take their two backpacks and one large duffle bag to the staging area.

Dave nods and smiles at her. "Give me a second." He walks over to Isabelle and Drew. They turn to watch the medic check the vitals on Drew. He quickly hooks up an IV bag. Dave helps Drew lie down in the support cage. Isabelle fusses over Drew and places extra padding around his head while the medic straps him into the harness. Dave looks right at Drew. "You're going to be fine. We will meet up when we get out of here. I put the contact information into your pocket, including the administrator, for the grant. Everything is taken care of. Don't worry." Dave places Drew's bag at his feet in the cage as Billy stands ready to take the other end of the cage.

Z grabs Drew's good hand. Tears are in his eyes. He can't say the words spinning in his head. Nothing more can happen to you, boy. Drew comforts him. "Don't worry about me, Uncle Z. I'll be fine. Just get the bat data. I don't want this to be in vain. I'm gonna have the best bar story for a lifetime with a badass scar to prove it."

The medic puts a padded sleeve on Drew's arm. Drew winces as he pulls it tight and releases Z's hand. The medic turns to Z. "He's going to the hospital in Kimbe. They have a trauma center there that is perfect for his injury."

Dave walks with them to the helicopter. "We'll keep you informed of our progress. Your job is to get better." Z and Billy lift the cage as Dave stands back. They slide the cage into the helicopter, and the medic follows. Dave raises his hand as a thank you. When he turns, the entire team is behind him, waving back at Drew.

The helicopter hovers before taking off. It spins once as the engine revs. The villagers watch. None ventured closer to the wind carnage from the chopper. Children huddle behind the adults. The braver ones in the trees laugh.

Dave turns back to look at Eric. He notices in the last six months, Eric's shoulders have broadened. He looks more like his grandfather, even with the several day-old beard. His sandy brown hair shows under the brim of his wide khaki hat. He watches Eric and Renee introduce themselves to the rest of the team. Then Dave and Eric talk rapidly to each other as they step toward the campfire. Renee follows, looking as if L.L. Bean expertly outfitted her. *She's pretty, a young Sally Field,* he thinks.

They all stop and turn as the helicopter returns and hovers above the ground. The door opens. A man jumps out from beside the pilot. He holds a large backpack and a well-worn baseball cap, which he quickly puts on. The helicopter takes off again. He steps lightly toward the group.

Damn it! Damn it! Dave feels a surge of adrenalin race through his body. Hold it together Dave. You don't want Renee to see you like this. The team freezes in place as the silver-haired gentleman approaches. Dave feels Eric's eyes on him. Their eyes meet for a second as Eric pleads for calmness.

Eric steps forward and puts his arm around the newcomer's shoulder as they meet. "Everyone, this is my Unka Rob, Dad's brother. He's a very experienced man in the bush, and we've come to see what else we can find out about the unusual sightings you mentioned."

"He'll probably go running off to get closer to the creatures the first time they appear, and we'll wind up having to rescue him," Dave mutters, deadpanned. Isabelle looks at him, surprised. "Sorry," he says, as he picks up his backpack and rummages through a pocket.

The resemblance to Dave is uncanny. He has the same strong

shoulders and long legs, but his hair is completely white, while Dave's has just turned gray. Rob tries to smile at the group, squinting with piercing-blue eyes. His focus is on Dave. Dave is tight-lipped. He stares intently at Rob, willing him to talk first so he can attack. The entire team feels the tension between them.

"Dad and Rob don't exactly see eye-to-eye, but he'll be glad to assume the research position your injured guy was doing. He understands Dad is in charge." Eric shakes everyone's hands. "Renee and I are just along for the ride, but we'll be glad to pitch in and help any way we can."

Eye-to-eye, my ass! Dave opens his mouth to say something but snaps it shut. *It's all his fault.* He told Eric about the sighting. *Why didn't I keep my big mouth shut?* His worst fears will be confirmed if he doesn't take a stronger role and it has his insides twisting like a hot poker. *Could the attendance of Rob compromise their research?* Their protocol methods will definitely be under higher scrutiny. Now, they don't have a choice. The truth of their new situation seeps in. He feels like he is drowning for a split second. Gossip spread easily in their profession. He will not let it taint their work.

Eric points to her collapsible shoulder bag and Renee drops the bag to the ground. She pulls out two large zip-lock bags of fried chicken and a box of Oreo cookies. Everyone freezes in place and looks longingly at the chicken. "I knew you'd be in a hurry to get going, so I brought us all a snack." She passes out the chicken legs to the team. "I'm vegan, so they don't work for me, but you guys look like you could use the protein." Billy watches the box of cookies intently.

She stops in front of Malcolm. "I've been told, you are THE MAN." She hands him the box of cookies that he cradles like a newborn baby. He nods "thank you" to her by putting one hand over his heart. She sits next to him.

Rob shakes hands with the members and introduces himself. He doesn't look at Dave. Eric takes one of the chicken legs and sits down at a log. He finishes it in three bites.

Through gritted teeth, Dave walks closer to Eric and leans over him.

"You failed to mention that Rob was going to join us when you called." He bites into a large chicken leg. "Thank you, Renee," he mumbles. The flavor explodes in his mouth, distracting him for a moment. *I've got to keep myself under control. I will not strangle Rob.* He fantasizes about leaving him here. Eric pulls him out of his daydream.

"Dad, it will be all right. Remember how much fun we had when we all went camping when I graduated from high school? It will be so much better having us along." He smiles sweetly at Renee. "You guys need to put the past behind us so that we can be a family again. I hate the tension between you two. You used to be best friends, talking through the night over your science hypotheses. It was magical." Eric watches Dave walk over to Malcolm.

For a moment, Dave doesn't say a word as he stands near Malcolm. "Everyone, we're off in fifteen. Finish up and join me at the trailhead." Dave grabs his pack and waits for the others to follow. Rob helps put out the fire pit as Dave watches him with an intensity that could burn through metal.

Dave replays over in his head, the funeral for Jeanne and the anxiety of not hearing from Rob. And the text messages that had hit a week afterwards when he finally contacted Dave. He changed his phone number, so he didn't have to talk to his brother. It was for the better, because Dave disconnected from everything afterwards and didn't want to talk to many people, just a few lab employees and the kids. The months ticked off. Then that article about cryptids made the rounds. The comments from his peers, the way the department head looked at him afterwards, and then the way Rob presented at the conference, chucking twenty years of research down the drain, and walking away from academia altogether, repeated in Dave's mind. Real people of science don't do that. People who are on the verge of a breakdown do that. And now Dave is looking right at him, a shell of the man he used to know.

The trail, while still deep in mud, is at least easier than it had been before. They walk for hours through glades of ferns, moss-covered rocks, and thick carpets of leaves. All the while, Dave keeps from looking directly at Rob. Z walks up next to Billy and motions for a break. "Could we take ten?" Dave nods his approval.

Malcolm halts the group and shouts back down the trek line. "Ten-minute rest for water." The guide walks over to a thick vine, cuts it off, and lets a stream of clear liquid drip into his mouth. He offers the juice to Renee, who accepts it with a big smile. "If you ever cut a vine, you aren't sure of and the juice is milky, do NOT drink it or let the vine touch your lips. We have several varieties that are poisonous."

"Good to know." Dave offers Renee a tube of sunscreen. "Get to know Isabelle. She's observant and knows the drill. If you don't mind, I'll keep close to you today until you get acclimated."

"Thanks." Renee flashes Dave a winning smile. "Sure, is beautiful out here. We went from one jungle climate to another. I've never been to this part of the world before. Guess we'll have to take a side trip to Australia before we head to the States. We're soooo close." She pinches her fingers, leaving a small gap. "Eric wants to get a world tattoo on his leg, then have the countries colored in as we visit them." It surprises Dave. "He doesn't like needles. I can't imagine him sitting for that long, can you?"

"No, I think it's a bunch of talk. But you never know with the Lane men, do you? So, have you seen the creature?"

Dave doesn't answer her. He notices that Z and Rob are deep in conversation. They have pulled Billy over and are reviewing footage on his camera. "They're probably showing Rob the claw from the village if you want to take a peek at it." He motions with his head at Z and Rob. "Oh." She gets up quickly and asks Eric to join her. Dave has his back to them when he hears Eric loudly exclaim, "No WAY! Let me see it again!"

The mood softens a bit as they take off down the trail. Billy and Eric exchange interests and are soon quoting Star Trek episodes to each other. The team has accepted them. Laughter floats in the air, then immediately gets sucked into the foliage. At the front of the line, Dave has trouble hearing anything behind him. Malcolm said it is a wonder of the jungle and a way people lose their way.

After an hour, they reached the summit, then began another descent along a gorge. Then another rise and another descent, and that keeps repeating for hours. Later down the trail, Isabelle visits Renee. "You must develop jungle eyes out here. Don't watch the patterns beside you. Focus further out and find natural breaks in the foliage. It will give you a headache if you try to focus on every little thing. Look through the jungle, not at it."

"Thanks, I'll try it." Renee adjusts her sunglasses. She takes in the vista of the web-like canopy overhead as it filters the light and invites them to paradise. The tall trees of the jungle wave in the breeze, welcoming them, but hiding their secrets in the depths below.

The late afternoon sun casts long shadows into the underbrush. A large brown Matschie Tree Kangaroo walks across the game trail in front of them, and Malcolm halts the group. The kangaroo is totally unafraid of the trekkers, and they watch him casually stroll over to a beautiful fig tree and climb up the side like watching a kindergartener cross the street.

"That's unnerving." Isabelle shades her eyes as she watches. "They are beautiful, yet so creepy at the same time. It's truly a wonderland out here." Her thick English accent rolls off her tongue.

Renee takes photos with her compact camera. "We've walked back through time. The animals aren't afraid of us at all." A small black and orange bird lights on the branch next to her. Renee offers her extended finger to see if the bird will sit on it. Z stops her just in time and shoos away the bird.

"That's a Hooded Pitohui, at least I think it is?" Z watches the bird fly away and they quickly catch up with the rest of the hikers. "He's poisonous."

Dave follows close behind.

"Are you sure?" asks Renee. "I've never heard of poisonous birds before." "Killer birds? You're kidding, right?"

Dave asks as he looks closer at the bird with his binoculars. He catches Rob's eye and turns away. *God, I can't even look at him without it turning my stomach.* "Let's get a move on." He turns to the group. "Guess that one wasn't in the informational packet. Please share the information with our new participants."

Z rocks excitedly on his feet. "Well, their feathers and internal organs are loaded with toxins. The same stuff you find in poisonous tree frogs. Just a touch and you'll go numb, then a burning, tingling will radiate from wherever you touched it." Z is almost giddy as he pauses. "Don't you just love batrachotoxins? They can keep you busy studying their methodology for years."

Rob nods. "We'll have to talk about bio-toxins later this evening. It's one of my specialties, too," he says under his breath. Z grins widely at Rob. "You're on!" He joins Rob on the trail.

"Batrachotoxins. One of my specialties too!" Dave mumbles as he repeats their enthusiasm with venom.

"I got hooked on the science of toxins back in college." Z turns to Rob. "So, what's your background?" Rob takes a deep breath. "Well, I have a Ph.D. in biology and taught in academia for a while before I got bored. Now I run a cryptozoology museum in upstate Maine. I love it." He flashes them all a big grin. "Takes a lot to change your life to happiness."

Yeah, and he's a laughingstock in the industry because of it. Dave shakes the thought from his head and swings hard on his machete, taking his frustrations out on the surrounding trees.

Their trek slows as they hit a prolific growth area where tangled masses of vegetation have reclaimed an old game trail. It resembles the Creature from the Black Lagoon as it drapes and strangles the underground. Malcolm calls out. "Okay, I think we're close to a platform area, but I don't see it. Everyone keep a close eye out for anything that could be constructed."

Malcolm slices through the interwoven thicket and addresses Isabelle. "Back in the '70s, a plane crashed near here and quite several people died. The government paid a village survey group to put up some of these platforms. Most of them are out near the World War II memorial site, but my map shows one right where we are."

Dave grabs a vine with a hidden set of irritating spikes on it. "Sheee-IT!" A spray of barbs stands at attention embedded along one finger.

Renee comes to his aid and pulls at it with her fingernails. Irritated, Dave studies the surrounding canopy while she works on his hand. He tries to pull it back until he finally succeeds. "I can get it! Thanks, I can get the rest." He moves away and looks closely at his finger. Damn splinters. It is swelling.

"Hey, Malcolm, this may be a brilliant spot to set up our netting." Z holds up his hand. "That vine over there has concave leaves clustering around those red berries. It looks like a type of vine growing in Cuba that bats love. We could try it since we're so close to the campsite. And we're close to that drop-off area." Z points to the cliff edge. "We've got good visibility here." He walks around the area in a big circle. The top of the mountain is another thirty feet above them.

Rob joins Z and cuts away brush to clear the jungle floor. "At least it's dry here." Rob drops his pack. "Is this camp?" he asks, in an upbeat manner toward Dave. "Yes." Dave yells to Malcolm, "Malcolm, let's stop here. There's a water source nearby. I can hear it."

Malcolm nods in agreement and sends two of the porters off to find the water as the others set up camp. Dave and Billy clear a base area for their tent. Dave holds his swollen finger out awkwardly. The needles have embedded themselves deep under the skin. "Damn vines," he mumbles as he sets up the shelter.

After setting up her tent and a hammock, Isabelle takes a break. She sits on a nearby moss covered rock. "Wow, look at that," she says to no one in particular. Behind her, a vista of rolling steep blue-green mountains layer across the horizon with skies streaked a deep orange. She takes several photos with her camera. Rob sits beside her.

Dave watches Rob put the moves on Isabelle. He doesn't know that she doesn't swing that way. *This could be interesting*, Dave thinks. He smiles at the expected rebuke he knows is coming. Rob works on his tent on the other side of hers. "Perfect territory for a Ropen." He unrolls his pack and scans the horizon with a high-power zoom lens. "Care to tell me more about what the natives have told you?"

"Not much to tell. They had some huge, and I mean HUGE, talons on display. I think you saw Billy's images. They said one talon came from a bird-like bat that tried to lift a boy out of the camp. His father cut off its foot, and it was this big," she says, holding her hands fifteen inches apart. "They call it the Black Death."

He just needles his way in, like he always does. Dave frowns as he marks an area for the campfire with a circle of stones. He watches them from the corner of his eye. The porters have their hammocks and tarps up in no time, so then they relax. Malcolm talks to them, and they each grab water containers and disappear into the bush. Over his shoulder, Malcolm yells, "Back in a sec, mate."

"Check out those flowers over there." Isabelle points to an extremely large white blossom. "I think it's a record rhododendron species. That bloom spike must be at least six inches across. And it smells heavenly." She steps over closer to the plants, clearing the ground near the edge of the drop-off. "I should be able to smell them from my tent." She points to the edge, mentioning, "Watch your step over here."

Just before dinner, Billy calls out. "Dibs on the first net watch."

Eric and Renee laugh as they set up. Rob checks out the hammocks the porters have set up and tries to replicate their knots. He walks back over to his ropes before giving up and putting up his tent. With a crunch of the leaves beneath his feet, Rob releases his frustration and anger. *This isn't how it's supposed to go. Things were reversed. Enough time has passed.* He wants forgiveness more than he thought, to go back to the way it used to be. He needed to clear his head and remain calm if they had any hope of reconciling. Seeing Dave is affecting him more than he expected it would. He seemed empty without Jeanne, and he didn't know how to take the first step. Saying "I'm sorry", won't do it. Dave has always been an action kind of guy.

Eric plops down next to Dave. "So, how are you doing? How's the finger?"

"How am I adjusting to Rob, you mean?" Dave huffs and takes a long drink from his canteen. He tries to bend the finger and it barely moves. Dave offers a drink to Eric and a flash passes before his face. Young Eric is still in there somehow, the mannerisms are still there. The way he poked his cheek and the little hop-skip he did when he got excited. He noticed the hop-skip after he viewed the talon photos. Now here stands a man who pushes through difficulties with ease. "I'm darned proud of you, Eric," he says as he pats Eric's leg.

"Thanks, Dad." Eric smiles easily. "You know, I hear you saying, 'Be careful!' in my head a lot these days." Dave ruffles the hair on the top of Eric's head. He nods in Renee's direction as they watch her helping Isabelle with her mosquito netting. "I'd rather talk about Renee. She's the one?"

"Yeah, Dad. Like no one I've ever met. We connect on so many levels. You will never hear her complain. She's smart, laughs at my jokes, and has an adventurous spirit, like me. I can't believe I found her."

He pauses. "Your mother would approve." Dave's thoughts turn to Jeanne. *She would love her. And would go on about how beautiful their grandchildren will be.* There is another pause in their conversation. "Yeah, Mom would love her." Eric returns Dave's canteen. "Talked to Mack last weekend. I think he's finally dating someone in North Dakota." He moves a rock around with his foot.

"Really? It's been a long dry spell for him. Did he say anything about going back and finishing his Ph.D.?" "No, just regular guy talk. He wasn't too chatty. You know how he gets." Eric picks up a rock and examines it as they talk.

A bubble of giggles comes from Isabelle and Renee. The men smile.

"Let's go join them, but I need to take off these boots for a bit and it won't be pretty." Eric walks over to the water. "I'll join you for a rinse off, and yes, we'd better do it before we go near the girls." Dave follows him.

Afterwards, Eric and Dave walk over to Isabelle and Renee. "Ladies, can we join you?" Eric plops down before they can respond. Dave shrugs and joins him without waiting for the invitation either. Isabelle moves her pack inside her tent, making way for Dave.

"I was just telling Isabelle that it's like a movie set: King Kong, the one with all the dinosaurs in it, except we keep running into real things. Have you always had such prolific sightings of animals along the trail?" Renee rubs her legs and adds a bit of antiseptic to a bug bite.

"I've noticed. It's increasing the deeper we go." Isabelle replies.

Renee smiles, looking out at the foliage and the mountains in the distance. The conversation lulls before Renee asks, "How did you join up with these guys?" She points at Dave and Z. "I work for the WWF, and part of our grant is paying for this excursion. I'm interested in palm deforestation." They all turn their heads as Rob and Z laugh loudly over something on the other side of the campfire. They can hear them going on about toxins from where they sit. Dave watches them intently. *They'll be talking about them all night, I bet*, he silently repeats in his head.

"Eric and I have been a couple for almost two years. We were in grad school together." She laughs as she continues. "I guess Rob just comes through association. Rob already had the trip to Venezuela planned a year ago, and Eric talked me into going with him. My family's foundation underwrites the research Rob has worked on in the past. My grandfather, Bruce, is a Cryptozoologist at heart. He's got the funds to put theories into action. It's how I met Eric." She flashes Eric a brilliant smile.

Dave kisses her on the cheek. "You are beautiful, Renee, and I'm happy to welcome you to the family. I've never seen Eric happier."

Billy, Z, and Rob cluster over the viewfinder of Billy's camera as he shows them his footage. They snack on a large bag of trail mix while they watch the show. Their enthusiasm matches those of three young boys with a new hand-held game.

Eric runs over to see what they are watching. In seconds, he is calling out, "Renee, hey Renee! Come and see this. Granddad Bruce will flip over this footage!" Eric waves frantically.

Standing nearby, Dave scans the horizon with his binoculars, then lowers the lenses. "Look, I can make out caves to the north a little higher up." He points in that direction and hands the unit to Isabelle. "Do you see it?"

She adjusts the lens and sweeps the area. Farther to the north, an area catches her attention. "Can these zoom in anymore?" She toggles a switch, but it does nothing. Her frustration grows as she tries the settings. Dave flips a knob on the side of the piece and adjusts the focus. "It can be tricky. Guess I've gotten used to it, but you are welcome to borrow them anytime."

"Damn it!" She turns and hands him back the binoculars. "There's an area of clearing back there. I hope it's not another path of widespread palm cutting. Will we be heading to the north soon?"

"We could, but that would take us closer to the coast and closer to the crocs. Let's see how our hunt works tonight. It might be worth a look or two." They both turn and walk toward the campfire. Dave's knees pop as he walks.

Malcolm motions that dinner is ready. "I'm starved," Dave and Isabelle say in unison. An array of food is arranged on banana leaves in front of the fire.

After dinner, Dave walks over to Rob with a length of netting in his hands. "Hey, be useful. Set up the second strand of netting over that large rock. I'm going to turn in early. Billy is already on the ridge. Wake me up if we get over two bats. The ELOD will scan the area for us. And I think Z may have another set of infrared goggles you can use." Dave heads toward his tent.

"Aren't we going to talk? I haven't seen you in—four years." Rob's voice is barely audible as he stands there holding the net in his hands. He doesn't move. Dave keeps his back toward him. "What's there to say, Rob? I think you said things pretty clearly when you didn't come to Jeanne's funeral." He turns his head, his eyes flashing with anger. "She loved you like a brother, always standing up for you, and you couldn't even stop your damn research long enough to do the right thing."

"You know, I would have, if I could." Rob turns to look directly at him.

"Yeah, Bigfoot called, and you had to meet him for dinner." Dave leaves Rob standing there holding the netting.

CHAPTER 6

"Hot damn, I think we've hit the honey hole," Dave yells into the inky darkness around them. His infrared goggles glow a neon green. "Whooo-IEEE," he hollers into the valley floor below. Billy hands him another bat for testing and calls out, "That makes number twenty-seven. I'm getting better at this. They don't scare me like they used to." Billy holds a bat firmly in a wide-angle grip. A small smile lingers on his face, barely visible in the moonlight, when he looks back at Dave.

They are getting into a rhythm of movement by processing the bats. The porter takes them out of the net. How he does it without getting bit perplexes Dave, but he doesn't question it? *It's working magnificently.* Billy holds the bat down with a stick, takes measurements, and puts the identification tag on. Dave takes the blood sample, writes the stats, and then releases them. *This is exactly what they are here for.* Most of these bats have been Otto's, too. Z is right. They are after the berries in the bushes nearby.

Suddenly, the jungle around them turns silent, except for the gentle tussle of leaves in the breeze. The eerie quiet falls around them like a heavy mist cloud. Billy looks around anxiously as he releases his bat. "Ya notice? It got quiet?"

A porter standing behind Billy scans the surrounding bushes. He looks wide-eyed as he struggles with the twisting bat in his hands. They all freeze for a second as they hear a loud, wing-flapping noise, "Swoosh, swoosh," from somewhere close. The porter crouches down low, dropping his bat, and leans below a rock overhang. As a precaution, Dave motions for them to step closer to the rock wall, away from the drop-off to the valley below. Suddenly, the trees shake violently, as if a microburst has hit them. Everyone looks around at once, trying to get a view.

"What the Fuck is that?" Dave yells above the noise, scanning the forest again as the trees sway with an intense velocity. Billy loses control of his grip momentarily and his large fruit bat bites down onto his glove. "Hey, hey!" Billy nudges Dave to help get the bat under control again, but it's too much and Dave releases the bat, pushing Billy against the wall firmly. "What is it?" he whispers to Dave.

He calls out, "What?" Dave scans the treetops. The words dissolve as he sees a flash of a large wing slip out of the canopy and quickly return. His mind rolls through the worst B-movie reels from the '60s of monster movie attacks and Raquel Welch running for cover. *Could a cyclops emerge from the foliage next?*

The swoosh sound continues a little more to the left before an unholy screech fills the air. It is so loud, that rocks come loose above them. It snaps Dave back to reality as a boulder narrowly misses him. Flashlights illuminate the tents thirty yards below as the rest of the science team flies into action. Dave focuses on Eric's tent with parental tunnel vision.

An angry screech fills the air again. "Holy Crap!" yells Billy.

"TAKE COVER!!?" Dave screams. Every neuron in his brain shrieks. This can't be happening!

Dave turns the echo equipment away from the valley to the skies above and the pocket of trees still swaying. A large, pixelated object registers on the green screen. "Do you see it? Where?" Dave calls out. He feels his heart beating loudly in his chest as he holds onto the monitor for a moment. *God don't have a heart attack now!!*

A palm frond crashes to the floor next to them. The porter takes off back to camp.

Dave takes a tentative step out away from the cliff wall and sees a bit of dark wing through the canopy branches above him. "What is that?" The trees arch, ache, and moan as the thing lifts off with one loud SWOOSH. He tries to get it on screen, but his hand is shaking too much to get it into the viewer. They listen as a third screech comes from a distance away. The flapping swoosh diminishes as it moves to the other side of the mountain.

Dave sits down hard on the ground, taking deep breaths. He notices his hand shaking visibly, and he tries to shake off the trembling in his hands. Billy is already sitting next to him, wide-eyed.

Eric is the first to scramble up with the others. "Did you see it?" his face alive with excitement. "I about peed in my pants!" He scans the horizon with his binoculars.

A disarrayed Rob arrives next. He's out of breath. "I may have gotten the sound on my recorder. Did anyone get a visual?" Rob looks to the group as they cluster around the flat screen on the echo unit.

Dave catches his eye. "I saw a bit through the trees." He grumbles. "I couldn't make out any more than a bit of wing, but we got a complete image on the echo." Dave gives his hand another shake, still trying to get his muscles back under control. *This is bullshit!* His mind screams a long "No, no, no." He watches Billy flip a switch and turn the equipment into red infrared imaging. He plays back the entire recording for the crew. They all stand there stunned, with mouths hanging open.

Getting up slowly, Dave scans the valley below with his binoculars, then turns to the data sheets for the evening. He picks them up and puts them in his pocket. Everyone is oblivious to the work they are supposed to be doing and concentrating on the new discovery. He watches Isabelle scan the horizon and watch the echo screen beside her. Eric is giddy with excitement and hugs Renee.

Rob exclaims to the group, "The image has the definite shape of an extremely large bat-like creature with a crested horn appendage." His breathing is quick. He says the words slowly. "It's registering close to twenty-five feet across."

Z puts his USB flash drive into the side of the unit and copies the image. "I'm not taking any chances."

SHIT, Just SHIT! I can't have them lose focus. This is NOT what we are here for. Dave's inner dialogue screams in his head. He stands staring straight ahead, face sagging. His mind flashes to the snickers of colleagues back at the university when Rob changed his focus to cryptozoology.

"I want a copy of that too! This is amazing," Rob says with awe.

"Simply amazing. So glad we're here." He gives Eric a knuckle butt on the side of his arm, then glances at Dave. Rob starts to say something, but Dave cuts him off, narrowing his eyes to him.

"Just don't talk to me for a while," Dave holds up his hand. All eyes are on Dave as he looks out over the valley floor. He turns his back on the team. His mind analyzed the situation. *Nothing could fly and disturb the trees like that or make that ear piercing sound. Nothing.* Behind him, two Ph.D.'s, each with a specialty in biology, were practically jumping for joy.

Eric eases over to his dad. "Dad--," he tries to calm him down. Dave walks away from him. Isabelle places one hand on Dave's shoulder as she passes, joining the others. Dave stops and turns back before addressing everyone at the equipment platform. "Let's get this straight. We are here to study and document BATS. Everybody got that! Our work is important. It could cure diabetes!" Dave huffs and moves to the netting. He untangles a line and resets it. "We pulled in twenty-seven bats tonight!" There is no response from the team.

Eric helps Dave reset the second line. Eric calls over his shoulder, "Everybody go back to bed. We've got this." A wave of exhaustion hits Dave. He stands still as Eric takes over. The group slowly walks down the trail back to their tents. Z remains analyzing the data.

"Dad, your shift is over. Go to bed. We've got it." He has to say it directly to Dave's face before turning and walking back down the trail. He doesn't go ten feet before Rob starts talking rapidly to Z and Eric about the sighting.

As Dave approaches camp, Rob comments loud enough for them to hear. "Ain't no way, I'm sleeping tonight!" There is a slight pause before he screams out into the empty night, "See, they are REAL!"

* * *

At dawn, a chorus of birdsong weaves through the canopy and stirs the campers awake. Dave steps out of his tent. He squints into a beam of sunlight as it breaks through a low cloud bank around them. He digs his sunglasses out and puts them on. They are all moving slowly today. Dave stands and watches Eric and Rob huddle with Malcolm over the breakfast fire. They are deep in conversation. Ain't no one getting anything done today, that's for sure.

Dave by himself, nursing his tea and then draining it. He keeps one eye on them as he scans the light on the water in the bay in the distance. He edges up behind the group.

Rob is so into the conversation that he doesn't notice Dave come up behind him. He jumps a little and snaps his tablet closed as he turns to see Dave. Rob looks at Dave apprehensively. "I've sent copies of the recordings and the echo data to my associate in Maine." He pauses as he hands Dave a cup of steaming water for his tea. Dave raises an eyebrow and accepts the water.

"We'd like to go up and see if we can find any evidence. Maybe do a small perimeter grid search of the area above the nets. Oh, we caught two more bats after you left last night." He pauses and lowers his voice. "Will we be staying here today or moving on?"

"We'll stay here another night. With the number of bats, we caught last night, we'll take it easy and catch up on some rest. Looks like we might be in for another long night." Dave pats Malcolm on the shoulder. "How are the porters holding up to the sighting?"

"Jodo is the only one who is upset. He sees the Ropen as a jungle spirit who must be appeased. To him, it's an omen. He wants to return to his village," Malcolm says, stoking the fire. "I told you they were a superstitious people."

"More shit." Dave grumbles and runs his fingers through his hair.

Renee loads up two banana leaves and walks toward the group.

Dave scans the camp. "You can do a grid search as long as you stay within 100 meters of the camp. You'll have to take a porter with you, probably not Jodo, though." Dave motions to Rob.

"I'll talk to the guys. I'll see if one of them will go with you." Malcolm lightly walks toward the porters and their hammocks. Rob follows him.

Renee steps to Dave and gives him a kiss on his cheek. "Morning Dad," she says with a big smile. She hands him one of the loaded leaves. Dave's eyes soften. "Morning, sweetheart. Sorry about being a little grumpy over all this. My science has always been very cut and dry. I rely on facts, figures, and biologicals." "Eric explained everything to me. I know it caused you embarrassment when Rob left the university and presented his Bigfoot data at that science conference." She gives him a hug and pours herself a cup of hot water. Dave hands her one of his precious, used tea bags.

She declines to take it. "No thanks, I've got herbal teas in my bag that I want to use. I know how much you enjoy your special blend. You keep it," she says, turning to get her supplies.

Stifling a big yawn, Z shuffles over and sits down. "Uhhhhh," he groans. "My brain is on fire with activity, but my body doesn't want to acknowledge it. I'm sore all over and I think I pulled a muscle in my leg in the confusion last night." He rubs his leg and looks longingly at Dave's steaming pile of vegetables, rice, and unknown meat.

"Take a bite." Dave offers breakfast to him. He sniffs it before taking a big bite. "What's the meat?" he asks after his second bite.

"You don't want to know." Dave finishes the last, wiping his hands on his shorts. "Think you could talk about exactly what you saw?" Z asks tentatively. Dave stands rigidly. "You know, I never wanted to be one of them. Those kooks who the rest of scientists talk about behind their backs. Rob has been on the edge all of his life, interested in the unexplained. He's always been chasing a Chubracabra, Bigfoot, or the Moth Man." In his irritation, he rubs his short beard. "You should have seen the stuff in his room when we were kids."

"Well, this time we're getting some documentation," Z says, then takes a swig from his canteen. Dave hesitates. "It was dark, leathery looking. I couldn't make out any feather pattern at all." He pauses again. "We heard it way before we saw it. There was a strange smell, kind of fishy in composition." Dave wraps his tea bag, takes a long drink, and downs the whole thing at once. They turn toward a clanking commotion on the trail.

Rob, Eric, Renee, and Gupty, the porter, wave as they saunter by with light packs and head up the mountain. Rob walks with the enthusiasm of a puppy with a new toy.

"Be back for lunch," Dave yells, as they disappear into the jungle. He scans the campsite to see Isabelle hanging her clothing out to dry outside her tent. She strolls over, joining Dave and Z. "You guys need to wash up a little, too. I can smell you from my tent." She wrinkles her nose at both of them.

"I'm thinking of following Malcolm over to the water source and checking things out. How about a quick shower? We can leave the other porters and Billy in charge of the camp," Dave says, stretching. "Then I want to come back and take a long nap. Billy snores so loud I'm not getting much sleep."

"Sounds great." Isabelle nods in agreement as the rank odor of unwashed bodies floats in the air. Isabelle eats her breakfast far away from Dave and Z.

Later, Malcolm leads Dave, Z, and Isabelle as they hike through a patch of dense forest. Dim bars of light stripe diagonally through an unbelievable collection of greens around them. After a ten-minute hike, Dave calls out, "I can hear the waterfall." Malcolm points the way. "Right over here." They walk another fifty yards before Isabelle says, "I didn't realize it was this close." A clear six-foot waterfall laps into a small pool and stream. She asks, "Is it safe here, Malcolm? Think it's okay to put my hand in the water?"

"Yes, as long as the water is free flowing, you shouldn't have a problem. I'll be glad to test drive it for you." Malcolm walks over, then balances on a rock to dunk his head under the stream. "Okay, we're all going to take turns on this. Me first."

Isabelle throws Malcolm a bar of soap, which he happily uses on top of his clothes, before he rinses thoroughly and strips down to his boxers. He calls out to Dave. "You know, mate, there will be a clear sky tonight. Should help watch for the creatures."

"That would be lovely." Isabelle smiles briefly and then shivers in the humidity. *What would her partner, Sarah, think of her in this situation?* She'd be yelling and screaming for her to get the F out of there! Their last conversation had been full of pleading and warning. And worry. They loved each other. She knew that to the depth of her soul, but this trip was something she had to do for her own mental health. Proving to herself that she can put something into action and help stop the mass clearing that is changing the landscape here.

"Stay for the show," Malcolm exclaims as he stands directly under the waterfall. She waves him off and turns her back to the waterfall. Isabelle, Z, and Dave examine the surrounding area.

"Let's take a step upstream," Dave holds Malcolm's machete, and slices through a green ribbon snake that is hanging on the branch behind Isabelle. He holds the carcass up to Malcolm.

"Lunch." Dave smiles at Malcolm. "I couldn't tell if it was poisonous. Just a reflex action, I guess." Dave swings the blade several times. "It's got a pleasant weight to it."

"My turn!" Isabelle yells to Malcolm as he steps out of the waterfall and shakes off.

Z scans the tree canopies around them while everyone bathes. He sighs. "It's a paradise out here. My adrenals are still high. I may just collapse in mid-step. Better take a nap when we get back."…Dave lounges nearby on a patch of moss. "Yeah, paradise with monsters." He winces and looks away.

"Your new daughter seems very nice." Z pulls debris from his pants and empties his pockets. "I need to know her better. Eric does nothing but talk about Renee. I think this is the first time he's chased a girl." Dave pats him on the back. "How is your son, Z? You haven't mentioned him in a while."

"He's ten now. Lives with his mother in Houston. Still don't get to see him often." Z stops scanning and tries to zoom in on an area with his binoculars. "Can't quite make it out—what do you think that is?" Z hands the lenses to Dave. "At 2:15,—in the fork of that tree. Down a little lower than us. It's not moving. Is that a foot?"

"A human foot?" Dave focuses the binoculars. "Sure looks like a foot." He adjusts the lenses again. "We need to check it out." They both stand as Malcolm joins them.

"Malcolm, after my bath, I'd like to hike to that grove of trees down there. Something's not right." Dave points to the canopy. "Guess we should all go." He looks up as Isabelle steps out of the water.

"Go where?" she asks as Z points down the cliffside. "Well, it can wait. Z, you need to finish that bath first." She holds onto her nose as she hands Dave the soap. She shakes herself dry and checks her feet before putting her Teva's back on. "Everybody wash their feet good?"

"Yes, Mom", says Dave, with a sly smile.

As they linger beside the waterfall and talk, Dave learns more about Isabelle. At thirty-three, she is a year younger than his son, Mack. She'd worked for several ecological organizations but found a home working for the World Wildlife Federation. Her goals include running the European offices by the time she turns forty. They have a crackpot group of scientists that get along well and support each other, sharing a little too much information about inner office politics. But underneath, he senses a deep loneliness running through her. There is a bit of fragility lurking there.

They stifle a giggle as Z walks out of the water. He shakes off like Isabelle had done, but it just looks ridiculous. Minutes later, Malcolm has them moving down the slope, through a series of granite boulders covered in moss in record time. Z is the last to arrive at the foot of the mountain.

After stepping in, Dave looks back up and motions for Z to stay. "Stay over there." Dave covers his mouth and nose with his bandana.

"So, what is it?" Z tries to see what the others are pointing at. He joins them, standing near the base of a large cypress tree, pinching his nose closed.

Mangled in the fork of the tree branches are the smelly remains of a man. The entire middle section is gone. A squadron of flies' buzzes around the body. The feet, hands and head are untouched, but the rest of him is nothing but tendons and bones. A length of intestines hangs off one side of the body. A trail of ants march up the tree to it.

Dave looks away, thinking about the poor guy being torn apart. The look of horror and shock on his face still registering on the man's face. Worry slithers through Dave. The wind blows in their direction. And everyone steps back, immediately covering their noses even more.

"Wow, he's ripe," says Malcolm. He doesn't look like one of our guys." Dave scans the corpse for identifying marks.

"Do you know what tribe he could be from?" Isabelle asks Malcolm. "Do you think it was the Ropen?" Her eyes water.

"Not much else could do this kind of damage. I see nothing particular that might identify his tribe." Malcolm says under his breath. "There isn't anything about him that stands out as unusual, other than a few of the tattoos on his face."

"There aren't any other large predators on the island." Isabelle steps back. "No cougars or panthers? No way it could be anything…other than…the creature."

"We were very thorough." Dave cuts her off. Dave's mind flashes to Eric under attack by a Ropen, off the trail. He flinches. "Right now, that is the only option. Unless you think a croc got him up there?" Malcolm steps back as Z photographs the body from several angles. "We need to notify the others and get back to camp." Dave moves toward the waterfall. He smells his shirt as they walk. "God, I can still smell that guy. I'm going to wash again, to clean this stink off."

"Don't you think we should bury him?" Isabelle stands firm. Dave turns back towards her asking, "I didn't bring a shovel, did you?" He takes a step and calls back over his shoulder. "I'll send the porters to take care of him." *We are getting so off track,* Dave thinks.

Malcolm raises his eyebrows. "Maybe that's not a good idea."

* * *

Later that afternoon, Dave has a long nap and then joins the others who are studying their own research data sheets near the campfire. He stretches and pops his neck as he walks over. Clouds are building once again to the north. The wind picks up. Dave looks around and frowns. "What's going on? Something feels different?"

"The porters. They've left. At least that's what we think. They could be out hunting." Z motions to the area that once held their hammocks. It's empty.

Dave quickly accesses the camp. "Malcolm, what do you think? Are they gone?" Dave asks as his mind screams *SHIT*.

"I'm afraid so. Thought I saw one of them follow us when we went to the stream. I'm sure he saw the body, but I went back and buried the guy."

"This is going to change things for us. We will all have heavier loads." Dave looks at each member of the group and smiles weakly. "We've gone through about half of our supplies, and we have three extra people to help lighten the load."

"We'll be glad to help," Eric motions for Renee and Rob to stand beside him.

"Z, I'd like you to be the only one touching the electronics," Dave says, directly to him, before turning to Malcolm. "Malcolm, are you feeling any doubt about continuing on with your guide contract?" Dave walks over and places his hand on Malcolm's shoulder. His respect for the man shoots up. His character and experience have been making the difference between life and death for everyone. They all look at Malcolm.

"No problem, mate. I'm with you." Malcolm grins and points to a cave opening above them. "It might be a good idea to put part of the camp in those caves a bit up the mountain, though. A portion of the equipment got wet yesterday. I would recommend we get things moving. Full moon, and it's going to rain tonight."

"Now that everybody's here, I need to tell you about our find below." He points to the valley floor. "We found a body, a human body, a native, partially eaten---parts of it, in a tree." Dave fidgets with items in his pocket. "The porters have gone. Your safety is my priority." He pauses. "I'd like to take a vote." Dave scans everyone's faces. *I've got to do this.* "Who wants to head back?"

Eric is the first to shake his head. "No." Dave looks at each member, as they all agree. He sighs, bends over, and puts his hands on his knees.

"I agree, with you all," letting out a deep breath.

Malcolm nods and walks up to Dave. "We need to pull everyone in on map locations. Let's all have a review on logistics once we set up in the cave. It's important that every one of you knows exactly where we are." Eric raises an eyebrow. "That cave isn't too big, but we might all squeeze in. I looked around at it yesterday. It will be a good place to set up the sensitive equipment."

Rob stands as if to say something. Dave looks at him and pauses. "Do you need to add something?" Rob nods. "Everyone, be careful. I'd like to give you an update on everything we know about the creatures once we're settled." Rob steps back and joins the others.

"Good enough," says Dave. "Let's strike camp and move up now." He unties the tarp over the fire. "But leave the fire burning." His eyes scan to a bank of thunderheads growing in size, filling the horizon. As the storm moves closer, and camp is set, Billy leans against the cliff side and fiddles with his slingshot. A rumbling sound from deep in the mountain catches his attention as a scattering of rocks slides loose around him. Eric holds Renee close to his chest. Everyone braces themselves as a small aftershock rocks the camp. Malcolm looks unconcerned, sitting beside the flames from the dinner campfire. He shrugs his shoulders at the team.

"Dude," Billy's eyes widen as he looks at Dave. "This place keeps surprising me. That was an aftershock, right? I'm gonna get the biggest beer when we are outta here."

"Yes, aftershock," Dave says, sitting down next to him. "We're going to take turns tonight keeping watch. Billy, you, and I will oversee the midnight-to-four shift. You'd better take another nap if you can. I already had mine." As Billy heads into his tent, Dave climbs over a large rock toward Eric and Renee. Almost immediately, they hear Billy snoring.

"How are you guys doing?" Dave joins them as they watch the storm approach over the bay.

Renee reaches into her pack and slips Dave a crumpled zipped bag of cookies. "For you." She leans in, whispering. "Don't tell anybody." Dave turns away from the others, hiding his precious gold.

Dave holds his hand over his heart and blows her a kiss before digging into the treat. "What else do you have in your pack?" He talks with his mouth full of crumbs. "I can feel the sugar rushing into my blood. God, I've missed it." Dave pours the crumbs into his mouth as Z enters and checks the equipment.

"We were just discussing the history of the Ropen. Do you know we've had the same reports of a flying creature in Big Bend National Park out in West Texas? That creature also had a long tail." Eric stirs the sand at the base of the rock. "And we've had reports in Alaska and Oklahoma, too." Eric's eyes shine as he talks. "And the petroglyphs in South America were amazing. This creature is still alive and we're going to get proof."

"What exactly did you find in South America?" Dave asks, tapping the remaining crumbs into his mouth.

"Just some carvings of an animal that looks like a Pterodon on crumbling Aztec monuments. Dad, you should have seen it. They matched those from an area in Peru that Rob found three years ago." Eric lights up with enthusiasm. "And Renee's grandfather has agreed to fund an Alaskan expedition in the spring. He's got more money than most third-world countries." He laughs. "Do you know he micro-chipped both of us before we left? We're kind of like his favorite puppies."

Renee grins and takes Eric's hand in hers as she intertwines their fingers. "You're my favorite puppy," she says, full of love. He kisses the back of her hand and looks deeply into her eyes.

Dave scoots away from them. "Young love," he whispers. *Jeanne, your boy is more than smitten.* "What's in Alaska? he asks as they pull apart.

Eric looks over to Rob who goes in and out of the cave. "You should ask him. I'm sure he'd love to tell you about it. Dad, he's been really great to us. I wanted you to know. I'm proud to stand next to him and you should be too." Dave rubs the top of Eric's head. *Guess he's too old for that now, too.* "So, how did you propose?" He asks in jest.

Around them, baseball-sized raindrops hit. "He didn't." Renee stands. "I did." Renee turns and enters the cave. Eric and Dave follow her.

"What? Dave's mouth hangs open. "What do you mean, E? You didn't ask this lovely creature to be your wife?" Eric steps into the cave as the storm increases. He shrugs. "I'm irresistible."

Rob joins them as he shakes off the rain from his ball cap and puts it back on. He scans the cramped space inside the cave and sits down in the corner. "Who's irresistible?"

Eric points at his chest and grins at his uncle. The mood has lightened since last night. Z catches his eye momentarily and Dave gives a "thumbs-up." He has set the electronic gear up perfectly. "See what you can do with some elbow grease?" With a flourish of his hand, he does a mock bow. "It's one of my super-powers."

As Dave looks over the gear, Renee asks Z, "Where did you do your undergraduate work?" He laughs. "Guess I've lost my Boston accent. Boston U, with my Ph.D. from Yale. That was a lifetime ago. Now, I work for a mega corporate identity on the south side of Philly and answer to a board of directors and a budget cutting administrator. This is my last forage out into the wild. I'm getting too old for this stuff. Dave, you've got to see the lab. Turned that decrepit barn into a real lab. It would rival any man cave. I'd put money on that. In fact, I promised Susan that you would visit after the trip."

"As always, you make it look easy. I'll take you up on that offer for a visit." Dave straightens his hair and tightens his ball cap. He rearranges the stack of backpacks, adding more floor space for the crew.

Z stretches up and touches the ceiling with his hand. "See, there are advantages to being short. I don't have to worry about hitting my head on the ceiling. Billy cannot stand erect inside this place, that's for sure."

Rob lights a portable LED torch near the opening. The cave's depth isn't over fifteen by twenty feet. A crack in the rock goes deep into the mountainside at the back. The cave is filled with a damp, musky smell, and dirt floor. Eric checks out the corners with his flashlight. After scouting the area, Rob heads back out next to Malcolm, who huddles under the canopy with Isabelle.

It takes a second before Dave realizes Eric is scoping out the area, checking for spiders. He smiles and shakes his head and motions with his hand to mimic a spider in Renee's direction, and she smiles back and nods an affirmative before Eric sits next to Dave and Renee.

Dave nudges Eric. "So, are you going to tell me about the proposal?" "I was going to ask her, but she beat me to it." Eric smiles at Renee. Haltom's is working on a custom ring for me. Hopefully, it will be ready when we get back." Renee snuggles against him. "Really, you were going to ask me?"

"Yeah, I looked at rings, but I couldn't find anything I liked." Eric kisses the back of her hand. "I didn't know your size and what you'd want?"

"When, when did you look at rings?" she asks. They murmur to each other. Dave smiles as he is closed out of the conversation. *He's a good boy, Jeanne. You'd be proud,* he thinks to himself.

Dave scoots over closer to Z. "How are we doing? We haven't had a chance to talk lately." Dave reviews the information laid out on a small printout strip. He analyzes the stats. A hint of a smile tugs on his lips as he reads.

"We've got promising preliminary stats on the blood samples. The metabolic rate on those bats is amazing. They're not any ordinary bats. They're super bats." Z grins widely. "At this rate, we might really find that key element the board is looking for." Dave lets out an audible sigh. He turns to tell Eric the news, but he and Renee are still deep into a couple's conversation.

Rob and Malcolm come into the cave dripping wet. "We've got both of the nets set up. I think Billy is still sleeping. He isn't moving." Rob sits on the other side of Z. "Dinner will be ready in fifteen, if we can keep the fire going." Rob wrings out his shirt. "Malcolm is one of the best guides I've ever had." He tries to get a look at one datasheet. Rob inches over, joining them as they scan the data stream. He is about to say something when Eric screams, brushes something off his arm, and runs out of the cave into the downpour.

"Get it off!!! Is it on my back?" Eric yells as he runs around. His eyes hold the expression of sheer terror. Malcolm calls out a warning to Eric before they hear Malcolm's laughter. "A spider? All that over a spider?"

Renee walks to the opening of the cave and calls back to him, "It's just a little spider, honey." They all look at her as she points to the spider crawling in front of her. She says, "He hates spiders."

Dave smiles. "You should have seen him when he was young. He'd leave overturned cups over spiders if he found any in the house. If I didn't dispatch them, he would leave them there for days."

"Z, is your research related to the molecular genetics of diabetes?" Rob asks as he takes one of the stat sheets closer to the lamp.

"Yes, it's going to be used in a study investigating insulin-resistant accumulation of toxic fats in heart tissue for Type 1 and Type 2 diabetes…" Z pauses before adding, "Good stuff. Ground-breaking stuff, and hopefully, a ride to a cure."

"Contrary to what my brother thinks, I still read the periodicals." Rob checks another column of data. He briefly catches Dave's eye before returning to his reading. "This looks promising," he says, as he continues to read.

Billy and Isabelle enter the cave. He groggily announces, "Dinner is about ready." He bends at an awkward angle to get around. "Geesh, it's not very high, is it?" He turns on his headlamp and scours the area. "Did anyone really check out this cave?"

"I did." Isabelle waves him off. "No worries here. Just animal bones back in the corner." She points to one section of the cave that narrows considerably. The dirt floor is bare except for a dusty cluster of small bones. "Some sort of bird, I think." Rob walks over to look at the skeleton.

After dining on roast pigeons courtesy of Billy's slingshot, Dave addresses the group. "I want both mist nets monitored. So far, we've caught a record forty-three bats, and twenty-seven of them have been Otto's. We've reached our milestone, but it won't hurt to get a few more. Work in teams, and I want everyone to stay with their buddy. Hopefully, the rain will lessen. If you hear or see anything that resembles the Ropen, blow your whistle. Billy and Eric have zoom lenses on their cameras for documentation. Questions?"

Z and Rob step forward. Z holds up his map with Rob's help. He points to the marker on the map. "I want everyone to inspect this tonight. Get comfortable with the island. If, for some reason, you become separated from us, your survival depends on knowing which way to go. Does everyone have their belt compasses?" Everyone looks and checks the small item. Rob has one tied to his shoelace. Renee has one, but Eric does not. "Put it on and keep it there."

Eric looks around at the concerned faces looking at him. "I've got one in my pack, promise!"

Dave stands up as Z refolds the map and passes it around. "Z and I checked through the specimen listing. We are past where I hoped we would be, but more samples only strengthen the results. So, excellent job everyone. I know it hasn't been an easy trek, but I appreciate the extra efforts you have put forth."

"I would recommend everyone turn in early." Z holds up one vial. "I'll stay in the cave working on the collection kit. When you've got something, bring it in. Rob and Renee, you're Team One; Dave and Billy, Team Two; and Isabelle and Eric, you're Third Shift. Malcolm is our floater should anyone need extra help. And, of course, I don't need to remind you to wear your gloves," Z says, firmly.

The downpour outside stops as if someone turned off the faucet.

With a slight hesitation, Rob turns to the group. "Billy has his zoom lens, and I've got a recorder. We'll keep the heat monitor right here inside the door. Please be ready and use your whistle if you see anything."

As they leave, Malcolm stops them. "Just a sec, mate. There is a cluster of razor palms to the east of net two. Don't go wandering off." Malcolm walks back out to the campfire.

Dave gently grabs Renee's arm. "Sure you're up for this?" "I'll be fine. I'm actually looking forward to it." She smiles graciously and pats him on the arm. "If I get a particularly wiggling one, I'll just have to blind it with my flashlight."

Hours later, Eric and Dave watch Renee deal with her first bat. Eric walks over to Dave after she finishes taking the sample. "Dad, can we talk for a minute?"

"Sure, I've always got time for you." Dave pats the ground next to him and Eric sits.

"This grant you've got on Type 2 diabetes. Did you know Rob has it? His levels have come down a bit. At least that's what he told me last month. He's controlling it with diet and medication." There is a long pause in the conversation before Dave responds. He is stunned by the news.

"I didn't know." Dave looks over to the cave entrance where Rob stands silhouetted against the night sky. *Just like Uncle Bobby. God, he went blind from it.* For the first time since his arrival, Dave takes measure of his brother, standing right there. He remembers how awful the end of life was for his uncle.

"When was your last check-up?" Eric says with concern.

"I'm fine. I had a complete head-to-toe check-up before I left Miami. It came with an array of shots for this trip." He watches Rob's every move as Rob zeroes in on a flock of birds flying past. "When was he diagnosed?"

"Two years ago. He told Mack and I last year." Eric fidgets before continuing, "You've got to get over this thing between you two. It's hurting all of us. Please? Nothing can be so bad that you two can't find a common ground once again. We're family. And family is everything."

Dave listens. *Where do I start?* Never one to give in first, he is asking a lot, but Dave knows it's the right thing to do. They are both bullheaded. Never giving the other an inch when the stakes are down. He remembers launching himself at Rob over a chess game. *What is wrong with us?* I don't want to be like that.

"Do you think you can patch it up enough, so we don't have so much tension? It's suffocating me, us." He grabs his dad's shoulders with both hands. "It's the wedding present I want most from both of you. I'm going to ask him for the same thing." Eric smiles weakly at his dad. "I want us to have nice family gatherings again." Eric walks over to help Renee with her catch. He mouths the words "please," over his shoulder toward his dad, then turns back to Renee.

Dave stands alone under the tarp at the campfire, watching the canopy of trees for hours that evening, just watching and thinking. *I hope I can do it. I've been holding on to it, and–it's hurting my kids. Let it go, Dave. Just let it go.* For a second he thought he heard Jeanne's voice on the wind, saying "Honey."

Finally, Malcolm walks over with a suggestion of a nap before his shift.

"I'm not sure I can sleep right now. Thanks anyway, Malcolm." Dave crawls into his tent and zips the netting closed. He is restless and tosses back and forth before finally falling asleep. He dreams of Jeanne and the boys and the last holiday dinner when magical laughter filled the room.

Hours later, Dave is instantly awake as a shrieking whistle call sounds. He grabs his camera and darts to the netting area nearest him. Isabelle runs up to him. Renee and Rob have their camera lenses raised and pointing to three dark objects with glowing orbs that flash on and off at six second intervals. They are flying above the tree canopy about a mile in the distance. In seconds, the rest of the crew joins them.

Billy's camera clicks incessantly. "Yes, I've got the zoom on!" he calls out to Rob who shouts back, "I've got it on video feed." His voice cracks with excitement as he whips his head toward the action.

"The Ropen?" asks Isabelle. "Finally, there they are. I'm a bit gob-smacked. This is brilliant."

"Bioluminescence, just like a lightning bug," says Z, under his breath. "Wow! Looks like the glowing is coming from an area under the wing. Billy, is that what you see?"

Billy adjusts the lens. "Yeah, I've got it zoomed all the way out. I hope the clarity is sharp enough." Billy continues to film against a pale and transparent moon low on the horizon.

Rob can hardly contain his excitement. His voice squeaks. "What's our altitude and longitude? We're in the jungle canopy of Papua New Guinea. It's now 11:20 pm. There are three distinct glowing orbs that are pulsing about every six seconds, twenty feet up from the forest canopy. Unknown objects. Large wingspan. Could be twenty-five feet across from tip to tip. The nearest settlement is a four days walk, about forty kilometers. We've been watching them for a minute." Rob looks at Billy. "Make sure you get some creatures in relation to perspective."

Billy adjusts the detection gear. "If they come a little closer, we'll really be able to see them. At the moment, they are just out of range." A distant Stone Age scream pierces the air as one globe moves into the canopy and flashes out. The other two orbs hover for a moment and then dive into the canopy in the same area.

Dave uses one of his military high-power lights to scan the tops of the trees in their direction. "It's still too far out," he says in desperation.

"I'm going to keep the video going, just in case." Rob plants his feet firmly apart.

Dave stands next to him. "Sounds like… is that the same scream you heard last night?" Rob takes a step back, so he can capture Dave on camera. "Come on, let's do an on-air interview, like the old days." Rob gives Dave his best smile.

Dave turns, and finger combs his hair. He nods an affirmative to Rob.

"Okay, rolling? Dr. David Lane, biologist. "Last night we had an encounter with a large, winged creature just above our research collection site. We couldn't identify the object, as it was over a thick wooded canopy, but we could hear a loud whoosh, wing flapping noise, and I saw a bit of its wing. There were no visible feathers. The skin is leathery in appearance. Site analysis of the area reveals no biologicals. A heavy fish odor accompanied the sighting," he says into the camera. "You should be the one on camera, Rob."

When he pauses, Rob zooms the camera back to the canopy. "Keep going," he says.

"It called out, a very high-pitched scream that exploded above us. The sound of a thousand eagles calling at once." In the distance, a shriek reverberated through the canopy. Dave turns and looks directly into the camera. "Just like that." Dave walks to the edge of the path.

In seconds, Rob joins him. Gingerly, Rob puts his arm around Dave as they scan the valley. "Thank you," he whispers.

CHAPTER 7

The next morning, Billy is lying in the tent with his feet pushed up against the netting. He fills the length of the tent. Nothing ever fits him. Next time, he'll be sure to get the longer tent. Sleeping curled up is getting old. His hip bones painfully dig into the dirt. He grins, thinking about the photographs he has taken so far on the trip. Last night, he spent an hour looking through six hundred images. They were exceptional. Getting the more expensive camera and lenses was the right move. He smiles when he thinks of how they will look on the big monitor when he cleans them in editing. This is Pulitzer Prize stuff, he knows it. He needs the perfect shot of the creature. It will make the cover of *National Geographic* for sure.

As a kid, Billy spent hundreds of hours looking through *National Geographic*. His secret dream was always to get jobs around the world for the magazine. *What would his mom say now?* She called his photography interests "his hobby," and never has come to any of his awards, even after he won a cash prize for some of his work. *Maybe now she will tell me I did a good job? Probably not. It isn't in her character to say words of encouragement.*

He thinks about the gallery on East Fifth Street back home, the one with the high-end artists. When they see his photographs, he'll get some gallery shows. Maybe the grant will fund a reception. His mind races through a dozen scenarios, maybe even a New York show. *I have to get THAT shot.* Lighting is important. *Will a full moon offer the opportunity?* He can hear Dave's morning coughing outside the tent and knows he will be called soon. He changes and steps out, strapping his camera around his neck.

Dave stirs his tea beside the campfire. Under hooded eyes, he watches Billy, giving him a little wave before staring lifelessly at the canopy below and out to the dark-blue expanse of the ocean in the distance. It's a breathtaking scene with the sun low on the horizon. But Dave's face is etched in worry. Dark circles under his eyes pair well with his blood-red eyes. He rubs them, then takes a deep drink of his tea. Behind him, Malcolm is busy making breakfast.

"I'll have something ready for you soon," Malcolm says as he stirs the coals. He nods a greeting to Billy before getting back to work.

Isabelle exits her tent and plops down beside Dave. "God, you look awful. Did you sleep at all? You've got to rest. That makes two days with little sleep." Isabelle bites into a mango and talks with her mouth full. "You get a little grumpy when you don't sleep." She offers him a bite.

Billy takes a mango from Malcolm's pile of fruit and bites into it. He snaps images of the breakfast fire, Malcolm, and the morning landscape. Dave looks at Isabelle and shakes his head.

"Are we staying here or moving on?" she asks, scanning the horizon of thin, clearing clouds.

Two large brightly colored hornbills fly by. The red bulbous crests on their heads shine in the morning light. They both watch the birds as they descend into the valley below. Billy captures them with his lens and smiles. *Another perfect shot for the gallery show,* he thinks to himself.

Malcolm brings Isabelle a cup of hot water. "Morning miss." He flashes her with a broad grin. "Bless you," says Isabelle as she drops a tea bag into it.

"Think it might be some sort of hornbill?" Isabelle inquires as she stirs her tea. "Those are gigantic birds." She points to the birds. Dave watches her.

"No, I don't. Look at the way those wings move. Our flying objects didn't have the same shaped wings. I've worked with bats long enough that I know the difference between feathers and bat wings." Dave takes a long drink of his tea.

Malcolm joins them. "Do you want to break camp?"

"Yes, let's get everyone up. I'd like to try heading to the north. Any settlements that way?" Dave asks.

Malcolm takes out a worn, folded map and lays it out on the dirt in front of them. "My map shows some sort of marker in that area, but no settlement." Malcolm points. "If we can make it past that mass of rock over there, the terrain should flatten out more. We've got only a few hills between us and the ocean. Progress could get soggy, and we might encounter more crocs. "This will be unfamiliar territory for me."

"Let's just make it to the other side of the rock and re-evaluate them. We already hit the numbers we are looking for. Last night's catch was a record. So, any further bat data is icing on the cake." Dave stands and brushes off his thin khakis. "I'm going to check on the equipment. Don't wake up Z yet. Let him sleep until we're almost ready to go." Z snores loudly behind them. The roar is weirdly comforting.

"Mmmmm," Malcolm says as he bites into a roasted plantain. "Cake, I haven't had cake in a longggg time," he says, smiling at Dave. "Well, you mentioned it."

"I'm going to get you a whole spread of fresh cakes when we get back. Whatever you want." Dave pats him on the back. "You've earned that and more.

* * *

Without porters, the team moves slowly, and they load each member with full backpacks and equipment. As they leave the safety of the cave area, Malcolm warns them to move carefully with each step. The pace is slow, methodical, and physically exhausting.

Z balances his load with the help of a sturdy hiking pole Malcolm fashioned for him. He balances his gear efficiently with his ninety-pound pack on his back. "It doesn't look too far. We should be there by early afternoon," Z says to Eric, as he almost falls into Dave.

Dave points at a site on the horizon 200 feet below. "Let's keep it nice and slow, everyone." Dave offers his hand to Z, but he declines.

"I've got it." Z pulls his hat down lower. His face is full of determination.

Navigating this terrain is outside the parameters of the team. Dave watches Z with concern. *Can he manage the additional load?* Billy stays close to Z, helping when he can. *There's been a definite change in the boy's demeanor. It's as if he has grown up overnight. The jungle can change anyone.*

And he's excellent in the lab. I might have to upgrade his work responsibilities when we get back, he thinks. Dave waits for the group's slow progress to catch up. While he waits, his mind replays Drew's encounter with the crocs now that they are inching back into the animal's territory.

Malcolm calls out as he drops his bag near a stream that is roaring from the heavy rains. "We will rest momentarily before we cross."

Isabelle looks to the water with concern. "Should we stay on this side? There might be an easier crossing ahead." Malcolm shakes his head and downs his canteen water.

Rob scans the deep foliage around them. The impenetrable mass looms in every direction. He leans over, catching his breath, waiting for Z and Billy.

Huge, ribbed roots on the river bank make for a life-sized "Chutes and Ladders" obstacle course complete with an encounter with a viper that Malcolm dispatches with his machete. It takes hours for them to go a mile in the thick vegetation. It surprises them when Dave steps onto a wooden platform out in the middle of nowhere. His boots echo on the worn boards. "Pristine rainforest, my ass," he says out loud. He stomps on the boards to free the mud from his boots.

"Hey, I think this is one of those platforms." Dave pounds the floor, dislodging chunks of clay. Several swipes from Malcolm's blade clear the area, displaying the complete platform and nearby, a small cleared area with a pig in a pen. An elderly couple emerges from the forest as if they have materialized from the jungle itself. Both sides stand in shock at seeing the other. Seconds pass before Malcolm speaks, to which the couple acknowledges in their native tongue. "We have overnight visitors." Malcolm turns to the team. "They're harmless, mates."

The others quickly follow, and they find a second platform close by. As their packs pound on the wood, the team releases a collective groan. "Are we nearing a village?" Dave asks, looking into the wall of the thicket in front of them.

"No, nothing in this area. I feel this couple likes the solitude." Malcolm talks to them in a local dialect that sounds like a major tongue twister.

"Do you think we should stay here tonight or go down to the beach?" Dave looks around as Rob joins them. Malcolm surveys the area and says, "If we go down to the base floor, it may be swampy. Then, there are the crocs to consider."

Dave nods. "You're right. How 'bout we stop here for the night? I, for one, am beat." Malcolm drops his pack softly. "Looks good. Okay, everyone. This is camp." He clears an additional area for the tents closer to the stream with several expert swipes of his machete. "I'll have a little conversation with Ma and Pa over there. Back in a minute." Malcolm disappears. His voice dissolves into the mass of green around them.

By the time Malcolm returns, they have set the camp up. "They've got a little place set up, complete with a fenced garden plot and tin roof. Careful, though, there are remains of a plane scattered in the area." Malcolm fills his canteen in the stream. "I'll hunt for dinner. I think we are close to one place the government built in the 50s. Everybody sit tight. I'll check it out." He turns and steps back into the emerald wall.

"That was some rack we trekked through," Eric says, as he rubs his shoulders where the pack straps dug in. "I feel like I've just finished a marathon. Guess there's jungle, and a whole new description for jungle?" Renee rubs his shoulders to his relief.

Dave finishes setting up his tent. "Hey Billy, do you think you could set up the nets? See that area just up from that bit of clearing?" He points to a bit of sunshine hitting a grove of trees arching over the stream. "Yeah, I can, but you've got bags under your bags. Take a nap. Rob and I will do it." Billy throws a section of netting at Rob. He doesn't argue. "God, I think I'm sleeping standing up and my body doesn't know it." Dave crawls into his tent and zips it closed.

* * *

Hours later, Dave emerges from his tent to find everyone sitting nearby eating pawpaw fruit from a woven basket. "Where did that come from?" he asks as he takes one piece and bites into it. Juice runs down his arm. Isabelle beams. "It's like finding a grocery store out in the middle of a desert. Have another. I've already had three." She eyes the basket, contemplating taking another.

"Malcolm made friends with the elderly couple." Rob stretches out on the platform. "Hold off, Isabelle. They can give you the runs." Isabelle stops her reach and throws the remains of the last one into the bushes.

"Dave, if it's all right, I'm going to barter for rice. I'd rather replenish now, since it's available." Malcolm stands and empties the basket of fruit. "They will sell you rice? Out here?" Dave licks his fingers clean. "Go for it."

Malcolm returns his smile and asks, "Should I turn down their offer of grub worms?"

Isabelle dry gags. "Please, no worms."

Renee shakes her head "no" as well.

Eric sticks out his tongue.

Malcolm laughs at the responses from the team.

After a dinner of German taro, rice, and boiled choko greens mixed with okari nuts, Dave sets the schedule for the night. "We'll keep the same teams as last night. Z, I want you to turn in. You look like you're ready to collapse. I will take your shift at midnight with Billy."

Rob raises his hand. "I'll run the station through the night."

Dave nods. *It's getting easier to be around him. Let it go, Dave, just let it go. One step at a time.*

Stifling a yawn, Z talks. "According to Malcolm, Grandma and Grandpa have been collecting food for a group that is doing some clearing half a day's walk from here. We might have company tonight or in the morning. I'm going to bed." Z drags his feet to his tent.

Dave looks for Malcolm. "Where's Malcolm? I want to know more about this 'group.'" They all look to where Malcolm had been sitting. "I've stretched the nets out and we're ready to go."

Rob collapses. "I think there are another ten pounds of mud on these boots." He tries repeatedly to get chunks of the clay to come loose from the sides. Using a stick, he flings mud into the dark bushes.

Malcolm steps out of the dark bushes of the foliage. His feet are so caked with mud that he looks as if he's wearing boots. "Hey, you just missed me," he says to Rob as he flicks one chunk from his thigh back at Rob in jest. "When I was a kid, it was a favorite pastime to fling mud at each other. I'm the King of that game."

"Oops, sorry." Rob leans back against a tree. He smiles playfully at Malcolm. Dave invites the guide over. "Hey Malcolm, could you talk to the couple to see if they've had any encounters from above? And who do you think is doing the clearing?"

A light breeze blows through the camp. With the wind comes the songs of the jungle. "That's a Bird of Paradise call." Malcolm points in the music's direction and smiles. "I'll ask them about the Ropen. I'm not sure who is doing the clearing. We'll know better once we see what they are doing. Hey, does anyone want to see the dance of love?" Renee raises her eyebrows. "The dance of love?" Billy runs to their tent and returns, adjusting a new lens onto his camera. He calls out, "Ready!"

"The Bird of Paradise is one of our jewels. The male birds fan their foliage and preen for the females. It's fun to watch. They are unique and colorful. You will see something special." Malcolm holds onto his shoes and whacks them against the side of a tree, dislodging a handful of mud with each hit.

Renee stands. "Come on honey, let's go see." She holds out her hand to Eric.

Billy is quick to respond again. "I'm game!" he says with a smile. "Hey, pretty good pun on words. Get it, game… birds?" Rob giggles. "I know I'll regret it tomorrow. I'm so tired, but yeah, I'll go."

Malcolm stands ready and offers a hand-up to Rob. "I'll talk to Grandma after we watch the birds. We only have about an hour left before dusk, and we need to finish getting everything ready." Malcolm, Eric, Rob, Renee, and Billy turn and dissolve into the jungle. Dave watches them go into the jungle as he sets up the equipment on one side of the clearing. Isabelle steps up beside him. "Hey," he says as he works.

"Hey, back at ya." Isabelle shakes her head. "I can't get your Texan accent right." She smiles. "Thanks for moving the camp. You didn't have to, but I appreciate it. The World Wildlife Federation just had a seminar on the illegal harvesting of exotic woods on this island. Like that grouping of Agarwood, we had at Enga Village. It validates my joining you on this trek. If I can find a second location, we might really stop some of this." She takes a deep breath. "The abundance of natural resources needs to be cherished. "There's extra water if you want to wash up a little." She points to a collapsible bucket and sits on the edge of the platform.

Dave joins her. He pulls off his boots and lets his blistered feet air out. Isabelle grabs his foot. "I wouldn't get too close. They are ripe." Dave leans back and away from his feet. He can feel the steam coming off them.

Isabelle inspects his heel. It looks inflamed. "Let's get you cleaned up and some antibiotic on that." She checks his other beaten-up foot and frowns. "Everyone's feet needs to be checked."

Z hobbles over with a noticeable limp. "That's not a bad idea," he says, as he jostles the boards, sitting hard, and removing his socks and shoes. His inflamed heel matches Dave's. "Kind of reminds me of going to camp when I was a kid." He smiles and scratches himself in the groin. "Remember how good the window air conditioner felt?" He elbows Dave. Isabelle looks confused.

"We went to a boy scout camp together wayyyy back," Dave says as he smiles. "Had a whole infestation of chigger bites. Now, I've got flea and skeeter bites driving me crazy." He scratches his leg in irritation. *Damn insects. No telling what parasites I've picked up as well out here.* A list of disgusting bug parasite cases flashes through his mind.

"What's a chigger? That a big bad Texas bug?" She snickers at them.

"A real pain. Not big, but it's bad. When you get them, they burrow under the skin… in sensitive folded skin areas. They might be so tiny but pack a wallop that makes you wanna strip your skin right off ya." Dave scratches his crotch at the memory.

Isabelle stands. "I'll be right back with the medic bag." She is just at the door coming out of her tent when a screech fills the skies above them. She ducks back into her tent and looks up. Dave and Z lie flat on the boards, not making a sound.

"Stay there Isabelle," Dave yells, then blows his whistle three times. He and Z both struggle to get their feet back into boots. Z rolls to the equipment and turns on the Echo, hitting the "record" button in record time.

The creature flies in a straight line just above the tree canopy. The wings are dark black-purple, and almost twenty feet across. Its beady eyes are dark, surrounded by bright aqua markings. The bald crested head is capped with a protrusion hump that angles away from its head. Dave focuses on the sharp beak of razor teeth.

"Are you getting this?" Dave motions to Z as they crouch-crawl over to the tent. Dave can't take his eyes off the creature. *What makes the sight so interesting? A dinosaur coming to life. I can't deny it any longer.* "Oh, my GOD," he whispers, his lips trembling.

Isabelle peeks out of the tent flap. Nothing has prepared her for the view before her right now. She vaguely could remember studying dinosaurs in grade school, but they never were a fascination. It shimmers from the way the sunlight hits the wings and floats so effortlessly. There is a beauty in its dance. *And it is alive. Definitely alive. Breathing. Observing.* Right over them. *Intelligence.* She feels its intelligence as it scans them.

"Pterodactyl!" says Z in awe, oddly calm. "Yes, I'm getting it. Must be twenty feet across, tip-to-tip."

The bird continues to soar. Its ribbed wings flap once before it disappears into the tree line and out of their sight.

On shaking limbs, Isabelle crawls out of her tent. "It had no legs. Three toes on each wing." "Four toes on its feet."

Dave adds. "Three toes on each wing."

Z tries to talk but can't find his voice. He fiddles with the equipment, checking to make sure the recording was taken. The rest of the crew explodes out of the jungle and hurries to the equipment desk. Rob and Eric talk excitedly between themselves. Dave chuckles at their excitement.

Sweat pours off Billy as he reviews his images through the viewfinder screen. "Check it out! I think it was only about thirty feet above us." The team watches the replay together. Rob's jaw drops when he sees the image. "Did you notice the smell?" asks Dave. "Fishy right?" Heads nod in agreement.

"The wings were black, oily, and thick," says Eric with enthusiasm. "I didn't see any feathers, definitely a leathery membrane of some sort." "Like wet Naugahyde," says Isabelle in a deadpan voice. "You could see light going through the wings when the sunlight hit them."

Rob turns to the group. "You know, there is so much we don't know about the Pterosaur family. There is a sizeable gap in the fossil record. Their bones were so fragile, that few survived. Think of what we can learn. So, what do you think, Eric? Didn't I tell you we would find it?!" Eric nods his head excitedly as they congratulate each other.

"Shouldn't we be looking out, making sure it's not coming back?" Isabelle scans the skies as they all huddle at the equipment. *God, what would happen if that thing made it to a population?* This is a predator like we have never seen before. *Think of what the media would do with the information and photos. Some rich influencers would bring tours or try to catch the thing. How many will die exploiting the creature? How many are there? Do they carry disease? This isn't Jurassic Park! No one will care about the flora and fauna when they have a real dinosaur to market and sell. Probably won't care about the loss of life with the natives, either.*

Isabelle can hear the arguments beginning with Z wanting to preserve the creatures. The government on the island is horrible to deal with. It is ripe with corruption and under the table deals are common. There would be devastation on a scale that her mind can't wrap around. They have confirmed the existence of a true master prehistoric beast that rivaled the biggest predators in the world. What will the next step be? How in the world can they protect the creatures and keep the rest of humanity safe? The world is changing too fast.

Isabelle and Dave's eyes meet. He doesn't understand the confusion that races through her mind. He steps closer to her. The jungle is still strangely quiet. She looks out. "It could be out there watching us right now, with its friends? Waiting to swoop down and kill us all in our tents."

"That's a scary thought, I know, but I think our scans will give us enough advanced warning." He watches the skies with her. "Our world just changed," he says, then exhales.

"Yeah, but did it change for the better, or the worse?" she adds as they watch the rest of the team.

Rob flips a switch on the echo equipment. He hits REPLAY. They watch it before Z inserts his portable USB stick and backs it up. The elderly couple stands inside the tree line and watches, unimpressed by the whole thing. Dave observes them out of the corner of his eye.

Rob motions to Billy. "Billy, bring your camera over here. I want to see if we can do an upload and send the data to my associate in Maine." Rob runs his fingers over the keyboard. "Let's interview Ma and Pa over there and get that on tape, too." He points to the elderly couple who are now settled, down at their campfire. They have their two pigs beside them.

"Great idea," comments Z, as he yawns. His eyelids are heavy and weighted after the adrenalin rush.

"Everyone, let's not forget your assignments. It's the bats we're after, not the Ropen," says Dave, as he grabs his binoculars and night goggles. *A laughingstock, we're going to be a laughingstock*. The mantra repeats in his head. Dave can't get the image of associates laughing when they present the data or images out of his mind. He knows there is no reeling-in Rob now that he has seen it.

Dave pulls Rob aside and hisses through clenched teeth. "Make sure nothing goes out to the press or ANYONE. Do I have your guarantee?"

"Yeah, promise. We will discuss how to present this after we get back. I'll do whatever you want." Rob's attention is diverted as Eric points to a detail on the screen.

Dave turns away, watching the older couple accept the evening's leftovers. He thinks, *maybe they are the lucky ones, oblivious to the outside world*. He puts on his poncho and hat and stomps off to the nets. Isabelle follows him as the sun sets behind them.

* * *

A heavy downpour diffuses the late morning light. Curtains of rain pound them, making them feel even more isolated. They know the storms with the westerly winds don't last long on the island, but still, the intensity can be unsettling. Everyone huddles underneath protection, waiting for the storm to pass.

Malcolm stokes the campfire, trying to keep the kindling dry with a small tarp. He huddles there and remembers doing the same thing as a child. He understands the jungle well. Humans are another question. He'd been by himself since the age of thirteen. At age five, his mother died, and his father worked as a guide for a large estate farther to the north. He often accompanied his dad to the estate and would take care of animals there. It was a perfect job for a child to do. Soon he became friends with another child who lived on the grounds. Life was good and happy back then. Until five years later, when his father caught a fever and died.

The work supervisor didn't hesitate and sold Malcolm to the oil employer nearby to work in the pits. It was like walking into Hell. He slept under a rock ledge by the pits. Digging in the slush piles, moving stones and dirt, and porting water for the larger men deeper in the pits, filled everyday morning to night for three years, until he could run away. He was skin and bones by that time. When he couldn't run anymore, he found refuge living on the outskirts of a tribal community that welcomed him. They had a thriving trade business going amongst other tribes in the area. Being adopted by the traders offered him the opportunity to learn languages and be out meeting new people. He is an expert at living off the land. A simple life suits him just fine. Miss Kennedy taught him to read and write over the years.

Carrying a bucket of water, Isabelle walks through the rain in her poncho. She enters the lean-to where Dave pounds on a folding keyboard inputting the data from the night before. "Let me doctor up your feet and then, please, take a nap," she says with one pat on his shoulder. "What's the plan for today?"

"Well, I want to take some of us and check out the clearing to the north." He yawns. "Everyone is still sleeping. I guess we're all exhausted."

Isabelle pulls off one of his shoes. "My sense of smell is off. Ever since the waterfall, I've not been able to smell much. I'm sure it's only temporary."

Dave waves her away and pulls off the other shoe. "Rob used to say I had 'Frito Feet' and I think I may have mold growing in the liner of my boot." He steps over to the rain pouring down and washes his feet. Wadding up his socks, he rinses them and thumps them several times against the support poles.

"Please check everyone's feet. I think it's a good idea before we go any deeper. I'll start." Dave offers a foot to Isabelle as she works on his blisters. He giggles a few times and pulls back his foot as she hits a sensitive area. "Sorry, I'm ticklish. Have you ever had an issue with your sense of smell before?"

"No, I'm indestructible. I don't even get sick. But my mom suffers from a loss of smell. Maybe it's hereditary?" Isabelle adds a thin stream of antibiotic ointment. "Let your feet air out a bit." She props his feet up on a log. "Do you have sandals you can wear?"

"Yeah, I've got a pair. I'll switch it up." Dave checks out her work. "Thanks, Belle—appreciate it."

Isabelle smiles. "My Dad used to call me that. Thanks, it made me smile."

* * *

After sleeping for two hours, Dave walks over to Z, who scans the data. He looks up as Dave sits beside him. "Got some of the slide breakdowns back from the lab. It's just preliminary, of course. Can't wait to really get this analyzed."

Z hands the thin printout to Dave, who breaks into a smile as he reviews the listing. "This is it. I knew it. How many slides are left?" Z pulls the box of slides out and counts the empty units. "A dozen," he replies. There is a pause in their conversation before Z asks, "What's next, chief?"

Dave looks over to see Rob watching him from across the camp. "Guess that's the big question, isn't it?" He gets up and motions Rob to follow him off the trail.

Dave waits as Rob walks over. Rob's eyes flash with excitement. "Hey, you didn't hear. Grandma and Grandpa told us they've had two recent sightings before. They saw a baby, so there's got to be a nesting site somewhere. We'd like to head out towards the coast. The birds seem to fly in that direction."

"What do you need to confirm the existence, scientifically?" Dave asks. He looks at Rob with hesitation. "Can't believe I'm actually asking you that question?" He picks at the barbs still stuck in his swollen finger.

Rob looks at him with a hopeful expression. "Well, any biologicals, of course, tissue, teeth, feathers, waste, recordings, film. Whatever documentation we can gather." Dave resists rolling his eyes and the sense of unease that hits him. Rob continues, "Bones, bones would be great, or even better, a nesting site." Dave listens and turns back toward the camp as Rob continues, "What do they eat? Life span? How high can they fly? Do they hunt in packs? Do they mate for life? What's their courtship ritual like? How fast do they fly? How big do they get? What is their endothermy?" He is still asking questions as they join the rest of the crew at the campfire.

The group is full of energy. Dave breaks into a big smile as he watches everyone. "Nice to see everyone happy." They are all wearing sandals. "I see that you've all gone for a foot inspection with Isabelle?" Heads nod across the team.

Dave pours himself a cup of hot water. Isabelle interjects, "Yes, all clear. Billy's got an area that we need to keep watch on. How are your feet feeling now, Billy?" she asks.

"Better." Billy holds up his left foot. "Really, it's much better."

"And make sure you do a good job washing out your socks as well. The rain should make the job much easier," she says, holding her hand in the rain. "Use your sandals for the next few days, at least."

Rob continues. "The Ropen the old couple saw glowed. We checked the images from earlier and we think we can see an area underneath their wings near their body that may be the source. Right here," says Rob as he points to a display monitor image. "We can see a shadowed area under the wing." "When the old man was a boy, he saw a nesting area on Umboi Island, near the crater. Can you imagine?" Rob says as bits of spittle fly from his mouth.

When we were kids, Rob could talk me into anything. Dave thinks to himself. *He's got the same look of anticipation that he had when he held that lighter before he caught that field of brush on fire.* They got a scolding from the fire chief and their dad.

Eric holds a map in his hands and points to the island. "Umboi Island is one of hundreds of small islands sprinkled to the north. It's not that far." Eric hands Malcolm the map.

Malcolm checks the location. "It would take us several days to get there."

"They feed on crocs," Eric interjects.

Dave questions him, "How do you know that?" Renee hands Dave a cup of hot water.

"The couple saw one flying with a crocodile in its mouth," Z says, beaming. "What a sight that would be!"

Dave raises his eyebrow, as he scans their faces. "If it continues to rain this hard, we won't catch anything tonight. I vote that we all get a good night's rest." Eric repeats himself. "Can you imagine what that looked like?" His face alight with glee.

Dave interrupts. "We caught nineteen bats last night. Thanks, everyone. Tomorrow, I'd like to see what's going on at the worker site. Isabelle, we might get you the information on the clearing. But, those workers might just walk in here, I don't know. Let's keep the Ropen news to ourselves. Rob, when you send out your data, who is it going to?"

Rob answers quickly, "Just my associate, Tim, who collaborates with me on my grant. Don't worry, he can be trusted."

"Z, can you get an update on Drew? I'd feel better knowing he is on the mend. Billy, you may have to help him get through on the line."

Malcolm raises his hand. "Dave, we need to check out the site down near the beach. It will give us an idea of what's going on down there. We've two hours of good daylight left. Should take us three hours there and back."

Dave nods. "I need some volunteers to stay here at the camp." Z raises his hand.

"No one else?" Dave scans the faces before him. "Rob, I'm volunteering for you to stay. You can rest up and help Z with the data." Rob looks dejected but nods. "Check your canteens and be ready to go in fifteen." Dave turns to his tent and grabs his daypack. He slides in a revolver when no one is looking. *Don't know what we are going to find. I can't believe I'm going to have to wear a gun.* In less than a minute, he is back to Malcolm and filling up his canteen.

"Grandpa is going to show us the way." Malcolm motions to the man standing at the edge of the clearing. He says, "They haven't seen the workers in over a week and that's not usual." Rob and Z wave "bye" to the team as they leave the camp. Rob looks a little dejected sitting by the campfire.

Less than five minutes down the trail, the rain suddenly stops, and a break in the clouds quickly spreads overhead. Isabelle looks up, smiling. "It happens so fast out here. Pouring and then blue skies."

"Everybody keep an eye out. We're in Ropen territory now," Malcolm says, with a look back at the team before he slices through the path with his machete.

Dave hears Eric say, "That is serious when it comes from Malcolm. I expected Dad to say it!"

Later, on the trail, Malcolm coaxes Grandpa to talk a bit more about the unknown workers. "Sounds like it may be a survey group," Malcolm says to the rest of the crew. "There are two white men, and they had four natives with them."

Dave walks close to Malcolm. "What can you tell us about what we might encounter, Malcolm?"

"I've worked as a guide in this area for seven years and I've seen clear-cutting areas, but never on this side of the island. According to the natives, they come in quick, do the work, and then are out within a brief time." Malcolm stammers. "But it's the m-mining o-operations that r-really take a toll h-here." He turns and waits for the others to catch up. "I used to work as a field guide for a large gold mining operation in the East Highlands. The money was good, but mentally I couldn't manage the atrocities." He pauses. "It was horrible. That mine is making money for someone, but the cost to humanity is..." He let the words die on his lips.

"Tell me more about this mining operation," Dave says, as Eric joins them at the front of the line.

Malcolm continues, "The Panguna, it's one of the largest, most productive gold mines in the world. It attracts a lot of migrant workers who work in the discarded waste pits. Violent raids into the active pit areas happen almost every night. I saw a dozen people killed at point blank range and gang rapes on some women. There are so many tribes working in the pits, so you can imagine the nightmare of keeping that in check, plus the huge security force personnel required. They do what they please, when they please, to whomever they please. I felt lucky to get out of there alive."

"How do they mine the gold?" Eric passes his canteen to Renee.

"It's a nasty and dirty business." Stepping quickly past them, Grandma and Grandpa move down the trail. Everyone listens to Malcolm as they pick up the pace. "They crush the rocks that have the gold inside them until it is dust, then they wash it and pour liquid mercury into the remaining material. The mercury sticks to the gold and makes a gold blend that they cook over a fire. They heat it until the mercury evaporates and then, mate, they have pure gold nuggets."

"What do they do with their wastewater? Do they have holding ponds like we use for oil drilling?" Renee asks, adjusting her hat.

"No, they just throw everything in the river," says Malcolm. "It turns the river red."

Isabelle calls out, "Wait." She catches her breath as she sees her first image of the cleared area. They cross to a vast swamp. "I've heard about that, mine. Human Rights Watch is active in the area. They've got no government regulation to stop the dumping or oversee the security forces. It's truly a horrific scene. I'm glad you got out of there, Malcolm."

Isabelle looks closely at the palms they pass. "Razor palm, careful."

Dave swings Malcolm's machete with greater intensity. "God, I hate what men do to fill their need for gold." He pushes away the dark feelings that wait to consume him. There is too much at stake and this team is depending on him.

"There is enough for everyone's needs, but not enough for everyone's greed." Isabelle reaches out, motioning. "We are in a big Garden of Eden, and we must do what we can for future generations, or it will be lost. There's no do over here."

Malcolm nods. "Glad to know others share my vision." He tips his hat to Isabelle.

The terrain changes as they move down to the flats. Mangrove and gum trees dot the area, and sandy ground becomes their base. Patches of razor palms are sprinkled throughout the area. Dave stops and shakes out his sandals. "That's why I hate these things." Walking becomes easier as the density of the trail lessens. Huge fern forests blanket the ground. Renee grabs a branch with a long thin bright green ribbon snake on it.

Eric takes photos of her smiling with the snake. Billy does the same.

Malcolm points out wild pig tracks and an abundance of mud crab tracks on the trail. "The crabs are especially tasty," he says as they continue. "We should try to catch some on our way back." "I'd rather you catch a pig," says Billy as he looks at Malcolm with puppy dog eyes.

"The natives believe that everything on the land belongs to Mother Earth. We are just tenants, but the government believes that everything below the ground belongs to the state." Malcolm halts the group. He sees a cleared area ahead, about sixty meters wide. He crouches down and lowers his voice. "Let's just watch for a while and see if anyone is about." Dave passes his canteen around as they fan out. He edges over to Malcolm and discretely shows him his pistol.

As they wait, an eerie quiet surrounds them. Even the bird songs have stopped. A small lean-to hut with woven palms hugs the tree line to one side of the clearing. Nearby, a stack of cut mangrove and gum trees are piled six feet high. The camp is deserted. There is an unusual grouping of large holes in the ground, which are now filled with water.

Malcolm takes a deep breath and shudders. He leaves the others and walks into the camp alone. He feels the campfire pit for warmth and calls out a greeting. It is unanswered. After surveying the area, he joins the others in the brush. Malcolm crouches low beside Dave. "I think a mining survey crew worked the area."

"Did they leave in a hurry?" Dave points to woven baskets of materials left in the open. Isabelle joins them in their huddle. "Those are sample pits." She motions to the pools of muddy water scattered throughout the area. Malcolm nods and explains, "See how burned the ground is to the side of the fire pit? They were doing something that required sorting. They could be looking for gold or copper. The rain has done a number on what's left."

"But why cut those beautiful trees?" Isabelle's eyes tear up.

"I don't know. Maybe they were to be moved out of here by helicopter or barge. Usually, crews just burn an area when they leave. I didn't go out with the survey teams when I worked for the mining company, but it makes me go cold to think they could look for a second mine location back here." He pauses. "There is nothing but wasteland, wastewater, and brutal survival in a barren pit of Hell at ANY mine, no matter where it is."

Chapter 8

Renee sits transfixed as Malcolm tells the story of the older couple to the team. "He's from the Baruni tribe and believes that the whites have violated the supernatural world. Only supernatural beings own the land. They live in caves or hollow parts of enormous trees. Legend says they can change into any living form and harass people for trespassing on their homelands." Malcolm translates the conversation from the elderly tribesman.

The words come out quickly from his lips. "That's why the Ropen is here now. He wants to take revenge for this disturbance." Malcolm stirs a tray of roast crab with mixed vegetables. "Don't get caught up in the politics of this area unless you have a big bank account to fight it." Dave looks at the dinner with apprehension, and says, "Trust me, being inside waiting on damned paperwork, phone calls, emails, meetings, and the never-ending politics of everything will crush your soul."

"How did they come to this place?" Renee motions to the older couple.

"They have been here for several months and will move on if the food supply runs down. These two are truly content." Malcolm continues. "Most of the natives I meet are happy. They are unconcerned with things outside of their lands." He looks hard at Dave. "They don't even understand the concept of politics."

"I'm on a board that is trying to stop the islands' introduction of registration of the tribal lands. Can you imagine telling these two ' happy people' that they must register their lands?" Isabelle shakes her head. "It's just what the multi-national corporations are hoping will pass so that they can come in and claim the lands themselves. Many of those big businesses break many, if not all, environmental protection laws and have scant regard for the rights of the local landholders. Who is going to watch them out here?" She drops her head at the brutality of it all.

"Can't the government pass a logging exporting ban? Eric says as he helps himself to a second serving.

"You'd think it would be that easy," Isabelle says sarcastically. "There is so much corruption in the local and national government that a select minority of decision makers that get the message out to the villages is a slow process. It rarely occurs. The villagers are only concerned with the trees they can see on their horizon. They can't comprehend the long-term consequences of logging."

Isabelle stands and dusts off her clothes. "I've got first shift with Z." She stomps off and then turns back to the others. "See if you can explain to 'Grandma and Grandpa' what registration and deforestation truly mean."

Dave and Billy walk over and start setting the evening nets. Billy adds a makeshift knot in his belt to keep his pants up as they sit low on his hips. But with every step, he grabs his pants as they inch over his butt and fall. "Man, I can't lose any more weight. Every time I reach up, they slide down. This diet of hiking and clean eating is making all my clothes fall off." Billy rolls his waistband.

"We could weave you some kind of belt." Z suggests as he joins them. "I bet Renee could do it. She braided a new shoelace for Eric." "Yeah," Billy comments. "Her smile about does me in. Eric is one lucky dude." He walks over in her direction, holding onto one side of his shorts. "That should about do it for tonight." Dave steps back to admire his work. "You should be all set. We're going to have another clear night. Hopefully, the harvesting will be good." Just to be sure, he walks over to the collection bay and checks the slides carefully encased in foam and the blood vials they have collected so far. He smiles and closes the lid.

As he steps back, he notices the ground beneath his feet has a bit of a bounce. It is spongy because of the leaves and moss growing abundantly in the area. All around them, the sand and moss pockets wind their way through the underbrush. The vibrant ecosystem surrounding them surprises him every day, but at this new location, his senses are now on alert for crocs on the ground and death eaters on the wind. Patting the box, he shakes his head to focus on the equipment before him.

Z takes a step forward and in sudden agony, grabs his leg. He stretches it as he works out the pain.

Dave watches him with concern. "Hey, are you alright?"

"No problem, no problem. I'm fine," Z says, as he works a kink out of his leg. "My knee has been locking up and acting kind of weird. I think an old sports injury has come back to haunt me." He moves around a little, with no hesitation. "See, worked the kinks right out of it. Guess we're both feeling our age."

They both finish checking the equipment and join Billy and the others at the campfire. Billy, Renee, and Eric are deep in a conversation. No one looks up as they approach.

"We're all set," Dave announces as he takes a long swig from his canteen. "What's up?" No one answers.

"No, *Star Trek* is totally better because it had more impact on the social issues of the time." Renee watches a lizard come close to the fire. "It addresses issues of racism, featuring the first black-white kiss between Captain Kirk and Uhura. And who can forget the Frank Gresham white on black/black on white episode?"

Dave groans. "Oh, my god, not *Star Trek*." *Kill me now.* When Eric was younger, and his family was stuck on the outskirts of a remote village in Mexico, Dave once listened to the same argument between his boys that lasted for two full days until he lost his temper and made them vow to be silent for the rest of the trip.

"Yeah, that was a good one." Eric holds out his finger for the lizard to sniff. "Yes, but the horrors of cloning are well expanded in *Star Wars*. The Imperial Army was based on a cloning exercise from Jango Fett," Billy says, with glee. "Hans Solo is the epitome of cool, while William Shatner is way too campy for my tastes."

Dave looks at Z and groans again. "Kill me now. Please kill me now."

"Billy didn't take the pledge." Z smiles and pats him on the back. He adds purification tablets to his canteen. "Eric will go right along with him.

They'll be talking about this stuff for hours. His best friend in school was a super *Star Wars* nut. For fun, those kids would repeat hours of dialogue. They would go back and forth when I took them to school. Every, single, morning." Dave and Z walk away from the fire. "I'm going to head in early and dream of things. If you hear me scream in the night, it'll be me attacking Billy."

Dave emerges from the equipment tent to see Eric and Billy still talking about *Star Wars* by the campfire. He heads for the command center as Rob finishes a call. Isabelle sits nearby.

"Well, Drew is on the mend. I finally got through. He had surgery yesterday and his prognosis is good." Rob stretches a little. "I'm eager and my palms won't stop itching." He rubs his palms vigorously and looks over at both of them. Both Rob and Dave say, at the same time, "Money is coming."

"Don't look at me." Isabelle pulls at her empty pockets. "I'm a flat broke researcher." She looks at the statistical data and his notes. She turns over pages of stats Rob has made notes on. Robs shakes his head. "It's nothing, just a theory I was working on."

He takes the notebook and checks the time. "Dave, we've had three hits so far this evening. I'm on the three-to-six shift. Gonna hit the sack."

"Did you feel as though we were interrupting him or something?" Isabelle asks with concern as she watches Rob enter his tent.

"Or something is right," Dave says, with a puzzled look on his face. "He's being evasive. That's not a good sign. Never is."

Later that evening, under a sliver of a moon, Isabelle and Z work the nets efficiently with Dave. He holds down the latest catch and takes the blood sample. Their green night-vision lenses glow an eerie lemony-yellow. "When Dave sent me the listing of different bat species to study, I did not know there could be so much diversity in such a small area." They each hold a distinct species in their hands. Z turns his bat toward the moon to get a better image through his goggles.

"What do you think?" Z stretches her bat out. "Is this a Flower-faced bat, or the Tube-nose fruit bat? Do you think you've got the uglier one?"

They both compare the bats as they walk over to Dave.

"Which one, Dave?" They try to get his attention, but Dave is deep in concentration on the testing materials around him.

Rob joins them on the trail opening. He looks up, then moves his head quickly to the right. "What the f?" He walks into the clearing and adjusts his focus. "Do I need to blow the whistle?"

Z looks up with alarm as well. "I thought I saw a light, up the hill a bit," Rob points and scans the palm line that sways in the gentle night breeze. "But now I see nothing. Do you see anything?" Rob calls out.

"He'd really like another encounter," Dave says out loud. Probably dreaming of riding one of those suckers into the night and keeping it as a pet? Dave finishes with the last bat and adjusts his binoculars.

Z strains to look through the thick tangle of branches. The bat in his hand flutters, and he loses his grip on the bat. It flies away. Frustrated, he takes one set of binoculars from beside the equipment and runs to Rob's side. From the lower camp, they all look up as the foliage parts and the old man walks over to get a closer look at what they are doing.

"See anything?" Isabelle calls out. Long seconds creep by as if they all are holding a collective breath.

Around them, the shadows of the night jungle turn from deep purple to light gray. The canopy quietens. Isabelle turns the low-density scanner to the area where a large dark mass appears just above the tree line. It moves as a swirling blob image on the screen.

"Rob, come here quick!" Isabelle motions as she keeps her eyes on the image. The old woman walks over and shakes Malcolm from his hammock slumber. He joins them. "Is that another Ropen?" Isabelle watches the image churn.

They all cluster around the screen. Soon, the creature's distinct crown appendage silhouettes. It flickers. Rob flips the switch on the unit to record. "Get Eric, but let's be quiet about it," Rob whispers to Isabelle.

The old man and Malcolm take the lead as they quietly move through the jungle. Eric is a bit out of breath as he joins Rob, Dave, and Renee. Everyone wears their night-vision goggles except for Malcolm and the old man. Rob's, Eric's, and Renee's more expensive units glow light blue. After twenty minutes of careful hiking, they stop. Malcolm motions for them to get down and be quiet.

Rob whispers to Dave about the more advanced system on his goggles. Dave exchanges units with him as they wait for Malcolm to return. Malcolm moves covertly and gestures for them to follow. "As quiet as you can," he murmurs as he ducks under a large branch. A ripping and tearing sound cuts through the foliage ahead and as Malcolm parts the branches in front of them, they see two Pterodactyls eating on something large high in a tree. The animals fight over a section. A human foot drops to the jungle floor with a loud THUD.

The animals are dark purplish-gray in the moonlight. Their sharp beaks break huge chunks of meat off as they swallow with one large gulp, similar to the way a pelican gulps. One Ropen has a larger head crest and is taller and heavier than the other. Both have light-colored markings around their eyes and partially down onto their beaks. They sit with their wings hunched around them. Large four-toed feet grasp the branches as they balance.

The slighter Ropen has a smaller, rounder crest on its head. Rob points to it. "Probably a female. Notice how wide her hips are."

"Upper jaw longer than the lower jaw. I make it, on the larger one, about three and a half feet long," Eric whispers to Rob, "Pteranodon or Pterodactyl?"

Rob points, saying, "Pterodactyl, they've got a small tail. Probably some new species, but closer to a Pterodactyl." Rob is practically drooling with excitement.

The old man talks low to Malcolm briefly. Malcolm jesters for Dave to come closer to him. "He said that he thinks the body may be a porter from the survey camp. His face paint is similar. It's still hard to tell. What do you want to do?"

"I'm stunned by what I'm seeing." Dave pauses. "He's obviously been dead a while. The smell is overwhelming." Crap! He flashes to presenting documentation at a scientific conference and how it would be received. No doubt about it, he'd be laughed at, ridiculed. He shakes the thought from his head.

"Maybe that's why the survey team left in a hurry?" Malcolm watches intently. Rob videotapes what they are seeing. The animals fight again over a different section of the body. The larger Ropen crashes his cranial crest down onto the smaller bird, who then illuminates a spot underneath her wings close to her body. It flashes a brilliant white-green color before winking out. The fighting speeds up and the coloring on the larger bird flares a deeper red around his beak. In a rapid burst of flapping, both birds take off into the night. Their shapes silhouette against the sliver of a moon as they soar to the north.

As the group still watches in awe, a distant rumbling noise comes from deep beneath their feet. A large aftershock gives everything a good twist. Flocks of birds take off from the canopy when the vibrations start. The surrounding trees dance. It is as if the whole jungle woke up at once. Noise comes from all sides.

Startled, Eric steps right into a large spider web and starts screaming, "Get it off me!" In an instant, everyone envelopes Eric in light and quickly removes the webbing, calming him down. As the tremor stops, Malcolm, the old man, Dave, and Rob step over to the remains and scan the area.

Renee stays on the trail as Eric tries to get his breath under control. "I'm fine," says an irritated Eric. "I'm going to have nightmares about that one. We're heading back." Renee and Eric step back onto the trail leading to camp. "I'm fine," Eric says, again.

Rob holds a large leaf in his hand that is splashed with a white liquid. He shows it to Dave. "Could be DNA." They both grin widely. Rob holds it like a trophy on the way back. An excited Z meets them at the edge of the clearing while Isabelle and Billy join them. "Let's meet at the fire in ten," says Dave. "We'll fill everyone in."

When Dave walks up later, Z is deep into a conversation with Renee. "Pteranodon are not dinosaurs but are a species of reptile," he says, in almost a whisper. "They could have survived in this remote area. I'm not sure they are the exact species that we have on record, but certainly very close relatives."

Rob puts on gloves and analyzes the white substance on the leaf. He drops a sample onto a glass slide. The smell burns his eyes the closer he gets to it. Eric and Renee crowd him. "Take a step back. This is liquid acid." Rob works quickly to isolate the material. "It's eating through the leaf. See how it's bubbling." He points to the material with a stick.

"I can't believe that I missed the sighting of the century." Billy sits down dejectedly. "At least the images are on my camera." He flips through the series again and keeps repeating, "Unbelievable."

Z walks over. "Billy, can I see it for a minute?" Billy hands it to him. Z pops out the memory card and downloads it to his laptop. "Taking no chances with this footage. This is Pulitzer Prize stuff."

Rob says something but stops as Z nods at him. "Yes, I'm sending it to your guy as well. We've got enough bandwidth to send here. Guess the planets have aligned correctly."

Everyone huddles around the campfire and the older couple has gone back to their place. Dave paces nervously. "Okay, a decision needs to be made." Dave huffs a bit and runs his hands through his hair. "Obviously, we are in the right place to make some amazing discoveries."

"Thanks for acknowledging it." Rob puts more of the white substance on a microscope slide, covers it, and puts it into his pants pocket. Rob gives Dave his best "hopeful" smile.

"These are dangerous animals. We need to take more precautions for our safety. This is priority one. Second, we've cataloged eighty-seven bats so far, more than double our criteria." I can't believe I'm going to say this. Dave hesitates. "I'd like to take a vote on whether we should investigate the Ropen situation further. Everyone think about it. We vote after breakfast." Rob tries to act calm but can't help but smile.

The ELOD beeps an alarm, as another bat hits the net. Billy looks toward the nets and moves in. Rob waves to Renee. "Can you bring it in quickly? I need to get back to making my notes," Rob says, without even looking up. "And send me a copy of the data in an email. I've got to forward it to Maine."

Eric yawns. "I'm heading back to sleep. Wake me if anything happens."

Renee pulls a long length of spider webbing from Eric's back as he leaves.

The next morning, as the first rays of sunrise lighten the skies, Z and Dave review a topographical map. "I think we should head out to the north and see if we can find more information on the Ropen." Z points to an area on the map. "We've been out almost two weeks. Our supplies are in good order. We could make it along the coast, and then decide which way to go."

Dave frowns as he looks at the map. Malcolm joins them as he puts another pot of water on to boil. "That was an exciting night. One I won't ever forget," Malcolm says. "I know. It was wonderful, wasn't it?" Z settles down with a weak cup of coffee. "I'm trying to state my case with Dave here on moving on today — up the coastline. We could use your input. How far is it on foot?"

"It's a bagarap, in some areas," Malcolm comments, as he points toward the coast. They look confused. "You know, Bagarap, poor goings. We could make it in two days if we don't get too much rain."

"Have you been that way before?" Dave clenches his jaw. They've all been moving with a combination of scientific discovery, fear, and an instinct to survive. The intensity is a unique mix for each of them, but today, the discovery side pulls them toward the Ropen and the unknown. Treasure hunters probably have the same mix of adrenalin.

"No, but I've been just east of here along the coast. There isn't anything there, but I've heard that an offshore company is doing some extractions in the area to the east, about fifty miles, off that cluster of islands." Malcolm sweeps the map area. "That information is a little old, as is this map."

"How far would it be for us to hike back to the Gimi Village where we landed?" Dave traces the trek on the map. Malcolm rubs his head vigorously. "Five or six days. There is a ragged ridge of mountains that cascades down to the water's edge between here and there. It might be better to head to the east once we get there. Easier to go back the way we came than to head over that ridge."

Dave stretches. "Let's go look at the coast. Roust the camp, Malcolm. We're heading out to the north." He pats Z on the shoulder. "After breakfast and our vote."

In less than ten minutes, the camp is down and Malcolm hands out the last of the breakfast items. Renee munches on fresh fruit and her trail mix. Dave motions everyone over and stands up. "I think this is going to be a quick vote, but we've got to do it. We are all scientists and explorers who care about the land, and I've seen that put into action. Thank you everyone. My job is to get you back home safely, and that is balanced against this new discovery. I am shutting down the collection of bat specimens and we can either go back to the Gimi Village, which will take five to six days of hard hiking or see what else is out in the great expanse as we look for biologicals and documentation on the Ropen. This vote will only be asked for once, and it must be unanimous. Remember, if we go after the Ropen, we are also entering croc territory and we all saw the speed of an attack. Drew is doing better, by the way." He looks at each member. "We've got about another two to three weeks out in the deep if we go after it. I think after the response from last night, that I know what you will say. Do we go back, or raise your hands if you want to continue after the Ropen?"

Hands go up quickly for everyone except for Isabelle, who slowly raises her hand. Dave nods and raises his hand as well. "Malcolm, you've got your mandate. We are pushing forward."

Rob practically goes airborne as he jumps up from a sitting position and does a mock Michael Jordan slam dunk into the air. Everyone laughs as he grasps Dave and lifts him up, spinning him around once. Even Dave laughs.

* * *

The crew hasn't gone too far into the jungle when they come across a flock of Queen Victoria Crown Pigeons who stubbornly refuse to move. The beautiful and majestic birds are the size of geese and after much "shooing" noisily honk out of their way. For about an hour, three of the pigeons follow them on their trail, much to the delight of Billy. Their blue crested fans on their heads bobble and sway as they walk like a bunch of pregnant women with fans on their heads.

The foliage around them changes from thick woodlands to more of a carpet of ferns overshadowed with tall palms. In open areas, sprays of bougainvillea vines hang down like roof shingles. Humidity levels rise during the heat of the day, and everyone remains soaked with perspiration.

Malcolm calls for a brief rest at the beginning of a peat bog area. "Go slow in here. Watch your steps." He hands out walking support sticks that he cuts from broken branches for when they will traverse over moss-covered logs. Queen butterflies are prolific in the area. Their brilliant-blue and black-iridescent colorings stand out in contrast to the deep greens of the valley.

"Amazing, simply amazing." Isabelle catches one butterfly on her finger. "How can anyone want to pillage such perfection?" she asks the butterfly as it gently flies off her finger. "God's, perfection, in all his glory."

"Everyone tank up, you need to replace those fluids," Dave calls out as he pulls a leech off his lower calf. "Leech check," he calls to everyone and pulls Billy over to inspect him.

"Those geese back there cracked me up." Billy tries to imitate their unusual head bob and walk. Eric joins him in clowning around.

Z sighs heavily as he watches them. "I don't have the energy for any extra movements. How much longer for today do you think, Malcolm? My stomach isn't feeling quite up to par today." His face is red and drips with perspiration. His face contorts with a pained expression.

"It's about three o'clock now, and we need to get camp set up by five, so we'll start looking for a decent place to bed down for the night. Those clouds are building up too. We'll have rain tonight, I'm sure. Let's get moving again." Malcolm walks off down the trail, calling back to Z over his shoulder. "I'll look for some ragwort to help your stomach."

"Almost there, everyone. Let's keep up with Malcolm," Dave says, standing to watch over his crews as they move forward again. Billy is the last.

Dave encourages him. "Billy, I'll take the tail. You keep up with Malcolm." *He's been better on this trip than I thought he'd be.* Dave feels a protective moment come over him. He recalls a slip in conversation where Billy called him Dad. Dave smiles.

After trekking for nearly three hours, they come across an old WWII bomber wreck partially overgrown with bougainvillea vines. Large worn script letters "Black Jack" are displayed against the faint gray fuselage.

CHAPTER 9

"Holy Cow!" Billy whoops and hollers at the find. There is no moving him once he starts taking photos. "This is sooo cool!" Billy says repeatedly. The bomber is broken into three pieces with the front end leaning forward into the earth and the rear of the plane leaning backwards. Its four enormous engines have crumbled deep into the jungle floor. Billy, Eric, and Renee drop their packs and explore the storage area inside the plane.

"What do you think, Malcolm? Can we camp here?" Dave asks. "They're kind of having a childhood moment," he adds.

Malcolm clears an area nearby. "Sure. I'll check the area for water." The rest of the crew drops their packs and scouts out tent areas. Eric sticks his head out of the pilot window. He waves enthusiastically as he puts on a leather Army Air Corps pilot cap. It doesn't quite fit and sits high on his crown. "Everyone must have gotten out because there are no bodies in here. But there are cool things to look through."

"We're definitely camping here," Dave says as he watches their enthusiasm. He grins. After twenty minutes of their tinkering and chattering, Dave calls to them, "You guys! We're staying the night but need to get camp settled first. Renee, see if you can find some kindling and you're in charge of water." Everyone works to get camp set up for the night. A weary Z collapses inside his tent as soon as it is partially up.

Isabelle walks over. "I have some chamomile tea in my bag that you can have," Isabelle whispers, as she checks his head for a temperature. "I hope you didn't pick up a parasite. Have you been using your purification tablets?"

He nods. "I just feel bad, like my stomach is on fire," Z says. "I usually can eat anything. My stomach is like a cast-iron skillet."

Malcolm builds the fire. "I'll make you something to soothe the fire in your belly."

Rob finishes the final setup of Z's tent. "You take it easy." He secures the last line. "I have some Tums in my bag that I'll get for you."

Billy and Eric arrive with old magazines from inside the plane. "Ah, man, I hate to burn 'em. Some of these are classics." Billy holds up a copy of *Life Magazine* dated October 1943. The binding disintegrates in his hands and pages drop around him, as he tries to get a handle on them. "It won't last much longer, anyway. Might as well get some use out of it." He drops it beside the fire pit Malcolm has started.

"We've got about an hour before the rain starts," Malcolm calls out to everyone. "I'm going to hunt for some dinner items, back in about half an hour. Rob, can you monitor the fire and feed it, so it doesn't go out?" Rob gives him the "thumbs up."

"Billy, help me with the tarps. I need your height to reach that branch." Dave throws Billy one tarp to hang. "Sure, it's always my job, anyway. I can reach the highest." As Billy reaches, Dave notices a woven belt cinched at his waist. "Nice belt," Dave says. "Did Renee make it for you?"

"Yeah, man, she did it in a jiff, too. She's very handy." Billy pats the belt with confidence. "It's the only thing keeping these pants on me. I've lost about twenty pounds."

Rob, Dave, and Billy finish putting up the rest of the tents and secure extra rain tarps over the workstation area as Malcolm returns. "That was fast!" Dave says, with a smile. Malcolm's arms are full of mangos, sweet potatoes, and some other roots that he doesn't recognize.

Eric, Billy, and Renee scurry back into the plane cavity with their flashlights as soon as the camp is deemed "together," their enthusiasm matches that of a bunch of kids heading out trick-or-treating for the first time. Sounds of finds "Ohhhh" and squeals of "Look out!" float across the camp.

Eric calls out, "Man, there must be a thousand lizards in here!" They move some heavy equipment and soon mock machine-gun-fire sounds add to their excitement. "We found part of a 50-caliber machine gun in here!" Eric walks outside with the remnants of the gun. "Check it out!" he says as he joins Dave and Rob by the fire. "It's pretty heavy, and a major piece is broken over here on the side." He flips a hinge that hangs loosely on one side. "I wish I could hang it over my fireplace back home." He sighs and leaves the gun with Rob.

Renee looks out through the window. She quickly goes back inside as Eric exclaims for the tenth time, "Check this out!"

As thunderclouds fire up overhead, Malcolm spots a possum and goes after it with his machete. "It'll make up a good stew. And, Z, I found something that might help your stomach ache." He holds up a handful of herbs. "I see our explorers have found some interesting items." He points to the gun still in Rob's hands.

Z smiles. "Yeah, don't get in their way. They're like kids in a candy store. I can't believe the plane didn't explode on impact. Do you see any burn marks on the plane or bullet holes?"

Dave lifts the gun from Rob and looks through the site marker. "Nope, I walked around it once and I didn't see any ash marks on it or anything resembling bullet holes. Maybe they ran out of fuel. That would explain why the plane didn't flame up. Personally, I'm glad there are no bodies inside. That would be a tough thing to see." Dave lays the gun back down. "Rob, remember Dad's brother was killed in WWII in the Pacific." Rob walks over and touches the plane with respect and says a silent prayer. Dave joins him for a minute before Billy runs over with a circular slide rule and maps that have been wrapped in plastic. He tells them to "add it to the treasure pile," before heading back for more.

Dave and Rob walk to the open fuselage. "You first," says Dave with a bow and smile. As soon as they enter the main body of the plane, Rob heads for the captain's area. Dave follows him. The right side of the cabin is crushed, but the left side cockpit seat remains in place. Rob quickly sits down and starts playing with the control column by flipping switches and pulling back on the steering wheel. "This is pretty cool," he says, with a big smile.

Dave scans the interior where the others are, with his flashlight. The beady eyes of a small rodent stare back at him. Eric scoots it out and tries to get it to run towards Renee.

"Eric, I saw that!" Renee calls out. He giggles as he attempts to catch it, but misses, and the animal goes into the insulation around the fuselage. Billy flips a knob on one side of the interior plane wall and a watertight olive-gray box falls out onto the floor.

Rob picks it up and dusts it off. "Hey, good job Billy. We've got a First Aid Kit." Rob opens it up and looks at the assortment of medicines, bandages, and a flare gun with two flares. He hands it to Isabelle, who by now is standing in the doorway watching.

Billy reaches into the wall of the plane where the kit had been stored and pulls out a second, smaller box. He opens it carefully and pulls out a 45-caliber pistol with one clip. "I've got a gun!" he exclaims to all who turn to see the gun. It gleams in the glare of two flashlights.

Malcolm calls in the distance that dinner is ready, and the explorers slowly filter out of the plane back to the campfire where everyone reviews the cache.

Isabelle opens the First Aid Kit and reviews the list of contents pasted inside the lid. An assortment of yellow boxes lists bandages, compresses, eye dressings, burn injury packs, disinfectant, suction kit, iodine, tape, scissors, surgical blades, and medicines with sulfur packs. "This could be really handy out here." As Isabelle puts things back into the container, she opens a bottle of aspirin and takes out two tablets to give to Z. "There's some Sodium Bicarbonate in here too, if you want to try it." She closes the box and walks over to Z.

"No, I'm already feeling better since I took a Tums." Z rubs his stomach and holds onto a steaming cup of broth Malcolm has given him. Peering at Dave through water-speckled glasses, Z gives him a weary grin.

Around them, the winds intensify, and everyone reinforces their tent stakes. Finally, Renee and Eric are the last to join the group at the fire. They accept their dinner and wrinkle their noses at the smell.

"What's in this?" Eric asks, making a disgusting face.

Rob smiles and says, "It's Possum, by gum; the favorite food of hunters in the South." He takes a big bite and smiles back at everyone. "Yum!"

"Gag," says Renee as she walks over to her tent and returns minutes later with three packages of Ramen noodles. "No offense, Malcolm, I just can't handle that tonight." She takes an empty pan and fills it from the water container. As she returns, the skies overhead release a torrent of rain.

Eric tosses Z a package of Ramen. "This will help your stomach more than a serving of Possum." Z gladly accepts it. "Bless you, bless you both," Z says, as Renee squeezes in under the tarp and hands Eric the pan. Dave puts his arm around her to dry her off.

"You radiate heat," she says as she snuggles up to him. Dave nods. "Always."

She looks up to see Eric engrossed in a story in a worn Marvel comic book from the 1940s. She whispers to Dave, "He found that in there too and won't let me touch it." Dave smiles at her and stands.

"Since everyone is here, let's talk about our plan for the evening and tomorrow." Dave shakes Billy's foot to get his attention. "Isabelle and Z will take the first watch, but with these winds and the downpour Mother Nature is throwing at us, we may not have luck seeing the Ropen. Eric and I will do midnight to three and Billy and Rob will do three to sunrise." Dave stirs the fire and adds a second log to the flames. "I'd like to get up early and be ready to go at first light. Renee, you're on call at the station for the twilight shift." He looks around at everyone huddled under the tarp. "Questions?"

"Any ideas on how long our hike will be tomorrow?" Rob asks Malcolm. "I can smell the ocean. I know we are getting close."

Malcolm looks up in the low light, and replies, "Yeah, we can already smell the saltwater in the air, but the trek will be harsher, especially with all this rain tonight. I figure eight-to-ten hours. It could be longer."

Everyone groans and after Dave assures them, there are no more questions, he suggests they all go back to their tents for some much-needed rest. The sound of cascading water against the metal sides of the plane makes an eerie "ping" that reverberates around them.

Before sunrise, when the rains lessen, Billy and Rob scare off a flurry of lizards that swarm out of the wreckage during their shift. Billy uses his slingshot to take a few minutes of target practice in the dim light. He scores several direct hits, which do nothing but add to the animal activity as the remaining lizards feast on the cadavers.

Z strolls up to the fire as dawn streaks across the sky. Renee is lying beside the fire, curled in a fetal position covered with a light blanket.

Z hands Rob the satellite phone. "Your office is on the line. You've only got five minutes, so make it count." Rob walks over toward the plane. Animated hand jesters and an occasional "I can't believe it either," come from Rob.

Malcolm adds the last bit of dry firewood to the fire, bringing back long flames that wake Renee. She opens her eyes and quickly shuts them as she tries to return to sleep. One side of her face has a path of mosquito bites on it.

Z looks at her with pity. "She's not going to be happy when she sees her face." Malcolm nods and starts the rice to cook.

"Where were you born, Malcolm?" Z asks, as he adds purification tablets to his canteen. "I'm from Chicago originally." He tells his story easily. "I was born in a village to the east of here. It's quite a way off. My mom died when I was young, and my dad a few years later. In my teens, I was raised by a village elder and a missionary from Iowa, Henry Watson. He was a great man and my true father. I went to advanced schooling at the Numonohi Christian Academy for two years. Miss Kennedy taught me to read."

Dave walks over to the fire, his hair standing up all over the place. He does not look happy. "Morning, Sleeping Beaut," Z says, and motions for Dave to pat down his hair. Dave sliced his hands through his matted hair. "I need a hot shower and my hat." He accepts a cup of hot water from Malcolm, who comments, "We all need a hot shower. My grime has layers of grime on top of it." He pulls his shirt out, sniffs it, and gags.

Rob finishes his call and steps over to the others. "That was my associate, Tim. He's having a heart attack over the footage we sent but has agreed to keep it under wraps." He elbows Dave. "Last night was a bust. No sightings."

Dave growls loudly and rousts the rest of the crew. "Everybody, up!"

"Yeah, he's been that way his whole life. We used to call him 'Crabby Appleseed' when he was little. He still doesn't do mornings well." Rob says. Malcolm looks confused and turns to Z. "Crabby Appleseed was a cartoon character who was grumpy all the time. It's an old cartoon," Z says.

The crew pulls down their tents and finishes their morning routine. Dave calls out for Billy to make sure he has a photograph of the tail of the plane for identification. Billowing white clouds blow across the morning skies as Dave barks orders, ensuring all the tents are down and rolled up.

Renee returns to the campfire with half her face slightly swollen and dotted with antiseptic. "Guess I missed a spot with my bug spray." She accepts her cup of hot water from Malcolm.

Bird calls sound around them as the sky brightens. "Let's head out as quickly as we can." Dave checks his shoes, which are caked in mud inches thick. "Great, just great," he mumbles.

Rob walks beside Billy and motions for a minute of his time. "Hey, I spoke with my associate in Maine this morning and he had a brilliant suggestion. If we get anymore encounters with the Ropen while you have a camera, try to keep distinguishing landmarks out of the frame if you can. We will need to protect this creature." Billy nods. "Got it. No sweeping panoramic mountainside vistas."

* * *

The trail is agonizingly slow as they hike through mud six inches deep in mud. Lush, green jungle bushes block their way. Malcolm is relentless with his machete as he hacks through clusters of thorny vines that seem to replicate every two feet. The air is sultry and humid around them, making breathing that much harder.

"This is hiking through Hell," Billy announces with frustration. After hiking for six hours, Eric finally drops the machine gun he'd been carrying and tosses it into some waist-high sharp Kina grass. "Man, that would have been sooo cool to have." He shakes his head and continues. A scream fills the air. Quickly, they all look up at the uppermost branches, to a cluster of Harpy Eagles watching them.

"They're like vultures waiting for someone to die," Renee comments. "All we are missing is for someone to key in the scary music."

Billy takes a series of photos. "Man, those birds are huge. The size of a six-year-old."

"The air is so thick here and the branches are like fingers reaching for you. I'm feeling a bit claustrophobic." Z leans against a branch. "I just need a bit of open air or a pretty vista to get my breathing under control." He swats away a swarm of mosquitos that end up attacking everybody.

Dave guzzles from his canteen. "The Harpies are a good sign that we are getting closer to the coast. But watch out for snakes. We don't want to meet any Taipan snakes. This is just the type of cover they like." He surveys the oncoming path that leads to the shallow waters of a stream, feeding into a larger tributary of a chocolate brown river. Malcolm squats down to scout wild pig tracks in the mud. "Looks like we might have roast pig for dinner." He licks his lips in anticipation.

Heavy afternoon rains pelt them as they once again move slowly forward. They pass a grouping of limestone caves naturally carved into the hills near a fork in a tributary river.

"Tribes use those as burial sites." Malcolm points to one that looks deep.

"Could we take a quick break? I'd like to look inside," Eric says, holding up his hand. Everyone stops, with a hope of resting.

Before he enters, Malcolm hands him a cut off, sharp piece of bamboo to use as a spear. Renee follows, and Eric quickly calls out, "Hey, everybody needs to see this. There are prehistoric drawings on the wall." A scattering of bones lay on one side of the cave. They take turns crawling into the cave, four at a time. Isabelle and Z wait outside enjoying the additional rest.

The rain lessens, then stops abruptly and, almost immediately, the forest erupts in bird calls. Dave says, under his breath, "Guess the birds are as happy as we are for that damn rain to end."

Using Malcolm's machete, Billy is in the front and hacks away at the branches in their path. He squeals with delight when his last whack reveals a large mango tree loaded with fruit. Closer inspection shows that the branches of the mango tree are covered with an army of ants. "Watch out for the ants," he calls out as he gathers the fruit. The crew loads up on the mangos, using their shirts as make-shift bags.

After another hour, Eric scampers up a limestone hill and exclaims with delight, "I can see the ocean!" He points towards a crushed, green, velvet thicket covered in more thorny vines.

Calling out, "That way!" Isabelle moans. Her exhaustion is showing in every step she takes. They are moving at a slower pace, as Z has had several emergency runs to the bathroom along the way. His face is ashen, and he holds onto his bloated stomach, but he refuses to stop the team.

"Let me cut a clearer path. Watch out for these nasty, saw-tooth, leafed bushes. They will do a number on your legs." Malcolm strikes with precision. "I think it's only about two more hours. Notice how it is flattening out." A sprinkling of sand appears on the ground in cleared areas and the tree line spreads out more. As they peek through the thick canopy all around, low misty curtains hug the mountains behind them.

The wind picks up, bringing a chill to their sweaty bodies. Renee zips her windbreaker. "I don't know whether to zip it up or take it off." Giant eucalyptus trees stretch to the skies around them like guardians forever on watch. She huffs. "At least the clouds are thinning."

"Yeah, check out the surrounding beauty." Billy shows her heavy beads of lichen, framed in his camera lens, which glisten in a ray of sunlight.

Isabelle shares his enjoyment and points at a spider web with pearls of moisture hanging on each strand. "I'm too tired to notice anything right now." Renee shuffles behind Eric. Z calls out. "Privacy break?" He heads off the trail slightly, but they can all hear him with explosive bowel movements.

Rob stays on the path nearby on alert, guarding Z with all the privacy he can give due to the circumstances. The rest of them step gingerly on the path through the tall grass, making sweeping motions with their walking sticks as they watch for snakes. A variety of wild orchids dot the grassy area.

With a quick jerk of his hand, Malcolm motions for everyone to stop. He moves slowly, with caution, into the thicket ahead of the others before shouting out an obscenity, "Sina gagai!!" Dave moves forward into the brush to check on him, then motions for the others to follow. "He almost caught a pig!" This brings a much-needed break from the monotony of their trek.

Everyone smiles as Eric smacks his lips. "Bacon!" He rubs his stomach. "I could eat a whole pig by myself. Ahh, pulled pork sandwiches, barbeque ribs, bacon, pork chops, bacon, ham, bacon--." He stops listing pork meals when Renee playfully hits him on the arm.

Rob steps forward and taps Dave on the shoulder. "At the next cleared area, let's set up camp. Z isn't complaining, but he's more than tired. I think he's done." They both look back at Z, who moves slowly. His face has no coloring and even seems white against the green foliage swimming around him. Stopping to wash his hands in the muddy waters at the stream edge, he leans heavily on his walking stick to get back upright.

"Good call." Dave watches Z and nods. *I will have to talk with everyone about Z's condition,* he thinks to himself.

Malcolm sharpens a bamboo pole with a few whacks from his machete. He shouts, "Five-minute break." He dives back into the undergrowth, silently, as if the leaves magically part for him. They hear an animal squeal in the distance, then a loud "thump" as Malcolm calls out, "Everything is fine." He returns holding up a dead tree kangaroo and some wild rhubarb. "Let's find a campsite," he says, as he smiles widely. "Lots of pig tracks in there, too. I want to set that trap."

Renee's eyes fill with tears as she looks at the beautiful animal

Malcolm holds by the tail. Its coat is a deep chocolate brown. "I think I want to go back to being vegetarian," she says under her breath as they start hiking along the widening tributary bank.

Eric looks at her and nods his affirmation. "I'll start watching for some wild roots." He looks over at Renee with a smile. "I'm getting lessons about them from Malcolm."

Z sets his pack down and sits on a boulder. "I don't think I can go any much further." He wipes his brow and closes his eyes for a minute. He's gasping from the exertion.

Rob picks up Z's strapped communication unit. "We're just about there." Dave smiles at Rob's kindness. *He's still in there somewhere. That kid I adored.* Dropping his pack, Dave points at an open area at the top of a steep berm.

Eric climbs up the vertical bank on his hands and knees, then walks around, surveying the location. "I think it will work!" The crew joins Dave at the base. "The incline should help keep the gators out, and we'll have a water source nearby." Dave touches the rock wall, rising twenty feet behind him. There is a natural overhang of trees, making a natural cover over the mounded area.

Malcolm and Rob give a "thumbs up" and each team member crawls up the embankment. Z needs help to get up into the campsite area and finally uses a moss-covered log and a collection of rocks and boulders to pull himself up. Once there, he collapses to one knee. Isabelle rushes to his side and feels his forehead. "He's got a fever," she calls out to Dave.

"And a severe case of the runs," Z says, not caring anymore who knows. "I'm going to need a latrine pretty quick." He groans and holds onto his stomach as it growls angrily.

Isabelle pulls out her First Aid Kit and quickly goes to work. "Don't worry, I'll see to Z." She catches Dave's eye as she closes the kit. Her look alarms Dave.

"This is NOT the place to have a sick person." Dave quickly puts up his tent and ties a tarp over the entrance to Z's tent. *No place at all to be sick.* He watches Z, then walks into the privacy of the jungle. He stands silently, leaning forward, head lolling, arms supported on his thighs. *I can't lose another one.* A shiver of dread spread through his body, spiraling around his heart and tightening.

CHAPTER 10

Dave barks orders out to the rest of the group. His nerves are frayed right up to his breaking point as he thinks about the danger Z could be in. They've been friends since middle school. While it didn't take much selling to have him join the team, Dave feels responsible for his condition. He can't get out of his mind, that flash of terror that crossed Z's face before he made it to his tent today. Nothing can erase the horror he is feeling for his good friend. The fear lingers as it swims through his mind. *Who will be next?* And, God, the smell is horrible.

Billy goes right to work putting up a latrine for Z and another for everyone else. He drapes them both with a tarp and adds cut branches to make a privacy area. Dave passes by, placing a thank you pat on Billy's shoulder. Eric and Renee collect an assortment of leaves, which they pile to one side near the pit before they go to put up their own tents at the other end of the campsite.

Rob quickly builds a firepit area and then helps Isabelle. "I'll see if there is anything in my kit that might help. He needs something like an instant cork to calm his stomach." He opens his pack right there and rummages through everything. "Ah, ha! An Imodium!" He holds up two very tiny white tablets and hands them to Isabelle. She holds them like gold and hands one to Z, which he takes.

Walking up behind Rob, Dave sees a zipped pouch of needles and blood testing supplies in his pile. *It's true. He does have diabetes.* Dave turns and finishes setting up camp.

Rob throws a T-shirt over the testing supplies but knows that Dave has seen them. Most insurance underwriters would not allow someone with Type 2 diabetes to forage in the deep jungle. It would be too much of a liability for them. He knows there will be an uncomfortable conversation coming from Dave yet again. He winces at the thought but returns his personal items to his bag, cursing under his breath while he does it.

On schedule, Malcolm returns with a pile of wild sweet potatoes. Rob is already unsuccessfully trying to start the fire. Malcolm nods his appreciation and buries the sweet potatoes in the dirt, then builds the fire over them using another of his reserve slivers of rubber. Malcolm steps off the trail to skin the kangaroo and returns with a very pink carcass. He calls out to the rest of the group, "If anyone finds kindling that is dry, please let me know."

Returning from a trip to the latrine, Z crawls inside the mosquito netting and onto his folded blanket as the net tests back over him. Down to his boxers, he lies on his pallet and moans. Isabelle steps around the perimeter of the makeshift medic area and sprinkles powder on the ground to keep bugs away.

When all the tents are up, and the fire blazes with intensity, Dave checks on Z. "He doesn't look good," he whispers to Isabelle.

"I'm afraid he's got a parasite. I've given him the medicine in our reserves, and there's other stuff I can give him from the First Aid Kit if needed. He needs plenty of liquids and rest. I'm afraid we're going to be here for several days. His temp is 103." Isabelle rubs her hands with a disinfectant lotion and looks at Z with concern as he runs for the latrine again. "I've got some antibiotics, but not a full course."

"My feet are killing me. Itching up a storm." Dave uses a stick to scratch, deep into his shoe. "Got any foot powder in that kit?"

"Take 'em off," she demands. "Now."

"Bossy," he says, but sits and removes them. The smell hits them, and they both recoil. "Wow," Dave says, with disgust. "How can that smell be coming off me?"

Isabelle covers her nose. "I've got news for you. All of us reek, but that's something on a whole new level." She points to the stream. "Give them a good wash and clean your socks, then come back here and I'll look. Guess I got my sense of smell back?"

Later that evening, Dave calls everyone to gather around. "Isabelle is going to check everyone's feet and do a general open sore inspection. We're going to be here for at least two days while Z recuperates. Take the time to catch up on your hygiene and wash your clothes. We need to be diligent in watching the skies and the monitors. Malcolm is setting up snares and doing some recon of the area. The beach is only about an hour that way." He points into the darkness. Lightning flashes in the distance behind him. "No one goes off on their own. In the morning, everyone will get a wash-up in the surf. We all need it." Dave scowls at the smell coming off the team. Everyone stands in bare feet as their hiking boots steam by the fire.

After dinner, Malcolm returns with a bundle of plantain bananas and weird shaped yams, which Renee is happy to see. She immediately spears plantains and roasts them over the fire. "These will be good for Z too," she says, as Isabelle joins her. "How's he doing?"

Isabelle speaks loud enough for the others to hear. "He's not good. But at least he had the shot series before we left. That will help him. Rest and fluids are the best we can hope for. I don't like that fever. I'll sleep close by. Could you wake me a bit early if I do fall asleep? I'm beat now, but I don't know that I'll be able to sleep while worrying over him." Isabelle watches him sleeping. "He's been incredibly careful with his water. I'm not sure how he became infected."

There is a pause in their conversation as Eric blurts out from across the camp, "I've got a blister on my foot that is infected." He hops over to Isabelle for a medical check and shows off a swollen area. Isabelle quickly puts ointment on it. "Wear your Teva's. Let it air out."

Dave snorts a loud snore from his tent. They all have gotten used to it. Renee giggles and pokes Eric in the ribs. "Guess I've got that to look forward to someday?" Rob is practically asleep where he is sitting. "Everyone should head in early. Eric and Renee, can you take the first shift?" They nod.

Isabelle pats Eric on the shoulder, telling him, "You'll need to look at your boots in the morning light, too. I'm sure that everyone has blisters or problem areas on their feet. That was a nightmare hike today. My ankles are so sore that they feel like giving out any second. I'm going to sleep barefoot tonight to let my feet air out."

Isabelle wiggles her toes and rubs her ankles. "Malcolm said that we might have fish tomorrow from the bay." They both smile.

"That would be nice." Renee bites into the plantain. "I can't eat another animal with beautiful eyes."

Rob checks the data and stretches. He talks through his yawn, "I'm going to head in shortly. Just need to check on the stats." He scans the horizon for Ropen using his night-vision goggles, talking while viewing. "Izzy, I'll check in at about two, for the night shift with Z."

Inside his tent, Dave awakens himself with a loud snore and adjusts his position. He listens to the crew as they talk amongst themselves, without his interference.

Billy and Malcolm sit nearby with the ELOD monitor. Malcolm's voice rises as he gets excited talking about a cryptid. "Actually, in Australia, the Aborigines in the Northern Territory have legends of a real animal called the Burrunjor. They describe it as a giant bipedal lizard that looks much like a three-toed carnivorous dinosaur. I heard it's like a huge monitor lizard, up to thirty feet tall. The Aborigines are afraid of it." Malcolm puts another log on the fire, and the flames spark with the new fuel.

"Wouldn't that be something!" Billy looks at Rob with wide-eyed wonder. Billy is animated. "I still can't believe the variety of species that are here. If I hadn't seen the diversity of this area with my own eyes, I wouldn't have believed it." He scans the skies as fingers of mist slither above them, around the mountain, and lower onto the jungle floor. "I don't think I can stay in a lab anymore after this. I definitely have adventure in my blood now."

"Told ya, you need to get out more." Rob smiles at the ease of their conversation.

"I've always dreamt of seeing something unknown—being the first to document the finding." Rob squats down next to Billy, and continues, "I've been thinking of heading into the Northern Territory in Australia after this to check on the Burrunjor sightings. Wanna go?" *And that's how it always starts,* Dave thinks to himself as he shuts his eyes.

Billy nods his head and uses his slingshot to shoot rocks up into the sky for the bats to catch. The alarm sounds on the netting. "I thought you weren't going to put any more nets up?" Malcolm questions them as Rob and Billy run to the net.

"Couldn't resist. We aren't going to assess them; just want to see what we catch." Billy says with glee. The bat is caught high in the netting, requiring him to climb to the top of the limestone cliff to extract the twisted meshwork. It is caught so tightly that they remove the ties holding the netting to get the bat loose. Billy narrowly catches himself to keep from falling.

"This is a big one!" Rob calls out. "Hold it still." Dave comes out of his tent to see what they have. Rob and Billy struggle with the massive bat.

"Let's lay it down on the ground," Dave says as they spread out the animal.

Rob takes a photo with his camera. "Check out the muscles in his wings." Rob points to the ligament. "Looks more like one of those hammerhead bats, big enough too." "Hammerheads are only in Africa," Dave says, struggling to hold the bat. "Could be a new species?"

"Let's document him with some measurements and images," Rob says as Billy grabs his camera. They quickly do their work and release him back into the inky night.

"What do you think it is, Dave?" Billy asks as they watch him fly. "Show it to Malcolm. Maybe he knows?" They look over to see Malcolm sleeping in his hammock holding onto a handmade spear.

"I have no idea." Dave yawns. "I'm going to turn in. Let me know if you catch more like him." He turns toward the campsite. "Had some nasty teeth, though," Dave says, over his shoulder.

* * *

Later, Rob joins Billy at the top of the cliff, and together they scan the tree line below. Billy points, saying, "Check out that mist bank rolling down the mountain on the right." Rob adjusts his lenses, and Billy does the same. The valley looks serene and lovely before dawn. "What time do you have?" Billy asks, as he repeatedly snaps images and adjusts the setting on his camera to let in more light.

Rob checks his watch. "A little before four."

With a mischievous grin, Billy asks, "So, you ever see any monsters since you've been hunting them? I'll keep the information to myself, promise." Rob looks out at the sliver of a moon and its reflections off the water.

"I've been interested in cryptozoology all my life, but followed Dave into biology. Just seemed like the right thing to do at the time. Came close to seeing Bigfoot once, I think. Back in middle school, got a call from a friend who knew I was working on a science fair project on Bigfoot, and he heard about footprints that were recent. We practically flew out to the site. There was four feet of snow on the ground and the roads had been cleared. The farm was in a field with nothing around it except for a small crop of trees behind the house about fifty feet back. We pull up, and I'm not lying. There are tracks going across the field."

Rob stops momentarily and pulls the lens down from his face. "And those tracks went right over the house. They didn't stop in the pacing, and my friend's dad couldn't match the stride. I tried to make a casting of the footprints before the sun got too hot, but I was just a kid and I screwed up the process. But we were about six hours behind the actual event. Guess I got hooked then, big time."

Billy looks at him wide-eyed. "The tracks went over the house?" They both get back to scanning.

"Yup. Of course, I've seen other things. Been on a few Bigfoot expeditions and once went looking for Mothman, but I tell you, the smell of a Bigfoot is something you never forget. As bad as Dave's feet." They both chuckle.

Billy snaps images and checks the settings on his camera before taking ten more. "It will take me weeks to get through all the photos from this trip," he says to Rob. Billy does a panoramic sweep with his lenses. "I think I might become a professional photographer."

"Whoa--," he says, as he pauses and refocuses. "Orbs... err Ropens. Four of them." The orbs flash in the distance, moving away from land across the water. He points. They are about two miles out. Billy snaps the images. "I wish I had my DLSR here. It would take better resolution, but I can't imagine lugging that heavy camera through what we've been through."

Rob turns on his recorder and watches the sky above them. The whirling "hmmmm" of the camera fills the surrounding air. "I can barely make them out." *Come on, let me see.* Rob tries to control his inner voice. He tries his own camera, which is zoomed out to maximum. *It's not enough!*

"Let me see! I can't stand it anymore," He pleads, as Billy hands him the camera.

Rob uses the zoom setting on high and follows the creatures as they move above the waters. Stunned, he watches one jet-dive into the water, similar to a loon, then come up quite a way closer to him and Billy, but a distance away from the other Ropens. The creatures cover the distance under the water in seconds. "Did you see that?" Rob says. This is so bizarre. "They dived right into the water." Rob hogs the camera as Billy nervously waits.

Rob hands him back the camera. "I would have, but you had the Canon." Billy quickly scans the horizon. He nods his head "yes" and continues to watch. "They are heading to the east." The lights blink off and on until they are out of sight. Both Rob and Billy stand shell-shocked without talking. It happened so fast. Rob shakes his head. "You get that?"

"Holy Hell!," Billy says, as they climb back down to base camp. "They are swimmers."

"We've got to get more biologicals," Rob says out loud.

At morning's first light, billowing white clouds shroud the highest mountain peaks behind them. Dave awakens to a smoldering fire and sits up quickly, looking for Malcolm. He goes to the untended fire and looks around with alarm, stokes the fire, and adds another log. Isabelle joins him.

The birds around them chirp and squawk in the morning light as the canopy stirs.

"He's still got a temperature of a solid 101, but he hasn't been running to the bathroom as much," she says, as she warms her hands over the new flames.

"That's good, right?" Dave looks around nervously. "Have you seen Malcolm? This is the first morning I haven't seen him at the fire at first light."

"Yeah, he left about an hour ago to check his pig traps," she says, as she notices a look of relief come over Dave's face. "What's up?"

"I dreamed that he left us last night, then I woke up and he wasn't here. I had a moment there that I didn't want to acknowledge." He looks meekly around to see if anyone overheard them. "He's been such a great guide. I've got to see if the foundation will give him a bonus." He throws a log on the fire and notices that Isabelle holds a ramen noodle package in her hands. "Some would pay quite a price for that?" He points to the meal packet and licks his lips in anticipation.

"I know... it's the last of my stored food stash. I'm donating it to Z. It's about all his stomach can manage, anyway." She caresses the package as if it were priceless.

"He might have to marry you after the way you're caring for him," Dave says with envy.

"Don't think his wife would go for that. All the good ones are taken, anyway." Isabelle sniffs the package and sighs contentedly.

"You're a good woman, Isabelle. How come you're not married?" She pauses before answering. "I am married. Well, at least it feels that way. I'm married to my work. I almost walked down the aisle years ago, but she wound up cleaning out my bank account instead. It was a painful time." Her eyes tear up briefly before she pushes the emotion away. "And I had an awful row with my girl before I left. She might not be waiting for me when I get home. Life is hard."

Dave pours her a cup of hot water and drops one of his precious, used tea bags in it. "For you, my dear." He hands her the cup. "Brilliant, mean, thank you." She accepts the steaming brew. "How 'bout you?"

"Married? I was. It was exceptional. The bar is too high. I don't think there will be another one." Dave pours a second cup of water for his own tea. It's still hard to talk about, after all this time."

"What do you want to do today?" She blows on the tea before taking a small sip. She looks up as Eric walks towards them.

He yawns and scratches himself as he stumbles in. "Coffee, I need coffee."

"I'd like to take a contingent to the ocean and scout around a bit, fish, and take a good scrub in the water. We'll probably let the others rest up today. We're all beat from that hike yesterday," Dave says, as he reaches for Eric's shoulder. "What do you think, E, want to go clean up a bit?"

"A… haaa." Eric yawns and collapses onto his back.

"Billy got more footage of a Ropen last night."

"Seriously? And nobody woke me?" Dave looks in Billy's direction. His feet are pushed up against the netting of the tent, in a relaxed pose.

Eric fans for Dave's attention. "Let him sleep. The camera is over at the station. Rob downloaded it already." Eric closes his eyes. "I've never been more tired in my life. I'm going back to bed. Unless someone has coffee." The words die in the wind as Rob rushes to the station and flips through the images.

Malcolm walks into camp barely holding a forty-pound black and white pig struggling in his arms. "Hey, could use a little help here," he calls out to Rob, who is mesmerized reviewing the images on the camera.

"Oops, sorry." Dave joins Rob and helps cradle it. "He's a little slippery, isn't he?" Rob grabs the back legs as it wriggles sharply.

"He's a young one. Meet my new friend. I'm going to call him 'dinner.'" Malcolm pats the pig. "And I even found a small pineapple patch, but I'll have to go back to bring some in. I think Renee will enjoy a breakfast of fresh mangos, pineapples, and bananas."

"Yeah, but don't let her see the pig," Dave says under his breath. "She'll probably want to adopt it."

Malcolm nods, and says, "It was strange out there hunting this morning. It's as if the animals haven't seen humans. They had no fear of me at all. Some of the easiest hunting I've ever done." The piglet wiggles in his arms. "Hold on to him for a minute, will you? I'll get vines to hold him. I'll need to string him up and let him bleed out, downstream, over the river. These guys can make quite a mess."

The swine squeals loudly. It echoes through the camp. Billy pokes his head out of his tent and smiles. "Bacon!" he yells with glee.

Later that morning, Dave calls a meeting to discuss the images from last night and to get volunteers to go to the beach. "Malcolm is going to get the pig draining down by the river, so that happens while we are gone." Renee flinches. "Sorry, Renee. Anyway, we'll be gone in about four hours. Take a light pack. Fill your canteens. Rob and Isabelle will stay with Z."

He looks at the crystal-clear skies above them and nods. "Skies are good today. Hopefully, we'll be back before the storms come in. I want to canvas the path to the beach, so we'll clear it as we pass. Rob, I think the walkie-talkies will still hold a charge. I'll be on Channel Two if you need us." Dave fiddles with the communication unit and clamps it onto his belt.

As they prepare to leave camp, Renee shields her eyes from the dead pig hanging over the riverbank. She hears Malcolm pat the carcass and closes her eyes tightly at the sound. She adjusts her Teva hiking sandals and checks her supplies to stay busy. Eric's outfitting matches hers, complete with color-coordination.

Dave walks over to them as they head out. "Where did you get the sandals?"

Eric shows off his sandaled feet, wiggling his toes. "Nice, aren't they? I think we can wear them today. My feet need to breathe," as Isabelle says, "and I'm tired of carrying them around." Renee smiles, munching on a granola bar.

"What else do you have in your packs?" Dave arches his eyebrows at Renee and whispers, "Any cookies?" Eric shakes his head. "I know. It's freaky. We keep finding stuff. Renee is a great packer. Wish I had a machete like Malcolm's, though. That is one thing I would bring on the next trip."

Malcolm works to widen the trail, and soon they are on the flatlands leading down to the beach trail. The trees in the area are a mix of tall sago palms, coconut palms, and large sycamore trees. They sway in the breeze that comes off the water. The beach is pristine other than a large colony of raised ant beds swarming near the tree line. In the sparkling-blue waters in front of them are the dots a chain of islands to the north. To the left, a large rigid backbone of a mountain cuts sharply into the water. To the right, a long stretch of open beach beckons them. At the water's edge, submerged coral make a dark horseshoe pattern under the aqua waves. Bright orange starfish can be seen moving under the water.

Eric and Renee drop their gear and prepare to hit the waves. They giggle in anticipation. Eric picks up Renee and takes several steps toward the surf until Malcolm calls out, "I don't think there are any crocs in this area. The coral reef should keep them out, but someone should stand watch just in case. The water here is the clearest I've ever seen." Malcolm grins as everyone starts undressing. He monkey-ups into a nearby sycamore tree as a lookout. "All clear," he calls out as the group runs into the water.

They play in the water for about an hour before Dave changes places with Malcolm. Renee sets up a shampoo station in the small side stream of fresh water and happily shampoos each of them one by one. Malcolm and Dave start canvassing the area in opposite directions.

Malcolm tries to get around the ragged rock cliff to the left and deems it too precarious. "That's one wicked mountain." He joins Dave back at the main area. "I bet there was some sort of volcanic eruption in this area not too long ago. Look at the mess these rocks made, slicing into my shoes." He leans over and inspects the tire soles to see if the damage is repairable.

"There is a long stretch of nothing to the east. I guess it's our new destination," Dave says, as his walkie-talkie squeaks at his waist. Static and more squeaking fills the air. He adjusts the nobs on the unit. "Come in Rob—O-over!" Dave repeats.

The garbled words, "Ropen ATTACK!" come through at one point. Dave quickly looks to the skies, rummages for his whistle, and blows it repeatedly. As the alarm sounds, Eric and Renee, who had been lounging on the beach, quickly ran for the cover of the trees. Billy stops taking pictures of the flora plants and joins the group as they huddle near a large fallen sycamore tree.

Silently, a Ropen emerges at the top of the tree line about seventy-five feet from them. It is a smaller Ropen than they have seen before, with a wingspan of about fifteen feet. Its leathery, gray wings glide with little effort as it passes almost right over them. In its beak, they can make out the pig carcass they left at base camp.

"Everybody okay back there? Over," Dave talks into the walkie. The predator flaps its wings twice and continues effortlessly out to sea.

"Whoa…!" Billy says, under his breath. "Dude, he got our pig!" Billy throws a stick toward the creature. The others watch in silence.

"We're okay. Over." Rob's voice is full of static.

Dave repeats the message, "We're okay, too. Over." He stands under the cover of the trees and uses the zoom lens on Billy's camera to watch the bird of prey as it continues to glide to one of the larger islands dotting the horizon.

Dejected, Malcolm joins Dave. "I will see if I can catch another pig."

The radio chirps back to life and the static filled comments from Rob scream out. "He took our pig, but we're okay. Did you see it? Did you film it? Over." Rob says with urgency.

Dave holds the microphone close. "We're fine. Yes, we saw it. We'll be back soon. Over." He lowers the unit and glances back at the islands to the north. "We may have a new destination." All they can now see is a small black dot as the creature hovers over the island and then dips into the canopy.

Later that evening, back at base camp, everyone huddles around the campfire and waits for Malcolm to finish preparing dinner. The mood is somber. Thunderclouds continue to build on the horizon, and the skies look dark and angry.

Billy grumbles. "Man, I can almost smell bacon."

Z sits with the others and leans against a moss-covered rock. His coloring looks better, and he is very animated as he talks with Eric about the encounter. "It made no noise, kinda like a raptor in its stealth mode or an owl. They are silent flyers too. I was sitting by the fire here," he says, motioning to his seat, "and Isabelle was in her tent. Rob had his head down at the station desk. That's when it swooped in from the side of the camp. I swear, it was coming for me. I could feel its eye right on me. For a second, I couldn't move or speak. It was like a waking nightmare. I hit the dirt and flattened myself as much as I could. It went right over me! I was too scared to panic." Z shudders. "Had to use my common sense."

He continues, "Rob did a Tarzan yell and threw a stick at it. Thankfully, it looked in his direction. I think Rob distracted it from me enough, that it went over the ridge and saw a tastier meal just waiting for it. I tell you what, I'm glad it took the pig and left me alone."

Dave smiles. "Seriously, you did a Tarzan yell?" He looks right at Rob. Eric and Renee giggle. Eric baits Rob. "Come on, do it for us, just once."

Rob ignores him. "It only flapped its wings once over that carcass, then was gone. The whole incident lasted about thirty seconds." Holding the camera in his hands, he continues, "I didn't have time to film anything. I just grabbed one of Malcolm's bamboo spears and threw it."

The fire pit crackles, and a stream of sparks overtakes the large lizard Malcolm is turning in the pit. He pokes the carcass and fluid spills out onto the coals. "You can use them anytime, mate." Malcolm picks up another bamboo stem and starts sharpening another spear. Billy and Eric join him in his efforts.

"I'd like to go over to that island offshore and see what's going on there," Dave says with authority. *I can't believe I said that out loud,* he thinks, surprised by the confirmation in his voice. *It is too risky. They won't want to go out over water.* There are hundreds of islands off the shore around the main island, but three times they've seen the animals go in that direction. *Something is there, I'm sure of it. Could there be a colony? Biologicals would be certain there.* His mind goes through a dozen scenarios.

The entire crew stops what they are doing mid-stride and looks at Dave, astonished. His mind whirls over what had happened the night before. "I'm canceling all bat research gathering for the rest of the trip." Dropped jaws and silence lasts an entire minute as they all stare at Dave.

"Well, I am. We've collected three times the amount I expected, and I only have a couple of vials left, anyway. If you're all still interested, I'd like to head to that cluster of islands where we saw the Ropen flying. We will need these vials for Ropen samples."

Rob, Renee, and Eric smile widely back at him. "And how do you suppose we get there?" Rob wiggles his toes against the warm fire rocks surrounding the pit. His eyes flash in quiet anticipation.

Malcolm and I have been talking. There are plenty of large sycamore trees down by the beach area. They make excellent cutout canoes. While we don't have proper carving tools, the lava rocks over by the mountain cliff will be an excellent substitute for axes. Just look at what those sharp rocks did to the bottom of Malcolm's shoes." Malcolm shows his torn sandals for everyone to see.

"If we work in teams, we'll be able to finish two dugout canoes in about three days. That will give Z more time to rest up." Malcolm pats Z on the shoulder. He holds up a prehistoric-looking axe made from one of the sharpened stones and ties it tightly with twine.

"If anyone would like to call rescue, to be pulled out, I'll be glad to send the alarm. Dave hesitates, "Z, I only want you along if you're up to it." *Please be up to it Z, I need your sanity.* Dave pushes his thoughts toward Z. He gets a return smile from him.

"We'll use the next few days to rest up, eat well, and let our feet heal." He pauses. "Leave the ant nests alone on the beach. Billy, I saw you poking them. Malcolm says they can give a painful bite." He looks at each one of them. "But I want those who continue to be wholly into it. We need to get some measurable biological samples from those creatures.

Something we can go to the scientific community with."

There's a long pause in the conversation before he continues. "Who's with me?" All hands raise in unison. Rob stands with both arms in the air and then dances a jig with Eric and Renee. They all collapse into a laughing heap.

As the camp dwellers crawl into their tents, Rob volunteers to be the first observer for the night. Billy joins him at the lookout spot. Eric joins Dave at the campfire. Malcolm is sound asleep in his hammock about ten feet away.

"Dad, that was something today. I'm proud of you." Eric rubs Dave's thigh. "Never thought I'd say it, that's for sure," Dave laments quietly. "It's a new path for me." *A new path for all of us*, Dave says to himself. They watch the flames before Dave asks, "So, tell me about the latest adventure with Unka Rob. How was Peru?"

"Ahhhh-mazing! We had so much fun. The petroglyphs were so clear, and in a cave, we found new ones. Can't wait until we get the dating back from the lab. They could be thousands of years old. One showed what looked like a spaceship and an alien with an elongated skull sitting inside. Have you ever been to the museum in Maine? It's actually pretty rad."

"Rad?" Dave snickers. "Haven't heard you say that in years." Through a break in the trees, Dave can see Rob using the heat sensor scanner. His enthusiasm matches the eight-year-old boy he once was, with his room full of dinosaur models, *National Geographic* covers, and illustrations of the beasts. Rob had his GI Joe's set to attack the monsters. It had been in his blood all his life. And now, the disease has transferred to Eric. His is more of a *Magic the Gathering* fantasy-dinosaur world building, but the core value of dinosaurs is there. *They are made from the same mold*. Dave smiles as he remembers the large dinosaur costumes he and Eric both had and the mock fights out on the lawn as Jeanne filmed them. Priceless family memories. And the laughter. He will never forget the belly laughs Eric made, as they pretended to fight and Jeanne's side-splitting laughter weaving through the air.

"I... was just remembering that time we had the dinosaur-costume fight out on the lawn." Dave wipes away a tear as he talks.

"You remember, Mrs. Peterson, down the street? She about had a heart attack when I showed up and snow plowed her driveway in costume. Best Christmas present ever, from Unka Rob. Now, look at us. Hunting a real creature. See, Dad, dreams do come true."

"I hope you still feel that way after we go to that island. A lot can happen out there. When you're a parent, you'll understand my hesitation. We've been blessed with a tight family that loves each other, and we both had happy childhoods. That's rare these days. I hope I can be the 'fun' grandpa at gatherings someday, but I think Rob will always one-up me on that. Love you, boy, more than you can ever know. Please, please be extra careful. You've got a lot of living yet to do." Dave pats Eric's leg and stands up. "Guess I'm going to bed. You turning in?"

Eric shakes his head. "Can't. I'm too excited. I'm gonna go up and watch the horizon. A storm is building. Probably will rain before morning. Nite, Dad. Love you too." Eric turns and walks toward Rob. Over his shoulder he says, "I'll be careful."

CHAPTER 11

By late in the day, the beach is under attack by the scientists as they sweep the area clean of debris. They've moved camp to the beach enclave complete with a covered latrine, make-shift shower, kitchen prep, and eating area. The tents dot the area in a circular pattern around the campfire. Two large trees are cut down and set apart from the others, ready for carving. Malcolm uses a large piece of charcoal to mark the cutting areas on one log they have already stripped of bark. He works quickly with his markings.

Dave and Billy make measurements on the second log and strip it of its bark. The heavy pulling is harder than they thought it would be. Eric enjoys using Malcolm's machete to finish the work. Isabelle and Rob are side-by-side on the first canoe, arguing as they work. "But we have to protect them at all costs. Can you imagine what will happen to this pristine ecosystem if it is swarmed by untrained idiots trying to get the latest photograph? Or capture a Ropen?" Isabelle uses her axe to take another section of wood out of the canoe.

Rob's arms bulge as he throws his weight into another whack on the canoe bed. Bits of wood fly in all directions each time he strikes the trunk of the tree. They both wear their sunglasses, protection from the bits and the sun.

"Hey, watch it!" Isabelle cries out as a wood chip lands in her hair.

"If you don't like it, don't get so close," Rob exclaims. He moves to the other side of the canoe and continues to carve. His words are a little biting as he talks, "My whole life has been lived trying to find scientific proof of unidentified animals. And now you want me NOT to announce the findings? I've got over eighty different creatures on my list of possible new species, and this case offers the most substantial potential scientific documentation of one of them. It would take years to do a census of animal life in this area alone. Heck, it would take an army of scientists to do it properly."

He beats the log with the axe, taking more chunks out of it. "The press has always made a laughing-stock of any minor documentation we've done so far. Cryptozoology isn't well thought of, yet without our questions and methodology study, we wouldn't have proof of the Tasmanian Tiger, Mountain Gorilla, or Giant Squid." Rob continues talking as he rests. "Look at the scrutiny they did of that movie reel of Bigfoot back in the '50s. No reliable scientific commission wants to tackle the problems of bringing a controversial new species to light. Nowadays, you've got to have biologicals you can hold in your hand. And, even with the proof, it can all go haywire in a second."

Dave, Eric, and Renee peel the bark off the second trunk nearby. Dave pipes up. "Protecting the new species must be balanced with proper documentation. A discovery can't end with a slaughter of the new animal."

Mumbling under her breath, Isabelle stands firm, "Have pity on them all, for it is WE who are the real monsters." She pauses before continuing, "But I think in this case it would end with a slaughter."

Eric casually strolls over. He listens intently to the banter. "I'll take over if anyone is tired." Everyone ignores him.

Rob pulls a section of wood debris out of the canoe bay. "There is at least one quarter of the total species estimated in the world yet to be documented. Taxonomists have classified only one-fifth of all invertebrate species. Four million insects have not yet been examined and named. Another half million spiders and their relatives are still unidentified. Rob closes his eyes briefly, taking a deep breath.

"I for one, am all for annihilating spiders." Eric grins.

Rob is on a rant, and he pushes full ahead. "Plus, hundreds of thousands of aquatic creatures, ranging from snails to sponges, remain mysterious. A *National Geographic* expedition just found amazing species in the waters around Antarctica; giant starfish and some bizarre octopi," continues Rob.

"I'm sorry, but I'd rather protect them than have the glory." Isabelle whacks the log with renewed vigor and goes on. "This isn't a cool species of starfish. It's a frickin' creature that most would associate with dinosaurs. It's a major find, and you know it!" A bit of spittle flies out of her mouth as she points her axe right at him. "One little leak and we'll have a plethora of news crews in the area!" She groans.

Dave steps over and calms them down by taking the axe from her hand. "Isabelle, why don't you start working on the second canoe over there? I'll work with Rob here for a while." Isabelle squares her shoulders and turns abruptly as she walks to the other tree that is, ready to be carved.

"High strung British female," Rob grumbles under his breath, as he attacks the canoe with bent-up fury. "What about the 'help to science' these new species provide? New medicines, cures for cancer could be right around the corner hidden in some leaf extract, sub-species of frog or in the digestive system of an iguana." He whacks the canoe.

"Hit it a little harder next time," Dave says, stopping to watch Rob for a moment before he works on the other side of the canoe.

"You hit it harder!" Rob says, throwing down a challenge. They both smile and work together for the first time in years. After an hour of sweating through their shirts, the others are astonished to hear them laughing and humming.

Eric elbows Renee and beams as he watches his dad and uncle belting out songs from the '70s while they chop through a huge section of the dugout. Awful renditions of songs by *Chicago* and the *Beatles* fill the air. Eric spies Billy's camera lying on a blanket nearby. He picks it up and takes several shots of them working. He whispers into Renee's ear, "I've always dreamed of seeing them like this." He waves at Dave, who waves back, saying, "I want that photograph on my desk."

Later that afternoon, Billy hails the workers on the beach as he shows off a string of assorted colorful fish and a good-sized sting ray. "Look everyone!" he calls out. "Malcolm showed me how to spear fish. I LOVE it!" He yells but he is too far away for everyone to hear clearly, so to make his statement heard, he belts out a Tarzan yell and beats his chest. Rob returns the Tarzan yell. Dave has to one-up him and Tarzan yells even louder. They all break into peals of laughter.

Isabelle and Renee secure a collection of broken branches in a safety area, to protect the group in case of another attack. Isabelle sings some *Harry Belafonte* tunes, and everyone sings along to the banana boat song. The mood has lightened up considerably in the last few hours.

Dave watches Z. The ELOD is on, and Z keeps his eye on it as he slowly moves around, picking up firewood for the campfire. Everyone is sweat drenched and working together as the canoe's finally look like seaworthy vessels.

"How much longer until dinner?" Dave calls out to Malcolm. "We're starving!" Malcolm stands with his hands on his hips. "Well, if I can get the fish from Billy, it would be sooner rather than later." On the beach, Malcolm practically wrestles the catch from Billy, who wants to take photos of every fish. Billy takes off running with one fish and his camera.

Eric stretches and tries to pop his shoulders and neck after the hours of carving. With a determined focus, Renee continues to work on her section of the trunk. Eric smiles at her resolve and soon scoops her up and carries her to the beach. He passes Billy.

"Hey Billy, we need a lookout." Eric throws a knife into the sand, puts Renee on her feet, and they run to the water. "Okay, but you have to watch out for me afterwards," Billy yells above the surf. He climbs a nearby sycamore tree.

Dave and Rob continue to make progress on their canoe. They are both soaked to the skin, rivulets of sweat run from each of them-chin, elbows, and hands.

"You know," Rob states under his breath, "Pterodactyls are bad at becoming fossils. Their lightweight bones are just too fragile. There are widespread gaps in the fossil record. No one knows what happened to the smaller species of Pterodon." He swings his axe and dislodges a huge chunk of wood.

"Yeah, and I remember, they were your favorite dinosaur. You had those models all over the ceiling of your bedroom. What did you make them out of? I forget." Dave stops for a moment and wipes his face.

Rob smiles. "No telling. Hmmm, I think I used popsicle sticks, toothpick parts, and tissue paper, then vellum paper when I got older."

"When you were thirty?" Dave teases Rob. "I think we're about done with this one. What'd you think?" Dave steps back and admires their work.

Renee and Eric join them as they drip dry. Eric runs his hand over the second canoe with care. "Dang, good job!"

The rest of the day is uneventful, other than Billy and Malcolm catching a large green turtle that they turn into a big meal.

Renee cries when she sees the dead animal. "A turtle, my favorite animal. I'm going to be sick." She throws up in the bushes outside of camp. Eric tries to comfort her, but it doesn't work. She is furious.

Billy fashions the shell into a shield using peeled bark as twine. He tries to soothe Renee as well and tells her the turtle had an injured flipper, probably from a shark attack.

She snaps back at him, "Great, now I'll be thinking about shark attacks as we head out." She waves the men off and steps over to Isabelle, who is busy weaving palm fronds into strips. Isabelle shows her how to twist and overlap the pieces. It quickly grows into a good-sized net that Rob gives a "thumbs up".

Later, Malcolm calls everyone over and shows them how to use fire to help burn out the interior of the log canoe and seal the surface against insects. They finish one canoe by the time the sun sets, and the second canoe isn't far off.

Malcolm, Dave, and Rob collapse around the campfire as they congratulate themselves on how wonderful their canoe looks. "It's a beauty. I think we should give her a name." Rob rubs his sore shoulder.

"I haven't worked on a dugout since I was about twelve." Malcolm scans the horizon, which is illuminated by a breathtaking orange and yellow sunset. The waters shimmer in the bay, but in the distance, they can make out three small black dots lifting from the island about five miles away and heading east of their position. Malcolm nods to Dave, who grabs the binoculars and watches the flight path of the creatures.

"They're on the prowl," Dave calls out to the others. "Malcolm and Billy, you've got first watch."

Rob holds out his hand for the binoculars. Dave hands them over. The group gathers as they watch the dots move slowly over the water. Dave turns to everyone. The outline of a plan takes shape. "Tomorrow, I want everyone to rest up a bit after we finish the dugout. We'll leave the day after tomorrow. I'd like to have a briefing around three tomorrow for all of us. We need to define our objectives and goals and make sure everyone knows their responsibilities." Dave shudders. His gaze darts toward Z, whose complexion is better today, but Dave knows his pain has been intense. He would need to have a serious talk with Z before they left. It would not be a comfortable conversation.

Standing with the others, Z says, "I'm ready. I mean, I feel up to doing my share again." He puts his hand out and shakes everyone's hand. "Thank you, thank you all for putting up with me. I won't let you down." Dave had to keep an eye on Z, to make sure he didn't do anything strenuous that day. "Just relax another day, please. We will all feel better knowing you are better." He doesn't argue and nods.

The night is uneventful, other than an anteater waking up Billy as it feasted at the ant mounds near them. Billy gets on his stomach to get some action shots and is pleased with himself when he shows them off at breakfast.

Malcolm whispers to Dave at the morning campfire, "There is pride in a day's work." He smiles as he watches the team relax around them.

Isabelle stands up and points to the canoes. "This should be a part of every corporate team-building exercise. We worked out some frustrations and inner feelings during that process."

Dave whispers back, "They're stronger now, and it shows."

They finish the second canoe by lunch, and they braid more of the vines and palms into make-shift seats for the dugouts. The crew stacks their supplies beside each canoe as they prepare to leave.

Dave pulls Malcolm aside. "What do you think about the plan? You're the survivalist here. Are we foolish to go off that way?" A million threats run through his mind as he looks pleadingly at Malcolm. *Things can get nasty quickly.*

"You're a brave crew, and smart. That's half the battle. They are more seasoned now after these weeks out here. I would recommend that we don't take all the gear with us. Try to get out there and back, with an overnight only if we need it. Fresh water will be our main concern." They both watch the team, while continuing to talk in hushed tones.

"Water is your priority? Not the creatures?" Dave asks. He holds onto his spear made from bamboo and looks at the sharpened tip.

"Water is always the priority. I'll put extra on to boil, but everyone needs to be responsible for their own water. We don't have room for extras. One backpack each. Leave the samples and electronics here." Malcolm is satisfied, so he sits back, letting Dave take in the information. *He's right,* Dave thinks. *Water - then protection.* "Okay, let's get organized," Dave calls out to everyone. "Billy, how are we doing with documentation? How much film do we have left?"

"No problem, I still have two cards unused, and I can download and clean an additional card tonight with our transmission." He holds out the cards for everyone to see and checks his camera gear for sand in the crevices. He blows out a stream of sand on the side of one lens. "I have room for another 100,000 images."

Renee and Rob show their cameras as well. "We'll have extra back-up if needed." Rob smiles at Renee.

Malcolm counts the food stuff supplies. "Everything is good on the food end. Everyone give me your water tablet count before dinner. I want to make sure our purification needs are stable." Rob waits for the computer connection to go through. "It's been acting a little shaky lately." He nods when the connection hits."

"Okay, let's try not to take any images that would offer an opportunity for people to pinpoint our location. No big landmarks or beach locale." Dave pauses. "We need to get scientific proof, organics, and biological evidence. Z, you, and Rob oversee biologicals. Renee, Eric, and Isabelle, you're on organics." Rob nods as the computer buzzes its connection.

"Rob, tell your associate what we are planning. He should keep everything close to his chest," Dave says, as Rob acknowledges his response. "I want to stash all the hard documentation we have on our bats before we head out. It will be safer knowing that I don't have to worry about it dumping into the ocean. Everyone, bring me anything you've got before you close it down tonight. I'm going to put it at the base of that log over there." Dave points to a large felled tree nearby. "All data has been sent, but if you've any slides or specimens, let's keep them together."

"Our aim once we arrive on the island will be to be invisible. This eco-system is unbelievable, but we've got to keep the balance where it is." Dave continues, "Malcolm, you're our native guide, so help us identify anything unusual. And I want you to continue to provide our meals." Malcolm gestures, and says, "I've made extra spears that can be used as walking sticks. I used fresh bamboo from back on the trail. These birds of prey may decide we're lunch, and you've got to protect yourself. Keep your spears with you at all times." Then he walks through the group, pulling out a spear for each of them.

He repeats "all times" to each member.

"Great idea Malcolm." Dave checks the strength of his. Renee hesitates before Eric coaxes her into accepting the spear. "I don't think I could kill one," she says. "You don't have to kill it, just injure it enough to leave you alone," Malcolm urges. "Your life depends on it."

Eric pulls out a handgun from a pocket on his backpack. I've got that loaded 45-caliber colt pistol from the wreckage. And I've got a flare gun, but we don't know if it's usable." Eric pulls the flare gun from the pack as well.

Renee quickly moves away from him. "How long have you had **that**?" she asks with concern, as she turns back toward him.

"Just the last couple of days. Z had it in his pack back at the last camp.

He asked me to hold it for him," Eric says, as he buffs the handle.

"Let me see that." Isabelle holds out her hand. Eric gives it to her. She quickly removes the safety, takes aim at a low-hanging branch on the other side of the camp area, and squeezes the trigger. A loud report causes an immediate evacuation from the birds in the surrounding canopy. The tree branch floats to the ground. It has been cut cleanly from the main part of the tree.

"Nice shootin', Tex," Dave says, in his best Texan accent. "Where did you learn to shoot?"

"My Father was a crack shot. He often took me to the shooting range." Isabelle comments in her thick High English. She tries to return the gun to Eric, who refuses to take it.

Eric shakes his head, saying, "You keep it with you. I think it makes Renee nervous." Isabelle tucks the gun into the top of her shorts.

"Okay, we'll be heading out across open water. Who doesn't feel comfortable in the water? Is everyone a good swimmer?" Dave scans the faces in the crowd. Billy raises his hand. He hesitates. "I can swim, but it's not someplace I feel really comfortable in. Just thinking about getting in the canoe and not being able to see land makes it difficult for me to swallow. I guess I'm just a little nervous about it."

Renee steps forward. "Dave, I used to be a competitive swimmer. Better put Billy in the canoe with me, just in case." He signals his agreement.

Dave looks out over the water to the islands, before continuing. "Okay, we'll set off after an early breakfast tomorrow morning. Tonight, we're going to take a quick ride and check out the seaworthiness of our beautiful canoes. Once we get to the island in the morning, our aim will be to land, then head to cover as soon as possible. On shore, let's keep the talking to a minimum. Everyone should be in stealth mode. We don't know how long it's going to take us to maneuver our canoes over and back. We might have to spend the night. You are each limited to your day packs. Only take your core essentials. And your most important item on this trip will be your water. Make sure you are fully topped off."

He turns, checking the faces of each team member. "I agree with Malcolm. Everyone needs to always keep their spears with them." He stands and dusts off his pants. "Any questions?" Heads nod in agreement as everyone clusters around the campfire.

Billy says, "Your assignment, Mr. Phelps, is to infiltrate the island, find out what's there, not get eaten, and return with proof." He pauses. "This tape will self-destruct in sixty seconds."

CHAPTER 12

Dave, Malcolm, and Rob make minor adjustments to both canoes. Behind them, the stash pile is wrapped in plastic sheeting, then covered with, and hidden behind clusters of branches. Earlier, Z made them dig deeper twice before he was satisfied the equipment would be safe.

Dave breaks out into a large grin for the first time in a long while as he watches the team efficiently move to the water's edge. His hand moves to his hip, where he has strapped the gun and holster found in the wreckage. It feels weighty and heavy, but comforting at the same time. Jeanne would have had a fit seeing him like this. Walking around the canoes, he holds onto a spear pole Malcolm made for each of them. A quiet ripple of anticipation races through the group as they each stand with their backpacks, waiting for Dave to move them on. Renee has a rolled netting under her arm. They all look ready to go.

Dave walks up to Billy. "Think you could put the camera on a timer and take a group photo? You all look great."

"Great idea!" Isabelle says, as they watch Billy balance the camera on a log. They all stand together in casual, relaxed poses as the camera alerts, then Billy races over each time to the group and is in place a split-second before it takes the shot. Five times he jogs back to re-set the unit.

As he gets back to the group for the final time, Billy has trouble standing still. The thought that *this could be the day that I get THE shot* bounces through his mind. His palms itch with an intensity that is difficult to ignore. He cuts the mood with a sarcastic note. "Feels kinda-*Survivor*-ish, doesn't it? Standing here with our canoes waiting to go, with our spears and cunning to survive the day?" He gives a Tarzan yell, which each of them down the line repeats, as they wait for Dave to go last. He puts added gusto into it and arches his back as he yells. The yelling releases some tension from the group. They all smile back at Dave.

"Let's go!" Dave motions them onward. Renee, Billy, Eric, and Dave are in the first canoe. Notches have been cut inside each canoe, offering a spot to keep the spears pointing upward next to each occupant.

Billy eyes the netting masterpiece. "Nice, Renee. Did you and Isabelle make it?" He slathers himself with sunscreen and adds a long-sleeve shirt over his t-shirt. "I burn easily. Being a redhead isn't easy."

"Yes," she says as she pats the bundle. "It was strangely relaxing to make." She strokes her work before lathering up on sun protection.

Eric and Billy pull their canoe out into the water up to thigh level and jump into the wooden vessel. Billy's long legs allow him to easily step into the canoe. Eric's transition isn't as effortless, and he lands at the bottom against the wood base, hitting his head against the side. "Smooth move, *Ex-lax*," Billy chimes as he watches Dave roll his eyes. Renee suppresses a giggle.

Next to them, Rob, Isabelle, and Z get a push out into the bay from Malcolm, then he hops in. The sea is like glass this early in the morning, smooth and clear. It takes practice strokes before they find their sea routine and rhythm. They are well-rested, and it shows.

Dave calls out, "Let's try to get back before those afternoon storms. I don't relish trying to handle rough seas in these things." They paddle for over an hour and rest when a large Great White Shark investigates and then heads back out to sea. Billy's eyes are wide as he watches it circle them a few times. The crystalline waters allow them to see deeply into the water. Renee gets lost looking down and loses her rhythm in paddling. "There's an entire world down there that we know little about." She points to a large grouper who watches them pass.

"Gawd, that shark must be close to twelve feet!" Billy has a white-knuckled grip on the canoe, as does Isabelle.

Malcolm holds up his paddle. "There's a bit of a beach area on the island that's on the east side." He points toward the smallest island. "Let's try that one first. Be careful as we come in. Cut across the waves, or ride them in."

Eric, Renee, Dave, and Billy are the closest, and they head in first with no mishaps. The island has clusters of mangrove trees in pockets with heavy razor palms spread under a canopy of sycamore trees. The ground is cluttered with rotten mangos. Billy quickly grabs a handful of ripe fruits from a nearby tree and places them inside the canoe. They've now pulled up and onto the beach as the second boat slides in next to them. Rob investigates the half-eaten body of a croc that has washed ashore and soon joins the group under a shade tree.

Dave whispers, "We are going to cut into two teams. Malcolm, Renee, Eric, and Billy, you head to the right. The rest of us will head to the left. If you go into the interior, don't go far. Stay on the beach as much as possible." He throws Eric a walkie-talkie. "This island isn't too big. We should be able to cover it quickly." Renee picks up her net and tucks it under one arm. She holds onto her spear with the other hand.

"Back here in an hour. ONE-hour." Dave holds up one finger. "If you see something, we are on Channel Two."

The team moves out, and Rob stops them. "Quiet, be very quiet," he murmurs. A loud flock of birds rises and settles next to them in the tree line. Rob raises an eyebrow as he watches them. He points and taps Dave on the shoulder. "I think we need to hit that one next." Rob keeps his eye on that island.

Dave watches the other team walk around the bend, then slowly joins his team, taking the rear position. *I should be with Eric*, he thinks, watching them disappear. He looks at the expanse of the main island and finally realizes, in his gut, just how far they have gone. It's now a sliver on the horizon. "Shit." He hurries to join his group when he sees the annoyed look on Rob's face.

Thin slivers of beach and coral make the hike slow. There is nothing out of the ordinary here as far as wildlife goes, and Isabelle is pleased to see a grove of palm trees on the northern bank. They follow a slight rise to the terrain, and they find themselves fifty feet above the water at one point. The squad rests briefly and re-hydrates.

"What do you think, Rob?" Dave asks as he takes a swig. "Other than that carcass on the beach, I'd say this is a miss?" Rob says, as he looks around cautiously.

Isabelle joins them. "Sure, it's pretty, pristine, and the view is to die for."

"Some billionaire would have all the isolation he wanted out here," Z comments seconds later. "The sound of the waves is so relaxing. There's even a breeze." He holds out his shirt to dry off in the wind.

Dave checks his watch as he halts the group. "We are nearly at the half-way point." Rob listens to the scanner. "No word from Team Two."

He points back to their landing area. "Okay, let's cut across back through that palm area to the canoes." Dave turns and heads into the foliage. "Hey, look, at least there's wildlife. Do spiders count?" A large, brown, tarantula-looking spider darts into a hollowed log near his foot. Rob walks past. "It's probably a new species as well. Especially with this isolation."

Isabelle tries to take a photo, but it's too deep inside the log. She pokes at it with a stick, but it doesn't move, only raises its front legs in alarm. "Guess this one is going to get away." She hurries up to the others and Z lets her go in front of him.

"Ladies first," he says, motioning with a sweep of his hand. "You know, spider populations are being decimated with the harvesting of so much of the palms."

"They nest in those fronds." Isabelle points to the canopy of trees around them.

Z nods. "Shush, we are supposed to be quiet." Looking guilty, she covers her mouth and keeps going. "I haven't been hushed since I was in grade-school," she says quietly.

Within ten minutes, they are back at the canoes, taking a rest under some trees, watching for the other team. Rob tries the walkie. "We are back at the canoes waiting for you. Over." He listens before static clicks.

"Nothing this way. We are heading back," Eric says. "Over."

Isabelle lays back in the sand. "Wake me when they show up," she says as she closes her eyes.

The calm sounds of the surf and the untouched beach relaxes them all.

Dave scans the island across from them with his binoculars. Rob holds out his hand for his turn. "I really miss my viewers. I lost my best pair on that last expedition." The words die on his lips as a deep rumbling from another tremor hits. Waves of intensity ripple out in the bay. Birds rise into the air behind them and across the bay at the next island. A herd of tarantulas exits the shade of the canopy and rushes out onto the beach about fifty feet away. There must be over a hundred dark spiders spilling onto the sand.

Isabelle jumps up and moves toward the water. "Holy Hell!" she yells, as she stands in the water up to her thighs.

In the distance, the second crew turns the corner, running toward the others. Eric is in the lead. He runs at full sprint. His mouth hangs open in horror as he points to the boats and motions for Team One to put them in the water.

Rob's feet splash into the surf. He pushes Eric's canoe out a little into the bay and holds onto it as Eric approaches, jumps in, and pushes out farther.

He is shaking. "Freaking nightmare! Look at those things!" He points to the spiders, who are now moving back into the shade at the tree line. The rest of the team gathers at the boats. Renee and Billy hold on to each other as they laugh.

Billy is laughing hysterically. "That may have been a world record! I've never seen–someone run–that fast!" He mimics Eric's running style.

Eric pouts in the canoe. "It isn't funny!" The rest of them can't hold it in and snicker.

Rob holds onto his knees. "Yeah, it is. I'm sorry, kid, but it reminded me of a cartoon or something."

Renee tries to look serious but can't hold it back and she starts laughing all over again. "I've got a great flashback!" She waves her hands and repeats his gestures, then says, "Sorry, honey."

"You know, when they show a character running and the sound happens afterwards," Dave says as he giggles, "you had your mouth hanging open the whole time you were running towards us."

"I did not!" Eric frowns. He watches the last of the spiders disappear into the green foliage. "Psssh, bet you'd have the same response in a zombie apocalypse," Billy howls.

"Okay, let's calm down," Dave says as he motions with his hands. "Stage Two is right over there. Everybody, settle down. We've got to be quiet as we get closer. Let's head out."

Isabelle looks longingly at the cover. "Guess I'll just pee in the water. I am not stepping foot back there now."

In minutes, the crew is paddling well, against a slight current at the coral shallows. Billy has trouble controlling his giggling, so now and then, they start laughing all over again. It only takes them about half an hour to paddle to the second island, which is a bit more rugged with rocky outcroppings. A landmark coral reef in the shape of a big crescent takes up one side of the island. Dave points them over toward an area to the side of the sharp rocks where there is a small beach.

Isabelle covers her nose. "Wow, that's a rank smell," she says as she dabs at her watering eyes. She sniffles. They all react to the overwhelming odor that increases as the breeze blows towards them.

Rob gives Dave a look of confirmation as he pulls up his bandana. "Smells like a million cat boxes," Eric says. "Never did get on with cats." He whispers to Renee. "Hope that's not a problem." She elbows him to be quiet.

Now they are there, on Ropen Island, as Rob claimed. Dave is sure of it. There is little cover, but at least the beach is empty. Malcolm leads them to the best spot under a tree with low-hanging branches. Dave is the last to finish pulling both canoes up onto the beach. This time, he secures them with Isabelle's homemade twine. He gives each an extra knot to hold them tight.

He notices a pounding ache in his chest and a tingling of the start of a headache. Stress always does that to him. Dave's hand goes to the gun at his belt for reassurance. He eyes the team. Billy lets out a low snort through his teeth as he suppresses a giggling fit. Eric slaps him across the chest in a gesture that is playful, but it looked a bit harder than that. Billy straightens up and nods at Dave to message that he is calm now.

Moving together, they move up the small rise on the beach into the canopy. The trees are a little more spaced out, with areas of hard granite stone dotting the landscape. Around them, rocks are speckled with gray and white algae and bits of moss. "Team up, but keep close," Dave says.

The smell gets stronger the closer they progress into the thicket. Most of them take out their bandanas and tie them around their faces, covering their noses. Isabelle examines some plants in the area and pockets a leaf that looks interesting to her.

They stop when Rob points to a dark shape moving slowly and awkwardly ahead. He creeps forward, keeping low, using a broken branch as cover. "Another Pterodactyl," he murmurs. The beast moves about twenty feet from them. Its broad shoulders and arms are tucked in as it hobbles along a rock. It shifts into place and sits back. This is a massive female with broad hips. She preens, using her long beak to move a rock near her feet.

Rob lies flat on the ground. "That's not a rock, it's an egg," he mouths to Dave. The only sound is the 'whirl' of his video recording. He plucks a small bright-blue feather from the dirt and pockets it. It matches the blue coloring around her eyes. Dave moves in close to him. "Female, notice the wide hips," he whispers.

Rob nods. "She's a beauty."

Cracking a branch nearby accidentally, Billy hides behind a tree as the female looks his way. She cocks her head to one side, then slowly shuts her eyes and rests her beak against her chest. Dave pokes Rob. "She's got a major injury to that crest on her head." A deep gouge and missing chunk have healed. Bits of skin hang down on one side. "Wish I could get some of that debris."

Billy motions that he is going to move further to the right and steps gingerly. Eric is right behind him, holding Renee's hand. They only move about ten feet from the others and stop. Eric motions a "thumbs up" to Dave.

Dave can't keep his eyes off the beast. *What is it,* he thinks, *that makes the sight so compelling?* He watches every slight movement she makes. Her eyes close and she goes to sleep, basking in the sunlight. It's a perfect shot, and Billy expertly takes about one hundred images of her. Dave can hear the slight 'click, click, click' of the camera spinning.

Her aqua feathers are short, as brilliant as a peacock. They run in a circular pattern around her deep-set eyes. Her beak is lacerated with sharp teeth edging out about a third of the way down, ending in a point. Her arms are relaxed, acting as a tri-pod to keep her large body from falling over. With her arms spread a bit, they can see the oval patch of discoloration under each wing. The skin is lighter there. The wings are a deep brownish-purple color. Blue feet and fingers with three-inch sharp claws complete the package.

There is no nest to speak of. The egg sits on hardened granite. It's a perfect oval, cream colored with a speckling of brown spots. Twice the size of an ostrich egg. "I think there may be more. We should move out." Rob remains silent, staring at the beast. "I am in awe, totally and completely."

Pointing to a break in the trees, Malcolm advances and Rob, Z, Isabelle, and Dave follow him deeper into the interior of the island. They stop in mid-stride as the meadow in front of them opens to a large nesting site with clusters of branches, twigs, and bones and several nesting Pterodactyls. There is a low crooning noise coming from the creatures.

Z motions the number "32" with his fingers after he quickly counts the number of birds on nests. Most of them appear to be sleeping. A racket of noise can be heard deeper into the tree line, and Dave moves. "Follow me." He grabs Rob to get him moving. Dave catches Eric's eye and motions for him to join him farther to the right and up a slight embankment. A large boulder blocks their way, and they take shelter to the side of it. A lip on one side of the rock acts as a roof.

"This is a good shelter, as good as any," Malcolm says as he pulls a fallen log over closer to them. "Gather any fist-sized rocks you can find and pile them up here." He snatches several from the terrain. "These trees might give us additional protection."

She clacks her beak, with a response sounding through the trees. Rob nods. "I'm sure there are more, I think a lot more, from the intensity of that sound. We've got to go farther inland."

"I agree, but we stay together. This is too dangerous for us to separate." Dave glances at Rob, briefly surprised at the look of suppressed excitement, almost triumph, on his face.

"Follow me," Rob says as he creeps forward. They follow in a single line, monitoring the sleeping creatures. Billy smears mud on his legs as he walks.

Renee asks, "Why are you doing that?"

"Covering up the smell of me. I don't want to take any chances." Billy wipes a streak of mud on Renee's cheek.

She surprises herself, turning and offering him a second cheek. "Thanks."

The trees thin as more of the rock base appears on the dirt path. Malcolm crouches down and points to his right. Suddenly, a throaty rumble roars up from the depths as another tremor hits. Frigate birds are flying out of a strand of trees and squawk loudly nearby, but they are drowned out by a large commotion coming from over the ridge.

Malcolm says, "I'm almost afraid to look." He holds onto a branch and pulls himself along.

The earth groans again, followed by a jarring blow that knocks most of them down to their knees with intensity. Billy crawls on his stomach. Several of the creatures fly up briefly in the sky, then return to their base. The air becomes even more suffocating, foul-smelling, and rancid. He shakes his head, trying to clear it, and ties a bandana around his head tighter, blocking the smell somewhat.

Dave pulls up next to him and nods. "Slowly, go slowly." They peek over the edge. Dave's words die on his lips as his gaze turns back to Rob. "Holy Shit," he mouths. Dave rolls on his back. For several minutes he lies on the cold damp stone, waiting for the others to catch up.

He inhales slowly, then again, a tremor, perhaps the leaping of his heart, seems to course through him. He rests his hands on his chest, commanding himself to calm.

"Holy shit!" He can't contain his words and wipes his hands across his lips.

A huge nesting colony is spread out before them. Rob moves to a stand of bushes that have drippings of white debris on them. He breaks off a section of a leaf and puts it into a small screw top container. He doesn't take his eyes off the creatures in front of him, a massive collection of Pterodactyls in varying sizes. The largest is a thirty-footer, wing tip-to-wing tip. A few of the young ones, six footers, look in their direction and squawk.

The constant camera clicking is the only sound coming from the team.

Dave struggles to keep his mind focused. *We should never have come. I've put everyone in terrible danger*, he thinks repeatedly. *Have I lost my common sense? This is reckless, irresponsible, dangerous-- on a level he didn't imagine.* He prays to God that he can get them back home safely. Dave motions for everyone to stay down.

After several terrifying seconds, Eric scampers up next to him. He watches the creatures and smiles. "I count about 135. Give or take a few."

"We've got to get out of here," Dave says, slowly. "This is too dangerous." His headache bursts to full-blown as the team does not respond to him. He watches Z move closer to the edge of their cover and reach for a broken eggshell. It's just out of his reach. He uses a stick to move it closer, breaks off a sizeable chunk, and pockets it.

Rob uses his binoculars to zoom in on the eggs the birds sit on. His hands shake noticeably. "Both male and female are sitting on the eggs." He points to a large male gently settling on a clutch of two speckled eggs.

"I'm trying to get my breathing under control," Renee says as she breaks off the strip of a shirt and covers her nose better. "Breath through your mouth." She points to a large mating pair to the side. "Notice that his blue markings flare brighter when he rubs his beak against the female." They all turn to watch the confirmation act.

"Everybody, back to the boats. I don't like our exposure here." Dave slides back down the hill slowly. He looks up to see Billy go over the crest toward the nesting site, away from them. No one else is following. "Shit, shit, shit!" Dave mutters. They watch helplessly as Billy moves several palm fronds in front of him, inching over to an empty nest that holds one shiny creamy-speckled, brown egg. He stands still for a moment and shifts, nervously scooting ever closer, ducking as three Pterodactyls fly overhead. The animals haven't noticed them and land with minor commotion from the flock.

Malcolm points to the clouds and the large thunderhead that is blooming above them. Dave motions frantically for them to follow him. Everyone but Billy and Eric starts back down the hill. Eric stands guard and gestures for them to head down without them.

Dave shakes his head "no" and points to the thunderhead growing rapidly. The wind picks up. Eric looks up to see Billy moving quickly toward him and away from the colony. In seconds, Billy and Eric turn swiftly and slide partway down the rock edge, but they lose their footing and slip on a spray of white waste, throwing them off balance. In what seems like slow motion, they sail over a small cliff and out of everyone's sight. Eric yells, then screams, followed by nothing but silence.

Dave groans and sinks to his knees. Oh Lord, NO. This time.

Rob grabs him by the collar. "Come ON!"

Renee crawls over to the edge without delay. "Eric----" she calls out repeatedly. There is no response.

* * *

Eric awakens to a throbbing at the back of his head. Reaching up, his hand comes back smeared with blood. He feels a cut over his eyelid, his other eye is partially swollen closed. With his fingertip, he pries it open and looks around and winces. A long section of his right leg is burned. His pants are ragged pieces of torn and dissolved fabric, as if scorched by acid. A searing bolt of lightning strikes overhead. He shrinks away from the thunderclap that follows. Rain falls in thick torrents around him.

"Billy," he calls out. "Billy, where are you?"

Eric slowly stands. He finds his defense pole nearby and uses it to support his movements. His back aches and he feels around as best he can to see if there is a wound there, too. Again, his hand comes back smeared with blood. The ground is a mixture of sand and broken fronds. He looks up to the twenty-foot drop he's just fallen from. There is no movement from above. Two large boulders block his path, and he squeezes between them.

Billy lies unconscious on the other side of a large rock. His foot is twisted at an odd angle. He isn't moving.

An advance nearby alerts Eric, and he is relieved to see Rob moving stealthily towards him through a curtain of rain. The rest of the group follows. Eric weakly waves at them before leaning back against the rock. "He's breathing, but I think his foot may be broken," Eric says, motioning to Billy. Isabelle rushes to Billy's side to check him over.

Rob takes Eric into a bear hug. "You scared us to death." Dave hugs them both, struggling with suppressed emotions. He sinks to his knees. "I thought I lost you." He turns and notices the burn on Eric's leg. "Are you okay?"

Eric shrugs. "A bit bruised and some cuts." He motions to his leg and the glob of white goo bubbling on the side of his hiking boot. "That shit ate right into me."

Renee pulls the rest of the fabric away from his leg and looks closely at the wound. A ten-inch stripe of burn runs down his calf. She winces and wipes the goo away from his shoe with a stick. "Sure, you're okay?"

Billy moans as he comes to. He opens his eyes to see Isabelle leaning over him. "Hi, what time is it?" He pauses. "You're pretty." He turns to Renee and says, "You're pretty, too."

Isabelle holds his hand. "You've had a nasty bump on your head, and I think your ankle may be broken. Do you think you can sit up while we check you out?" Billy smiles. "Give me a second." He looks at his foot and frowns. "Whoa, that doesn't look too good." His foot angles off unnaturally.

Eric stands up, a little wobbly on his feet, and looks around. "I'll probably be extra sore tomorrow, but we've got to get off this island."

Dave gives him another hug, finding it hard to release him.

Malcolm walks forward and puts his hand on Eric's arm. "We can't go anywhere with this storm brewing. It would be suicide." He looks up into the rain. "We can only hope that this storm will pass, and the seas will calm, so we can get back to the mainland." He pauses. "This rain is a good cover for us. Why don't we try to move closer to the beach?"

Billy tries to move, but his eyes bulge when he moves his leg. "Yikes, nope. I'm going to need support for my foot." Malcolm observes the trees around until he finds a thick sycamore tree and cuts off a section of bark. In minutes, he is back with a brace and vines to use as ties. "Nature always provides," he says as he drops the material close to Isabelle. She quickly fashions a cast.

"I'll try to be as gentle as possible." Isabelle works quietly as Rob helps support his leg. Her voice quivers as she talks. A shiver runs down her back. *If I focus on doing something, maybe the overwhelming sense of panic will lessen. They don't have to know how completely terrified I am.* When she finishes Billy's make shift cast, she looks over the edge at that mass of creatures below, to a moment of complete white out fear. She took shallow breaths. She lies there next to Dave, on her back, willing her body to fix itself. Her flight instinct is on full alert. It screams, "Run!" over and over. *Is it a panic attack? Yeah, where better to have a panic attack than on a deserted island full of monsters with only a spear to protect myself? Oh, and I can't see anything clearly.* Thankfully, her vision returns a few minutes later.

Z notices a bit of shell hidden in some leaves and walks over, uncovering an unbroken egg. He quickly picks it up and shows it to everyone.

"My egg," Billy exclaims. "You found it!"

Z turns it over, examining it. "I can't believe it isn't broken." He weighs it in his hands. "It's heavier than I thought it'd be. Nothing better for biologicals than an actual egg." His eyes shine with excitement.

"I tried to protect it while we were falling." Billy winces as Rob helps him to his feet.

"Lean on me," Rob says as Billy wraps his long arm across Rob's shoulder. Isabelle supports his other side. Another loud crash of thunder booms above them and they all crouch down in unison.

"This way," says Dave as he helps Eric step over a bush. With his hand still shaking, Eric thinks as he tries to give his dad a re-assuring smile. *"Dad, I'm okay, really."*

CHAPTER 13

The team clusters under a tree near the edge of the canopy. They are all drenched. Their boats bob in the surf nearby. Farther out, the seas are a swirling mass of wickedness. The rain lessens directly overhead.

Malcolm walks to the canoes and looks back over the island. He scans the clouds, then joins the group again. "Should only be another fifteen minutes. The storm is moving to the east, and the seas will calm shortly. I recommend we start heading out now, before the evening shift begins at bird central," Malcolm says, motioning to the colony area. "The tide will be to our advantage."

"I've lost all sense of time," Eric whispers. "How much longer until dark?"

"It's about 5 o'clock now, so we've got a good two hours," Z says, looking at his watch.

"Okay, everybody, we're going to change the pairing." Dave runs his hands through his wet hair and readjusts his hat. "Rob, Malcolm, Isabelle, and Billy in the first canoe. Eric, myself, Z, and Renee in the second." He looks at everyone's face for confirmation. Heads nod. "We are not expecting the injured to paddle. You guys will just be on look-out." Dave helps Billy get onto his good foot. "Come on."

Z fills his pockets with fist-sized rocks as Dave finishes talking. Isabelle grabs stones, then steps into the boat. "Good thinking," she says, looking directly at Z. They all advance to the canoes. Z constantly watches the skies for the predators. He gently places his backpack behind him in the canoe and secures it with one of his stones.

"My heart is racing," Z says as he settles in and picks up his paddle. "We're going to have to pull hard to get through that bit of surf." Dave's team is the first to attack the waves and moves out in front of the rest of them. Renee says, "What's that old saying? I don't have to be fast, just faster than you? We need not be the last on this expedition. Pick up the pace, Z. I believe in you."

With each dip in the surf, Billy grumbles, "Shit!" as his foot is jarred or banged against the side of the canoe. He finally pulls his leg up closer to his chest to keep it from jarring in the waves.

As they reach the edge of the bay and deeper water, they look back and see a handful of Ropen flying away further to the north toward a dot of islands. Eric watches them carefully with his good eye. The thunderhead that passed is massive and now covers a large section of the main island with sheets of purple rain. With each paddle stroke, Ropen Island recedes in the distance. Both canoes pull alongside each other. "How are you doing, Eric?" Isabelle calls out.

"Better than Billy, I guess. My leg hurts like hell, but it's manageable pain. My eye has swollen shut again. I feel like a pirate watching those birds with only one eye. Arghhhh." He does his best pirate imitation for Isabelle.

Isabelle scans the shoreline, noticing that when she stops paddling, her hands are still shaking. She is eager to get to shore, but it's as if their progress is even slower than before. There is nothing distinguishable, along the miles of green hills, in front of them. The beach is still a sliver on the horizon. "Where are we going to pull in, Dave?" she asks.

Malcolm points to an area further away. "It's over there."

Dave pulls hard on his make-shift paddle. "We need to make it back. Come on Renee, show me your muscles." He taunts her efforts that are working well, and, with renewed vigor, she slices her paddle even harder.

A large manta ray moves by one canoe and Renee points to it. "I can't get over how clear the waters are, such a beautiful crystal-blue." The animal stays with them, then turns back toward the open ocean. The battered survivors move in a jagged formation toward the main shoreline. Malcolm's crew takes the lead. Underneath them, majestic seamounts dot the landscape in brilliant color. With each tower, a plethora of animal life circles and dances in the current.

Eric shouts "Incoming" and points to a Ropen moving in their direction. Above the island they just left, now in the distance, dark shapes move and twist in a primitive waltz, oblivious to their audience.

"Shit, everyone, stay down low in your boats and have your poles ready," Dave says with urgency.

Isabelle releases the gun and checks the number of bullets. "That sound may carry for quite a distance over water. Don't use it unless you absolutely have to." Dave grabs his pole and holds on tight. "We don't want the cavalry coming this way."

They watch the creature approach as it circles once above them. This one is mid-sized but still deadly. It cocks its head and cries out one loud screech, bulleting towards them with a speed that surprises them all. Z throws one stone, hitting it on the head. The bird flinches, flapping its wings hard above the water, then lifts off again. Z roars at it, as it climbs. The beast replies with a deep-throated, hurling roar.

Isabelle raises the gun, keeping a close eye on it.

"Not yet, Isabelle," Dave calls out. The bird cries out again, a piercing call that makes them shudder. It circles wider. Isabelle tries to throw rocks at it but misses. It slopes closer to her. At the last second, it turns its head sharply to the right and dives into the sea, making a turbulence of displacement waves as it moves. They watch in disbelief as it catches a manta ray in its beak and breaks the surface again without changing stride. It flies off, back toward the island. The wings of the manta flop back and forth as it struggles in vain in the jaws of death.

"Everybody paddle like crazy!" Rob calls out, as his canoe begins a sprint toward the main island. Everyone follows his double-speed pace. They push hard, as if they are warriors returning from battle. As the depths lighten closer to shore, Dave urges them forward. They are totally exhausted when they finally pull into their abandoned camp. Isabelle and Renee collapse on the beach next to Eric and Billy.

Isabelle rolls to her stomach and sobs into the crook of her arm. Renee rolls over next to her and pats her on the back. "That was pretty intense, wasn't it? A once-in-a-lifetime experience." She keeps an eye on Eric as

Dave moves him to sit under a tree. Beyond, the jungle closes in on them like a twisted cocoon. Tiny shafts of light stab through the dancing shadows in the breeze like a thin stream of smoke rising through the trees. There is a comfort to being back where cover is available.

"Thank God for trees," Isabelle says as her breathing regulates.

Malcolm points to the smoke. "I think I'll check on Grandpa and see if he's got any extras for dinner." He disappears into the jungle. Z, Rob, and Dave joins the team on the sand, as they all breathe heavily.

"By the grace—of God, we all got back here," Z says, between breaths as he kneels with the others.

"He's right, we aren't the Marines. I've got to get medical attention to our crew." Dave pants from the exertion, noticing a line of blisters on his right hand. "How are you two doing?" He turns and looks at Billy. Eric gives him a "thumbs-up" but lies on the sand without opening his good eye. He moans with effort.

Billy's white as a ghost. "Just nobody touch my foot," he says, twice. Swollen and purple-blue, his limb looks painfully un-human. He flinches when Isabelle comes closer.

She checks Billy for a fever. "No fever yet, but it won't be long until he'll spike one. That's a really bad break." She looks over at Dave. "Can we call for a pickup?"

Dave shakes his head. "I don't dare call in a helicopter this close to the nesting island. Can you imagine what would happen if the nest were disturbed?" He pauses. "We're going to have to move farther, away from that island."

Z rummages through his pack and pulls out the map. He spreads it out and uses rocks from his pocket to hold it down, so the wind doesn't take it. He points to a spot on the chart. "We're about here." He looks closer at the illustration. "The islands aren't even on this drawing."

Rob looks it over and marks it with a bit of charcoal from an old campfire. "We need to have Malcolm look at the coordinates. Don't want to get this wrong." Heads nod in agreement.

"There's an old mining station on the coast here." Dave points to a plot. "I don't know if it's still active. Supposedly, there are only two mines still operating on the entire island, after legislation passed years ago. This one is supposed to be closed, but there may be shelter there. I don't know." He looks carefully at the map. "The closest town is where we came in, almost 100 miles back through the brush." From the background, Billy moans, "I can't do that."

Cradling the egg, Z makes a little nest for it with some branches and rocks to hold it secure for now. He takes an old T-shirt out of his pack and wraps it around the oval. "Don't want it to get blown over." He smiles at everyone. "I expected it to be larger."

"I can't believe we got an actual egg." Dave shakes his head. "It's big enough, that's for sure."

"I think it's viable. It's heavy. We can do a nesting by fire tonight and see if anything is visible." Z pats the egg and sits next to Isabelle.

"Let's get into some cover and take a nap," Eric says, sleepily.

"I've got it." Rob walks to the nearest palm and cuts off fronds. He puts the ends into the sand over Eric and Billy. "Everybody go forage, and let's make a shelter for them right here. They need the rest."

In minutes, a teepee of fronds covers Eric and Billy. Z sits nearby. "I'll take watch," he says, as the rest of the group moves to set up camp.

Later that evening by the fire, Malcolm sits, turning the last sweet potatoes into the hot coals. "We are just about ready," he calls out, to the waiting crew.

Dave walks up to Rob. He surprises him by catching him getting ready to check his blood levels. Rob tries to hide it but knows Dave has seen him. "Aren't you going to say something?" Rob asks as he puts the testing gear away.

Dave grabs him gently by the arm. "When were you going to tell me?"

"I didn't know how to tell you?" Rob zips the pack away and turns to Dave. "I got really sick a few years ago, in Cuba." He hesitates. "At one point, they thought I was going to lose my leg. I had all the classic signs: thirst, elevated blood pressure, blurred vision, and a sore on my leg that wouldn't heal." Rob takes a long drink from his canteen. "You know how stubborn we both are about going to the doctor. I'm a bit more stubborn. It got pretty bad. I was in the ICU for a while."

"Why didn't you call me?" Dave probes.

Rob shakes his head. "I was stupid, and embarrassed. My sugar levels were off the charts." He pauses again. "It seemed easier to deny the changes than deal with it. Have you had your levels checked lately?"

Dave watches Rob check his blood with a prick and testing strip. "Do you do that every day? I'm due for my checkup when I get back, but I haven't had issues with blood pressure or sugar levels. You know how bad it was for Uncle Shad. It runs in the family."

Dave takes the canteen from Rob and finishes it. "Not every day, just in stressful situations. Regular medication keeps it under control, plus I lost that weight around my middle. It all helps." Rob pats his stomach. "You could lose a little around the middle too."

Dave stops and asks, "When did this all happen?" Rob flushes red and turns from Dave. "A few years ago."

"WHEN?" Dave's voice is firm.

"Let's not go there, okay? Leave it alone." Rob walks off as Renee approaches with a sweet potato wrapped in a banana leaf. Dave says loud enough for the entire camp to hear, "**WHEN**?" Everyone stops and looks in their direction.

"**When Jeanne died**," Rob says as he walks into the jungle holding his spear. The camp quiets in an awkward silence as they watch Rob disappear into the thicket.

Dave turns to watch Malcolm securing a dozen spiked bamboo poles to the top of a shelter near his hammock. He sits down hard on the sand.

Isabelle moves her bedding underneath the shelter. "Mind if I join you?" she says, in her most perfect English accent. "I can't get that vision of the colony out of my head."

Malcolm smiles. "No worries. Just taking additional precautions. I've been thinking, if they didn't make such a racket with their screams, they'd be the perfect predator. Almost completely silent as they glide through the air." He watches the skies overhead as he talks.

Dave moves to join them for the night. He checks in on Billy's snoring and unrolls his bedroll next to Isabelle. "We've got to get him out of here, and Eric's bruising around his eye is wicked. Did you find the salve for his leg?" he asks calmly now that his temper has subsided. The pain in his chest still bothers him and he stretches to ease the muscles.

"Yes, in that old First Aid Kit. There was some boric acid that I put on it, but it's probably non-effective after all this time." She pauses. "He'll probably have a nasty scar to show for it."

Dave bows his head, and says a little prayer, "We probably need to give thanks for surviving this far." She takes his hand and joins him. Z walks over and wraps his arms around both their shoulders. "Amen," he says, loudly for everyone to hear.

Rob disrupts them from over at his own tent, with a loud outburst. "Damn it!" He slaps the bottom of the tent with his shoe, then throws a dead lizard out of his enclosure. They watch Rob re-secure his tent before he zips his tent flap shut and is down for the night.

"Rob has been going after the unknown since he was a kid. He must have been ten and working on his merit badge, Boy Scout stuff, anyway. We had just returned from a camping trip out in Washington State and heard about some Bigfoot tracks on the police scanner. Dad took us both to the location, and we saw huge bi-pedal footprints in the mud along a river bank. There were these strange groupings of trees in the area, too. I remember seeing a tree that had been uprooted and was now upside down on a stand of trees that were crisscrossed together. Rob was never the same after that." He pauses for a while.

"We've got biologicals, samples, the egg, and video. Everything we'll need to present this as documentation of a new species." Using a stick, he draws the outline of a Bigfoot print in the sand before he stabs it with his stick. "I never wanted to be THAT scientist. I saw what the ridicule did to Rob's reputation."

"Dave, we've got to protect them." Isabelle moves closer and puts her hand on Dave's arm.

"Damn it, I know. Conservationists will go ballistic. The government doesn't have a set conservation plan for raptors, does it? Heck, no country does." Dave looks straight at Isabelle as he brushes off her hand. "This could change a lot of things in the science record."

"It's going to change everything in the science record." Z finishes his drink and heads to his tent.

"The Papua New Guinea isn't the most progressive and they are extremely slow to act on anything. Remember, I'm the plant girl. But I do have connections that I'm sure will help. With our documentation and proof, it will be interesting to see how things go." Isabelle looks up to see Renee walking towards them. She pats the blanket next to her and motions for Renee to join them. She does.

"Hey, well, they are both out cold and snoring." Renee sits next to Isabelle. "I don't think I'm going to get much sleep tonight. Eric's eyebrow is now purple-blue, and he is moaning in his sleep. When I left them, Eric was snuggling up to Billy." She smiles. "They look pretty pitiful."

Malcolm sits up in his hammock. "What's the plan?" Dave nods. "Good question. I think we should head out at first light in the canoes." He hesitates. "To that mining camp."

"I can get thicker bark sleeves for Billy's foot in the morning. It should help with the jostling in the canoe, but we may need to get donations of old T-shirts from the rest of the crew to wrap his ankle." Heads nod in agreement as Malcolm continues. "We've got to keep watch tonight. I know everyone is exhausted."

"Malcolm, how long will it take us to get there?" Renee stretches out and pops her neck. "Might be two days. Depends on the weather." They all watch the blinking of three Pterodactyls out over the ocean. "What about the second nesting site on Umboi Island, the one the couple mentioned? Do you want me to take you there?" Malcolm asks, as Dave watches the creatures heading out to sea.

An exasperated Z walks back over to them. "I'm too hyped up to sleep."

Isabelle shakes her head. "I'm not going back to any nesting site. I didn't say anything, but I was truly paralyzed with fear out there. It took everything I had just to put one foot in front of the other on that island." She hesitates. "I don't think I could do it again. Maybe it was a panic attack? I don't know. I never want to go through that again."

Renee runs her hand through the sand in front of them. "You know, I bet my grandfather would get an elite force together to document anything we need." She looks directly at Dave. "He is going to go nuts when we reveal the footage and specimens. I mean, really go nuts with excitement." She smiles. "I can't wait to see his face."

"You didn't ask, Dave, but he is the reason we got here as quickly as we did. He sent his private plane and a small team of survivalists out to find us when we didn't report back. I don't know how they got there that quickly, probably from the trackers we have?" He rubs her wrist where a small square is revealed under her skin. "I think we were meant to be here with you. Within two hours of your call, we were on the plane racing here. I've never seen Rob move so fast. He talks about you all the time, you know." She pauses, before continuing, "I would appreciate putting in a call to him, back in the states, when the opportunity presents itself. I did promise."

Silence fills the air. Z checks everyone's faces before saying, "The Marines. We need the marines, or Rambo, or someone like that, and a metal submarine to approach an island. Not these flimsy canoes." Z stretches out his hands. "A big ass submarine." He checks his watch. "I'm beat. My heart needs a good rest."

Malcolm nods at him. "I'm taking the first watch. Get some rest. You too, Dave. I'll wake you at two." Everyone disburses for the night without argument.

As the first slivers of light on the horizon glow, Dave shakes the foot of Malcolm, still sound asleep in his hammock. Dave throws a log on the fire, which crackles to life.

His eyes opening quickly. Malcolm is awake in an instant. "Blimey, mate, you scared me to death!" He sits up and rubs his eyes. "Thanks for stoking the fire. Guess I needed those last minutes." Isabelle sleeps undisturbed underneath Malcolm's hammock. One arm is over her face. It is caught in the mosquito netting she had draped over the two of them.

"I'm just glad that we had a relatively quiet night." Dave pours distilled water into a saucepan and puts it over the flames. Rob exits his tent, relieves himself at the edge of the clearing, and joins them. "So, are we leaving?" He rubs his hands together to warm them and stretches. "Did I miss anything?"

"Yes, we are leaving as soon as breakfast is done," Dave says as he throws a mango at Rob. "Go take that to Renee and check on the boys. Be nice. Don't eat it." Rob looks at the mango with desire and almost takes a bite. "Do we have any more?" he says, over his shoulder, as he walks off.

"If you want to go look for them," Malcolm says. He turns to Dave and points at Rob. "Let's make sure he takes first watch tonight."

Rob waves and walks over to the medical bay. Dave and Malcolm can see Renee sleeping between the two men. Somehow, she had elevated Billy's leg, which was now suspended on a rope tied to a tree.

Dave smiles. "I like the way you think," he pauses, "and thanks for helping me save my boy."

Malcolm nods. "No worries, mate."

Later, there is a sudden noise behind them as they sit around the kitchen fire. Rob jerks to attention, nearly tripping. Isabelle pulls her gun. A doe and fawn step out of the shadows, nibbling on green sprouts. The doe looks at them without concern and continues to eat. A collective sigh goes through the crew. "Haven't seen many deer here," Rob comments under his breath as he finishes eating cut pineapple and passion fruit. He throws the last of his breakfast into the brush.

"Help Renee get the boys ready, will ya?" Dave says to Rob, helping Malcolm put out the fire. "Let's get going in ten minutes, everybody," he calls out to the rest of the team. The old native couple watches them leave from the protection of the canopy. They turn and disappear into the jungle without a wave as they step into the canoes.

Eric waves to the couple but sees they have already left. He adjusts himself in the middle of the canoe. "Guess they aren't big on goodbyes," he says, as he motions to the space where they had been. His eyebrow has a deep cut and is inflamed. Yellow-green and blue bruising completes the surrounding palette. "I'm gonna sit facing away from you, so that I can keep watch on our backs."

Watching with a father's concern, Dave winces when he looks at Eric. "Really, how's your eye? Can you see better today?"

Eric squints. "I can see some. Better than yesterday, but that burn on my leg is a little more sensitive. I got some salt-water on it getting into the boat. Stings a bit." He flinches. "Actually, stings a lot." He pulls his hat down and, with his sunglasses, covers up his facial injuries.

Renee settles in beside Eric. She talks to Dave. "The swelling around Billy's ankle is worse today." Billy has elevated his foot, propping it up on the side of the canoe. It is wrapped in an old T-shirt. Dave watches Isabelle encourage Billy to lie down and rest. He slowly leans back out of view as the boats move down the coast.

"As soon as we're far enough away, I can call in the heli." Dave looks toward the island and sees several black dots on the horizon riding thermals over the island. "Let's move."

The team makes progress keeping close to the bay. Thankfully, the water is calm and glassy for most of the morning. After five hours of pushing hard, Dave motions for them to head onto the beach. They pull into an area with a long stretch of thin beach. A spiny anteater watches them approach and continues to dig into an insect mound.

"Let's take a half an hour break, stretch our legs." Dave watches the beach with alarm as a flock of birds leave the canopy all at once. "What do you think, Malcolm?" he calls out.

"Let me go check." Malcolm grabs his machete and heads into the brush. A second stream of birds exits back in the canopy, followed by the howl of dogs.

"That doesn't sound reassuring," Isabelle says, moving closer to the boats.

Billy pipes up as he lies on the beach. "Those are singing dogs. They are native. Man, I wanted to get photos of them." He pauses and closes his eyes. "You know, more like a dingo."

Isabelle plops down next to him. Dave joins them. "How are you feeling?" he asks, as he looks at Billy's twisted foot.

"Already tiring of people asking me that question." He covers his face, draping it with an extra T-shirt. "I can't look down. It makes me sick to my stomach." This trip had been his dream, but never in the dream did he have an injury like he had now. That was never part of the plan. What other beautiful shots would he miss, now that he was out of commission? *I can still take photos if they would prop me upright, couldn't I? Or maybe they could get me in a bed next to Drew? With a cute nurse? Yeah, that wouldn't be bad. And something to knock the dreams out of my head.* He had horrible nightmares last night, so gut wrenching that he could only remember snippets of it all, a Ropen tearing his insides out. He was still alive as it ate him.

"We're moving farther down the coast, so we get clear of the Ropen nesting, then we'll call for a heli. I'm going to go look for mangos. Think you could eat one?" Dave smiles at him with encouragement. Billy nods. "Yeah, they sit good in my stomach." He leans up and looks at his leg again, wincing in pain.

"Sorry, I know we're all tired, but we're more than half-way there. And the storms aren't building on the horizon. We can get there by dark." Dave looks out as Malcolm emerges from the foliage holding in his hand a dead creature by its tail.

Dave says, to Billy, "Look, the drive-through is open. I'll have a burger ready for you shortly. Just rest. I'll go talk to Malcolm and see how things look. You're doing great, kid."

Rob lights the campfire. He smiles as Dave approaches. "I'm getting good at this. Guess my merit badge work wasn't a waste of time." "Yeah, but we're only staying for lunch, then we're back on the road. Your fire doesn't have to be perfect." Dave's words make Rob stop re-arranging the rocks encircling the flames.

Behind them, Malcolm skins a wallaby. Dave turns his back on the chef's preparations with the first hard whack of the machete. "Hey

Malcolm, we'll just wait here while you get lunch prepared. Do you want me to peel potatoes or something?" Rob grimaces as he watches Malcolm.

Dave turns just as a long rope of intestines is pulled out of the wallaby. He quickly turns back around. "Guess I shouldn't have looked."

"If you two will do a walkabout for mangos, that'd be great. But stay together. I don't want to go looking for you. Give it a good American try. Be back in forty-five minutes. Renee has a bag you can use." Malcolm points to Renee, who is sound asleep next to Eric. Rob shakes his head. He grabs his backpack and empties it on the ground.

"Hey, don't wake her. We'll make do." Rob straps a bowie knife to his leg, saying, "Be on the lookout."

"No shit, Sherlock." Dave chuckles and Rob joins him as they step away from the camp.

"So, our first excursion together." Rob breaks a branch, allowing Dave more room.

"Our first excursion *in years*." Dave corrects him. He watches the canopy for movement. "I'm a little jumpy. Guess my nerves are still on edge after the island."

"So, wanna talk about it?" Rob continues ahead on the trail they are making. There is a long pause before Dave responds.

"What do we say? This whole thing has been overwhelming." Dave checks a branch for fruit, but there is nothing worth taking. Silence flows between them like at an awkward family reunion dinner party. He steals a glance at Rob through the branches and thinks, *how much older does he look now?* He notices the first age spot is on the back of his left hand. *Strange how men don't normally notice things like that. Jeanne would have noticed right away with her eagle eyes.*

"Let's start with an easier conversation." Rob turns and holds out his hand. "Peace- Bury the hatchet?"

Dave stops, closes his eyes, and when he opens them, he accepts the handshake. "Don't do anything stupid." He squints. "Sorry, it just slipped out. Let's do that again. Peace." He says as they shake again.

"Better. Now, for the immediate need. I'm worried about Billy. I think we should call the medivac." Rob looks right at him, before turning down the trail. He checks his watch. "I know, but I'm hoping we can get to the mining camp, call for the evac, and then have them show up first thing in the morning." Dave breaks off a branch that swings in his direction. "Eric's eye doesn't look good either. Think we should urge him to go, too?"

"Good luck getting him to go into the helicopter. He told me last night that he wants to set aside time to work on the biologicals from the Ropen." Rob stops and turns back toward Dave. "He's hooked, you know. Ain't no way he's leaving. Probably all my fault." Rob gives him a guilty look.

The snap of a branch sounds in the distance ahead. Rob and Dave both stop mid-stride. Rob unstraps his knife and pulls it from the sheath. A strand of bamboo is on one side and with one step, Rob slices it into a stalk and hands the new spear to Dave. "In under 10 seconds," he winks, whispering to Dave.

"Impressive. Have you been practicing that move for a while.... in your head? Johnny Quest would be proud." Dave smiles. "Might be some of those dingoes that Malcolm mentioned earlier?" Rob turns and holds up his hand for quiet as a snort echoes from ahead on the trail. Both men crouch down and move stealthily through the brush. An Axis buck steps out. It stands at alert, its massive rack blending into the landscape. The animal is agitated and hooves the ground with a stomping motion. The deer looks into the thicket of bamboo off to their right, as a trio of wild dogs snarls in the depths.

"Shit." Dave moves in closer to Rob as he grips his spear with a death grip.

The stag snorts loudly and runs in the opposite direction of the canines. It's off like a bullet with the dogs tight on its heels. In seconds, the woods return to silence with only needles of barking echoing in the distance.

Rob stretches and pounds his spear into the dirt a few times. He watches and listens for a moment before walking on. Aren't you gonna say something, about that?" Dave asks as he leans on his pole.

"Not much to say. At least we know there are Axis deer out here. They're good eatin'." Rob licks his lips as he watches for the deer to return. "Would be nice if they chase him back this way."

"Yeah, but I don't want to battle those dogs. Did you see the teeth on that black one?" Dave nods. "Kind of reminds me of Blackie. He was a clever dog."

Rob grins and points to a tree. "I think that may be a mango tree. Let's check it out."

Dave smiles as they approach the base of the tree. "Eureka, we've found the mother-lode." The tree is loaded with yellow mangoes. The ground is filled with rotten fruit and a swarm of flies.

Rob kicks a mango aside to see a pile of wild boar scat. He gets some of it on his shoe. Rob mentions, "Watch where you step." He opens his backpack and loads up the bag with hanging fruit from above. "Make sure they are a little soft. Don't get the hard ones. They aren't ripe enough." Dave tests several of the large fruits.

"Picky, picky. Hey, do you remember when we fed Blackie all those peaches?" They both laugh. "That dog had the runs for a week." "Poor boy." Dave giggles as he adds the last mangoes to the bunch. "I think that'll about do it. Time to head back."

"Think you know the way?" He pats the bag as he zips it closed. "What ever happened to Blackie when I went to college? I don't remember."

Rob frowns. "Don't ask."

"What do you mean, don't ask? Come on man, forty years have passed. It's not gonna matter." Dave urges him on. "I think I can handle it." "Really, you won't get upset?" Rob says, as he points down the trail and to the way out.

"Yeah, I can handle it." Dave tosses a mango up in the air, grabs it, and takes a big bite.

"I accidentally ran him over coming home from a party." Rob turns back and shrugs.

Dave stops in his tracks.

"Seriously, you knew how I felt about him. I've never had a dog as great as he was." Dave holds the mango he had been eating in his hand, looks at it for a second, and then throws it at the back of Rob's head, where it explodes into a slimy mess. "Asshole! That's for Blackie!"

Rob turns again. This time, his face is red with rage. "I'm going to give you a pass on that one, but don't push me again. We're all on the edge. The past is in the past. Guess you couldn't handle it after all." He sneers at Dave and heads to the camp, adding, "The dingoes can have you." Dave grumbles behind him.

In minutes, they are back in camp. Rob walks over to the kitchen area, dumps the mangos, and walks directly into the surf to clean up.

Malcolm raises an eyebrow when he sees the steam coming off Dave, as he unloads his fruit.

"Don't ask," Dave says, as he turns and sits on a log by himself. Out of the corner of his eye, he watches Billy sleep, Isabelle with her obvious concern over his care, and Rob who is dunking under the water and cleaning off.

"Great, just great," Dave mumbles. He berates himself with strong inner dialogue over his leadership abilities and walks to the water's edge, where he strips down to his boxers and dives in.

CHAPTER 14

The afternoon sun beats down on them as they try to paddle with smooth strokes. Z checks uncovers the lab samples and checks on the egg nested in with the gear. He watches Isabelle carefully apply sunscreen to Billy and covers him back up with a re-wetted t-shirt. His fever is spiking. They can all hear his teeth chattering. The crew paddles, keeping the dugouts hugging the shoreline, all the while with an eye on the sky. Without Billy's upbeat comments, their progress is silent and focused. Dave is in his own world. He strokes his paddle with a fierce intensity that says everything.

The truth of Rob's words hit Dave afresh. Rob killed Blackie. That all happened about the time he met Jeanne and fell head over heels in love with her on their first date. He should have paid more attention to the story about Blackie when went home for Christmas that year. Dad had been evasive when he asked about Blackie. He remembered that now; they didn't even tell him when it happened. But Dave had loved that dog with an intensity that made people smile when they saw them together. Before college, the dog was always with him. During his first semester, Dad would call him and put the phone out for Blackie so that he could hear Dave's voice and howl a response. They all laughed hard at that. And Blackie was smart. Smarter than most humans.

Finally, Dave comes out of a fog as Eric calls out to him, "Dad, can you take it down a notch?" Dave stops paddling and looks over at Eric. The bruising of his eye and cheek shows along the edge of his sunglasses. It's turning blue. Dave nods.

"It would be appreciated. I can't keep up with you much longer." Z rests his paddle across his knees. He breathes heavily as he tries to get in more air. "Just don't kill me, okay?" Without waiting for a response from Dave, he turns and checks on his egg balanced among dirty laundry at the end of the canoe.

Z asks, "How much farther do you think, Malcolm?"

Malcolm stops paddling for a moment. "I'm guessing, about an hour. Those clouds are building on the horizon. We'll be in for rain tonight."

Isabelle scans the sky with her viewers. "All clear above." She passes the binoculars to Billy, who motions to see, but all that comes out in response is a deep moan as he accepts the lenses. She wets his foot to cool him off. "Maybe I should dangle it over the side," Billy says as he moves to get more comfortable. "A croc could take a bite out of it and put me out of my misery."

"Let's put things in perspective, Billy," Eric calls to him. "You just secured the best bad-ass story on the planet. No one is going to top you when you tell them about breaking your leg as you ran away from Pterodactyls! Think about it! Every chick on the planet is going to want to talk to you! That's gotta count for something as you move forward in healing. Keep thinking about that!"

"Thanks, Bro," Billy says, with a hint of a smile on his lips before the next pain wave hits him.

Rob hydrates, closes the cap and nods to the others. "Let's keep going. We could find the site around the next curve." He slathers up with more sunscreen.

The group takes off again and floats past an inlet with a trio of large salt-water crocs sunning themselves on the beach. Everyone watches them closely. Billy moves his foot inside the boat as the team paddles past. The crocs don't move.

Malcolm points to a fresh-water stream nearby. "Everyone good for water?" Isabelle shakes her head. "You aren't considering going ashore to get water with those crocs so close, are you?"

He shrugs his shoulders. "They won't bother me. I know how to move on land. The breeze is coming from the other direction. That's important to remember on this journey." Malcolm nods as he returns to paddling.

"Good to know," she says.

Renee looks to Isabelle. "Good information to remember."

"Malcolm, could you give us a new safety meeting after dinner tonight? Now that we've been out in the wild for a while, we see things a bit differently than when we first started. Maybe it will help ease some of this tension," Dave asks, across the water.

Looks are exchanged between the members, knowing that Dave is causing some of that tension. The waters calm around them, making paddling easier.

"Sure thing, mate. Hey, I think I see an electric pole on the horizon?" Malcolm points east. Everyone looks. Isabelle uses binoculars with the best zoom, focusing into the distance while also scanning the carpet of green tree tops for more Ropen.

"Yes! It's there. Civilization!" Excitedly, she hands the viewers to Billy. "Hold on, we're almost there." They all paddle with renewed strength.

The station sits on a coral reef in a shallow bay. As they get closer, they notice the area's state of dis-repair. The dock juts out into the bay about forty feet—past the coral reef. A twenty-by-twenty building is at the end of the dock with a small decking area. A broken piling causes part of the dock to slope down into the water. The dock looks like it hasn't been used in years.

On land, there are four small cabin-like back at the tree line. A pile of cut palms lies on one side of the area. No one is about. In the distance, behind the huts, a cleared area can be seen. "OMG, I've got to get over there and check out that field. I think we've found a test site." Agitated now, Isabelle strokes her paddle straight to the dock. She is the first to touch the old wood.

Dave and Rob come in behind her. "Wait, let me check the sturdiness of the dock," Rob calls out as he steps first onto the dock. The rest of the crew holds on to one piling. He walks gingerly over to the door to the shack and opens it. A pelican flies out, scaring him. They hear him yell.

Dave sits on the dock, gets up, and takes a step toward him. "Rob, you, okay?"

Rob runs out of the doorway, brushing off his pants and looking a little embarrassed. "Nothing like getting scared to death in a dark room. I thought a baby Pterodactyl was coming at me! All I saw was that beak!" Renee laughs, saying, "Come on, that's funny." No one else laughs. They look at her. "Well, I thought it was funny. Can we get out?" she asks.

Rob jumps up and down a few times, checking the sturdiness of the dock. "I guess it's okay." Dave grabs some of his gear and places it on the deck. "Everyone sit tight a moment. You can start piling the gear beside the boats. Let's get Billy inside and out of the sun. Z, you set up the electronics on the beach. We need to get that heli coming asap."

Rob opens a modest-sized outside closet door of the building where he finds a small, rusted generator that's covered in spider webs. "Baby generator here–maybe we can get it going?"

Eric walks over next to Rob. "Dang, I'll look, but it's gonna be with one eye."

Dave pats him on the back. "No, you go inside and get out of the sun. Hydrate, you still look puny." Dave points to the hut.

"I'm not puny," Eric says as he turns and walks inside the shelter where they've already laid Billy on a table. Isabelle carefully lifts Billy's leg onto a bundle to get it elevated. She presses her palm on Billy's forehead. He is sweating profusely. "I think your fever is even higher than it was. Can you drink some more?" she asks.

Billy nods. "Just no one touch my foot for a bit, okay?"

Dave grabs his pack and walks toward the beach. One section of the dock walkway leans into the water. He jumps over that section, then makes it to land. He walks over to Z, who has made a makeshift desk out of two palm trunks. Dave helps him hang a tarp over the equipment. "How's the gear and the samples?" Dave asks, while reaching the higher ties. "I should have asked after you dug it up back there."

"So far, good. I've got it charging for that call now. Should be ready to go in about twenty minutes. Glad to be back on land, but we're awfully close to those crocs. Malcolm has already gone searching for dinner. You could start making the fire pit. What do you think about over there?" Z points to a cluster of rocks. "I'll let you know when we're ready to transmit."

Dave clears the area that Z suggests, setting rocks in place. He takes stock of their surroundings as he works. "Looks like they've cleared several acres back there." He motions with his head to a distance behind them as Rob approaches.

"Yeah, they've planted and cleared quite a bit. I'm sure Isabelle isn't going to be pleased. Think I'll dig a second fire pit over there close to that open area. We've got to set up an area for the heli to land. Probably gonna rain hard again tonight."

Rob frowns. "Maybe a bonfire instead? Bet those logs will burn well," Rob says, then walks over to look at the wood.

Dave hesitates as he watches Z wince with pain in his shoulders. He calls out to Z, "Sorry about going all out on the boat today. Hope you won't be too sore." He gives Z a hopeful look as Rob gets started on the bonfire area.

Z gives Dave a half-hearted smile. "I think my arms might turn to jelly tonight." He stretches his shoulder. "This might be my last excursion out into the wild. I'm getting too old for this stuff. My muscles are screaming and the muscles under them are screaming even louder. Lots of joint cracking going on, too." He continues to stretch and holds onto his lower back.

"I know what you mean. My brain doesn't keep up with the way I feel. It keeps telling me to do stuff. I will pay for it afterwards." Dave finishes the digging and looks for rocks to encircle the opening of the firepit.

Wiping down the electronics, Z also briefly turns on each unit's switches. He glowers at the main satellite phone, willing it to charge faster. "Guess that's all part of the aging process. But I know it gets worse if I stay too inactive too. It's a sharp-edged knife, anyway you slice it." Z blows off a layer of sand from all the gear. "It's been killer keeping the gear clean out here."

Dave finishes the area surrounding the firepit and looks up to see Isabelle walking his way. She frowns as she looks at the pile of palms stacked by some rusted equipment. A garbage pile of remains from processed fruit is piled next to it. He follows her and tries to spare her feelings from the explosion that he knows is coming. "Izzy---!"

She stops when she gets to the cleared land and SCREAMS. It reverberates throughout the area, echoing off the mountainside. A flock of birds flies off from the tree line. She has daggers in her eyes as she turns to Dave. "Do you know what this means? When they come in an annihilate acreage, they change the eco-system. It affects everything. Pollution, slave labor, land grabs." She paces in her anger.

Birds circle above them, including a large Harpy Eagle.

"Looks pretty organized, doesn't it?" Dave reaches down and picks up a discarded palm root. Rob comes running towards them with his knife out. Dave motions that it's okay and Rob joins them. "She's letting off steam." Dave watches her pace.

Rob stops. He scans the area. "Dang, that's pretty messed up. Looks like they left equipment behind, too." He points to a rusted shredder in one corner of the field. They walk towards it. Isabelle stops when she finds a carcass of a spiny anteater left to rot. A tear falls down her cheek. She wipes it off, smearing dirt across her face.

Rob and Dave take their time walking to the machine. It's large, about the size of a Volkswagen Beetle. Heavy, thick cutting blades lean down into the soil. Dave slides into the driver's seat and slides right back out. "What do you think?" Dave asks, as he opens up the engine compartment. "It might help get the generator going? You were always better at that sort of thing," he says, looking over to Rob, hopeful. "There's a little shed over there. Might have more equipment in it?"

"I'll look at it after we get settled. Lots to do in a little time," Rob replies.

Dave closes the cover and walks back toward camp saying, "I'll join you. Hopefully, Z's ready for a transmission." He puts his arm around Isabelle as they all walk back towards camp.

She brushes off his arm as they approach camp. "I'm fine. Its gotta be a testing site. Too small to be anything else. But thank you." She turns and walks away from him without looking back.

Dave collects some large limbs for a bonfire, and Rob drags one out as well. They leave divots in the sand as they move closer to the water. "Hey, we should use the palm logs. Bet they are loaded with oils and they're right there." Rob points to the stack and walks over, returning with one skinny log. "I haven't done this in a long time. Didn't the Aggies dig a big hole first, then stack the wood from there? What do you think?" Dave looks at the logs. "You game for making our own Aggie bonfire?"

"Gig 'Em." Rob smiles, leans forward, and puts effort into a louder version of "Gig 'Em!"

Isabelle frowns as she watches them from the edge of the dock ramp. She motions for them to be quiet before walking toward the shed.

Dave mumbles, "Guess we need to build quietly," as they place the wood into the pit. He scans the camp, listening to Z make the transmission for aid, and smiles with relief. Rob brings over vines, so they tie the trunks together in a teepee format, but the trunks keep slipping. Frustrated, Dave takes a section of the rusted chain he found over by the equipment, and they adjust the last pieces tightly, securing it all. When they finish, the bonfire ceiling is almost nine feet tall.

Rob wipes his brow. "Glad the heli is coming." He steps back to admire their work. Dave adds brush for kindling at the base. "Great idea. Aggies around the world are applauding our effort." They sit beside the pile and share a canteen of water. The jungle sounds float around them as Malcolm steps out onto the beach from a shield wall of thick vegetation. He holds a skinned carcass in one hand.

"Wonder what it was?" Rob asks, as he and Dave look around.

Out at the dock, Renee sits and fishes with a cane pole. She catches something and laughs as Eric tries to help her bring it in. She pulls hard on the pole and the fish goes flying, knocking him in the chest. He catches it and holds it up like a trophy. Rob points the fish catch out to Dave as they continue to rest. They both laugh together. Rob says, under his breath, "Nice to hear you laugh again."

Dave silently acknowledges that. He turns and warily watches the skies as storm clouds increase in intensity on the horizon. He raises one eyebrow at Rob. "Kinda like the calm before the storm."

* * *

As the sun dips lower on the horizon, Malcolm walks into camp with two huge, dead, coconut crabs. They each measure two feet across. He holds them up for Rob and Dave to see. His muscles strain with effort. "Whoa! That's some mighty fine eatin' there!" Rob exclaims as he runs over. "Never seen crabs that big before!" Rob follows Malcolm to the prep area, where he drops them.

Malcolm looks over his shoulder at Rob. "Come on, you can help me carry the rest of them." Rob scurries behind him. "Rest of them?" he says as he walks into the jungle. Dave pulls one up and gives it a close examination. "Dang, that's impressive." He turns when Isabelle walks by and says in his best English accent, "Got any butter on you?" She smiles and continues out to the dock.

Several minutes later, he follows her. "Didn't mean to make you uncomfortable back there." She shrugs her shoulders. "No problem. Just needed to let off steam, you know. And maybe a good dose of stress. I'm still thinking about that nesting site." She shudders.

They enter the shack on the dock. Billy dozes, leaning back against the wall. His wet clothes cling to his body. Eric and Renee are lying next to him. Eric has a wet T-shirt folded over his eyes and has dozed off, but Renee is still awake. She quietly gets up. "Shush, they both finally fell asleep. Have they made the call?" She motions for them to walk with her, back outside of the hut.

"Yeah, Z nodded it went through. I don't know how long it will be. We've got the beginnings of a bonfire set up to help vector them in. Did you get Billy to drink more?"

She watches Billy from the doorway as they whisper. "He finished the last of the canteen and we are out of anything viable from the First Aid Kit. It's only going to get worse for him. Eric is doing better, though. Thankfully, his injury is closer to bone than eye socket." She eyes the fish she caught earlier. "I've got dinner covered."

Dave grins at the fish. "Pretty impressive, but Malcolm has pulled in some HUGE coconut crabs." He rubs his stomach.

She shakes her head. "No thanks, I'll have plantains and yams, but you're welcome to the fish. It's starting to really attract the flies. Could you take it back to the kitchen?" Isabelle comes in after wetting a T-shirt and wringing it out.

"I'll take over for a bit, if you'd like a break?" Isabelle whispers to Renee, who follows her. Both women look at the injured men and sigh.

"No, I'm fine," Renee stands at Eric's feet, watching him sleep. "Could you get more water? She hands Isabelle the water canteen, she nods, throws the strap over her shoulder, and starts walking out. "Do you think Malcolm's back yet? I don't want to do any exploring for fresh water with those crocs so close," she says as she passes Dave.

Dave scans the tree line on shore, looking for Malcolm before looking back to the dock. Isabelle hops over the broken planking. Below him, movement catches his eye under the dock as a large barracuda takes shade there. He turns back to Renee. "I'll take the fish off your hands." He walks back, holding the dead fish by the tail.

Renee observes Dave's navigation down the dock, now swaying more than it was earlier. The enormous eye of the barracuda focuses on her, and its large, toothy grin makes her shudder. She stomps on the decking, frightening the fish away. But, in the evening light, she can still see its eyes on her as it moves back into the shade under the hut.

Back on shore, Z checks an array of gauges. He lowers his eyes to the small display screen and watches the meter. He takes off his headphones when Isabelle approaches. "What's the news?" she asks as she kneels down next to the log he is sitting on.

"Got sand in every nook and cranny. It's a wonder that it's working at all. But the copter is being readied. Hopefully, it will be here in about two hours. Might be closer to three." He smiles at her with a nod of his head and covers part of the equipment from the wind. The egg is carefully wrapped in two T-shirts and nestled in a small hole by the workstation. He touches it as he moves past.

"You doing, okay?" He pats the log next to him and moves over, making more room for her. Isabelle joins him.

"Guess I'm a little wired. I haven't slept much since we left the nesting site. You don't have any Xanax do you?" She holds out her palm, which shakes slightly. "I hope it's mostly sleep related." He shakes his head "no." He looks to the clearing behind them. "It's the palm acreage, isn't it?"

"Makes me so mad, I might have an adult outburst, so incredibly mad. It's greed, nothing but greed," Isabelle says, "but I think I also have a heavy dose of exhaustion.

"My tent is right there. Go ahead. Take a nap. I'll stay right here so you won't be bothered." He smiles at her and pats her on the leg.

"Really? That would be wonderful. What about those huts? Have you checked them out?" She gets up and opens the door to one. The door hangs partially loose on one side. An old army cot is inside with a crate, for a table, beside it. 'Homey," she says, deadpan.

They hear Rob exclaim, "EUREKA!" from somewhere in the area behind them as lights flicker from strung lights weaving through the trees to each hut. In rotation, the lights continue on the way out to the hut on the dock. They watch Renee exit the hut and look around excitedly. She gives everyone a "thumbs up" before returning inside.

In moments, Rob walks through the opening in the foliage with one large coconut crab smiling ear to ear. "I found the master switch."

Dave pats Rob on the back. "Great job!."

* * *

Over four hundred miles away, at a small warehouse encampment across the island, lights flicker on a display panel for JVO International. It goes unnoticed for several minutes, as Jessica checks her phone screen and works through a pile of emails on her double computer screen monitors. Her fingers fly across the keyboard efficiently. The other two desks only have one monitor and are staffed by two locals in their thirties.

A window panel next to her overlooks men busily working in a warehouse filled with racks of equipment and supplies. They use forklifts as they move products onto trucks. The men in the office with Jessica banter between themselves. "Gonna go to Hickima Beach this evening. Having a barbeque with the guys. You guys wanna join us?" Willie looks over at Jessica with hope.

She shakes her head and finishes emailing. She hears a low BEEP and looks around her desk. It sounds again before she looks up at the display board and the blinking light there. She walks over to it and taps the light once. It BEEPS again. "Huh?" she says as she grabs a manual from the top of the filing cabinet and returns to her desk.

Willie walks over and inspects the board while Jessica flips through the pages. She scrolls through data lines. "What's the last four digits again? 5654?"

Willie gets close and takes off his glasses to see better. "Yeah, 5654."

"That's Station 54. It's been closed for six years. Why is it alerting?" She looks through more data on Station 54 and turns the page, reading more. The alarm BEEPS again. "How do we turn it off? You guys know? They both shrug their shoulders.

Jessica slams the binder closed, hard, and pushes back her chair. She takes a deep breath. "God, going to tell Barker." She bats her eyes at Willie. "You wouldn't like to go tell him for me, would you, Willie?"

He quickly returns to his desk, averting his eyes. "Nope." Both men type on their keyboards. "Got this report to get in tonight."

Jessica stands and pops her neck before returning the binder. The alarm BEEPS. She switches several buttons on the main board. The beeping stops, but the light continues to flicker. She turns to the guys. "Wish me luck." She turns and walks down the hallway, stopping in front of a door. She knocks. A booming voice on the other side says, "Come in."

Jed Barker, an ex-pat from the states, sits behind a leather covered desk. His muscles bulge tight in his shirt, showing a massive developed chest. He looks up, surprised to see Jessica. "Jessica, you have the oil report ready?" He looks her up and down, then returns to his keyboard. She feels naked standing before him. Most of the time, he looks only at her chest.

"No, sir. I'll have it for you tomorrow afternoon, but I wanted to bring something to your attention. We've had an alert at Station 54."

He looks over to a large map on the wall of Papua New Guinea. It has an array of colored push pins scattered over the map. "54? Isn't that over on the south side?" She nods and points to a spot on the map. "Maybe it's just someone checking out the site." He frowns at her. "Get me a live satellite feed, NOW!"

She is startled but moves to his keyboard and types the commands. She zooms in when she pulls up the location. He pushes her hand aside when he sees people there.

"What? Those are white-skinned people, and women?"

"Looks like four, no, make that five." She points to a figure coming out of the tree line.

Baker scans and looks for boats in the bay. He zooms in on their canoes.

"Canoes? They look pretty primitive. Get me information. I want to know who they are and what they are looking for. Why are they there? Do we have anyone in the area?"

She shakes her head. "Closest is Bogata Bay. Maybe eight hours away by sea."

He continues to scan the area. "I don't see any equipment. Why are they in canoes?"

"Sir, the link costs fifteen-thousand dollars a minute." She looks at him.

He slowly looks up. "I don't care what it costs. Get someone down there, NOW!" She backs up, says, "Yes, sir," and quickly exits the room.

CHAPTER 15

The sun sets in majestic streaks of orange and pink feathering across the sky. Large purple clouds move off to the east on the horizon, close to Ropen Island. Z remains vigilant beside the radio. Behind him, a pile of crab carcasses is stacked. Sitting across from Z, Dave pats his stomach. "Now, that was good eatin'." Dave looks at the mess.

Rob picks up a plank board and walks over to Malcolm. "I'll dig a trash hole. You did enough for the day. Put your feet up." A contented Rob smiles and takes the body cavity of one large crab with him. "Or do you think we should use them for something else?" Malcolm sets up his hammock and turns back to Rob. "No, go ahead mate, they'll be stinking up the place pretty quickly." Malcolm's worn and scarred feet face the men. They have all the pit marks of a moon landing.

Rob shakes his head as he takes in the detail of Malcolm's feet. *How in the world could he let his feet look like that? They are past rough and scarred, more like looking at something you'd find in a horror movie set's back lot. Would a manicurist scream if he sat down at her station?* He looks at his own sandaled feet. *I'm definitely displaying feet that need some love, too. I've only had a pedicure twice in my life. Guess it's time when we get back? Maybe even a good massage.*

Dave fills his arms with empty crab legs and follows Rob. As they get a distance away, Dave turns back to look at Malcolm. "Did you see his feet? They are pretty rough. Closest thing I've seen to troll feet."

"Wonder if he ever played baseball or soccer? You ever seen ball-player feet? They break most of their toes. Another reason I wasn't a player." Rob stops and surveys a section of sand. "I think this is as good of a place as any." He makes his first strike into the sand with the board. Dave watches for a moment until Rob stops and looks at him.

"Well, go get the rest of the mess. Don't just stand there watching me." Dave gives a smirk of a smile and returns to the kitchen trash pile as Rob digs. In minutes, they've dumped all the carcasses into the hole and covered it up. When they finish, they both scan the clear skies above. Out on the dock, Renee stands and watches the horizon. Both the men watch her for a moment. Dave pats Rob on the shoulder as he walks past.

"Let's get back. I want to stay close for the heli. He did fantastic with that one," Rob says, as he nods at Renee. "Yeah, I noticed. All I can think of is how much Jeanne would have loved to meet her. I remember her running up to me in the kitchen when we got a postcard from one of their first trips together. She was so excited that he had found someone that matched his spirit of adventure." He sighs and walks to the kitchen area where they find Z slowly walking around the fire, cradling the egg.

"Aha! They've returned. It's time to check whether 'CHESTER' is alive." He holds up the adorned egg for everyone to see. "We need the light to dim just a bit more, I think."

Dave looks at him. "You named.. the egg, Chester?"

"Sure, why not?" Z carefully holds the egg close.

Malcolm smiles from his hammock while Isabelle sits on a log near him.

"Any word on the heli?" Dave walks over to the equipment area, but before he can flip a switch, Z stops him. "Don't touch! And no updated ETA since the last time you asked ten minutes ago. They'll get here when they can." Z holds the egg out in front of the fire. An image of a dark curled up embryo is revealed inside the shell. Z turns it slightly and the object moves.

"AHA! Outstanding! We have a viable egg!" Z does a little dance, but carefully puts the egg down, and then explodes into a dance celebration. He pulls Isabelle up and she joins him. They are both laughing and dancing when Eric walks up and asks, "I could hear you all the way out there. Is the heli close?"

Z claps Eric on the back and answers in a song. "We have a viable embryo!"

Eric looks at the egg and carefully lifts it. He moves it so that it is backlit by the fire and examines the creature inside. He continues to turn it while everyone watches.

"I've named him CHESTER. Of course, if it's female, I'll name her...." He looks at Isabelle and kisses her on the cheek. "IZZY! I'm just so excited!"

Eric carefully wraps the edge of a T-shirt around the egg. He puts it back in the nest. "Glad I went over the edge to save her, but it's really Billy's doing. He's really getting uncomfortable out there." Eric looks at the equipment. "Any news?"

Dave looks up at him. "Not yet. We're waiting and watching, just like you. I know you don't want to go with him, but you should get your eyes checked out. Don't have any spare ones to give you." He smiles at his son with a hopeful expression on his face.

"I know, but my vision is almost back 100%. It looks bad but doesn't hurt like before. I'll get it checked out once we're back, promise. Keeping my shades on helps. Do you think we should light the big fire?" He eyes the tall bonfire stack nearby. Rob looks over to Dave, who nods. "Yeah, fire it up!"

Eric nods and pulls a burning stick from the kitchen fire. Rob and Dave follow him to the stack, and he lights the wood. It goes up in a WHOOSH as the palm oil lights. They stand back several feet because of the intense heat. Eric puts on his sunglasses. Rob smiles at the construction and looks over to Dave. "Do you remember daring me to light my cigarette on the Aggie Bonfire? I worked hard on that project."

"I'll feel so much better once we get him onboard." Dave is distracted. "What did you say?"

"Never mind, I agree. Our focus needs to be on Billy." Rob turns back toward the pier. On the water line in the distance, about fifty feet offshore, is a pair of reflective eyes. He points to them. "See those eyes out there? Probably one of those crocs! What else do we have to deal with?"

"I'll let everyone know, especially Malcolm. He might know how to get rid of them." Dave walks over to Malcolm while Rob and Eric stay by the fire.

Eric looks back at Rob, saying, "Really don't want to go back out on the pier. It's getting ricketier and one misstep and I'll be going swimming with that barracuda. I'd like to get Renee back onshore. Would you mind heading out there and staying with Billy for a while?"

Rob pats him on the shoulder. "I should have offered. Let me know if we get a call. I'll send her back." He grabs one of his spears and walks to the dock platform. He barely clears the submerged section as it wobbles with his weight. Minutes later, he is helping Renee navigate across the open water area. Using the spear pole as a steadying mechanism, she crosses safely into Eric's outstretched arms.

After another hour of watching the skies, the radio cracks to life. Z is on it in a flash and answers the incoming call. He turns to the others and yells, "ETA ten minutes!" The crew walks to the open beach to watch. Dave uses his binoculars to watch for orbs over the sea. Eric yells across to Rob on the pier, "Ten minutes!"

Rob steps outside and takes the cane fishing pole from the hut and places a bit of crab leftovers on a hook. He drops the line into the water as he watches the reflective eyes in the distance. They haven't moved. Now, a second set of eyes beckons.

His pole is only in the water for a second when he gets a big strike. The tail of the barracuda flashes on the surface as the pole bends hard. Rob struggles with it, then slowly makes his way toward shore. Each step brings the large fish closer. Dave walks across the sand to the edge of the submerged planks and reaches toward the pole. The weight of the fish pulls Rob to his knees.

"Uh-oh! I didn't expect it to strike right away, but at least we can get it out of here while we transfer Billy! Grab the pole!" Rob returns to his feet and stretches with all of his might as he hands the pole to Dave. Eric helps him take control of the pole and they drag the fish to the beach area. It's almost six feet long, with rows of razor-sharp teeth protruding from its large, thin head.

With one swift strike of Malcolm's machete, Dave cuts off its head. They leave it bleeding on the beach as they all stand around looking at it.

Its scales reflect blue-purple in the fading light.

Rob calls out, "The heli! I see it!" He points and everyone turns to see the red and white flashing lights of the machine as it comes into view. Isabelle claps her hands. They all watch in amazement for a good one minute before jumping into action.

Dave helps Z cover the equipment and holds down the plastic sheeting with rocks. Z moves his egg out of view into a corner behind his tent. Collectively, they gather to one side of the beach area as the winds pick up around them. Sparks fly off the bonfire toward the group. Rene and Eric move one log off to the side of the beach, increasing the landing area. Rob stands on the pier outside the hut and holds onto the side of it.

The helicopter circles once and lands. Two technicians step out onto the beach. Dave walks toward them as the rotor blades slow and come to a stop.

"Dr. Dave Lane. Our injured guy is out in the hut on the pier. He's in terrible shape with a compound fracture. We haven't moved him much." They move toward the pier and stop when the reflective eyes of two crocs reveal themselves within striking distance — about twenty feet from the entrance of the hut.

One technician runs back to the helicopter and returns with a loaded handgun. Malcolm stands next to him with a fistful of homemade spears. "Those are some large crocs," the technician says under his breath. "They can launch pretty far out of the water."

Rob meets the medic on the hut's side of the pier with his spear. "You can grab onto this pole to help get across. Whoever has the drugs needs to get here first. He's in pain, acute pain." He looks at both of them. The technician with the medical bag goes first and jumps across the open pier. Rob helps him to his feet, and they run to the hut. The crew watches the water ripple in the bay as the crocs circle closer.

The pilot exits the chopper with the rescue gurney. He maneuvers it over to the edge of the pier. Dave pulls the technician aside. "Do you want to hover over the crocs to get a better shot?"

There is a flurry of activity as the medics and pilot go into rescue mode. The medic responds, "I don't know. Let's use the gurney as a platform to get across. We're going to have to strap him. Let me get more blankets and an immobilization sleeve for his injury." He runs back to the heli and returns quickly. Rob is back at this end now, so he and Dave help the second technician get across the pier. Rob returns to the hut with him.

"Malcolm, what do you think?" Dave points to the bleeding barracuda body. "We could throw it back out there?" He smiles. "Let me get something first. We've got to make sure they won't come back." He turns and runs into the brush. When he returns, he cuts open the barracuda with one swift stroke of his blade and lays several bulging branches inside the cavity. He is careful to only use the blade's edge. He ties a thin cord to the tail of the fish and drags it over to Dave.

"What did you put inside?" Dave whispers. His mind rifles through a variety of known toxins and what they do to the human body. "A powerful poison that will have those crocs out in minutes. It's stuffed. Don't touch any of the tubers if they fall out. It absorbs into the skin quickly." He grunts with the effort to get it onto the dock. "And be careful. Those crocs can launch themselves far out of the water if they're hungry enough, and now they've got the scent of blood." He secures the foliage with the last bit of twine tied to the tail.

Dave picks up the plank board Rob used to dig the trash pit and lays it under the fish. "How do you want to launch it? We could both take an end and throw it out as far as we can?" Malcolm nods. He is careful not to step on a root that falls off the fish.

Billy yells from inside the hut, "That still hurts! Just knock me out."

From the tree line, Eric, and Renee watch. Isabelle is right behind them. Z chats with the pilot.

Rob steps out of the hut with his spear in hand. He watches Malcolm and Dave navigate the sloped pier area onto the main dock area. They slowly pass behind Rob to the end of the pier. Rob looks up in the distance to see an orb faintly blink in the distance. Rob raises his eyebrows at Dave, then motions with his head in the island's direction. "Let's get this thing into the water. You ready, Malcolm?" Dave sets his feet firmly on the deck.

"No worries, mate. It's dinnertime." Malcolm watches the crocs as they position with their noses pointed right at them. "Seems they are interested. On the count of two. Give it a good shove." "One, Two!" yells Dave, as their muscles strain with the effort. The barracuda flies off the board to the middle of the bay. Both crocs attack with a voracious swish of their tails. They fight over the carcass, each taking a good section before they sink under the choppy waters.

One technician comes out of the hut in time to see the crocs sink back down into the water. "What did you give them?"

"A good dose of Angel's Trumpet," Malcolm says, with pride. "They'll be dead within five minutes." The technician nods his head in approval. "We've got him strapped in, just waiting for the pain relievers to hit his system. We'll be out of here in a sec. Anyone want a ride back? I've got room for one more passenger."

Turbulence below the waters strikes as the crocs move out into deeper waters. Dave watches with satisfaction. "No, I don't think so. Everyone wants to continue. We're almost done with our survey. Hey, we've had wicked winds blow up from the east. You are heading out to the west right, away from those storm clouds?"

"Yeah, we don't want to jostle him any more than we have to." He looks at their primitive canoes. "Do you need us to send a rescue boat? You could paddle your way to Dolok in three to four days if the currents are with you."

Dave shakes his head. "Thank you for coming. It's a relief knowing that he's going to get back on the road to mending. We'll keep going to the next community. There's nothing to the east, that's for sure. What hospital will he be taken to?" Dave sighs and thinks about Drew recovering from his croc bite.

"We'll stop at the Victoria Hospital. From there, they might transfer him. Depends on the number of beds available," the medic replies.

Isabelle listens to the medic's conversation. She wonders what the level of care for Billy will be in this third world country. Would he ever walk normally again? This will not be a simple leg setting. He will need major surgery and the rehab that goes with it. She once had a bad viral infection and had to be hospitalized in Haiti. It was awful. No medicine, no nurses, no resources, no options. She got out as quickly as she could.

A great splashing is heard from the water, as the crocs thrash and one goes belly-up.

"Please let him know that we'll check on him once we get to Dolok. Do you have any pain reliever packets that you can give us? We've used everything we had on him." Dave helps Rob take one section of the gurney as they all help maneuver back to the beach area. Billy lies unconscious. He is hooked up to an IV that is clamped to the gurney.

Isabelle and Renee each kiss him on top of his head before they slide him into the chopper. "Maybe I should go with him?" Isabelle whispers to Renee. "He looks so defenseless." Renee responds with a shake of her head 'no'.

"I can hand you a vial of morphine, but that's it. We're on a tight budget." The tech digs into his bag and slips Dave a vial before turning to the crew. "Last chance, anyone want a ride back?" Dave scans the faces of the crew. Both Renee and Isabelle smile back at him. Everyone takes at least one step back as the rotors move. "You're ready! Thanks again!" He waves to the pilot and the technicians as Billy is secured in and the door shuts. The helicopter lifts off and makes a wide arc over the lagoon and away from Ropen Island.

In the distance, the second croc goes belly-up out in the bay, past the surf line.

Dave notices everyone is closely watching the helicopter. Eric has his arm around Renee's shoulder, giving her a squeeze. Isabelle makes the sign of the cross on her chest as the machine blinks off in the distance.

A strong breeze blows through the camp, loosening the plastic covering on the equipment. Z runs to cover it up. Dave helps him and returns to the crew, all huddling around the fire. "Hey, let's have a staff meeting around the bonfire in ten. Guess we need to discuss the next few days." Heads nod. "How's the equipment?" Dave looks directly at Z.

"All good." Z disengages as he is momentarily lost watching a flock of birds fly out of the tree line nearby. Their cry is deafening. The birds fly off, deeper into the mainland.

Dave's exhaustion hits. He lets out a slow breath, staring straight ahead. *Can I keep the group's cohesion together?* The logical part of his brain takes over. He's been through enough intense situations to know that even when you make all the right decisions, people can still get hurt. *Would they still follow me?*

Dave grabs his pistol and one of Rob's sharpened poles, which are spread throughout the main beach area. He keeps his eye on the tree line as he talks to Z.

Z says under his breath, "Sorry, got a bit distracted." He adds another rock to the top covering of the equipment. "Getting a bit more sketch each time it's exposed to the elements. This delicate equipment isn't meant to be out in these conditions. I'm doing the best I can, but I make no guarantees anymore. Each time it fires up, I breathe a breath of relief." Beneath it all, his compressed knowledge of electronics suits the team, but if the system goes down, he doubts he could fix it. He pats the unit affectionately. "We've been through a lot. Oh, and the samples are secure. You haven't asked in a while, just wanted you to know."

"I appreciate you, Z. We'll have you back with Drew and on your way home soon. I promise." Dave pats him on the back. "Come join us at the fire." He turns and walks over to Rob, who has pulled a log close to the bonfire. Rob and Dave sit together. He puts the vial in his shirt pocket and leans over, whispering in Rob's ear. Rob gets up and lifts a pole from the sand over by the cooking fire. He returns and stabs the sand around the bonfire with each staff the team had left lying on the sand. Rob sits back down with the approach of Eric, Renee, and Malcolm. Isabelle is the last to arrive.

"Thanks, everyone, for taking such great care of Billy. Isabelle and Renee, you went above and beyond." Dave walks over and hands Isabelle the vial. "Got a bit of morphine from the medivac crew, just in case. We've used up our allotment of injuries so far." *Who's next?* he thinks as he looks at everyone. Isabelle holds the glass cylinder like a priceless object. "But we can't breathe easy yet. I'd like everyone to keep a hand on one of Rob's spears if you're out walking at night." On cue, the birds screech, then settle back into the treetops. "Something is agitating them." Rob hands each member a spear.

Malcolm uses his machete to sharpen more poles as Dave talks.

"There is a community to the west that we can get to in about three days, but it might be longer. I don't know what kind of reception we'll get there or how large of a place it is. Malcolm says it's nothing major. Hopefully, we can charter a boat to take us back to an area with an airport." Dave holds up the map and points to it. "Malcolm recommends we sleep in hammocks, not on the ground, this close to that group of crocs. Or you're welcome to sleep out on the dock, but they can easily launch right out of the water and onto the dock."

Malcolm gives everyone a quick smile. "I'm going to make a circle of stakes around our sleeping trees to give us added protection." His teeth reflect a yellow hue in the firelight. Isabelle shivers, rubbing her arms as if she is cold as she says, "Anyone want to sleep out on the dock?" She looks at the group with pleading eyes. "On the table?"

"I'll join you, Isabelle, if it will help you sleep," Z nods in her direction. "As long as we sleep on the tables and with the door shut. I don't want any crocs knocking at the door."

"We've got our samples. Billy is on the road to recovery, and our trip is ending. Any thoughts?" Dave looks at each of them as worry tugs the back of his mind.

Malcolm looks up. "Those tubular stems I put into the croc are VERY powerful. If you see any on the beach, don't touch them."

Eric looks up at his dad. "Are we done? That's it?" Eric shakes his head, not seeming to comprehend it all. Renee squeezes his hand.

Dave lets out a slow breath. "We have the bat samples that need to get back for research. Finding a lab to handle the biologicals might be difficult. Not to mention what to do with Chester? We've been out three weeks now. Aren't you ready to head back?"

"But if we could stop some of the deforestation, shouldn't we take steps to do so?" Isabelle looks at each member of the group as she brings it up. "We need documentation. I've taken the images from here, but if you see any more cleared areas or places where something looks odd, we need to check it out. This corporation is counting on staying under the radar, as they have for a long time. It would be worth this trip if we can do something good."

Malcolm stands up. He faces them. "I have seen horrific human trafficking, child labor, and total disregard for nature with these corporations. They have to be stopped, or at least identified to the public. I will help any way I can." His mind flashes through experiences he has seen. He closes that door to the horrific imagery and stokes the fire.

Rob stands beside him. "Me too." Eric and Renee straightens up next to Rob. Malcolm grabs Rob's hand. "We four." Z is the last one sitting on the log. Everyone looks at him. "Well, count me in. I'm moving slower, but I signed on to work with ALL of you. If we need another week, so be it. Let's do this right!" He stands up.

Isabelle cheers. "Brilliant!" She raises her hands to the heavens.

Dave looks out over the water. "We need to do some undercover work to find out about the land ownership in this area. We've got to protect the Ropen. Isabelle, do you have connections in the Department of the Interior for New Guinea?"

She shakes her head. "I don't, but I know someone who does. I don't think we should say much over the phone lines. There have been issues with phone tampering in the past by some of the larger corporations. They have infiltrated most areas of government. If we can get secure email connections to get things going, I think that's our best route for now." Everyone nods affirmatively to her.

Renee looks up. "Get me access to secure emails. I bet my grandfather will jump over bridges to come along for THIS ride. He's got deep pockets and is bored to death. He will buy up everything we need if I ask." She looks longingly at the communication gear. "Think I could put in a quick call to him? I won't tell him about the find, but he needs to hear from me."

Z nods at Dave. "When we're done here, Z will fire it up, but keep it short. Only ten minutes. "He watches Eric squeeze Renee's hand in happiness. They both are beaming. "Dad, you've got to meet him."

Dave looks at her and smiles. "Thanks, Renee. Let's keep it cryptic. The less people that know about it, the better." He pauses, letting out a slow breath. "Before we turn in, I'd like to say something. Malcolm, we wouldn't have come this far without you. Thank you, my friend, for being the calm in our storm and the dial on our compass." He walks over and shakes Malcolm's hand. Each member of the team follows Dave, thanking Malcolm. Renee kisses him on both cheeks. He giggles as they head in.

Malcolm calls over to Dave, "I'll keep the bonfire going, though. It should help deter the critters. Everyone be ready to go after breakfast in the morning."

Renee kisses Dave on the cheek while Eric watches. "Thanks, Dad, for letting us join the expedition. I will never forget it." They look up to the carpet of stars above them, brilliant in their display. "Should get some Milky Way photos while we are out here." Eric squeezes her shoulder. Turning back to Billy's gear, Dave hands Eric Billy's camera. "Your new job, or Renee's." They nod and look over the gear.

Rob holds out his hand for Dave to shake, but Dave pulls him into a big bear hug. "We're good, right?" Rob pats him on the back and whispers, "I missed you, too."

The quiet of the night is interrupted by Renee's phone call. Her enthusiasm and kindness comes through with every word on the line. Dave smiles at the nickname of "Puppy" her grandfather uses to speak with Renee.

They each take their spears and disburse for the night. Isabelle sits next to Dave, both in quiet contemplation. The lapping of the water is hypnotic and soothing. After several minutes, she says, "It's truly magnificent out here. One of the last places in the world, untouched, the way God made it." He has no response for her as he watches a comet fly across the sky. A few minutes later, Z finishes and then walks Isabelle out onto the pier.

Dave remains sitting on the log, looking out across the waters, and listening to the soft sounds of the surf. "You should see this, Jeanne, it's spectacular," he says under his breath. "I know you're with me." With all its intensity, the Milky Way shines brightly across a carpet of stars above him.

CHAPTER 16

A lone twenty-four-foot aluminum raised bow fishing boat moves slowly along the coast just past the surf line. Its engine smokes and sputters. Jose, the captain, a weathered local, stands and leans against his chair. He smokes a cigarette and taps on one dial as the boat slices through the water.

Behind him, Percy, a teenager, and John, in his early twenties, doze in their seats. John has his baseball hat over his eyes. Percy drools into a folded towel and is curled up in an uncomfortable position. One of Percy's hands drips into the water, barely breaking the water line.

Jose looks back at both of them, disgusted at their laziness. The boat is a double-lined aluminum twenty-four-footer with seating for four and a small bow front. A small canopy covers the first two chairs. Fish locator mounts are in the front and back. He rides the boat dark, blending into the water seamlessly. The puttering of the engine echoes across the expanse. He pulls out his cell phone and makes a call. It's a long time before it is answered.

"Hello? Como?" says a voice on the line.

"This is Jose. We are about an hour from the location. Any change?" He takes a long puff on his cigarette and blows the smoke out across the water.

"No, we've identified six people there. A helicopter picked up someone. Management wants them off the property, but find out what they are doing there. Use force if needed. You know the drill." The line clicks off.

Jose looks at his rifle on the floor and re-secures the gun strapped to his belt. Both are ancient pieces that are worn and well-used. He had to take the job. Money was scarce and Luca would leave him and take the kids. He knew it. She'd threatened so many times, but the look in her eyes had made him realize he was out of time. There were too many fishing trips without a catch these days. Bringing Percy wasn't part of the plan, but he owed too many people.

He steers the aged boat into the open ocean, away from shore, where he idles it and wakes up the crew. A dark shape follows the boat under the water. His attention is diverted to the carcass of the crocodile floating belly-up.

He kicks the bare feet of both men.

"What?" says John as he adjusts his hat. He looks to where Jose is looking. "That's a big croc. You woke me for that?" He shakes Percy awake. "We're getting close. Put your sandals on and wake up." His voice is gruff. Both men look around the floorboard for their gear, which has shifted during the journey.

A tremendous WHOOSH sounds as a large Pterodactyl comes up from the depths, and with large flaps of its immense wings, hovers at the back of their boat. The men turn as water drips heavily onto them from the creature.

They stare for a moment, shell-shocked. "AYE!" yells Percy. He falls, lies flat on the floor, and reaches for the rifle. Before he can get his hand around it, the bird lands on the back of the boat, rocking it badly, threatening to sink it.

Jose releases his gun from his belt and fires at the bird. He hits it in the chest.

The bird SCREAMS and impales Jose in the chest with its beak. In one swift motion, it lifts Jose, opens its beak, spitting him in half. The lit cigarette in his hand is still smoking when it lands at Percy's feet. The other half of the body lands in the water. His gun goes with it.

Percy and John race for the rifle, now among the mess of entrails and blood covering the floor. The boat rocks as the beast rises toward the front of the boat. A wing hits John. He pushes it away.

Blood drips from the bird's chest wounds. The beast screams louder and breaks apart the steering wheel column and front windshield when it lands on the front bow. One deadly, dinner-plate eye focuses on Percy as the enormous bird takes a step forward. Its footing is rocky against the broken canopy and with the metal supports twisted around it.

It **SCREAMS**.

Percy yells, "**GET THE RIFLE**"! John is closer to it. The boat rocks with the weight of the beast listing everything to the right. "**DISTRACT IT!**"

"How? It's already looking right at me!" Percy fumbles with his towel and throws it at the animal. It lunges toward Percy, missing, and swishes its beak side-to-side before hitting the side of the boat with a loud BANG.

John gets his hand on the rifle and shoots it point blank in the head. It explodes. The colossal head flies off to the side, splashing into the water. The rest of the body lies sprawled across the bow. Both men look at each other in astonishment.

"What the Fu....?" Percy collapses back in his seat and looks at the enormous feet of the animal as they twitch in death's muscle spasms.

Both men have small pieces of Jose splattered on them. Percy kicks the leg of Jose away from him. He eyes Jose's bulging wallet and reaches down, taking it. "Don't judge me," he says, as he catches John's eye. "We need to get rid of him. You know he wouldn't have hesitated to get rid of us if it were us lying dead back here." They throw the larger human parts overboard, suppressing a gag reflex.

When finished, they both look at the creature. "What is, it?" John takes a step closer to the front of the boat. He pokes the quivering blue foot with the end of the rifle.

"Alien, got to be some sort of alien-thing." Percy hyperventilates. He closes his eyes for a moment and looks back to the receding coastline. He peels off his filthy T-shirt and throws it at the engine. Percy bends over and holds onto his knees. His breathing is rapid. He experiences a strange feeling of unreality, as if he dreamed the whole thing. Looking back at John, he steps forward and touches the wing of the bird. "OMG, that whole thing was real!" Percy looks up at John. "I'm not dreaming, right?" In seconds, he is vomiting off the port side.

"Keep your eyes open!" John screams as a ripple water line passes by the boat. John has his gun ready as a large fish swims by. "There could be more!"

John touches the leathery wings, then takes out his phone and starts snapping images. He pushes the creature off the front of the boat. It slips into the darkness below, barely making a splash. The boat rocks back into place.

He can't explain it. *Nothing makes sense. It came shooting out of the water, then hovered before landing on the boat. It looked at me as if I were dinner. And it killed Jose. Didn't even eat him, just split him in two? The thing was overwhelming in size, too. What was it? Did it breathe underwater? Are more down there? God, I hope we won't be stranded out there with more creatures coming in. What in the F — am I going to tell the corporation? God, we are good as dead, right here, right now if we don't get out of here.*

"Give me a minute," Percy says, his voice quivering. He pulls out his phone, but he is shaking so intensely that he loses his grip on the phone, and it goes into the deep waters with a small PLOP.

"SHIT!" echoes across the water.

John throws the canopy pieces into the water and looks at the damaged captain's area. The steering wheel is bent in half. Part of the dashboard is missing. The throttle against the side of the boat is untouched. He kneels into the captain's chair and tries to start the engine. It won't start. He notices loose wires sticking out of the control panel. He twists one set back together and tries the engine again. After several tries, it sputters and starts.

"Thank God," John says as he pushes the throttle slowly toward shore. He looks down into the water as they move. "Keep an eye out. There might be more of them down there."

"Now what?" asks Percy, as he sits in his bloody seat. He gags once and throws up again over the side of the boat.

"We finish the job." John moves the throttle harder, and they move toward the camp. "We don't have a choice."

Up ahead, after fifteen minutes, they see the lit pole shining at the top of the dock. John slows the engine to idle and moves closer to shore.

Before long, he pulls in silently on the other side of the bay. Percy pulls the boat up onto the sand. John helps him with the last heave of the boat. They both look at the damage to the side of the boat briefly before looking toward the camp. The light of the diminished bonfire burns low in the clearing.

Pulling the rifle over his shoulder, John takes the lead and moves toward the sleeping hammocks he can barely make out through the outcrop of trees. "Stay behind me and keep quiet," he whispers to Percy.

The darkness is intense, but there is a bit of illumination coming from the dock and the campfire. Percy can't see his hand in front of his face, but he follows the dark figure in front of him. A light wind is at their backs.

They are ten steps into the thicket and jump over a narrow stream that leads to the open ocean when Percy lands and twists his ankle. He makes a slight "oh" sound before stepping forward.

A guttural, throaty ripple sounds from the area nearby. Both men freeze. They recognize the sound of a croc. They look around anxiously to see eyes reflecting from the firelight. Those eyes are less than ten feet from them.

The crocodile explodes from a stationary position and locks its jaws onto Percy's leg. Immediately, it spins and rolls, taking Percy with it.

Percy SCREAMS and reaches for anything to grab ahold of. Branches slip from his grasp. "Help me!" he yells. The croc releases his leg and clamps onto his hip, right by his femoral artery. A loud CRUNCH sounds as the bones are crushed it its massive jaws.

Percy **SCREAMS** louder.

John lights up the area with his phone and shoots with his rifle. The bullet goes through the back of the skull on the animal's skull, and the croc lies still. John looks up at a series of spears pointed right at him and Percy.

"Don't move!" Dave is in the lead, with Malcolm and Rob right behind him. Dave holds his gun in his hand.

Blood gushes from the mouth of Percy's mouth. He coughs once, then stops moving. John drops his rifle and holds his hands up. Eric holds up a burning log from the bonfire, closer to John, to see the full extent of the carnage. He sweeps the area with the light. The twelve-foot croc is on its side, dead. Percy's eyes stare unblinking. He is on his back in a dark puddle of blood. They scan the area for more crocs. There are none.

"Out of there. Over to the campfire. Don't make any sudden moves." Dave motions with his gun. Isabelle kneels down next to Percy and says, "He's just a kid."

John keeps his hands up and walks through the trees into the open. Eric grabs John's rifle and follows everyone back to the camp area.

"On your knees," Dave orders John down. "Do we have anything we can tie him up with?" He looks to Malcolm, who shrugs his shoulders. Z rummages through the electronics and finds one zip tie. He hands it to Rob, who quickly pulls John's arms behind his back and zip ties him tight.

"Start talking." Dave stands over John.

A menacing Malcolm stands behind the zip tied man, with his machete in hand.

John looks around the area carefully before responding. "We were attacked by an alien creature out on our boat. We came ashore when we saw the light on your dock. It killed our captain. Honest, that's what happened." John squirms against the ties. His shirt is a mess of dried blood and bits. "Look at my shirt! It was horrible!" His voice quivers. "Who are you people?"

Dave leans in. "And why were you out this way—in the middle of nowhere, in the middle of the night?"

The man answers. "We had boat engine issues. Have been out for three days." John hangs his head. "If you've got anything to eat, that'd be great. My name is John." He glances at the guys, hoping they believe him.

"Okay, John, where did you start your journey?" Rob paces nearby.

"Boku, across the Solomon Sea. Do you know it?" John looks believable.

Malcolm spats in the dirt. He takes his knife and holds it under John's jaw, who now doesn't move an inch. "Now, how about you tell the truth?

You don't have the accent for Boku. And no one would attempt to cross in that beat-up boat you were in." Malcolm looks over to Dave. "He's lying."

Eric searches for John. Finding John's phone, he pulls it out and checks the last call made. He holds it up for everyone to see and dials it, putting it on speaker. It rings several times before someone answers.

"Hello? John, Jose? Done already?"

Eric takes the phone and tries to imitate John's voice. "Had boat issues. Everything's fine." The voice on the phone asks, "Who are the people on-site?"

"No worries, mate, just some fishermen who lost their boat. They're leaving in the morning."

"Check on Station 25 on your way back." The phone clicks off.

Eric throws the phone deep into the woods behind him. "Answer carefully," says Malcolm as he points the tip of the machete into the front of John's neck.

"Let's try this again." Dave squats down next to John. "Why are you here?"

John looks at their fearful faces. "I—I work for Newcastle, Newcastle Corporation. They own this research site. They wanted to know what you were doing here."

"That's one of the big industry takeover companies," Malcolm says, and looks over to Dave. "They are into gold mining. Chinese-backed. They want to dam-up the rivers. They are disgusting, every single one of them." He eyes John with malice. "So, they sent you out here to find out what we were doing? How did they know we were here?" Rob continues to pace.

"The electricity. It alerted one of our satellite offices." John watches Rob walk alone into the tree line, turns on his flashlight, and works his way back toward the mass clearing area.

"Tell me about the attack." Dave pulls the tip of Malcolm's blade back from John's neck a few inches.

He talks rapidly. "This thing came out of the water and attacked us.

Had massive wings, a huge head, and a long beak. Must have been some sort of alien. Bluish black. It reeked."

The lights go out in the camp all at once, followed by a strong seismic rumble. Birds fly out of the canopy behind them.

Malcolm holds his blade tight. "Don't even think about moving. Everyone here will tell you I'm quite skillful with this thing, mate."

In seconds, Rob is back and out of breath. "That was a big one. There are wild dogs at the back of the cleared area. I turned off the main switch."

John looks over Rob's shoulder with concern, and says, "Those dogs can be vicious."

Isabelle steps forward. "Now that he's here, what do we do with him?"

Dave gives her a blank stare, then he turns to John. "Where's your boat?" "On the other s-s-side of the bay. We beached it. I c-c-can show you." He stammers a bit in his response.

"Well, we probably won't sleep anymore tonight." He looks at his watch. "It's about 4:30. Let's gather our things and get moving. Malcolm, can you get breakfast going? I'm gonna tie him up over by the bonfire area. That should keep him tidy for the next two hours until we decide what to do." Heads nod in agreement. Malcolm takes a net and his machete and steps off into the tree line in a huff.

Eric pulls a linked chain he gathered earlier from the dock and throws it down near the bonfire. He takes a palm log, wraps the chain around it, and leaves the end, waiting for them to secure to John. Rob watches him and then helps John over near the bonfire.

John looks up to Rob. "I won't run away. You don't have to do that. Where would I go?"

Rob sneers, "Well, if you had been honest with us at first, this probably wouldn't be necessary." He hooks the end of the chain around John's ankle, then, taking a lit branch off the burning pile, says, "I'm gonna walk over to his boat. Anyone want to join me?" Renee and Eric follow Rob down to the beach.

Z, Dave, and Isabelle sit back down near the kitchen fire pit. They clean out bits and arrange kindling for the breakfast fire. "What are you thinking?" Z asks Dave in a whisper.

Isabelle responds, "What a horrible, horrible way to die. That kid couldn't have been over sixteen."

Dave gazes into the jungle depths, his mind projecting through the trees to the cleared area. "I'm kind of thinking we should just leave him here, but then they would send someone to investigate, and it could lead to another Ropen attack." Dave runs his hands through his hair. "I think Malcolm would be happy to skin the guy alive."

"Well, we have to take him with us," says Isabelle as she watches John.

"I don't think the Ropen attack was too long ago. The blood on his shirt looked pretty fresh. I think I'd like to find out more from our guest, and what he does for Newcastle." Dave brushes off his pants and walks over beside John. He sits down. "Guess we need more information from you. How old are you? How long have you worked for Newcastle?" Dave smooths the sand beside where he sits.

"I'm twenty-two. Have worked for Newcastle since I was sixteen." John looks up.

"And what do you do for Newcastle?" Dave scans the water, looking for running lights from a possible other boat. "I'm on the survey team. I was at the closest site to this one when we got the call. Your guy was right. They are more concerned with gold mining than palm oil production." John shifts uncomfortably in place. "I think that's why they abandoned this site."

"Are they mining around here?" Dave looks him right in the eye. "They did. Had one mine about a day's ride, err, six hours by boat. But they closed it years ago. I think there was a problem with land rights. That's Station 25. I don't know the politics on these things. I just go where they tell me."

"What do you know about THIS area?" Dave motions with a sweep of his hand.

"Here? Not much. It's kinda of a mystery. It's sort of a forbidden area by the natives. This whole side of the coast is. We had to buy the boat we used to get here because none of the locals would bring us out this way."

"When did the creature attack you?" He looks at John's shirt and bits of skin still attached to it. "Must have been a little after one, in calm waters. There was a dead croc floating, though. That was weird. I was sleeping before we stopped, so I can't give you the details." Dave pauses. "You sure you didn't get into an argument with the captain and kill him?" Dave throws him an unexpected question.

"No, man. It's like I said. This thing came out of the water. Had a huge wingspan." They look up to see the boat with Rob, Renee, and Eric coming into the bay.

Dave gets up. "I'll be back." He walks out on the pier to meet them and helps tie the boat against the dock. After securing it, they all walk into the hut, leaving the door open for ventilation. Dave pulls out a chair and sits down.

"Well, I've been talking to him. He's on the survey team, twenty-two years old, and is just a grunt. How's the boat?"

Dave looks right at Rob. "It's pretty banged up, but I think we can use it. We can tie the canoes, full of our supplies, to the back and tightly fit in the boat if some of us sit on the floor. Just thinking out loud. Oh, and it's got an extra gas reservoir in the back. I think we'd be okay for a while."

"Eric, what are your thoughts as to our guest?" Dave sits back. "Thanks for asking, Dad. Let's take it slow with him. We might need someone to help be our lookout once we leave the island. He might be good to hire for undercover work."

Dave nods. "Renee? You get input, too."

"I agree with Eric. We were talking about it on the walk over. He's strong, been here a long time, and can blend into the scene. But I think we need to check for weapons and keep everything out of his reach until we can trust him more." Dave looks at Rob. Rob calmly states, "Ditto." He smiles and nods his head to agree.

"Let me talk to Isabelle, Z and Malcolm. Malcolm's the one that is going to be hardest to convince. I understand where he's coming from.

Did you know Malcolm was sold into slavery into that same company when he was ten?" Dave gets up. "Let's head back. I don't want to leave them alone with John any longer."

Rob steps over toward the boat. "I'm gonna do a sweep for anything that could be used as a weapon. Be with you in a minute." He hops into the boat, checking all the nooks and crannies. Taking a rag, he dumps water onto the floorboards, washing away blood and body part debris. By the captain's chair, he finds a long knife in a sheath in a hidden floorboard compartment under the steering wheel. He holds it up in the dim light, examining it before he ties it to his outer thigh. He pats it as he heads to the beach.

* * *

Rob walks back to the group with the swagger of Crocodile Dundee. Dave eyes the knife wrapped to his leg and smiles. "Mate, that's a bad ass knife. Got any more of those?" He shakes his head. "So, what's been decided?" John sits on the beach as everyone joins them with their supply bags. Malcolm works on the kitchen fire nearby.

John looks up pleadingly. "I'd like to know too." He smiles.

"Okay, here's the deal. We're going to cut you loose. You're going to join us on the boat as we make our way east. You will not ask us what we are doing here or anything about our excursion. We'll load up the canoes with our gear and pull them behind the boat. Eric, you will be our boat's captain. I know those years out on the lake give you the skills to drive it. Everyone will take a six-hour rotation from seat to floor. There's seating for four. We'll leave after breakfast. Any questions?" He scans the crew member's faces.

Rob raises his hand. "I'd like to know more about Newcastle." He takes his knife out and cuts the zip tie behind John's back. "So, we may ask YOU lots of questions."

John nods his head. "Thank you for taking that off. It was a bit tight. Whatever you need. You're in charge." John takes a quick glance at the communication gear on Z's make-shift table as Z wraps it in plastic and secures it. He notices Malcolm's eyes on him and turns away. His thoughts turn to the satellite phone he thought he saw tied in amongst the gear parts. He runs several scenarios on how best to get his hands on it.

Renee picks up a handful of mangos from Malcolm's pile and returns to the group. She wraps them in her shirt as she holds onto her spear. She hands John and Eric each one as Eric releases the chain around John's ankle.

"Thanks," John squeezes the mango, splitting the skin on it, and takes a big bite of the flesh. I'm starving." Juice runs down his neck. "Would it be all right to wash out my T-shirt before I get in the boat?" He talks with his mouth full.

Isabelle steps forward. "Let me have it. I'll give it a wash in the surf." In one quick motion, John pulls the shirt off and holds it up with two fingers. "It's pretty nasty." He hands it to her. "Thank you."

As Isabelle approaches the waterline, the ground rumbles with an aftershock. Birds squawk in the distance. She turns and looks at the tree line and the brightening morning skies. In the distance, over the valley, are two gliding Ropen. Their bellies flash in the dim light and they are coming in their direction. She points and calls out, "Incoming!" and runs into the nearest tree line as everyone scatters from the open areas.

John follows Eric and Renee to cover. He calls out, "That's what attacked us!" John picks up a large branch. Eric and Renee hold their spears and watch from behind a tree.

In two quick flaps, one creature lands beside the bonfire. It studies the fire and cocks its head side-to-side. Pushing against a partly burning log, it roars as the fire licks part of its beak. "GAWK!"

The second, larger Ropen circles the area before landing on the dock. The beak on it measures over six feet long. It poops, making the dock smoke where the acid eats through aged wooden planks. It splashes into the water. The creature takes a step forward. The entire dock shudders.

It lifts off and, with one stroke of its wings, lands on the beach. Its head turns quickly, scanning the area. The animals make a clicking sound back and forth between each other and move toward the tree line where

Eric, John, and Renee have taken cover.

Eric dashes for the other side of the bonfire, grabs a burning log, and throws it at the smaller raptor. Its feet burn until the whole body goes up in flames. Eric jabs it in the stomach with his spear, narrowly missing a swipe from its razor teeth. The larger male takes a step towards Eric, then stops. It watches Eric struggle to dislodge the sharpened instrument as he pulls before it comes loose. The smaller creature falls into the bonfire, knocking the burning structure to the ground with a thud.

Dave and Rob join Eric and rush to his aid. They confront the larger male who comes at them. Rob yells as loud as he can. **"HEY, UGLY! OVER HERE!"**

The coloring around the male's eyes turns a brilliant blue. It screams loudly at them. Its eyes focus on John, and its glowing belly lights up as it rears back. Behind it, Renee creeps up. With all her might, she stabs the beast in the back.

"Get out of there, Renee," Eric screams, as the beast turns, knocking Renee to the ground with one swipe of its beak.

Malcolm hurls four spears at the creature, and each one takes hold.

It **SCREAMS!**

Renee struggles to hold on to her spear. She ducks as the Ropen narrowly misses her with its wing.

John yells as he runs out from the tree line, clobbering the beast with his large branch. It breaks apart at impact, splintering pieces into the sand. Now, standing there unarmed, the creature tosses John onto the beach with a swish of his wing, narrowly missing the burning embers.

Rob takes his twelve-inch knife from the sheath and pushes it all the way into the beast. Malcolm, Rob, and Dave repeatedly stab the creature, until Malcolm slices through its neck, almost decapitating it. The bird flops to the ground and stops moving, its mouth open in a death scream. Rows of razor- sharp teeth reflect in the firelight.

The team is out of breath as they look up to see Isabelle run towards them. They are all panting heavily. Eric helps Renee to her feet, pulls her into an endless hug.

Dave and Rob assist John, who holds onto bruised ribs. John pants, "Yeah, that's what attacked us before, but I have a feeling you knew they were here. Glad I landed on the beach and not in that fire."

"Look at the size of that thing!" Dave puts his foot on its beak and gets a closer look.

Isabelle gingerly walks over to Renee. They embrace as she sobs. "I couldn't... my legs wouldn't move." Renee holds her until she stops shaking.

"It's okay. We're okay." Renee comforts Isabelle.

Everyone gathers around the bird carcasses as the earth calls with another aftershock. The trees dance as if answering.

"Time to leave." Dave turns toward his bag, picks it up, and looks to the others still standing around the bird. He squeezes Eric's shoulder as he passes.

"Hold on a sec." Z takes close-up photos of the bird with his camera and runs a glass slide over a bloody area. He seals the sample and adds it to his pack. Checking through pockets, he finds a second blank slide and does the same thing, getting as close to the burning creature as possible.

"You guys coming?" Dave calls out as he turns toward the dock. His eyes naturally scan the horizon for any objects. "John, can you stand watch while we load up?" John nods and walks to the water's edge. He picks up his T-shirt, which Isabelle left, and rinses it in the water. He takes a couple of hands full of water and dumps them over his face, never taking his eyes from the sky.

Malcolm lights the larger bird on fire and throws a heavy log on top of it. He calls out, "If you've got extra hands, we can take breakfast with us. Fresh water is in the pot. Everybody needs to fill their canteens."

CHAPTER 17

"Please, can we stop? My backside feels bruised," says Isabelle after three hours of heavy winds, whitecaps, and an incredible jarring ride. The first seven hours weren't bad, but that was before the winds picked up. Dave and Malcolm nod at each other, then Malcolm points to a sliver of a beach coming up. "That one should work. Pull in there," he says to Eric. "Let me do a brief scouting before we tie up." The boat lurches onto the shore. Malcolm jumps off the boat with his machete in hand. The rest of the crew gather on the beach next to the boat, stretching.

Malcolm descends into a sand berm area that runs parallel to the beach. His eyes dart through the brush, identifying foliage, animal tracks, upturned trees, roots, and any signs of humans. He reads it all in a flash. Something is bothering him, and he can't put his finger on it. *Maybe John is too happy or too compromising?* Malcolm's gut aches when he looks at him. He stops and sits in the sand for a moment, listening to the noise in the jungle. *What is it telling me?* The soft coos of birds floated around him. He hears a monkey scampering up a tree nearby, or maybe it is another aye-aye? *Dave was too easy to accept John's story, but he trusted Dave. After hundreds of scouting missions over the years, this team is one of the few that stands out. And it isn't because of the Ropen. The family bond that intertwines between all of them is genuine. They care. They are good people who are trying to do the right thing, but the island can change you in ways you'd never thought possible. Right now, it feels good to be by myself and think.*

Back at the boat, John winces as soon as his feet hit the sand. Isabelle notices his pain and pulls up a section of his T-shirt, revealing a spreading blue bruise across his side and back. "Let me look. Ouch. With all the knocking around on board, I don't know how you weren't screaming. I bet you've got bruised ribs. It's a wonder you're still coherent."

"I gritted my teeth through it." He pulls his shirt down and tries to stretch. He pulls Dave aside. "What can I do to help? Need me to scout for firewood?"

They both watch Malcolm's form silhouetted as it moves through the trees. "I'm happy to help." Dave motions for him to stay put. "Just chill." Eric and Renee scout the beach area for shells as they wait.

A blast of humidity hits them when the wind subsides. Heat radiates from the sand they are standing in. Dave slaps his leg, and he notices sand fleas jump. "That's a problem," he says, under his breath. To the right, long shadows cover the beach toward a patch of hibiscus plants under a canopy of trees. A loud screech bellows from the depths beyond, sounding like some sort of monkey. They all look in that direction. Rob joins Dave and John near the boat.

John is rattling on. "I'm pretty good in the bush. If you need a guide." His look is close to pleading. Rob shakes his head, saying, "I'd do whatever you can to stay away from Malcolm." Dejected, John takes a quick dip in the crystalline water, scrubbing his skin clean. "As you say, mate."

Splashing through the surf, Dave's nerves are frayed as he stomps in the waves. He keeps a safe distance from anything in the tree line as best he can make out. He twists his head at movement in the tree line. *An animal is hiding there*, he's sure of it. Dave grips his spear tightly, constantly watching for Malcolm. He is taking longer than normal to scout. Dave imagines *another big bull Ropen landing in front of them. This one is about the size of the biggest we've seen on the island. It screams as it looks in Eric's direction and knocks him over with one big sweep of its wing. My legs can't move fast enough. It's as if I am running in quicksand to help Eric.* He shakes his head to clear the image.

Rob steps closer. "You look mad. You okay?" He pats Dave on the back.

"Just reliving that Ropen attack. I think we all may suffer a bit from PTSD. Or I'm just exhausted."

Isabelle walks in to her knees, then steps farther in. She stops to pick up a beautiful shell with a filigree edge. "Beautiful." She points to the feather clouds overhead. "Going to be a spectacular sunset tonight with those clouds, if they hang around."

Eric scrambles back to the boat and stands on a seat watching for crocs. He holds a spear in his hand. "Thanks, Eric. The water is so crystal blue here," Isabelle says, as she sighs, looking into the water.

Renee floats next to her in quiet bliss. "Let peace and calmness float with you," she whispers to Renee.

John heads out deeper, diving underwater before coming back to shore. "Don't want to take any chances." The water stings on his open cuts but cleans them at the same time. It's worth the pain.

Walking away from Dave, Rob adjusts his knife and turns away from the others, relieving himself quickly. He shakes his canteen and takes the last bit of clean water. He calls out to Dave. "Got any water left?"

Dave nods and hands him his canteen. "Not much, but you can have it." He checks the wrinkles on his fingertips for dehydration. "We all need to drink more."

Rob groans. He resists the urge to push the canteen back at him. Instead, hands it back with a light touch. "Thanks. That was one bumpy ride. I hope the seas calm soon. At least I haven't seen any crocs in a while. That's a good sign, isn't it?"

Dave slaps his thigh. "Maybe, but sand fleas have infested this area. No one will sleep on the ground tonight." His response is curt.

Down the beach, in the distance, a cassowary bird struts and stops. It turns its blue head in their direction before heading back into the tree line. This beach isn't as pristine, instead is scattered with old palm fronds for miles in each direction.

Dave stands next to Rob, searching the trees for signs of movement. Rob coughs. "I want—to say something. Hear me out." He pauses before continuing, "I'm feeling more comfortable with John. Do you think you could have a conversation with Malcolm, tell him to ease up a bit? Makes things difficult on the boat in such close quarters."

He smirks and nods. "Yeah, I've been thinking about the same thing. But I'm still not ready to talk all about it." They both turn back to see Z fussing with the canoes. For the thousandth time, Z caresses the egg, wondering *how the little guy is doing?* He knows this find, still alive, would have the entire world buzzing. How would they raise the creature? Would it even be allowed to mature? And where could it be kept secret? Word would get out eventually and then it would be a zoo with media coverage, news journalists, and elite members of the science community. The thought makes his stomach drop with a bit of anxiety. I won't be able to apply for grants without revealing the context of the request, so that's out. Maybe Dave has connections to a strong benefactor or lab he could use? The farm in Vermont we've always dreamt of had a barn. Could we convert it into a lab? Z talked to the egg. "Don't worry, little guy, I'm now your protector. Going to keep you safe." Z pats the egg lovingly before wrapping it back up and pulling the canoe up to shore.

John watches him with interest but can't see exactly what he is doing.

Dave and Rob pull the second canoe to shore. They all stand waiting for Z to join them. Rob asks, "How far you think we came today?"

John and Eric tag team with a high five. Eric and Renee jump into the water as John moves into lifeguard position. He takes off his shirt, revealing rock-solid abs and a spray of bruising. Even Isabelle looks. Rob and Dave watch them as they talk.

"Made good time, better than I thought. At least the wind was at our back, even if it was rough. Hope it's that way tomorrow. I'll ask Malcolm. Should we get the map back out?" Dave whispers. "Make sure John doesn't see the entire map. We marked the island on it."

Rob looks up to see Malcolm waving everybody over. "Guess we're here for the night." They move to pull the canoes even further up onto the beach and tie them with vines to the nearest trees.

As dinner is cooking, Malcolm takes a lit log and slowly passes it around a circular area six feet from the fire. Rob watches him perplexed. "What's that for?" he asks when Malcolm sits back down. "Old trick. It helps keep the fleas from the area. Tonight, before we head in, I'll do the same thing around the hammocks, but everyone needs to set their beds higher and use their nets. If there's extra charcoal, put it under your bed.

It repels them." Rob steps back. "Okay, I'll tell the crew." He walks over to each member, as they are planning where to hang their hammocks.

After a feast of roasted monitor lizard tail, sweet potatoes, rice, pineapple, and pawpaw fruit, the crew set up their sleeping hammocks. John uses Billy's ex-long hammock.

Rob and Dave return from the surf line, wet from a quick dip. They stick their spears in the sand beside the firepit. "The water feels fantastic. Z, did you want to take a dip?"

His eyes hold a deep fatigue. "I'm pretty tired. The sun took a lot of energy out of me today. Got a bit sunburned. Guess I'll clean up in the morning." Z finishes setting up his bed. He looks even older with a layer of grime on him.

"I'm gonna sleep like a baby tonight," John says as he finishes his hammock lines. He eyes the canoes in the distance, thinking about what might be in them. *If I can get to the satellite phone or whatever looked like a phone, maybe I can save my job.*

Rob, Dave, and Malcolm sit around the fire, looking at the carefully folded map. They call John over. "Malcolm hasn't been this way in a while. Do you know the area?" Dave points to a section of the map. "We should be about here."

He studies the map carefully. And using Dave's pencil, marks a location. "I haven't been this way in about ten years. The company usually takes the route overland." Using the pencil lightly, he draws the road route in the area and then points to a river tributary noted on the map. "We haven't crossed that yet. So, we can use it as a marker. That's Station 25." John taps the map at the spot.

Malcolm exhales. "Wildlife is abundant here. I practically picked that lizard up. So, I'm guessing, people haven't been around. No croc signs, but that doesn't mean that they aren't around. Did you see that twenty-footer sleeping back there, mate?" Malcolm watches John but talks to Dave. "Tell us what you know about Station 25," Rob says, looking at John.

"Not much. It was active about ten years ago when the company was bought out by a group of Chinese investors. That was before I signed on. They dammed up a section of the mountain and got into open pit mining, but it didn't produce enough, so they closed it." He looks at them. "That's about all I know, if I'm even remembering right."

"Let's see what tomorrow brings. I think we're all ready for an early night." Rob brushes off his shorts, takes a section of mosquito netting, and hangs it over his bunk. Rob nods and yells to the others, "I'm heading in. Night."

Eric and Renee are already snuggled together in their hammock.

John looks at Dave. "You gonna tie me up or something? Other than getting up to pee, I'll be sleeping like a rock."

He narrows his eyes at him. "No, but I'm a light sleeper. I will hear your every move." Dave turns and smiles. "Thanks, Malcolm, another sumptuous meal. Next time, though, don't tell me it's lizard."

Later, Dave lies watching the night sky as he listens to the crew sleeping around him. His mind races with visions of Ropen Island and Eric falling off that cliff. He watches Eric and Renee sleep, hoping he isn't being creepy. Malcolm had stoked the fire with kindling before he turned in. It snaps and spats regularly. After an hour, sleep eventually overtakes him.

In the early morning hours, a sliver of moon illuminates the bay as the wind dies, turning the water into a glass reflection. John stirs from his hammock and quietly slips out. As promised, Dave is sleeping close to him. His regular low snoring regulates his breathing. John steps toward the tree line, watching the crew members rather than where he is going. The fire embers are red hot, giving him some light. There is no movement anywhere, even the jungle is quiet. John steps closer to the canoes and then relieves himself on the beach, glancing into the canoe contents while he does. As he zips up his pants, he looks up to see Eric watching him from the tree line. Giving him a little wave, he walks back to his hammock and goes back to sleep.

What was John doing? Eric listened to his movements, which was a good thing, but left him feeling a bit anxious. He could hear the blood pounding in his own ears. The darkness of the camp is absolute, other than the firelight. He wishes he had some sort of weapon other than his cane pole. Should he wake up Rob and let him know, or was John simply taking a leak? He quickly checks the time on his lit watch and makes a note to bring it up in the morning. Dave's snoring reverberates across the camp. It takes about an hour for him to fall back to sleep.

Before dawn, Dave, and Malcolm work together to get the fire going. The night's embers are still warm, and it flames up easily. A persistent mist hangs along the mountain range behind them. Malcolm grabs his knife, takes a step, and turns back to Dave. "Wanna go?"

Without thinking, he says, "Yeah, in fact, I do. I can't get over how you do what you do. Will be nice to watch the master in action." Dave grabs his spear and follows Malcolm into the dark.

"Stay right behind me. Try to step where I step." Malcolm gives him a wry smile. His voice holds a steely hardness and edge to it. "And keep quiet."

After pointing out edible sweet potatoes, Malcolm stops. He listens to the quiet of the jungle as it comes alive. The twittering of birds sounds close to them. He turns to a tree in front of them and looks up. "Most of them either sleep during the day or are settling down to sleep the day through. It's the perfect time to hunt." His whisper is so light that Dave strains to hear it. Malcolm whips a string with weights on either end through the air, snagging a tree wallaby from the upper branches. The animal screeches as it falls from the tree. It shudders before lying still.

"Damn, that was fast." Dave steps back, trips over a log, falling hard on his knees. "Ooops," he says as he brushes the debris off his legs. "Not as nimble as I once was." He gathers the sweet potatoes back into his shirt. Malcolm helps him up.

"Hey, while we are away from the others, I wanted to talk to you." Malcolm raises an eyebrow at Dave as he secures the wallaby and skins it with an expert swipe from his knife. "Yeah?" he says under his breath. "Can you not be so hard on John?" Dave takes a deep breath. "I know it's asking a lot, but the tension is high on the boat and that could lead to accidents."

"Always the peacemaker, aren't you?" Malcolm doesn't look at him but looks wounded.

"I have to be. I'm trying to do what is best for the entire team. John did not cause your experiences." He pauses as they walk on. "I'd like to hire you full-time if you're interested? I need someone I can trust to help us protect the Ropen. If you want to slow down, settle somewhere. We can help with that. Will you think about it?" He stays focused on Malcolm. "We're going to need a base location somewhere on this side of the island. I'm sure we can work something out that we are both happy with once we get back."

With a swish of his machete, Malcolm says, "I will think about it." He steps toward the deeper thicket.

Dave follows, careful to step exactly where Malcolm steps. Dave smirks as he watches the back of the tracker. His senses are on high alert, better than a cup of tea any day. Up ahead, there is a faint crack of a broken twig. He can barely make out his hand in this low light, much less see any animals. *How does Malcolm do it?* Dave slowly opens his pocket knife, keeping a firm grip on it. It locks in place with a faint click.

Malcolm stops at the sound and looks over his shoulder at Dave. Seconds tick by. A slight rustling comes from the brush down near his feet. Malcolm turns, sweeping the brush with his machete. The "thud" of contact and the small squeak of an animal is the only confirmation of a hit. Dave touches his display watch, illuminating a small grapefruit-sized-body of a prickly echidna lying at his feet. He whispers to Malcolm, "What is that?"

"Good eating," he says, as he picks the animal up by its tail. He glances at the small knife in Dave's hand and shakes his head at the effort. "Gotta get you an actual knife, mate."

Back at the campfire, Eric sits uneasily, waiting for Rob to come over. The rest of the camp is still sleeping. He watches Rob's flashlight within his tent as Rob unzips and exits and throws another log on the fire. Rob relieves himself, then walks over to Eric. "You're up early this morning.

There's another hour before breakfast is ready if you want to go back to bed." Rob watches the sky while talking. "Any sightings?"

"No, but I wanted to talk to you before Dad gets back. I think Dad's out hunting with Malcolm." He scoots over on the log, making room for Rob.

"What's up?" Rob asks. "Something weird last night. I heard John get up in the middle of the night, 2:35 actually, and instead of walking to the tree line away from us to pee, he walked down by the canoes. I think he was checking out what we have in there. It was covered up, so he saw nothing, but don't you think that was odd?"

"Did he see you?" Rob asks.

"Yeah, he waved at me, then went back to his hammock. My whole radar went on alert. Maybe I'm just too jumpy after hitting the island." Eric runs his hands through his bed hair. "Thought you should know. I didn't want to tell Dad or Malcolm, but I think we should still watch him." Rob pats his knee. "Thanks for telling me. Didn't we have anyone on night watch last night?"

"I think Z was supposed to be, about then, but I didn't go over and shake him. He might have been awake. He did wake me around four." "I will set up next to him and do watch with him tomorrow. Best to be cautious."

* * *

After three hours by boat, they pass by the abandoned mine of Station 25. The jungle has reclaimed part of the landscape, but the scarring of the pit mining and everything right around it has turned the area a slate, dingy gray. An ore tailings disposal streak leaves an ashen line in the water as it snakes out into the bay. The whole mountainside is a carved mess of dull against brilliant emerald-green trees beyond. It's a contrast of death and the green of life.

They are all stunned by what they see.

Isabelle comments as the boat slows. "Yeah, and the levels of cyanide, mercury, and heavy elements are still flowing from here into the ocean after ten years." There are three vast dump sites of waste rock piled across the area. Dotted in between are a scattering of abandoned huts and rusted equipment sluice lines. The forest is strangely quiet.

"What a depressing place." Eric turns the throttle up, moving them past.

Renee wipes away a tear and turns her face away from the others. She'd heard of dig sites before, but seeing and smelling the devastation cut her to her core. *The wanton excess and greed sting. How can this be legal?* She takes a deep breath and looks out toward the sea, not turning back until they are far away from the area.

Malcolm observes the tree line. "Notice, not even the birds are singing." He takes Renee's hand in his and they sit in silence. Memories of his life in the mine flicker through his mind. Even with the years behind him, the smell of the area brings everything rushing back. He tries not to breathe it in.

"They've got to be stopped," says Dave as the mine shrinks behind them in the distance. He doesn't realize he's said that cutting comment out loud until it's too late. He looks strongly at John. Rob shoots him a serious look. His voice is barely over a whisper, "Gonna, take some deep pockets to make a dent in anything we do."

* * *

It takes an additional day before they arrive mid-afternoon at the bay of Dolok. The tension has eased slightly since Malcolm stopped looking at John as if he were going to murder him in his sleep. They strain their necks to see stone-lined streets, telephone poles, and the novelty of larger boats at the marina. A collective sigh passes among the crew.

John doesn't see any of the company's boats in the harbor, but he still scopes out each vessel and the occupants standing around.

Malcolm says softly. "And we're back to civilization."

Renee looks down at her filthy clothes. "I desperately need a hot bath and clean clothes." Eric sniffs her shirt. He smiles. "Guess my sniffer is out of commission. I can't smell a thing." She hits him in the arm playfully and snuggles up against him.

"We all do. Let's see if there's a hotel. I want to check on Drew and

Billy. We can hope for an internet café of some kind." Dave is the first to hop out onto the dock. "Malcolm, can you talk to the marina and arrange for our docking fees? Let me know what they say. I'll be back in about an hour."

He nods, steps out of the boat, and walks up to the locals congregating at one end of the dock. Malcolm blends in easily with them, and the crew can tell who is talking by the hand gestures of each person. They watch Dave walk farther into town and out of view.

A boatload of chickens in stacked cages comes up beside them in an open bow boat. The birds smell. Isabelle covers her mouth and nose with a scarf. They watch the captain grab six birds by their feet and step off onto the dock.

Eric and Renee walk over to the rock embedded road thirty feet from the boat. They stretch and look at the continuous curtain of green around them that also includes the draping of vines over the buildings. "Doesn't look too bad." They watch two men cut up fish at the make-shift fish station across the bay. The water churns with activity as the men throw fish pieces into the clear waters. Renee points to a shark fin circling the flying bits.

"I doubt they will have internet here," she says to Eric. "Looks like they are still back in the '50s." They watch a donkey pulling a cart go past on a side street. "If Billy were here, he'd be out taking photos right now. I actually miss the guy." Eric rubs his itchy beard. Pointing to a bank sign on the side of a building, he says, "But there's a bank. Surely they have internet for transfers." They walk back to the others.

John finishes tying the boat. He checks the gas level in the tank, refills it, and sits back, relaxing. He covers his face with his hat, crosses his arms, and settles in for a nap. *Best to stay put*, he thinks as he listens to the surrounding community. It is an old trick he learned early in life. He knows the pace is slower in these small towns. Opportunities will present themselves if you learn to listen.

A police officer in a worn uniform makes his way down the hill to the marina. Malcolm steps over to meet with him. From their view on the water, the conversation includes a crash course on hand gestures. Malcolm calms the man, and together they walk to the harbormaster and out of view.

Rob whispers to Isabelle, "Should I go over?"

She shakes her head. "No, let him handle it. We need to secure the equipment. I'm sure if we left it for a second, it would disappear." He watches as desperate eyes keep watch of their set-up from a bank of boats to the left.

Z pats his pockets. "Do you have any cash? There's a food cart over by that big boat." He motions with his head. Sweat glistens across his forehead. He fights the urge to just walk over there. "God, I would kill for a cold drink of any kind." He wets his lips. "Sugar, any kind of sugar. I'll go into shock when it hits my system."

John replies, keeping his hat in place. "I think we all would."

Isabelle pats her pockets, then turns to her bag. She finds a small roll of currency and hands it to Z. "I'm not sure on the conversion rates. Use it wisely." John sits up and pushes his hat back. "I'll go with you. You'll need an extra hand to carry the drinks back. And I can speak a little of the local dialect."

Z gives Isabelle a grateful smile. Not waiting a split second longer than needed, John is out of the boat in a flash. He cinches his belt, following Z.

Rob busies himself doing a quick check on the electronic equipment and Chester. He pats the egg before sitting back down. "I'll take anything that isn't too sweet!" he yells at Z.

Isabelle shelters her eyes from the sun. "Hey, a coke would be great if they have it." Her eyes catch a vendor selling illegal bird feathers. She recognizes the brilliant coloring on them. "Gawd, takes all kind," she mutters, under her breath. *Maybe I should switch my specialty to birds? No, not birds. Better stick to the plants. They don't try to kill you.* She shudders again, thinking about those last two Ropen attacking them by the bonfire. *They are all suffering from some sort of PTSD.* The nightmares will be with her for years.

Rob follows her line of vision. "Looks like that guy is a regular. Guess the police look the other way here." His cart also includes carved wooden items, made from exotic wood.

Renee and Eric follow Z and John as they walk to the cart. Eric is practically skipping. Straightening up the equipment, Rob leans over and points to a small blue item in the boat. "Huh? What is that?" He cleans his sunglasses, which are a smeared mess.

"Let me." Isabelle steps to the cleared area in the bow. She inspects a splattering of membrane hanging in the bow underneath the boat's rim ledge. She looks closer. A tiny, brilliant-blue iridescent feather is stuck to the underlying boat coating. It's only about an inch long. She holds it and studies it carefully. Her mind connects the brilliant-blue of the angry Ropen attack head feathers to the sample she now holds. The bird had changed its skull feathers from mahogany brown to brilliant blue with an adrenaline rush. She lays it inside a worn piece of paper in her bag and folds it up tightly. *Might need it,* she thinks, as she pats her bag. Rob doesn't say a word as he watches her work.

When the crew gets back with armloads of cold drinks, Isabelle has already done a thorough inspection of the entire front of the boat with Rob's help. They sit back, satisfied, and accept the drinks happily. John rubs the cold glass bottle over his bare chest, between sips. "That doesn't work for me, but I think the women within a four-block radius are all watching," she says, and points to women standing on a balcony on the corner.

"Heck, it works for me. It feels great!" John smiles and finishes his drink.

The owner of the chicken boat returns without his birds. He unties from next to them and turns his boat back to the west. Isabelle sighs with relief. "Thank God." She waves the air in front of her and pulls down her bandana covering.

They all turn to watch a commotion taking place as a voice is raised at the bird feather vendor. A local woman knocks one tray of feathers to the ground. It looks as if she is going to attack the cart owner, who tries to gather his items before the wind takes them. The small man yells back as the police officer slowly strolls over.

The woman holds up one of the bird of paradise long feathers from the ground. "Looks like a kindred spirit lives in Dolok." Isabelle smiles at her antics. The police officer tries to calm the woman who storms off up the street. He helps the man arrange items from his cart before walking off.

Malcolm passes the officer and comes back to the boat, where John hands him a cold drink. He hesitates before taking it, then downs the whole thing at one time. He returns the empty bottle to John. "We're good for two days. Has anyone seen Dave?" They all shake their heads.

"There's a hotel here, probably not much other than a clean bed. We'll be lucky if they have hot showers. Thanks for the drinks." Malcolm looks at everyone before Renee points to Isabelle. "Appreciated." One unopened drink sits on the floor of the boat. Everyone eyes it as they watch for Dave.

Another hour passes before they see Dave's silhouette coming up the street. By this time, the sun has dipped below the tree line. He walks to them in mock exasperation. "Took a bit longer than I expected. We've got lodgings at Casa Puente. We have the whole place to ourselves. It's up the street and to the left. I've found a bank, and they are wiring funds. We should have a charter in two days to Puerto Del Brazo, then they'll fly us to the capital. See, I've been busy." He stammers when he sees the puddle around the drink, which has turned tepid. "W-w-was that for me?"

Rob nods, saying, "Thank Isabelle. We've been staring at it for over an hour in this heat." He hands it to Dave with all the bravado of a golden cup.

Dave continues, "Dinner, lodging is all on my tab. The kitchen is already working on it. Come on, let's get the gear inside." He hands Malcolm a wad of folded bills. "For the harbormaster, or whatever he is called. We can sell the boats. Can you switch the drink for a cold one?" Malcolm smiles and takes the money. "No problem, mate."

The shadows in town lengthen as they haul the last bit of equipment to the hotel. Z gently takes the wrapped egg to his room, putting it down in the corner. The rest of the equipment is spread out around it. He grins, hearing Renee exclaim from down the hall, "There's HOT water! Oh, my Lord!"

His room is sparse, with mosquito netting over a full-sized bed, a small nightstand with a lamp, and two awful paintings on the walls. Exhaustion creeps up on him full blast. He sits and strokes the lumpy mattress before falling back onto it. He closes his eyes for what he thinks is a second until he hears Dave call out, "DINNER!"

As the team walks down the stairs, Dave's head is full of questions. In particular, how to inquire about the ownership of the land east without arousing suspicions. He decided that his cover story of being on a scouting mission for a new mining entity would work well in this scenario.

A room off to the side of the living room acts as a dining room downstairs. Dave has iced cold drinks sitting in a bin on the floor as an array of flour tortillas, vegetables, cheese, fruits, and meat simmer in a large pan in the middle of the table. His hair is still wet from his shower and shave. He holds court like a king with each member. "Help yourselves, man it's good."

Malcolm walks in wearing a fresh shirt and pants. He shifts awkwardly when Renee smiles at him. His nubby beard is gone. "Wow, Malcolm, you look great," she says. Eric gets up quickly and holds the chair for Malcolm. "Sir, you are our guest of honor." Malcolm sits and rubs his shaved face. Rob hands him a cold beer. "Thanks. There's a clothing store around the corner. Here's to a hot shower for all of us." He slicks back his hair with his hand and rubs his shaved chin.

The celebration is light-hearted as they all eat their fill. By the time the dessert arrives, a chocolate flan concoction, they are all a bit drunk. The cook has prepared a special chocolate cake that she places in front of Malcolm. She flirts with him and winks, taking the tip of her finger along the side of the cake and then into her mouth. Malcolm is embarrassed as the crew teases him. "Told you I'd get you cake," Dave says with a big smile.

Isabelle keeps saying with each bite, "Oh, my god." She slowly chews each morsel. Dave clinks a beer bottle with his fork. "Okay, we have a new public corporation, Lane Enterprises. Thanks, you for your excellent skills in site location and analysis. Malcolm has agreed to sign on as our first full-time employee. He will oversee the establishment of our corporate office and do recon into promising sites as we move forward." Everyone raises their glasses for a toast.

"You're sure you're okay with staying here and setting everything up?" Rob clinks his glass with Malcolm. "Yeah, I need a break and Dave has outlined what he wants me to do. I'm not sure about the politics of all this, but I'm willing to learn. I know little about computers." He takes a deep drink of his beer. "Guess I'm going back to school."

"Don't worry about that. We'll get you set up and have computer training included." Dave straightens to address the group. "He's going to stay with us all the way to the capitol, and then return here. We could use help to find an office location and a home base, though." Dave looks at the faces around the table. "We'll split up into teams."

Rob raises his hand. "I'll head up the office search." Eric and Renee nod.

"Malcolm, why don't you lead the home search team? We have little time to get a lot done." He nods his head and runs his fingers through his hair. "Z is charging the satellite phone and we'll put in calls to check on Billy and Drew in the morning."

John raises his eyes at hearing the news of the satellite phone, but then softens and gives the team a defeated look. "And what do you want me to do?" The activity stops for a moment and all eyes are on John. "There aren't many opportunities for guys like me on this island, but I'd welcome a chance to do something meaningful with my life. If you'll allow me."

"That's a good question." Dave looks at him hard. "How would you feel about doing undercover work? It pays really well." Leaning forward,

John catches his eye. He smiles. "How good?" "I'll talk to you about that in private, but I noticed Newcastle has an office here in town. Would be nice to know what they are doing here? Since you're already an employee, could you ask around discretely and find out what their expansion plans are?" Dave hands him another cold beer.

John cracks open the beer by catching the lid on the edge of the table. He smacks it with expertise. "You know, I've seen you guys in action. You're all right. I would do the undercover work for free if it would mean you hire me on for the next trip." He eyes Malcolm, who finally gives him a little affirmation. "Oh, and I took out the spark plug for the boat. It's not going anywhere." Malcolm clinks his beer to John's in affirmation.

Eric and Renee stand and say good night. Isabelle follows them up the stairs.

Z slowly rises, taking his time. His voice is a bit slurred, "I'm worried about safety for the gear. Can we have someone keep watch? I'm sure everyone in town knows about our arrival."

Rob stands with him. "Let's fix up a little booby-trap in case you get night visitors." He looks back at Dave. "Thanks for tonight. It was much appreciated. I'll take care of the equipment."

"So, tell me more about how I can help." John leans forward to hear the plan from Dave. He smiles at John. "I think you're gonna like it."

CHAPTER 18

Sunlight streams through the window as Dave ends the call on the satellite phone. "You heard?" He turns to Z. "Drew is going to meet us in Puerto Del Brazo. Shouldn't you give your wife a call? I did promise that I would keep you in contact."

Z exhales. "Yeah, think I'd better. Anyone you need to call?" Z fiddles with a bank of knobs on the system.

Dave leans against the wall, watching. "No, just waiting on that call back from the hospital on Billy." Dave looks around the messy room. "Sorry, they dumped everything in here."

Z smiles. "I'm not. I slept better knowing that I could see it. Go ahead down to breakfast, I'll catch up. Still got a headache from the alcohol, or just a bit too much of everything. I'll stay here today and rest and monitor the equipment." He looks up as Dave closes the door to head down the hallway.

Renee, Eric, and Rob are at the downstairs table drinking coffee. Rob gets up to pour a coffee as Dave walks down the stairs and over to them. He hands Dave the fresh cup. "Thanks, I could smell it two floors up. That and bacon always get my attention." Dave eyes a thick slice of bacon, grabs it, and bites into it. "How did you guys sleep?"

Eric talks with his mouth full. "Like the dead. At least, I did. Renee tossed and turned all night." They both look at Renee. "That dig site really affected me."

Dave looks up, surprised. "That bothered you? Not the island adventure?"

She shakes her head. "When we get back, I'd like to contact my grandfather. I think he could help. He's looking for a project to be interested in after closing on that big IT buy-out in the states, and we could be that project. He was always telling me fascinating stories about monsters, giants living in mountains, Bigfoot."

Rob smiles. "I'd like to meet him. Sounds like my kind of guy." He takes a long drink of coffee and looks at Dave. "What's the word on, Billy?"

Dave starts a cup of tea brewing before answering. "He's in surgery now. They had to go back in. Waiting for the call-back from the hospital. Drew, on the other hand, is doing great. He's going to meet us in Puerto Del Brazo."

Rob talks in a hushed voice, "I'd like to make a call to my office, if that's okay? My guy used to work in top-level security. He'll be able to find out more information on Newcastle, for sure. I won't go into any comments about our biologicals. Hey, how'd it go with John last night?" He stuffs his mouth with a fork full of scrambled eggs and vegetables.

The hotel owner's wife brings Dave a huge omelet, which she places in front of him. He smiles at her and blows her a kiss. She blushes and heads back to the kitchen. "You don't look at food the same after coming in from a long trek, that's for sure." He takes a big bite before answering Rob. "Yeah, you can call, but wait until after lunch. We made calls this morning and Z is talking to his wife now. It will need a re-charge."

"And John?" Eric asks, holding his coffee cup to his lips. "Well, he's on. Gonna head to the office first thing and see what he can find out." He checks his watch and looks around the room as someone walks by the open door slowly. "He's already on site. Hey, let's watch our language. Never know who might be listening. Z is going to stay today to keep watch on the equipment. Has anyone talked to Isabelle?"

Renee laughs. "She's taking her second hot shower. If you hear groaning from the bathroom, it isn't me." She stands and puts her hand on Eric's shoulder. "We should get going. I'm sure Malcolm has already scanned properties out there." Rob stands with them.

"It's only about four blocks of buildings, so it shouldn't be too bad. I'm going to head back to the bank. Let's regroup in Z's room before dinner, 'bout 6 o'clock?" Dave watches them leave and pours himself a third cup of hot water. He rubs his hands together with excitement as he scans the array of tea flavors in a basket before choosing one and pocketing two more.

Rob looks over a three-story brick building down the street that is at least fifty years old. Eric and Renee catch up to him. "This looks like the only decent place around. Let me talk to these people. Why don't you scope out if there are any other options in the area." He heads inside to find building management. Three local men lounging against the front of the building watch him enter.

Eric and Renee do a loop around the four blocks of the city of Dolok. It's a mix of empty buildings and things you would expect in an economically depressed area. There are a couple of two-story buildings, but most are one-story. The road is made of stone pressed into dirt. Motor scooters and motorcycles are the preferred methods to get around. People watch them as they pass. They keep their eye out for Malcolm, without success.

Renee enters a clothing store that has a bit of everything. She buys a pair of khaki pants for each of them, woven sandals, and thin T-shirts. She looks at more shirts while Eric heads to the bank across from the store. He notices two men watching him as he crosses the street. One man has a barrel of a chest and thin legs. The second is stocky with bulging muscles. They look like they should work for a traveling circus. He chuckles to himself.

The men are still watching as Eric returns to the clothing store. He steps closer to Renee, and whispers, "Hey, I think we're being trailed. There are two goons outside. Stay close to me." He adds a second shirt for Z to the pile and pays for their goods before they exit.

As they walk back to the hotel, it's obvious everyone in town seems to be watching them. Nervously, Renee whispers to Eric, "Glad we're leaving tomorrow." She stops at a street vendor selling hats and buys one while carefully glancing around to see the goons coming down the street in their direction. She elbows Eric, and with a slight toss of her head, she motions toward the men. "Those goons?"

He nods his head. "Yeah, they don't look too smart, though. Might be the muscle in this town. Let's go."

As they approach the hotel, they see Isabelle walking by herself farther up the street. They call out to her, but she doesn't respond. Eric hands the bags to Renee and tells her to go inside the hotel and stay there.

He takes off on foot toward the goons, but it is too late. He sees large muscular arms grab Isabelle from a doorway as she is pulled inside. The goons wrestle Eric as they all get to the doorway at the same time. They push him to the ground, against the wall. They bar his way, speaking in a local dialect.

Eric hears Isabelle scream. Looking through dirty front windows of the building, he watches them put a cloth around her mouth. She kicks one of the men who is holding her in the groin, and he drops to the ground in pain. She is fighting like a banshee.

The taller goon grabs Eric by both arms and picks him off the ground. No matter how he struggles, the man's grip holds him firm. He watches helplessly as they pull Isabelle through a doorway, in the back of the building, and into a waiting truck that speeds off.

The goons notice their prey has been secured. The smaller one smiles, revealing broken and missing teeth. When the larger one releases Eric, they both kick him into the street before heading back up the street, laughing.

Stunned, Eric rolls to his side, narrowly being missed by a motorbike. He gets back on his feet and hurries to the hotel entrance. The hotel owners help him into a chair as he comes in. Renee checks him over for injuries. "Call the police," he says under his breath. "Policea, por favor!" He urges the homeowner to act. They both try to communicate with the couple without success. Renee runs up the stairs to get Z. They return from upstairs in less than a minute.

Everyone speaks at once when John walks through the door. "What's going on?" Eric stands up, holding onto his side. "Goons just kidnapped Isabelle out on the street. We need them to call the police." Renee is shocked. Z sits down hard on the second chair.

"I'm afraid it's probably worse than that." John quickly steps over to talk to the hotel owner in the native language, who then runs down the street to get the official. "He's getting help. They don't understand Spanish here." He paces. "Where's Dave? Kidnapping is another way for them to make money down here. Her life is in genuine danger. Depends on whether there is heavy drug use involved. I've heard horrible stories."

The concern on Renee's, Eric's, and Z's faces is real. "What do we do?" asks Z. "It's all I could think of in the situation. I panicked," Eric says. Bruising fingerprints appear on Eric's arms. "This big guy picked me up and held me while they took her. There was nothing I could do."

John turns to Eric. "Describe them to me and the vehicle they took her in." After getting the description, John turns and runs down the street. From the doorway, they watch him catch up to the hotel manager and then turn into the police office. Z paces.

"Where's Rob?" "Over at that three-story building around the corner," Eric says as Renee looks at his bruised arms.

Z starts for the door, saying, "I'll go get him." Renee stops him. "I know we need him, but I don't think any of us should go alone, even if it's just around the corner." Renee plops down next to Eric. "And if you two go, then it leaves me here alone. The manager is gone, remember?"

Renee and Z decide to wait at the doorway to the hotel. They constantly scan the area for members of the team. After thirty minutes, John and the hotel manager return, shaking their heads. "There's not much hope in getting their help," John says, exasperated. "He took the report and said he would look into it, then went across the street to a bar. I don't think he's going to do anything."

"Jesus," Z mutters. Suddenly, to him, the situation seemed a bit coincidental. "I bet he gets a kickback from the kidnappers. John, you, and Eric run over and find Rob and Dave. Stay together. We'll wait here." They nod and practically fly out the door toward the bank where Dave was last seen.

At the entrance to the bank, Eric looks at John. "Hey, man. Really appreciate your help. She's a good person." John nods back to him. "I know," he says, entering the bank. In minutes, they find Dave talking to the bank manager in a private office. They both rush in without knocking.

Dave quickly looks up. "What?…" He barely has time to finish one word when they quickly retell the chain of events. Dave looks at the bank manager, who speaks fairly good English. "This happen often in your town?" The guy shrugs. Not waiting, Eric pulls Dave to the doorway. "We need you now!"

Dave turns back to the manager. "Get that transfer done immediately. I'll be back."

In minutes, they find Rob and run back to the hotel. The tension is high as the team re-groups. Rob flexes his hands while he paces and mumbles. In his mind, Rob goes through scenarios to spin the ransom request, but now, looking at the team, he decides to lay it out straightforwardly. "We've got to go along with their request, whatever it is."

John runs his hands through his hair. "The police said to expect a ransom note sometime tonight. They've done this before."

"She's a British citizen. Shouldn't we contact the consulate office?" Renee pleads to Dave.

Eric squeezes Renee's hand. "God, if they hurt her…-Dad, I might not be responsible for my actions."

Dave looks over to John. "Any ideas?" He nods his head. "Actually, I do. I'm going to hang around the Newcastle office. I made calls while I was there to my field office, so I'm expecting a call back, anyway. Let me see who the players are around here. Obviously, don't go anywhere alone. The laws of the jungle still apply here." He puts his sunglasses on and walks out the front door.

"Anyone heard from Malcolm?" Dave scans their faces. His thoughts race with a million ways they could hurt Isabelle. His face turns beet red in frustration.

At that exact moment, a motorbike pulls up to the entrance of the hotel, blocking the exit. Malcolm steps off the bike. He's all smiles until he notices the concerned faces. "What happened?" Dave explains the situation to him. "Give me some time. I might know where to start looking." He gets back on the bike and takes off.

Dave paces. "Okay, let me fill you all in. The money transfer should have come in by now to cover our charter, the hotel tab, and a bit more. Guess I'll have to go over there and get even more." He shakes his head. "There's no real government in town. It's run by a few wealthy people, or at least folks better off than most, with connections back to the larger cities. We're really on the edge here. Kinda like the old west."

Rob leans against the large table. "Found suitable office space. Let me rephrase that. Found what is good office space around the block in that three-story building. It's one room with electricity, a closet, and access to a shared bathroom down the hall. They even have wi-Fi, but it's expensive." He pulls out a lease contract and throws it on the table.

"Did the police tell you how much they usually ask for in a ransom? Aren't they looking for quick cash?" Dave looks over to Eric. "Could be as much as fifty-thousand dollars. It varies." Eric slumps his shoulders. "I've read reports about this scheme." Dave winces. "That much? Damn it!"

Z looks up. "I've got to contact her employer and let them know. Perhaps they can help with the money?" He turns to go up the stairs. Renee stops him.

"Dave, let me help. I can call my bank and get the wire transfer sent right now if you have your banking info available. We can work it out later. Money isn't a problem for me." She blushes as she looks at Eric. "I'll talk to you about it later, promise."

"Good news is that Billy is out of his second surgery and is expected to have a full recovery." Z sits back down with a deep exhale. "The phone is charged."

Dave nods to Renee. He writes his banking information and hands it to her. "Don't have a choice right now, but we'll talk about it when everything has calmed down, and she is safely back with us. Thank you." Rob follows her. "I'm going to call my office as well." He follows Z and Renee up the stairs.

Dave plops next to Eric. "You sure you're okay? Did they hurt you?"

Eric shakes his head. "Fell on those same ribs. It's sore, and a little bruised. I'm fine." He pulls away from Dave and stands in the doorway, watching. "That could have been Renee they took." He bends down, hands on his knees. "I couldn't deal with that."

"Neither could I." Standing next to Eric, Dave pats him on the back. "You kids are all I have. When you're a parent, you'll understand the depth of that statement." He bows his head and says a silent prayer for Isabelle, knowing it isn't enough.

* * *

Back at the Newcastle offices, John leans against the wall in the reception room. A local, pretty girl is behind the desk. She fidgets with items in her desk drawer before sneaking looks at John when she doesn't think he's looking. He keeps his mirrored sunglasses on, knowing the effect he is having on her.

She answers the phone when it rings, then looks at him. "It's for you, John." She gives him a coy smile and poses in her simple cotton dress.

"Thanks, I'll try to be quick." He answers.

"This is John." After answering affirmative to the questions over the phone, he returns the phone to her. She hangs up. "So, who's got the fastest boat in the area?" He pulls his sunglasses down so that she can see his eyes.

She barely hesitates. "Well, that would be Obi. He's always trying to get me out for a ride." She looks at him, giving him her best smile. He leans even closer to her and whispers in her ear. "And, if I needed to make someone disappear, who would you suggest I see

She sits back, looks around to see that no one else is in the room, then leans forward and whispers, "Bruno, and Escobar. Up on Medias Street. I would take you, but it's not somewhere I should be. People would ask questions." Her eyes quickly scan the room again.

"What does Bruno look like?" John runs his fingertip along her jaw. "And where is Medias Street?"

"Well, he's big. Big chested and very strong, but with a teeny waist. He wears suspenders. The only guy in town who does." She stops and runs her fingers down his arm. "Medias is north of town, where the stones stop and turn to dirt. Take the turn to the right at the top of the hill. Don't go after dark."

He pushes a stray strand of hair back behind her ear. "Know where I can rent a scooter?" She nods, stands, and takes his hand as they leave the office.

An hour later, John parks his scooter in front of the hotel entrance and walks inside with confidence. Dave and Rob anxiously look up, and John says, "I need one of you to go with me. I have a location where they might have taken her. Who has the gun?"

John watches Rob pull the gun from the back of his waistband under his shirt. "Put it back. Has Malcolm returned?"

Dave shakes his head. "I should stay here. Rob, are you okay about going with him? Where exactly are you two going? Please stay together."

John's voice is quiet and low. "Up Medina Road to a big guy's place. Sounds like he might be the guy who held you up. Name's Bruno. I'm gonna go look around, or at least drive by to see what it looks like, or if we can see the vehicle. Was he wearing suspenders?" Eric nods.

John continues, "Yeah, I think he was. Do nothing that puts you at risk. Watch for Malcolm." He sighs heavily. "Only an hour, okay?"

They'd been gone an hour when Renee, Eric and Z walk back downstairs. Z sticks his head out the hotel door and looks up and down the street. Renee sits next to Dave and whispers, "The transfer has been completed. At least we'll have access to the funds. Did you talk to anyone at the bank?"

Dave raises an eyebrow at her. "Good idea. I'll head over and talk to the bank manager."

"What if they got Malcolm too?" Eric looks around at the anxious faces. "It's not like him to be gone for so long. He's so efficient at everything he does."

"You're right." Z squeezes Eric's shoulder.

The hotel manager brings out a tray full of different alcohol bottles. His wife follows with a tub of cold beers. They put them on the table before returning to the kitchen. "I don't think a drink is what we need right now." Z looks at the cold beer longingly and instead chomps loudly on a chunk of ice.

Thirty more minutes have gone by, when Z points to Malcolm coming down the street. "Thank God." Everyone clusters around him once he is inside. "We've been worried."

Eric clasps him by the shoulders. "You're family to us." Malcolm purses his lips. "Well, I couldn't leave my protected spot. Had to wait until they changed workers, but I know where they are keeping her. She is tied up and throwing every curse word she can think of at her captors. Saw Rob and John drive by at one point."

Renee nods, "I bet she is. It's a relief to know that she is alive."

They turn to the commotion at the entrance as John and Rob return, parking the scooter inside the lobby area. "I think we need to monitor it, too." They both walk over to the team. "All eyes are on us wherever we go."

"Where's Dave? Any word?" Rob looks around outside to see Dave hurrying across the street back to the hotel. "He's coming now. Glad you're back, Malcolm." Rob stands at the entrance watching Dave. As he approaches the entrance to the hotel, a boy, no more than six years old, intercepts him. He walks right up to Dave and hands him a note before running back down the street. Dave's hands shake as he opens it. In broken English, it asks for seventy-five thousand US Dollars for her safe return and gives an account number to transfer the funds to.

His worried expression says it all. "Well, there's no secret about it. They finished setting up things at the bank. The funds have been transferred. And it's interesting that they've asked for the exact amount that Renee transferred to us seventy-five thousand dollars. We have our ransom note. Someone at the bank is definitely helping them."

Rob looks up and down the street. "Maybe we should put our offices in an area that is a little less noticeable?" Dave pats Malcolm on the back. "It will be your choice, mate."

"He's seen Isabelle, or rather, heard her. He knows where she is." Rob looks up to Dave with hope in his eyes.

"That's some good news." Dave checks the door to the kitchen to make sure they are alone. "John, can you drive me over to the police office? Let's see what the officer says, and if it's not up to par, I'll suggest that while we're gone, you work up a plan to get her ourselves." He checks his watch. "We've got two hours to make the transfer. Let's make them count." The team huddles together with Malcolm as they question him further about the layout of where they are keeping Isabelle.

John pushes the scooter back out onto the sidewalk and hops on, revving the engine. Dave slips his leg over the seat and he and John are off in a flash.

* * *

Slim shafts of light illuminate the dirt floor around Isabelle. Her hands are tied up over her head with a twisted rope. They gagged her with a dirty rag. Her eyes are fueled with rage. She watches a rugged man wearing stained clothing observe her from the doorway. Bits of fluff and small feathers float in the air around her. The area she is in once sheltered chickens. Her pants are stained in chicken poop. She repeats a mantra of, "Don't cry," and closes her eyes.

The rugged man barely acknowledges her. Occasionally, he steps outside and swings his machete at the bushes before returning to his position of leaning against the side of the doorway. He chews tobacco, or some other dark liquid, that he spits into the dirt in her direction. Clearly, he isn't happy doing guard duty.

In the back of the shed is an enormous crocodile, almost fifteen feet nose-to-tail. It wears a thick rusty collar that digs into its skin. The croc is chained to a metal pole. Now and then, it hisses at Isabelle, letting her know it is there. She jumps every time it moves. Her eyes track from the croc to the doorway repeatedly. Sweat and tear lines track down her face. She scans the area deeper into the forest, hoping to glimpse Malcolm.

"*I must have dreamed it,*" she thinks, as she squints into the distance. She works the ropes over her head again, straining against them. "Please, God, let them find me."

A door slams in the distance and a pair of heavy foot-steps approach. Bruno enters by turning his body sideways. His massive shoulders don't fit through the regular door frame. He motions for the guard to take a break and once inside, reveals the carcass of a dead wallaby that he holds by the tail. The croc alerts and opens its mouth, swishing its head side to side.

Bruno talks to Isabelle, but she doesn't understand his language. He stands at her feet, watching her. He kicks her foot to get her attention.

The croc rumbles and snaps his jaws shut with a loud SNAP. Bruno talks lovingly toward the creature. He teases it then swings the wallaby over into the corner of the shed. The croc catches it before it lands on the ground. The crunching sound of breaking bones fill the space as Bruno steps back out.

Isabelle gags in response and swallows a sharp tang of bile. Time is running out. She can feel it deep in her bones. But there is no way she is going to go quietly.

Two men walk by. They talk to the man outside and laugh as they get into a vehicle. She can hear their footfall and the start of their car engine. She tries to concentrate on that rather than the crunching.

"*It will be over soon,*" she repeats in her head. "*Stay cool. Wait for the opportunity.*"

Bruno calls the guard back in and motions for him to cut her loose. He smiles, watching the gator tear apart the meal. The guard spits once more beside her and, with one whack of his blade, slices through the binding. Her arms fall like dead weights as she scoots to get away from the beast.

Bruno says something to the guard. They each take one of Isabelle's arms and pull her out of the building. They mumble to each other as they move her. Isabelle tries to get her feet underneath her, but her legs are asleep. Outside, they throw her to the ground as Bruno winces, holding onto a section of his back.

She pulls the rag out of her mouth and, on her hands and knees, has a raking coughing fit. She wipes her mouth with the back of her hand,

and they jerk her to her feet. "Don't hurt me!" she calls out to them.

Around them, a slight earth trembling sounds. They all stop and listen to the earthquake. A tile falls off the roof of the building nearby before the rumbling fades out.

Bruno looks down at her in disgust. "You stink!" he says in broken English. Then he laughs at his own joke. They throw her into the back of a beat-up pickup truck, its paint so faded that its color barely registers. Bruno turns and walks into the house.

The guard pulls her to the corner of the truck bed, near the window of the cab, and ties her hands to a loop. He takes off his sweaty bandana from around his neck and covers her eyes, tying it tight at the back of her head. He spits beside her before jumping off the truck bed.

She hears him walk away and slam a screen door. *Now what?* Isabelle tilts her head awkwardly, barely making out the things around her by looking through a slit of space under the bandana. She coughs loudly. Her raw throat screams in pain.

Nearby, voices rise in the house and soon the guard stomps outside. He stops at the side of the house, turns on a hose and Isabelle watches him take a drink. Then, he turns up the intensity on the nozzle and, while walking around the truck, cleans each tire. He stops for a moment and then opens up the tailgate. He sprays Isabelle hard with the hose. She opens her mouth to say something and receives a dousing with water. He laughs and jumps back out.

* * *

Back at the hotel, Renee and Eric analyze an old map of the area. Malcolm and Rob join them at the table in the dining room. There are still no other guests around. Malcolm hesitates, "I don't know. It's too risky." He paces nervously. "I should get back up there." A new, long knife flashes on his waistband.

Renee checks her watch. "It's almost four. Any sign of Dave?" She cranes her neck to look out the window. A local woman walks by with a pet pig on a leash. She holds a whip on a stick in the other hand and catches Renee watching her. The pig squeals and runs, pulling the woman behind her. Large flocks of birds take off from the mountainside.

Seconds later, the ground shakes with a minor tremor. Everyone braces themselves as people swarm into the middle of the street.

Rob holds onto Eric and Renee.

Several tiles fall off the roof of the three-story building down the block. The mountain screams a response with a vigorous shake. They look up to see John and Dave approaching, bouncing along on the scooter. John stays on and motions for Malcolm to come over. The tremor subsides.

Eric and Renee stand in the middle of the street watching the events around them. They take a step towards the team, but Dave motions for them to stay put.

Malcolm and John whisper to each other, then he gets on the scooter behind John, and they take off up the hill. Dave says a quick word to Rob and walks over to the bank with the bank employees that had been standing in the street. He calls out to the bank manager and disappears inside.

Rob motions for Renee and Eric. "Let's get back to the table." He keeps his voice low and watches their faces as he says, "It's in motion."

The table in the lobby is now covered with dust. A new crack snakes up the wall behind them. Renee touches it as they sit, getting back to the map.

Rob coughs, then whispers, "The police were no help at all. Dave thinks he may be in on the whole ransom deal, so getting help from any government entity is out. What is in, though, is that Dave talked to Isabelle's director. They gave us suggestions. We're getting her. Dave is wiring the funds to a separate account that will be released once she is safely back with us. This keeps the bank manager and all the other 'insects' from getting the funds." Renee shakes her head. "I don't care about the money. For me, it's about getting her safely out."

"Let me finish." Rob strokes the back of his arm. "Hear me out. We have to get to Puerto Del Brazo as soon as possible. The Foundation is sending a plane for us there. Malcolm will drop John off to get the new boat. Then, Malcolm will get Isabelle. We're to meet John down at the dock. See if you can borrow that kitchen cart from the hotel owners. I'll pay the bill. Do it quietly. We need to get ALL our stuff now and wake up Z. Dave will be back any minute to help."

Renee looks up in alarm. "Oh, my god, we left Z upstairs during the earthquake!"

Eric rises. "I'd better go up and check on him! Wait, Malcolm is going in all alone with the kidnappers?"

Nodding, Rob continues. "He knows the situation better than we do. He's getting help from some locals." Rob stands and motions for them to follow. "Let's get packing."

* * *

The dirt road John takes follows the curve of the bay. The address he is racing to, and the map he uses to get there, are scribbled on the back of his hand. He stops at a lean-to that is propped up with 2x4's and a water cistern that seems to keep the building upright. A local man in his twenties, wearing shorts and no shoes, steps out onto the porch. He fits the description of the boat owner, Obi.

After talking a bit, Obi motions to the dock area that is behind the house. A gleaming three-year-old speed boat floats happily at his make-shift dock. John and Obi walk over to it. *The boat is a perfect fit for them. Room for five in the cabin*, John thinks as he looks it over.

After negotiating the price, he charters the boat with Obi as the driver. John doesn't hesitate and hops onto the boat with him. Obi rev's the engine and, after a tight turn, speeds the boat back toward town.

* * *

Back at the hotel, Rob hustles up the stairs and helps Renee on her way down with an armful of backpacks. She stays with the items as he races back up for the last bags.

Z struggles with his wrapped egg and the communication box and two back packs as he hobbles down to her. "Well, that's all my stuff and Isabelle's." He drops the backpacks on the floor. "Any word?"

"I'll do a final check." Dave drops what he thinks is the last of the gear and heads up the stairs one more time.

The cook hands a netted woven bag to Z and smiles at him. He takes the gift and smiles back to her before she walks back to the kitchen.

Renee smiles. "I think she likes you." She looks up in time to see Eric coming through the door, out of breath. "Nothing yet. Mr. Trey is bringing his truck for us. Should be out back any second." He points to the back door. "We should move everything back there."

Renee helps Z loop the bag over his head to make a "baby pouch" for the egg. They nestle it, still wrapped in T-shirts, into its new cocoon sack. "This works perfectly." Z holds the pouch protectively. "Feel kinda pregnant."

* * *

Isabelle bakes in the sun watching mosquitos feast upon her arms. She twists, trying to get them off, but they fly back on. She sends psychic messages to Malcolm to get her out of the situation. Keeping one good eye focused on the house, she waits for the guard to walk her way. He leans against the wall, whittling with a big stick and large pocket knife.

A pebble "dings" against the side of the truck. She turns her head quickly, scanning what she can. The guard looks up briefly before returning to his carving. Inside the house, Bruno can be heard talking loudly on the phone.

Isabelle re-positions herself as best she can in the truck bed. She looks back toward the sound and catches her breath when Malcolm quickly appears out of the brush. He stays crouched, running to the side of the vehicle. "You okay?" he whispers to her.

She nods and strains against the rope. "I'm going to cut you loose, but keep your hands up," he says. She hears quiet movement in the brush but doesn't look. Instead, she coughs, covering up any sound.

The guard looks up briefly.

She leans as far away from the binding as possible, giving Malcolm more access. He slips over to her without making a sound and slices through the binding with one quick motion before returning to his hiding place.

The sound of arrows piercing through the air zips past Isabelle as the guard is hit once in the chest and once in the throat. Malcolm runs to him, slicing across his neck and moves him into the brush where he lies still. Isabelle covers her mouth in horror and scoots over the side of the truck, falling onto the ground with a thud. Malcolm helps her up and takes her into the tree line.

"God, Malcolm, I knew you would come." She kisses him on the cheek. "We don't have time."

At that second, Bruno steps out of the house. The screen door slams behind him. He calls for the guard. There is no response, so he stomps over to the truck, kicking it when he sees Isabelle is gone. He swears and pulls a long switchblade from his pants. Opening it, he scans the trees.

An arrow flies and hits him on the shoulder. Bruno races into the brush in the direction the arrow came from and is hit with three more arrows at once. He stops and looks down with surprise. He pulls one arrow out, wincing and keeps moving forward, now at a slower pace.

A teenager steps out from behind a tree. He stands defiantly and sneers a profanity at Bruno before launching two more arrows that hit the bullseye of his heart. Bruno goes down in a lump, piercing two of the arrows out his back. The teen walks over to Bruno, takes the arrows, kicks Bruno, then dissolves into the jungle.

It happened so fast that Isabelle barely had time to register what she saw. Malcolm pulls her along. "Hurry, we must get out of here," Malcolm urges.

"Who was that?" Isabelle looks back in the direction the teen moved.

"You don't need to know. Bruno raped and killed his sister. Revenge can be sweet." Malcolm pushes bushes away. "Everyone is waiting at the marina. We're leaving now!"

* * *

Dave paces on the dock and checks his watch. John stands next to Obi in the boat, securing life vests. His heart races as he remembers watching each member sign their travel waivers and thinks of the magnitude of the situation they are now in. He has put their lives on the line too many times. Isabelle's calm smile and the way she teased him those first few days floated into his memory. Things would have turned out differently had she not been on the team. They had to rescue her. There wasn't another option.

Rob sticks his head up from the cabin. "Can you see them?" he calls out.

"No, not yet. I'll let you know," John replies, as he scans the horizon before reviewing the route map on top of the engine block. He swallows the urge to say, "*nothing since you asked five minutes ago.*"

Dave watches the bank manager walking down the street toward them, followed by the police officer. There is a lot of gesturing being done between them as they walk.

Finally, in the distance, Malcolm and Isabelle appear on the scooter. Dave calls out to the crew, "They're coming! He's got her!"

Obi starts the engine with a loud roar. Rob looks up from the cabin and steps onto the deck.

From the other end of town, Escobar's stocky form emerges from a truck. He heads straight for them and is followed by two burly men also walking toward them. The men split off from Escobar and go to a boat tied at the dock.

Dave calls out to those below deck, "This might get dicey. Everyone stay below. Rob, be ready to push off."

The police officer tries to wave Malcolm down, but he zips past. The police officer and bank manager start running after the scooter.

Rob stands at alert with John. They have untied the moorings and are holding the boat to the dock.

Dave looks at Obi. "John, tell him, if he gets us safely to Del Brazo, he can have the whole seventy-five thousand dollars!" John relays the message. Obi smiles wickedly and agrees.

Malcolm screeches to a halt on a grass strip and throws the scooter in park, while Dave helps Isabelle off. John helps her step into the boat while Dave jumps in. They both give the boat a good push from the dock.

The police officer calls out for them to "halt" and shoots his gun into the air.

Everyone dips down with the gunshot and brace themselves as Obi pushes the throttle forward. Malcolm shouts, "STILLMAN!" to the officer and holds on tight, sitting down next to Dave. He looks at Dave and says, "I called him a thief!"

The team watches Escobar make a run to his boat as the goons now have it ready. He flips off the bank manager as he passes.

Obi expertly navigates the boat as it roars out of the marina. The wake capsizes one small boat as they race by. John points out a log floating in their path so Obi zips to one side, then takes the boat out into the bay.

Renee and Eric help Isabelle inside the cabin. It's a rough ride until the boat planes and smooths out. In the distance, Escobar, and his goons race after them. The goons make up a bit of the distance, and Escobar fires wildly toward Obi's boat. Three bullets "ping" off the boat. Obi curses at them and then takes the boat at full speed, increasing their lead.

Dave steps into the cabin. "Everyone okay?" He looks at Isabelle, who is already shedding her filthy jeans. Renee holds a pair of shorts for her to put on.

Isabelle's hands shakes as she holds out the dirty jeans for Dave to take. "Throw them overboard. That smell is never coming out." He gingerly takes them, between a finger and thumb. His eyes flash relief to Isabelle during the transfer, but she won't look at him.

"Incoming," Rob calls out as he helps John navigate down the cabin steps. John holds one hand to his chest where blood is blooming across his shirt.

John murmurs, "Must have been hit by a stray bullet."

"Help me get him inside." Rob pursed his lips under the weight.

"Hold on, Buddy," Dave calls out, as he helps John. Eric and Renee move to make room for John.

John looks at his shirt in surprise. "Mate, doesn't even hurt. Why is that?"

Renee presses a folded towel against his chest. She whispers to him, "Just stay calm. We're gonna get you help."

Dave turns back to Malcolm on deck. "Ask Obi how long it will take at this speed?" Z fumbles with the satellite phone gear. He fires it up. "Can call in just a few minutes. Give me a sec."

Eric looks up to Dave. "Are they still following us?"

Dave steps out, scanning the horizon. "They are slagging behind. Won't be able to catch us. We're flying ahead." He looks over to Malcolm, whose face is etched in worry. He holds out his hand for Malcolm to shake. "Thank you. I don't know what you did... shouldn't know, but I'm sure glad you got her out."

Malcolm speaks to Obi. "It's gonna take at least four hours to get him to Del Brazo at this speed. The boat can handle the speed, but I don't think John has that much time." Malcolm looks to the inner cabin where Isabelle and Renee work on John.

Eric steps out onto the deck. "It looks bad. He's coughing blood. Z can call for an emergency pick up by heli. The phone will be ready in less than five."

Rob motions to the boat following them. "They know where we're going. Is there anywhere we can pull in?" Malcolm repeats the words to Obi, who shakes his head in response. "There's nothing between here and there." Malcolm looks over at Dave.

Dave shakes his head. "No, there's no stopping, but I can have the heli meet us in Del Brazo for immediate transfer to the hospital. I will not risk the entire team by stopping." He pauses. Normally, he would discuss it with the crew, but there isn't anything normal about the situation they are in. He reminds himself that *as the leader of the team, sometimes you have to make hard choices.* He remains silent, not trusting the words that might come out.

Malcolm slumps to the floor of the boat. He opens a bottle of water and downs it. "If it were Eric shot, what would you do?" He looks at Dave hard.

"The same thing." Dave turns and goes into the cabin. He looks into everyone's eyes as he enters. Z keeps his head bowed. Isabelle wipes the brow of John. Renee looks for another towel to hold back the bleeding as the first towel is almost drenched.

John shudders, opens his eyes, and looks at Isabelle. "Thank you," he whispers, breathes out once and then doesn't take another breath. Renee tries to revive him, but there is no response. She takes the new towel and places it over his face. His wound no longer pumps blood. It's over in less than a minute.

A heaviness fills the cabin, it clings to the stifling humidity.

"He's gone?" Dave asks, looking right at Renee. She nods and steps back before heading up the stairs and into Eric's arms. Dave sits across from Isabelle. She holds her arms crossed in front of her and scratches her mosquito bites. Dave tosses her a bottle of lotion. She lets it land on the cushion beside her and looks at him hard. "So, now I'm responsible for John?"

"That was a wild accident," Dave says softly. His thoughts replay the series of events as they raced for the boat. Z turns off the equipment and touches her shoulder as he passes. He steps out onto the deck.

She holds up her hand. "Just don't talk to me. I'd appreciate a transfer back to my field office base as soon as possible. I'm done." She lies down and closes her eyes, sobbing.

Dave steps back onto the crowded deck. Eric and Renee sit on the floor beside Malcolm. Rob sits in the corner by himself. The boat following them is a dot on the horizon. It is enhanced by a beautiful thunderhead, backlit by streaks of orange and pink from the setting sun. They all watch and sit in silence.

Darkness has fallen when they pull into Puerto Del Brazo. Dave calls out to Obi, "Marina Mercado? Do you know it?" Obi nods and continues on, passing three marinas. Their destination marina has four bays in the front area, but over fifty spread out across the inlet, complete with a small mechanical dock and a one-pump gas station in the middle. A scattering of people are out with their boats, including a white man in khaki pants who stands out as someone of importance. He waves at the boat from near the gas pump.

Obi pulls into Marina Mercado and slows at the gas pump station.

The man in khakis walks over to them as Dave and Rob step onto the dock. He calls out to them, "Dr. Lane?" Both Rob and Dave answer, yes." They elbow each other. "I'm Dr. Dave Lane and this is my brother, Dr. Robert Lane." Dave shakes the hand of the stranger.

"Nickolas Tuttle, with the World Wildlife Federation. We've got transportation waiting for you." He looks up to see Isabelle's red lined eyes. "Isabelle?"

"Thank you, Nick. We'll talk later." She brushes by him and heads to the restroom door. Renee follows her.

"We need to unload quickly and pay our captain. One of our crew didn't make it. He's wrapped in a sheet down below," Dave says, helping Z step out onto the dock. He brings a dolly cart over to the boat. Eric hands him items.

"Whoa, sorry, I didn't know. But we've got the payment as you requested. It was really difficult to arrange. The plane is ready and waiting." Nick watches them load the cart.

Dave motions to the way they came in. "There was a boat following us. They aren't friendly. Need to get going fast."

Malcolm watches the horizon as he pushes backpacks to the cart loading area. "Obi is going to manage taking care of John. We don't have time to argue."

Dave nods. "Thank you. Have Obi follow us to the plane, and we'll pay him there."

In his haste, Obi fumbles with the gas pump. Malcolm goes over to talk to him. They argue, then Malcolm looks up. "He won't leave the boat. We'll have to bring payment to him."

Nick takes a step back. "The plane is about a seven-minute van ride away. Let's take this pile of gear and two people. I'll come back for the rest of you and bring the payment." Rob watches one boat in the area as a man drinking in the back of his boat watches them.

"Take Renee and Eric," Dave says as he motions for Eric to go. "And, Isabelle, if she will go with you."

In minutes, the van is packed. The whole while, Isabelle refuses to look at Dave.

Rob squeezes Eric's shoulder as he shuts the door. Renee sits on Eric's lap. Isabelle has squeezed in. She is covered in backpacks and electronic equipment. Z gives her a peck on the cheek as he closes the door. "We'll be right behind you."

"You'd better," she calls as the van heads out.

Rob walks over to Dave as they head back to the boat for the last of the gear. "Don't worry, I gave him my pistol, just in case."

Dave scans the area. "I can't even think about that. Let's station the gear past the tree line." He points to a large tree. "It's a bit more hidden there."

They watch Z struggle up the hill, carrying his egg in the sling pouch around his neck. The ground is slippery from the recent rain. In his other hand is the satellite phone gear. He is completely drenched in sweat by the time he makes it all the way. "I'm gonna enjoy a long, cold drink when we get there."

Finally, they have the gear off the boat. Obi disables the boat by removing a spark plug. He follows the men to the staging area at the top of the hill and talks to Malcolm in a hushed voice. "He says that these people might have look-outs in the area. We need to be careful." Obi fidgets nervously.

"Any minute," Dave calls out as they watch the road and the water's edge. A boat slowly passes the marina and collectively they all hold their breath as it continues on. Malcolm squats down close to Dave. "Guess we can cancel the idea of having an office back there?"

"You're right on that," Rob answers.

The van comes toward them. It turns off its running lights and headlights, arriving in the dark. Nick steps out of the van and looks around, confused. He can't see them waiting a bit up the hill.

Dave steps out with bags in hand, and everyone follows. Then Obi stays with Malcolm, who takes the money bag from Nick. They open it to check the contents and, with a quick nod, Malcolm hands it to Obi, who runs back to the boat. In less than a minute, they are all in the van pulling out.

"Man, I really didn't see you when I pulled up. I thought something bad had happened." Nick turns onto the main dirt road and turns on his headlights. The road is filled with potholes. Z braces himself by holding onto a strap while he holds the egg pouch in the other. Rob is sandwiched tightly next to him. He follows Z's line of sight to the vehicle's light.

"Could you go faster?" Rob asks, as he sees new headlights in the distance coming their way. Sweat drips off them in the humidity and from being closed up inside the van. Dave cracks his window. "Everything okay at the plane?" he asks Nick.

"Yeah, the props are spinning. We'll make a run for it."

Rob turns to see the vehicle behind them. "Looks like we'll all need to make a mad dash. Z, I'll take the satellite phone. You keep your hands free to hold on to Chester."

Nick frowns and looks back. "Who's Chester?"

"No worries, it's just a name we've given some of our specimens." Z tries to sound calm, but there is a bit of a quiver to his voice. He stays silent, his face betraying nothing in nervous agitation as he bites off a fingernail.

They turn into the parking area. A tricked-out jeep is parked to one side. It turns on its lights, illuminating their vehicle. Two men are inside. One is on his phone.

Nick drives the van closer to the plane. Dirt sprays as he stops the vehicle. The plane doors open. Nick takes a photo of the chase vehicle. The crew enters the plane. They move so fast that Rob and Dave practically lift Z onto the plane. Nick is the last one in. They all watch a heavy-set man step out of the chase vehicle as it arrives.

The plane engine roars and turns onto the taxi-way. No one says a word as the pilot taxis the plane forward and takes off into the night sky. They quickly move out over the bay where they watch the chase boat pull into the marina. The space Obi occupied at the dock is empty.

Dave sighs heavily. "That was a bit too close." He catches the pained look of horror on Isabelle's face as she turns away from the window and the scene below. Z pats her hand in comfort. She avoids looking at Dave.

CHAPTER 19

Three days later, the crew sits around a large conference room table. Isabelle's seat is empty. Out the bank of windows behind them is the city center of Port Moresby. Joining them at the table is a corporate lawyer, Tim Tindale. A large video screen shows an aged man, Bruce Butler, sitting behind an elaborate desk. He listens in on the proceedings.

Next to Dave is a private security agent, Titus Wells, oozing intimidation. Mr. Wells is dressed all in black.

Mr. Butler cuts into the conversation. "I understand Isabelle is taking a leave of absence from her job? I'll have Miss Cathy send her a year's salary to tide her over until she is ready to return to work."

"She was an integral part of our mission, saving the lives of three of our crew in the process," says Dave. "We wouldn't have been able to finish the mission without her. She is going to need counseling." Dave watches as Butler ponders the statement. Then responds, "I'll get her the best therapy money can buy."

Butler looks at Tindale. "Tindale, you've finished setting up the corporation?" Mr. Butler shoots out statements fast and furiously.

Tindale holds a stack of papers in his hand. "Yes, sir, almost a million acres, set apart as a game preserve. Gifting them back to the country of Papua New Guinea after one hundred years. We've got an option on another two hundred thousand acres. I've run it past one of our members of parliament, t and they are going to add it to the next legislation docket. The land won't be touched, and access will be denied to any outside entity or organization. Mr. Malcolm will function as liaison agent yearly. The codicil amendment to include air rights was put up with some hesitation, but it should pass." Tindale shuffles through his paperwork. "We will set up Malcolm's offices at his discretion at a location of his choosing."

Dave watches Butler on the screen, then turns to Malcolm. "Malcolm, keep it small. We can even build a bunker if that is more advantageous for you. Mr. Butler, you've been more than generous with the stipends." Dave looks right at Butler. "You're sure no one will find out our true mission?"

Wells interrupts, "Leave that to me, Dr. Lane. My security team is top-notch. Anyone looking further into this corporation will be led to an array of misdirection. Your mission and board are totally confidential." Mr. Wells speaks clearly and confidentially. "You understand, all documentation and images must be run through our field office representative." He passes documents around the room. "This is part of protocol. It is your understanding that all images are part of the corporate entity. Please read through it and sign before leaving today. Miss Isabelle signed her approval earlier today. It is imperative that we have ALL signatures."

Dave takes a long drink of water. "All image files have already been sent. We will send back separate files for your own personal use. When the time is right. That takes a load off of us and will protect the creatures. We want to keep the public away from the area."

Butler leans forward until his face fills the screen. "So, how is our little Chester?" His animation shows nothing but excitement. All eyes look toward Z. He stammers. "Snug as a bug. But what's the next step for him?"

"So glad you asked." Butler beams. He pushes back from his desk. "Dr. Zahir, I would like to invite you and your family to come and stay at my estate out on Kennebunkport. I'm not there much. It's isolated and there is a fabulous greenhouse that we can convert into a lab." Dumbfounded, Z looks wide-eyed at the screen. "Really?"

"Of course, you'll have a generous budget to work with. Got to get those biologicals analyzed and categorized and set up a nursery for the baby. It comes with a salary you can't turn down." Butler raises his eyebrows comically at Z.

Renee giggles. "Grandpa, that's so kind of you." Renee reaches for Z's hand. "He means it too." She pats his hand.

"Having a lab so close to my offices in Portland works perfectly. I'm sure you're going to enjoy collaborating with my guy," Rob interjects, as he signs the confidentiality agreement. The attorney takes the paperwork.

They all look up when a knock sounds at the door. Wells motions for them to stay seated. He opens the door to Billy in a wheelchair and Drew standing behind him. Everyone starts talking at once as they all quickly get up to greet Billy and Drew.

Z turns to the screen. "Yes! I'll take you up on the offer!!!" It takes a minute before Dave gets everyone to calm down.

Dave apologizes to Butler. "I'm sorry for the disruption. We've been concerned about these two members of the team that were injured. That's Billy, our photographer in the wheelchair, and Drew, Z's nephew, and lab assistant, with the cast." Dave points to the men and beams with happiness to see them. A flood of relief passes through him, making him feel lighter. The coloring on both men is good. Drew wiggles his finger in his cast, showing off the healing.

"I'd like to talk to you and Tindale alone," Butler says above the din.

Z quickly dials his phone, Facetiming Isabelle for the rest of the crew. The crowd sings out "IZZY!" when they see her image.

Dave sits back down, facing Butler. "Give me a moment." Butler nods, catching Renee's eye. With a quick flip of Butler's hand, Renee gets up as the team moves to the adjoining room. Dave whispers to Rob, "Let me talk to him for a minute. He wants to meet with me and the attorney." Rob nods his head and ushers everyone out. Wells closes the door and silence fills the room. Dave takes a deep breath.

The muted voices of the team seep through the walls.

"I am impressed with you and your team. Had an exceedingly long call with Renee last night. Someone's got to be lead for the foundation, and I'd like to offer you the position." Butler sits back, waiting for Dave to respond.

"You mean the corporation, don't you?" Dave looks over as Tindale opens a separate folder. He slides it across the table to Dave. He slowly opens it and reads.

Butler continues, "No, a new foundation. The corporation is for the Ropen. This foundation is something else. I've had so much fun watching Eric and Renee romp around the world living my dream. I'm getting too old to fly these days. Oh, by the way, I'm sending my private plane over there for everyone to come back state-side. Makes covering our tracks easier. The plane will be on-site tomorrow afternoon. Tindale will give you the information. Make sure Chester is on it!"

"This...-this foundation is for us?" Dave flips through the pages, not believing what he is reading. His hands shake with excitement and awe. *Rob is going to have a heart attack!* He pours more water from the stainless pitcher in front of him.

"I don't think Renee will sit still for any length of time, and your boy Eric is a perfect match for her. They need adventure. It's in their blood. I know you will protect them, and with your brother Rob along for the ride, it's what is needed. If you want more funding, simply ask for it. I've been lucky in my business life and at this point in MY life, I want to make a difference. I've also sent a generous stipend to the Diabetes Foundation in your wife's name." He pauses. "Go search out reports of the weird, the unknown, and document what you can. I only ask that all biologicals go through the lab I'm setting up with Dr. Z. And I have one stipulation." Butler pauses and leans forward on screen. "Yes?" Dave gulps.

"That Renee and Eric are not to go on any trips without either you or Rob accompanying them. Oh, I have them micro-chipped, and I would like the same done to you and Rob." Butler sits back, satisfied as Dave nods. "I'll be glad to pay for additional security or trackers on any research project." Tindale points to a line on the document for signature.

"What do you say?" Butler is anxious.

Dave flips through several pages. "Tell you what, give me an hour to look through this? I don't see a problem, but I don't sign anything without reading it." He smiles at Butler.

Tindale gets up from his chair. "Just let me know when you're done. I'll be in my office down the hall."

Dave stops him. "Would you send Rob in?" He looks at Butler on the screen, who is moving slowly, getting out of his chair. "Thank you, Mr. Butler. You have been so generous. I'm sure there won't be any issues."

"The plane is yours to use as you need it. Make the most of this opportunity. I'd like to celebrate your successes while I'm still alive. But call me Butler. All my friends do." He clicks off the screen.

Dave is still sitting there shell-shocked when Rob comes in the door. He has a large, iced soda in his hand that he puts in front of Dave. "So, what else? Billy is doing really well, and Drew is already talking about the next trip. You should have seen his face when Z showed him some of our footage. I know we should have waited, but—". He notices Dave isn't moving. "What? What is it?" He sits down with a plop. Dave slides the document over to Rob while watching his face.

"What?.. -What?…--What?!!" Each page he turns, he looks up to Dave. After reading the last page, he pushes back from the table. "Holy shit!"

"Now, sit there and let me read the whole thing. He wants me to run lead on this. Think carefully, can you take orders from me?" Rob crosses his arms and pouts a bit; he's grinning from ear to ear.

* * *

Almost a year later, Rob and Dave are at a medical conference. Together, they step down from a podium before a room full of Ph.D.'s and sponsored medical corporations. The crowd gives them applause as they walk back to the end of the room. An executive from a medical research firm pulls Dave aside and tries to engage him in a conversation while Rob stands next to him, accepting congratulations from his peers. They both move out of the main conference room into an annex. A small crowd follows them.

Dave elbows Rob and whispers, "See, this is what good science can get you. I'm not all about accolades, but there is required protocol to get funding. No grant is going to happen if they are laughing at you. Our results may make a difference in the world. Maybe even save YOUR life. I feel that I've honored Jeanne. We've honored Jeanne."

Rob stands immobile, staring at Dave.

A man in an expensive suit interrupts them. "Fascinating, the cellular connections. You've found it, a genetic therapy-based cure for diabetes." The executive is animated in his response, talking very quickly.

"Not yet, but we are hopeful the viral vectors gene works, may shield them from the immunological assault." Dave beams as he talks. Other people listen in.

An attractive woman steps forward. She flirts as she asks him, "Dr. Lane, what made you test bat blood?"

Dave pauses before answering. "My wife suggested it, after looking at a cellular connection. You never know where a lead will take you. This is all thanks to Dr. Jeanne Lane. Excuse us."

Dave moves from the crowd.

Rob follows him and when they are alone, he grabs Dave's arm. "You did THIS for ME?"

Dave is all business, as he responds. "It didn't start out that way, but I had time to refocus out in the deep. I saw what it did to our extended family." His eyes soften. "And you're the only family I have left. Nancy doesn't count."

Rob tears up, wiping away a tear as he looks away from Dave. "It IS what Jeanne would have wanted." He lets out a long sigh as they walk out to the lobby. "Thank you," he says as his phone beeps. He holds up a text message from Eric.

Dave puts on his glasses to read it. The message reads, "Call me! Great footage of a SKUNK APE in the Everglades!" Dave looks over his glasses at Rob. "Seriously?"

Rob is a bit giddy as he plays the video. "Whoa, we gotta go!" He looks over to Dave with puppy eyes.

"Oh, for heaven's sake...." Dave watches the video and zooms out on it. Under his breath, he says, "You know that people have been trying to verify the existence of Bigfoot, Yeti, Sasquatch, and the Skunk Ape for more than a hundred years?"

Rob nods quickly. "Unh, huh." Dave stops and looks at him hard.

"And you want to go into the swamps again?"

"Unh huh, yes!" Rob says in a flash.

Dave plays with the image on the phone, then hands it back to Rob. "Let's get our physicals done and if your results are within range, we'll go. But, only for two weeks. I've got to work on the next paper." Dave lets out a deep sigh.

Rob shouts, "WHOOPIEE!" Many of the people in attendance turn and look. He doesn't care and does it again. "WHOOPIEE!"

Dave puts his arm around Rob's shoulder as they walk out the conference doors. "Guess the Lane Foundation is off on its next adventure!"

THE END.

The next adventure continues with...
RIVER OF GRASS

EVERGLADE CITY, FLORIDA

Since starting the Lane Foundation six months prior, biologists now turned cryptozoologists, Dr. Dave Lane and his brother, Dr. Robert Lane, squeezed into the booth at a local dive fish market that has seen better days.

The heavy aroma of fish covers the smell of their sweat from being out all day in the swamp.

They have learned to expect anything, deep in the Everglades. Being on site for five days has taught them that speed bumps might not be made of concrete and speed limit signs are everywhere protecting wildlife. Every truck has a gun rack, a water cooler, and the permeating suspicious eyes of locals. You don't dare speed or be disrespectful. But despite that, it is a magical place to be. You can feel the energy, the life of the place. Early mornings are especially tangible and have a pulse. It pulls you in and makes it difficult to leave, even for dinner.

But the bug swarms were a whole different situation they still struggled with.

The entire day had been spent canvassing the Loop Road, an area known to locals, where observing wildlife in their natural habitat allowed them to weave through the swamp in their vehicle this close to the dry season. They had stayed too long and were starving. Handmade signs announcing the "Seafood Festival" were going up around town and their hotel reservation would only give them another three days before they would have to find other accommodations. Dave licks his lips as he reads through the paper menu.

Rob slaps down his menu and motions for the server to come over.

Rob calls out to Dave, "I'm having the hushpuppies and grouper. Sounds perfect." He drinks the entire glass of water the server had left earlier and motions for another as she approaches. "You ready?" he asks Dave, who is still reading through the listing.

"Give me a sec," Dave says, without looking up. He listens to Rob ordering, then looks at her pleasantly before asking, "What's fresh?" She rolls her eyes, smacks her gum, and responds, "Everything. What'll ya have?"

"Well, that's promising, isn't it?" says Rob, with a smile. "Could I also have a large icedtea without sugar?" She nods and waits for Dave to order. She looked too young to be working, with a pimply face and her hair in two long braids.

Dave's eyes go wide as he reads the fine print on the back of the menu. "You've got snake? I knew there was a big snake issue in this area, but you're eating them?" "Yeah, they're real popular too." She keeps her pen poised to her pad, ready to write. He hands her the menu. "I'll have the hushpuppies and grouper. And a large, really large, iced tea." She turns quickly and walks to the kitchen area. Dave watches her. "Guess it's hard to get kids to apply to jobs here. She looks bored to death."

Rob leans over and whispers, "That's cuz she's a teenager." The scientists sit quietly for a few minutes before Rob pipes up. "Are you excited about going to the site tomorrow? I can't wait to talk to the Wilsons." He pulls out his phone and watches the video for the hundredth time.

They are back in the swamps with the alligators and crocs. Dave knows firsthand how difficult the terrain can be out in the mud after spending six weeks in Papua New Guinea last year. His crew of biologists, photographers, and electronic engineers had documented rare blood taken from species of bats found only in that area of the world. And it looks as if the science research is leading to a cure for diabetes. Beta testing had started back at the lab in Massachusetts. He itched to get back to the research, but loves being out in the fresh air, too.

Time had flown by since their return. His son, Eric, married a wonderful adventurous soul, Renee, and their honeymoon would end when they arrived in the Everglades at the end of the week. The research team in the lab had expanded to a staff of six, but now they also have top security protocols and a barrage of inquiries from a secretive government agency that wants, no demands, access to their lab. A law firm dedicated to their cause is fighting the fight for them, but his time at the lab in the last two weeks had been nothing but meetings with the legal team and their benefactor. There had already been two suspicious encounters at his home with government agents crossing the line and while he was gone, the corporation was going to scan his home for listening devices.

The government wants their live specimen, a baby Pterodactyl.

Dave looks around the small restaurant. Outside, there's a dock with a line of colorful boats tied up, floating on the glassy waters. Across the canal, the shell of a burned-out warehouse watches over them. In the early evening light, it's hard not to watch the shadows and birds sitting on the abandoned fencing.

Music blares from the outside speakers. He watches a server busily serve people sitting in their boats. A heavy amount of alcohol traffic is moving back and forth. "Must be the place to get a beer." Dave scans the people around, looking for government operatives that might track them. *How did it ever get to this point?*

Rob holds onto his stomach. "I don't want a beer. Thank goodness that urge left me years ago." He tears into a saltine cracker from their basket on the table. "But I might consider a snake out here. I'm that hungry."

Pulling out his phone, that "dings," Dave checks for messages. "The Wilsons can meet us at 8:30. He's got to go to work, so we'll only have about thirty minutes with them. I doubt we'll get much out of him. He's probably tired of all the questions from people."

Rob talks with his mouth full, "Did the lab finish the analysis of the video? Man, if that were my kid on the playground, I would move to... I don't know where. There are Bigfoot sightings everywhere in the U.S.," Rob puts the phone down, face first. "I can't keep watching it."

Dave scrolls through his emails and stops, looking at Rob. "Just got some emails, and one is from the data lab. Let's see what they say?" Quickly, Rob scoots over next to Dave, and they read the message together. "Analysis is clear. The video has not been altered. Light filters have changed the image, making it clearer."

He clicks on the attachment and plays the new video feed. He stops when the face of a Skunk Ape clearly comes into focus. The creature is massive. Standing two feet higher than the six-foot frame of the metal playground. The arms are long, and muscular, and drape down to its knees. A coat of matted, ochre, long hair covers most of its limbs, with shorter hair on its chest. There isn't a neck, just a slightly elongated head, bulging eyebrows, and thick shoulders. It's the clearest shot of a Bigfoot-like creature they've ever seen."

A five-year-old girl had been swinging on a swing prior to the sighting. A high-end game cam caught the whole thing on video. The creature walks to the swing-set, while the chain is still moving, and pushes the empty swing before turning and heading back into the forest. You can clearly see the muscles rippling with the slight movement. It looks incredibly light on its feet for the size it is. The soles of its feet reveal toes, all the same length, and a flat instep.

Rob almost hyperventilates. He is so excited. "Dang." He pushes back and returns to sitting across from Dave. "Can you forward that to me?" Rob nods and watches the video one more time. "Good thing Wilson used to work for a camera company, or else it would have been just another blurry photo to add to the pile."

For a few minutes, Rob strums his fingers on the table with nervous energy. "Think it's still out there?" His voice is clipped as it catches when he speaks. "Guess I'm pretty excited about this one!"

Dave smiles as the server returns with his iced tea. "Wish I could put it in a vein." She doesn't say a word or return the smile, just goes back into the kitchen.

"Thanks," he says, louder than he meant to. Several of the other customers look in their direction. Dave shrugs and tries to look pleasant.

"Feel like we're getting the once-over. Guess we stick out as non-locals?" He strums his fingers on the table in irritation and watches Rob replay the video.

The town's population is small, less than a thousand. Clusters of homes dot the area, usually over a random bridge to the small islands in the area. Naples is over an hour away by car once you get through the protected Florida puma area. It feels very rural here, as if people rarely go to the larger cities, and that they liked it that way.

Eric and Renee, his son and new daughter-in-law, would arrive on Wednesday with their large RV bus and combination home-base trailer. How awkward will it be joining them in an RV? Dave tries to shake the visuals that creep in.

The server arrives with their plates of food. She doesn't look up, but says, "Enjoy!" as she quickly returns to the kitchen. They dig into their food with gusto. Rob pops several hushpuppies into his mouth without dipping them in the sauce they came with. He stops halfway to his mouth with the second forkful as a muscular, 6'6", Rambo-looking man steps into the café. He is head-to-toe in camo gear. His eyes go right to Rob and Dave. Rob quickly looks at Dave. "Oh, oh, think they've found us."

Dave turns to see the man approach. He stops at the table, pulls a folding chair over, and sits down with them. "Gentlemen, you are hard to find. Butler sent me to stay glued to your side while out on your recon. You can call me Ace." He holds out his massive paw for Dave to shake. Rob plops a handful of hushpuppies into his mouth and shakes his hand as well.

"Figured he might do that." Dave takes a bite of his grouper that had been cooked inside a small paper bag. He sighs when the mixture hits his lips. "Man, this is really fantastic." Rob does the same. He looks at the server and motions for her to come over. "Can you get another one of these for our guest? You've gotta try it. Melts in your mouth."

Dave covertly texts a message to Butler, their benefactor, as they talk.

"Thank you, appreciate it. Haven't eaten all day." Ace watches them eat.

After several bites, Rob moves the paper tray of hushpuppies closer to Ace. He stares at the biceps on Ace and casually asks, "Those real?" Ace flexes one arm, straining the seam of his short-sleeved shirt.

The text response from Butler is immediate, with a confirmation from Ace.

"Yeah. Your trackers are working. Had to activate them after spending the entire day traveling the back roads looking for you." Ace downs a tall glass of water the server brings him. With the comment, both Rob and Dave rub the inside of their wrists where the trackers had been inserted. "I'm highly valuable for this mission and can track just about anything. Grew up in the deep swamps of Louisiana, but I live outside of Tampa now. How is it going?"

"Well, would have been nice to get a text before you arrived, but it's part of the agreement we made with Butler. Tomorrow morning, we're interviewing Wilson at the site. So far we haven't found any tracks. Would like to talk to locals in the area." Rob talks with his mouth full. He turns over his phone and loads the video for Ace to watch, before taking another bite.

Ace zooms out the image as much as he can while he watches it twice. "Good clarity," he says before he passes the phone back to Rob.

The server stops by their table with drinks and a huge basket of hushpuppies, tartar sauce, and melted butter. Ace gives her a hint of a grin, which makes her blush. She stumbles past a chair as she leaves and covers her face in a cloth napkin in embarrassment.

Dave looks up and smiles. "She's texting every teenager for miles around with your image. Not much to do in this small town."

"Are you kidding? This is a great place. I'd have an airboat and be out all the time!" Rob looks longingly at an airboat tied up at the dock behind them.

"Can you fill me in on exactly what you are trying to accomplish down here?" Ace asks, popping a handful of hushpuppies into his mouth.

Rob watches him answer before Dave can say a word. "We're out to see if we can get definitive proof of Bigfoot, the Skunk Ape, or a new bipedal species. The government has become quite interested in our lab work, so there might be roadblocks with the local police or other entities. We're out for two weeks of exploration." Rob looks at Dave for confirmation.

Dave gives a slight head nod to Rob before taking the last bite of his grouper. "That was five-star. Remind me to have that again while we are here."

Ace leans in and lowers his voice. "I've already caught two government cars in the area trying to blend in. I'll be even more alert."

After getting to know each other over dinner, they are surprised to see the local sheriff pull into the parking lot as they are leaving. The officer watches them get into their vehicles and calls back to his office with his chest mic. Ace follows Dave's truck back to their hotel.

The next morning, Dave and Rob find Ace standing beside his own truck as the sun peeks over the tree line. "Come on, we're grabbing a quick coffee at a roadside trailer, then off to the interview. Where'd you stay last night?" Dave interjects while noticing the full parking lot.

"In my truck. It's fine. After years in the military special forces, I can sleep anywhere, but I might need to borrow your shower later." Ace fires up his tricked-up vehicle and follows them out of the parking lot.

Dave slows as he approaches the address for the Wilsons. Three police cruisers are parked near the entrance of his sandy-dirt driveway. The mobile home sits back from the main road about fifty feet. It is set in a cluster of tall pines. A trampoline is off to one side, covered with a corner section of the house, and that piece of the roof is resting on a crushed trampoline armature. Mr. and Mrs. Wilson stand near the front door holding their two children in front of them, a girl about five, and a boy maybe seven.

"Oh, that doesn't look good," Dave says as he parks the truck. "Was there a tornado last night? Storms? I didn't hear anything?" Rob and Dave walk over to Ace. A police officer sees them and starts walking in their direction. Dave holds up his hand. "Let me do the talking," he says to Ace and Rob.

"Officer, Dr. Dave Lane, Dr. Robert Lane, and our associate Ace--?" Dave looks at Ace. "Ace Henderson, National Guard Superintendent, Ex-Special Forces, and tracker." They all shake the officer's hand.

The officer starts unraveling a yellow crime scene tape roll. "Sorry, we've got a crime scene here. You'll have to back out and come back later," he says as he takes a step away from them, extending the tape.

"We had an appointment with Mr. Wilson this morning. He'll verify it. Could you let us know what happened?" Dave asks, as they watch another officer check the perimeter.

"A bear tried to get into the house through an open window. Took off that whole section of the house like it was tissue paper. Luckily, Wilson hit it with buckshot, and it took off. Almost got that little girl." The officer wraps more of the tape around the area.

"Can we wait over here, to talk to Mr. Wilson? We'll stay out of your way. If you could tell him we are here, sure would appreciate it." Dave hands the officer his business card.

Almost an hour later, Wilson frees himself from the officers and walks over to the group. His face is grim as he approaches. "So sorry about the wait. Guess I'm not going to work today. This is so f-d up! They want me to tell you a bear tried to get in." Wilson runs his hands over his scalp and puts his old baseball hat back on.

Dave shakes Wilson's hand. "Dr. Dave Lane, my brother Rob, and our tracker, Ace." They nod greetings to Wilson and step away from the police tape.

"We got enhanced video back for you to see, from last week, but could you tell us what happened last night?" Rob interjects without consulting Dave. Rob opens his phone.

"I'd like to see that." Wilson leans against Dave's truck and lights a cigarette as Rob pulls up the feed. They all review it again together. Wilson exhales the drag from his cigarette, and says, "That ain't no bear. There were no claws on it. I know fingers when I see 'em."

Rob hands Wilson his phone to play the video feed again. His eyes go wide when he sees the clear face of the creature. "Holy shit!! That's it!

That's what I saw last night!" Wilson looks around for his family. "I've got to get 'em outta here. It's not safe, but — I don't have the funds to set up in a hotel. I gotta work."

Dave looks sternly at him. "Do you have friends you can stay with? Family?" Wilson's hands shake as he takes another puff from the cigarette. "No, maybe I can get Lester to let us use his houseboat for a while? I work as a mechanic over off Fifth Street, Delany's. Everything is booked for the festival. They bring big-name bands in."

"You've got to get your family safe. That's the most important thing right now. Rob pats the guy on the shoulder. He puts out his smoke.

Wilson looks at them sternly. "It was growling and banging on the side of the house. I think it was using one of the tree trunks. Cindy was screaming. I ran so fast into her room, to see this long hairy arm reaching for her. Had to be at least seven feet tall. Oh, and the smell made my eyes water worse than a cottonmouth. She's gonna need counseling or something. She won't talk and just holds onto her Momma."

"Are you insured?" Ace asks him. Wilson nods. "Barely. They keep raising the premium."

"Okay, for us to walk around the perimeter and take some photos?" Ace holds up his camera. Wilson nods.

"Do you think it's the same creature? It seemed a little smaller than the one from last week. Is there a family of them?" Wilson asks as he lights another cigarette in nervous energy.

"It might be. Do you have Venmo?" Dave asks Wilson.

"Yeah, we use it at work and for some of the side jobs." Wilson looks at Dave as he pulls out his phone.

"What's your number?" Dave asks as he pulls up the app.

"Wilson-Everglade23," Wilson says, as he watches Dave pull up the information on his phone.

"This you?" Dave points to the account and Wilson nods. "I'm sending you five thousand dollars to get out of this place. Get help for your girl. You need to secure what you can, then stay away for at least a month. Can you do that?"

"You are?" Wilson watches the transfer go through. He shakes Dave's hand over and over. "Thank you, man. Thank you."

"Let's look at the area outside before techs show up." Ace leads them away from the main area.

Wilson walks with the men, past the two officers that are still there and over to the corner of the house, staying away from the police tape. The grass in the area doesn't lend to footprints, so they scan out back to the tree line, where Rob finds an impression in the dirt.

As they gather around looking at the footprints, Wilson whispers into Dave's ear, "There are two kids missing in this county and the sheriff's office is doing nothin' about it. Same method of taking kids. Right through their windows at night. Big hairy arms. Talk to Jensen over on Pier 23. His son was taken last month. Ten years old. They're keeping it out of the news. It ain't right."

Wilson leaves the men and returns to his wife and kids on the porch. They watch his wife go into the house with Cindy holding her hand, followed by Wilson and his son. They all return in minutes with bags of clothing, get into their truck, and peel off down the road.

Dave stands straight and waves "goodbye" to them. Rob finishes taking measurements and scouts the area farther back into the woods. Dave clears his throat and says to Rob, as he approaches, "This just got a bit more urgent."

Both Ace and Rob look at him, as he says. "Seems the creature is stealing children."

Rob's jaw drops, horrified. "They don't do that. They stay away from human interactions."

"Well, this one isn't like the others? Maybe, like humans, there are a few bad ones in the mix."

Ace looks out, deep into the woods. "I think I need to call a friend of mine to help."

Rob breaks into the conversation. "We've got that meeting with a local tracker at two."

Dave stands next to him and puts his hand on Rob's shoulder. "Yeah, we might need more… more what? I don't know."

The next adventure continues with **RIVER OF GRASS**.

To be continued….

If you have enjoyed this series, please go to my website, LoisBuchter.com and sign up for notices of new releases. I'll be glad to send you a free copy of one of my monster short stories. Also, I'll let the readers decide what adventure story I will write next!

Will **greatly appreciate** reviews of the book as this helps with ranking on the different sites.

And, I would love to hear from you if you enjoyed this book. Drop me a line at Info@loisbuchter.com and more information on my writing projects and scripts.

I must say, I thoroughly enjoyed writing this action-adventure monster story with the Lane brothers and will be doing sequels of their explorations into cryptozoology.

ABOUT THE AUTHOR

Lois Buchter ("Book-ter") is an accomplished artist and teacher of art and creativity. Buchter works to capture stories that inspire people to value life. From her Northern California home, she is working on paid writing assignments in screenwriting and new novel projects in her monster action/adventure specialty.

Lois happily writes with an aged puppy at her feet, good friends around, and a twinkle in her eye. She has a keen eye for the unknown, mysterious, and weird, all wrapped in a reluctant hero's journey.

https://LoisBuchter.com

Instagram: LoisBuchter
Tiktok/@LoisBuchter.BeastHunter
LinkedIn: @LoisBuchter
Twitter:@LoisBuchter
Facebook: Lois Buchter – Author

www.ingramcontent.com/pod-product-compliance
Lightning Source LLC
Chambersburg PA
CBHW031550240626
47153CB00002B/454